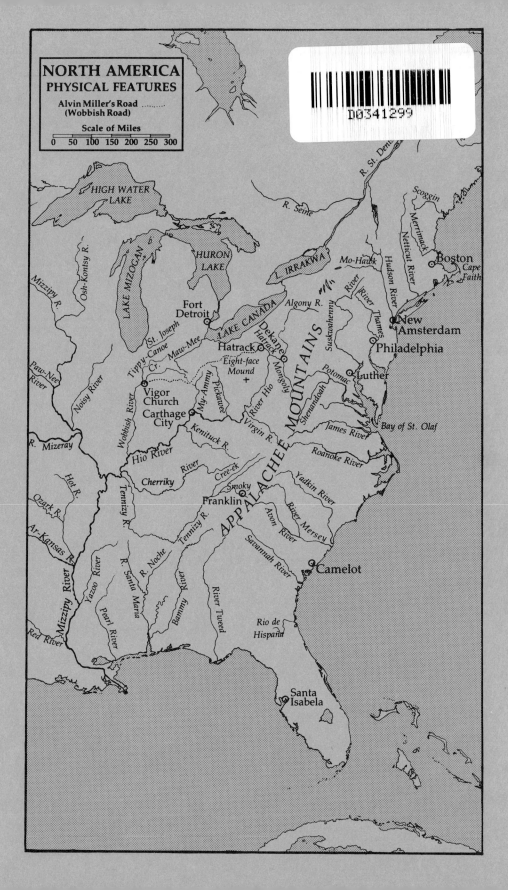

NORTH AMERICA
PHYSICAL FEATURES

Alvin Miller's Road ....
(Wobbish Road)

Scale of Miles

0   50   100   150   200   250   300

D0341299

HIGH WATER
LAKE

R. St. Denis

R. Seine

Scoggin

LAKE MIZOGAN

HURON
LAKE

L. IRRAKWA

Mo-Hauk

Merrimack

Netticut River

Hudson River

Boston

Cape
Faith

Mizzipy R.

Osh-Kontsy R.

Algony R.

Suskwahenny

River

River Thames

**New
Amsterdam**

Fort
Detroit

St. Joseph

Tippy-Canoe

Maw-Mee

LAKE CANADA

Dekane

Hatack

Philadelphia

Paw-Nee
River

Cr.

Hatrack

Eight-face
Mound
+

My-Ammy

Pickawee

Mongoty

River Hio

Shenandoah

Potomac

Luther

Noisy River

Wobbish River

**Vigor
Church
Carthage
City**

Virgin R.

Kentuck R.

James River

Bay of St. Olaf

R. Mizeray

Hio River

River

Cree-ek

Roanoke River

Hot R.

Tennizy R.

Cherriky

Smoky

Yadkin River

Ozark R.

Franklin

Tennizy R.

Avon River

River Mersey

Ar-Kansas R.

R. Noche

R. Santa Maria

Savannah River

Camelot

Mizzipy River

Yazoo River

Pearl River

Bammy River

River Tweed

Rio de
Hispani

Red River

**Santa
Isabela**

APPALACHEE MOUNTAINS

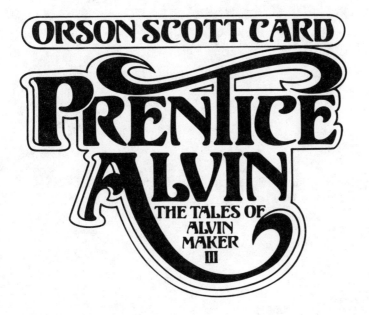

ORSON SCOTT CARD

PRENTICE ALVIN

THE TALES OF
ALVIN
MAKER
III

TOR

A TOM DOHERTY ASSOCIATES BOOK
NEW YORK

PRENTICE ALVIN
Copyright © 1989 by Orson Scott Card
All rights reserved, including the right to reproduce this book
or portions thereof in any form.

A TOR BOOK
Published by Tom Doherty Associates, Inc.
49 West 24 Street
New York, NY 10010

Library of Congress Cataloging-in-Publication Data

Card, Orson Scott.
Prentice Alvin / Orson Scott Card. — 1st ed.
(The Tales of Alvin Maker : 3)
"A Tor book"—T.p. verso.
ISBN 0-312-93141-7 (St. Martin's Press)
I. Title.   II. Series: Card, Orson Scott. Tales of Alvin Maker : bk 3.
PS3553.A655P74   1989
813'.54—dc19   88-39927
                                                                CIP

First edition: February 1989
0 9 8 7 6 5 4 3 2 1

For all my good teachers, especially:

Fran Schroeder,
fourth grade, Millikin Elementary, Santa Clara, California,
for whom I wrote my first poems.

Ida Huber,
tenth-grade English, Mesa High School, Arizona,
who believed in my future more than I did.

Charles Whitman,
playwriting, Brigham Young University,
who made my scripts look better than they deserved.

Norman Council,
literature, University of Utah,
for Spenser and Milton, alive.

Edward Vasta,
literature, University of Notre Dame,
for Chaucer and for friendship.

And always François.

Acknowledgments

IN THE PREPARATION of this volume of the Tales of Alvin Maker I have, as always, depended on others for help. For immeasurable help on the opening chapters of this book, my thanks go to the gentlefolk of the second Sycamore Hill Writers Workshop, to wit: Carol Emshwiller, Karen Joy Fowler, Gregg Keizer, James Patrick Kelly, John Kessel, Nancy Kress, Shariann Lewitt, Jack Massa, Rebecca Brown Ore, Susan Palwick, Bruce Sterling, Mark L. Van Name, Connie Willis, and Allen Wold.

Thanks also to the Utah State Institute of Fine Arts for awarding a prize to my narrative poem "Prentice Alvin and the No-Good Plow." That encouragement led to my developing the story in prose and at greater length; this is the first volume to include part of the story recounted in that poem.

For details of frontier life and crafts, I have used John Seymour's wonderful book *The Forgotten Crafts* (New York City: Knopf, 1984) and Douglass L. Brownstone's *A Field Guide to America's History* (New York City: Facts On File, Inc., 1984).

I'm grateful that Gardner Dozois has kindly allowed pieces of the Tales of Alvin Maker to appear in the pages of *Isaac Asimov's Science Fiction Magazine,* allowing it to find an audience before the books appeared.

Beth Meacham at Tor is one of that vanishing breed of editors with a golden touch; her advice is never intrusive, always wise; and (rarest editorial trait of all) she returns my telephone calls. For that alone she may be sainted.

· ACKNOWLEDGMENTS ·

Thanks to my writing class in Greensboro in the winter and spring of 1988 for suggestions that led to important improvements in the book; and to my sister, friend, and editorial assistant, Janice, for her work on keeping story details fresh in mind.

Thanks most of all to Kristine A. Card, who listens to me ramble through the many versions of each as-yet-unwritten book, reads the dot-matrix printouts of the early drafts, and is my second self through every page of everything I write.

Contents

1 The Overseer 1

2 Runaway 13

3 Lies 50

4 Modesty 73

5 Dowser 78

6 Masquerade 91

7 Wells 99

8 Unmaker 112

9 Redbird 117

10 Goodwife 133

11 Wand 139

12 School Board 143

13 Springhouse 154

14 River Rat 177

15 Teacher 198

16 Property 224

17 Spelling Bee 238

18 Manacles 257

· CONTENTS ·

19 The Plow 297

20 Cavil's Deed 319

21 Alvin Journeyman 327

1

The Overseer

LET ME START my history of Alvin's prenticeship where things first began to go wrong. It was a long way south, a man that Alvin had never met nor never would meet in all his life. Yet he it was who started things moving down the path that would lead to Alvin doing what the law called murder—on the very day that his prenticeship ended and he rightly became a man.

It was a place in Appalachee, in 1811, before Appalachee signed the Fugitive Slave Treaty and joined the United States. It was near the borders where Appalachee and the Crown Colonies meet, so there wasn't a White man but aspired to own a passel of Black slaves to do his work for him.

Slavery, that was a kind of alchemy for such White folk, or so they reckoned. They calculated a way of turning each bead of a Black man's sweat into gold and each moan of despair from a Black woman's throat into the sweet clear sound of a silver coin ringing on the money-changer's table. There was buying and selling of souls in that place. Yet there was nary a one of them who understood the whole price they paid for owning other folk.

Listen tight, and I'll tell you how the world looked from inside Cavil Planter's heart. But make sure the children are asleep, for this is a part of my tale that children ought not to hear, for it deals with hungers they don't understand too well, and I don't aim for this story to teach them.

Cavil Planter was a godly man, a church-going man, a tithepayer. All his slaves were baptized and given Christian names as soon as they understood enough English to be taught the gospel. He forbade them to practice their dark arts—he never allowed them to slaughter so much as a chicken themselves, lest they convert such an innocent act into a sacrifice to some hideous god. In all ways Cavil Planter served the Lord as best he could.

So, how was the poor man rewarded for his righteousness? His wife, Dolores, she was beset with terrible aches and pains, her wrists and fingers twisting like an old woman's. By the time she was twenty-five she went to sleep most nights crying, so that Cavil could not bear to share the room with her.

He tried to help her. Packs of cold water, soaks of hot water, powders and potions, spending more than he could afford on those charlatan doctors with their degrees from the University of Camelot, and bringing in an endless parade of preachers with their eternal prayers and priests with their hocum pocus incantations. All of it accomplished nigh onto nothing. Every night he had to lie there listening to her cry until she whimpered, whimper until her breath became a steady in and out, whining just a little on the out-breath, a faint little wisp of pain.

It like to drove Cavil mad with pity and rage and despair. For months on end it seemed to him that he never slept at all. Work all day, then at night lie there praying for relief. If not for her, then for him.

It was Dolores herself who gave him peace at night. "You have work to do each day, Cavil, and can't do it unless you sleep. I can't keep silent, and you can't bear to hear me. Please—sleep in another room."

Cavil offered to stay anyway. "I'm your husband, I belong here"—he said it, but she knew better.

"Go," she said. She even raised her voice. "Go!"

So he went, feeling ashamed of how relieved he felt. He slept that night without interruption, a whole five hours until dawn, slept well for the first time in months, perhaps years—and arose in the morning consumed with guilt for not keeping his proper place beside his wife.

In due time, though, Cavil Planter became accustomed to sleeping alone. He visited his wife often, morning and night. They took meals together, Cavil sitting on a chair in her room, his food on a small side table, Dolores lying in bed as a Black woman carefully spooned food into her mouth while her hands sprawled on the bedsheets like dead crabs.

Even sleeping in another room, Cavil wasn't free of torment. There would be no babies. There would be no sons to raise up to inherit Cavil's fine plantation. There would be no daughters to give away in magnificent weddings. The ballroom downstairs—when he brought Dolores into the fine new house he had built for her, he had said, "Our daughters will meet their beaux in this ballroom, and first touch their hands, the way our hands first touched in your father's house." Now Dolores never saw the ballroom. She came downstairs only on Sundays to go to church and on those rare days when new slaves were purchased, so she could see to their baptism.

Everyone saw her on such occasions, and admired them both for their courage and faith in adversity. But the admiration of his neighbors was scant comfort when Cavil surveyed the ruins of his dreams. All that he prayed for—it's as if the Lord wrote down the list and then in the margin noted "no, no, no" on every line.

The disappointments might have embittered a man of weaker faith. But Cavil Planter was a godly, upright man, and whenever he had the faintest thought that God might have treated him badly, he stopped whatever he was doing and pulled the small psaltery from his pocket and whispered aloud the words of the wise man.

In thee, O Lord, do I put my trust;
Bow down thine ear to me;
Be thou my strong rock.

He concentrated his mind firmly, and the doubts and resentments quickly fled. The Lord was with Cavil Planter, even in his tribulations.

Until the morning he was reading in Genesis and he came upon the first two verses of chapter 16.

> *Now Sarai Abram's wife bare him no children: and she had an handmaid, an Egyptian, whose name was Hagar. And Sarai said unto Abram, Behold now, the Lord hath restrained me from bearing: I pray thee, go in unto my maid: it may be that I may obtain children by her.*

At that moment the thought came into his mind, Abraham was a righteous man, and so am I. Abraham's wife bore him no children, and mine likewise has no hope. There was an African slavewoman in their household, as there are such women in mine. Why shouldn't I do as Abraham did, and father children by one of these?

The moment the thought came into his head, he shuddered in horror. He'd heard gossip of White Spaniards and French and Portuguese in the jungle islands to the south who lived openly with Black women—truly they were the lowest kind of creature, like men who do with beasts. Besides, how could a child of a Black woman ever be an heir to him? A mix-up boy could no more take possession of an Appalachee plantation than fly. Cavil just put the thought right out of his mind.

But as he sat at breakfast with his wife, the thought came back. He found himself watching the Black woman who fed his wife. Like Hagar, this woman is Egyptian, isn't she? He noticed how her body twisted lithely at the waist as she bore the spoon from tray to mouth. Noticed how as she leaned forward to hold the cup to the frail woman's lips, the servant's breasts swung down to press against her blouse. Noticed how her gentle fingers brushed crumbs and drops from Dolores's lips. He thought of those fingers touching *him,* and trembled slightly. Yet it felt like an earthquake inside him.

He rushed from the room with hardly a word. Outside the house, he clutched his psaltery.

> *Wash me thoroughly from mine iniquity,*
> *And cleanse me from my sin.*
> *For I acknowledge my transgressions:*
> *And my sin is ever before me.*

Yet even as he whispered these words, he looked up and saw the field women washing themselves at the trough. There was the young girl he had bought only a few days before, six hundred dollars even though she was small, since she was probably breeding stock. So fresh from the boat she was that she hadn't learned a speck of Christian modesty. She stood there naked as a snake, leaning over the trough, pouring cups of water over her head and down her back.

Cavil stood transfixed, watching her. What had only been a brief thought of evil in his wife's bedroom now became a trance of lust. He had never seen anything so graceful as her blue-black thighs sliding against each other, so inviting as her shiver when the water ran down her body.

Was this the answer to his fervent psalm? Was the Lord telling him that it was indeed with him as it had been with Abraham?

Just as likely it was witchery. Who knew what knacks these fresh-from-Africa Blacks might have? She knows I'm here a-watching, and she's tempting me. These Blacks are truly the devil's own children, to excite such evil thoughts in me.

He tore his gaze from the new girl and turned away, hiding his burning eyes in the words of the book. Only somehow the page had turned—when did he turn it?—and he found himself reading in the Song of Solomon.

> *Thy two breasts are like two young roes*
> *That are twins, which feed among the lilies.*

"God help me," he whispered. "Take this spell from me."

Day after day he whispered the same prayer, yet day after day he found himself watching his slavewomen with desire, particularly that newbought girl. Why was it God seemed to be paying him no mind? Hadn't he always been a righteous man? Wasn't he good to his wife? Wasn't he honest in business? Didn't he pay tithes and offerings? Didn't he treat his slaves and horses well? Why didn't the Lord God of Heaven protect him and take this Black spell from him?

Yet even when he prayed, his very confessions became evil imaginings. O Lord, forgive me for thinking of my newbought girl standing in the door of my bedroom, weeping at the caning she got from the overseer. Forgive me for imagining myself laying her on my own bed and lifting her skirts to anoint them with a balm so powerful the welts on her thighs and buttocks disappear before my eyes and she begins to giggle softly and writhe slowly on the sheets and look over her shoulder at me, smiling, and then she turns over and reaches out to me and—O Lord, forgive me, save me!

Whenever this happened, though, he couldn't help but wonder— why do such thoughts come to me even when I pray? Maybe I'm as righteous as Abraham; maybe it's the Lord who sent these desires to me. Didn't I first think of this while I was reading scripture? The Lord can work miracles—what if I went in unto the newbought girl and she conceived, and the Lord worked a miracle and the baby was born White? All things are possible to God.

This thought was both wonderful and terrible. If only it were true! Yet Abraham heard the voice of God, so he never had to wonder about what God might want of him. God never said a word to Cavil Planter.

And why not? Why didn't God just tell him right out? Take the girl, she's yours! Or, Touch her not, she is forbidden! Just let me hear your voice, Lord, so I'll know what to do!

> *O Lord my rock;*
> *Unto thee will I cry,*

Be not silent to me:
Lest, if thou be silent to me,
I become like them
That go down into the pit.

On a certain day in 1810 that prayer was answered.

Cavil was kneeling in the curing shed, which was mostly empty, seeing how last year's burly crop was long since sold and this year's was still a-greening in the field. He'd been wrestling in prayer and confession and dark imaginings until at last he cried out, "Is there no one to hear my prayer?"

"Oh, I hear you right enough," said a stern voice.

Cavil was terrified at first, fearing that some stranger—his overseer, or a neighbor—had overheard some terrible confession. But when he looked, he saw that it wasn't anyone he knew. Still, he knew at once *what* the man was. From the strength in his arms, his sun-browned face, and his open shirt—no jacket at all—he knew the man was no gentleman. But he was no White trash, either, nor a tradesman. The stern look in his face, the coldness of his eye, the tension in his muscles like a spring tight-bound in a steel trap: He was plainly one of those men whose whip and iron will keep discipline among the Black fieldworkers. An overseer. Only he was stronger and more dangerous than any overseer Cavil had ever seen. He knew at once that *this* overseer would get every ounce of work from the lazy apes who tried to avoid work in the fields. He knew that whoever's plantation was run by *this* overseer would surely prosper. But Cavil also knew that he would never dare to hire such a man, for this overseer was so strong that Cavil would soon forget who was man and who was master.

"Many have called me their master," said the stranger. "I knew that you would recognize me at once for what I am."

How had the man known the words that Cavil thought in the hidden reaches of his mind? "Then you *are* an overseer?"

"Just as there was one who was once called, not *a* master, but simply Master, so am I not *an* overseer, but *the* Overseer."

"Why did you come here?"

"Because you called for me."

"How could I call for you, when I never saw you before in my life?"

"If you call for the unseen, Cavil Planter, then of course you will see what you never saw before."

Only now did Cavil fully understand what sort of vision it was he saw, there in his own burly curing shed. A man whom many called their master, come in answer to his prayer.

"Lord Jesus!" cried Cavil.

At once the Overseer recoiled, putting up his hand as if to fend off Cavil's words. "It is forbidden for any man to call me by that name!" he cried.

In terror, Cavil bowed his head to the dirt. "Forgive me, Overseer! But if I am unworthy to say your name, how is it I can look upon your face? Or am I doomed to die today, unforgiven for my sins?"

"Woe unto you, fool," said the Overseer. "Do you really believe that you have looked upon my *face*?"

Cavil lifted his head and looked at the man. "I see your eyes even now, looking down at me."

"You see the face that you invented for me in your own mind, the body conjured out of your own imagination. Your feeble wits could never comprehend what you saw, if you saw what I truly am. So your sanity protects itself by devising its own mask to put upon me. If you see me as an Overseer, it is because that is the guise you recognize as having the greatness and power I possess. It is the form that you at once love and fear, the shape that makes you worship and recoil. I have been called by many names. Angel of Light and Walking Man, Sudden Stranger and Bright Visitor, Hidden One and Lion of War, Unmaker of Iron and Water-bearer. Today you have called me Overseer, and so, to you, that is my name."

"Can I ever know your true name, or see your true face, Overseer?"

The Overseer's face became dark and terrible, and he opened his mouth as if to howl. "Only one soul alive in all the world has ever seen my true shape, and that one will surely die!"

The mighty words came like dry thunder and shook Cavil Planter to his very root, so that he gripped the dirt of the shed floor lest he fly off into the air like dust whipped away in the wind before the storm. "Do not strike me dead for my impertinence!" cried Cavil.

The Overseer's answer came gentle as morning sunlight. "Strike you dead? How could I, when you are a man I have chosen to receive my most secret teachings, a gospel unknown to priest or minister."

"Me?"

"Already I have been teaching you, and you understood. I know you desire to do as I command. But you lack faith. You are not yet completely mine."

Cavil's heart leapt within him. Could it be that the Overseer meant to give him what he gave to Abraham? "Overseer, I am unworthy."

"Of course you are unworthy. None is worthy of me, no, not one soul upon this earth. But still, if you obey, you may find favor in my eyes."

Oh, he will! cried Cavil in his heart, yes, he will give me the woman! "Whatever you command, Overseer."

"Do you think I would give you Hagar because of your foolish lust and your hunger for a child? There is a greater purpose. These Black people are surely the sons and daughters of God, but in Africa they lived under the power of the devil. That terrible destroyer has polluted their blood—why else do you think they are Black? I can never save them as long as each generation is born pure Black, for then the devil owns them. How can I reclaim them as my own, unless you help me?"

"Will my child be born White then, if I take the girl?"

"What matters to me is that the child will not be born pure Black. Do you understand what I desire of you? Not one Ishmael, but many children; not one Hagar, but many women."

Cavil hardly dared to name the secretest desire of his heart. "All of them?"

"I give them to you, Cavil Planter. This evil generation is your property. With diligence, you can prepare another generation that will belong to me."

"I will, Overseer!"

"You must tell no one that you saw me. I speak only to those whose desires already turn toward me and my works, the ones who already thirst for the water I bring."

"I'll speak no word to any man, Overseer!"

"Obey me, Cavil Planter, and I promise that at the end of your life you will meet me again and know me for what I truly am. In that moment I will say to you, You are mine, Cavil Planter. Come and be my true slave forever."

"Gladly!" cried Cavil. "Gladly! Gladly!"

He flung out his arms and embraced the Overseer's legs. But where he should have touched the visitor, there was nothing. He had vanished.

From that night on, Cavil Planter's slavewomen had no peace. As Cavil had them brought to him by night, he tried to treat them with the strength and mastery he had seen in the face of the fearful Overseer. They must look at me and see His face, thought Cavil, and it's sure they did.

The first one he took unto himself was a certain newbought slavegirl who had scarce a word of English. She cried out in terror until he raised the welts upon her that he had seen in his dreams. Then, whimpering, she permitted him to do as the Overseer had commanded. For a moment, that first time, he thought her whimpering was like Dolores's voice when she wept so quietly in bed, and he felt the same deep pity that he had felt for his beloved wife. Almost he reached out tenderly to the girl as he had once reached out to comfort Dolores. But then he remembered the face of the Overseer and thought, this Black girl is His enemy; she is my property. As surely as a man must plow and plant the land God gave to him, I must not let this Black womb lie fallow.

Hagar, he called her that first night. You do not understand how I am blessing you.

In the morning he looked in the mirror and saw something new in his face. A kind of fierceness. A kind of terrible hidden strength. Ah, thought Cavil, no one ever saw what I truly am, not even me. Only now do I discover that what the Overseer is, I also am.

He never felt another moment's pity as he went about his nightly work. Ashen cane in hand, he went to the women's cabin and pointed at the one who was to come with him. If any hung back, she learned from the cane how much reluctance cost. If any other Black, man or woman, spoke in protest, the next day Cavil saw to it that the Overseer took it out of them in blood. No White guessed and no Black dared accuse him.

The newbought girl, his Hagar, was first to conceive. He watched her with pride as her belly began to grow. Cavil knew then that the Overseer had truly chosen him, and he took fierce joy in having such mastery. There would be a child, *his* child. And already the next step was clear to him. If his White blood was to save as many Black souls as possible, then he could not keep his mix-up babes at home, could he? He would sell them south, each to a different buyer, to a different city, and then trust the Overseer to see that they in turn grew up and spread his seed throughout all the unfortunate Black race.

And each morning he watched his wife eat her breakfast. "Cavil, my love," she said one day, "is something wrong? There's something darker in your face, a look of—rage, perhaps, or cruelty. Have you quarreled with someone? I would not speak except you —you frighten me."

Tenderly he patted his wife's twisted hand as the Black woman watched him under heavy-lidded eyes. "I have no anger against any man or woman," said Cavil gently. "And what you call cruelty is nothing more than mastery. Ah, Dolores, how can you look in my face and call me cruel?"

She wept. "Forgive me," she cried. "I imagined it. You, the kindest man I've ever heard of—the devil put such a vision in my mind, I know it. The devil can give false visions, you know, but only the wicked are deceived. Forgive me for my wickedness, Husband!"

He forgave her, but she wouldn't stop her weeping until he had sent for the priest. No wonder the Lord chose only men to be his prophets. Women were too weak and compassionate to do the work of the Overseer.

That's how it began. That was the first footfall on this dark and terrible path. Nor Alvin nor Peggy ever knew this tale until I found it out and told them both long after, and they recognized at once that it was the start of all.

But I don't want you to think this was the whole cause of all the evil that befell, for it wasn't. There were other choices made, other mistakes, other lies and other willing cruelties done. A man might have plenty of help finding the short path to hell, but no one else can make him set foot upon it.

⚹ 2 ⚹

Runaway

PEGGY WOKE UP in the morning with a dream of Alvin Miller filling her heart with all kinds of terrible desires. She wanted to run from that boy, and to stay and wait for him; to forget she knew him, and to watch him always.

She lay there on her bed with her eyes almost closed, watching the grey dawnlight steal into the attic room where she slept. I'm holding something, she noticed. The corners of it clenched into her hands so tight that when she let go her palm hurt like she been stung. But she wasn't stung. It was just the box where she kept Alvin's birth caul. Or maybe, thought Peggy, maybe she *had* been stung, stung deep, and only just now did she feel the pain of it.

Peggy wanted to throw that box just as far from her as she could, bury it deep and forget where she buried it, drown it underwater and pile rocks on so it wouldn't float.

Oh, but I don't mean that, she said silently, I'm sorry for thinking such a thing, I'm plain sorry, but he's coming now, after all these years he's coming to Hatrack River and he won't be the boy I seen in all the paths of his future, he won't be the man I see him turning into. No, he's still just a boy, just eleven years old. He's seen him enough of life that somewise maybe he's a man inside, he's seen grief and pain enough for someone five times his age, but it's still an eleven-year-old boy he'll be when he walks into this town.

And I don't want to see no eleven-year-old Alvin come here. He'll be looking for me, right enough. He knows who I am, though he never saw me since he was two weeks old. He knows I saw his future on the rainy dark day when he was born, and so he'll come, and he'll say to me, "Peggy, I know you're a torch, and I know you wrote in Taleswapper's book that I'm to be a Maker. So tell me what I'm supposed to be." Peggy knew just what he'd say, and every way he might choose to say it—hadn't she seen it a hundred times, a thousand times? And she'd teach him and he'd become a great man, a true Maker, and—

And then one day, when he's a handsome figure of twenty-one and I'm a sharp-tongued spinster of twenty-six he'll feel so *grateful* to me, so *obligated,* that he'll propose himself for marriage to me as his bounden duty. And I, being lovesick all these years, full of dreams of what he'll do and what we'll be together, I'll say yes, and saddle him with a wife he wished he didn't have to marry, and his eyes will hunger for other women all the days of our lives together—

Peggy wished, oh she wished so deep, that she didn't know for certain things would be that way. But Peggy was a torch right enough, the strongest torch she'd ever heard of, stronger even than the folk hereabouts in Hatrack River ever guessed.

She sat up in bed and did not throw the box or hide it or break it or bury it. She opened it. Inside lay the last scrap of Alvin's birth caul, as dry and white as paper ash in a cold hearth. Eleven years ago when Peggy's mama served as midwife to pull baby Alvin out of the well of life, and Alvin first sucked for breath in the damp air of Papa's Hatrack River roadhouse, Peggy peeled that thin and bloody caul from the baby's face so he could breathe. Alvin, the seventh son of a seventh son, and the thirteenth child—Peggy saw at once what the paths of his life would be. Death, that was where he was headed, death from a hundred different accidents in a world that seemed bent on killing him even before he was hardly alive.

She was Little Peggy then, a girl of five, but she'd been torching for two years already, and in that time she never did a seeing on a birthing child who had so many paths to death. Peggy searched up all the paths of his life, and found in all of them but one single way that boy could live to be a man.

That was if she kept that birth caul, and watched him from afar off, and whenever she saw death reaching out to take him, she'd use that caul. Take just a pinch of it and grind it between her fingers and whisper what had to happen, see it in her mind. And it would happen just the way she said. Hadn't she held him up from drowning? Saved him from a wallowing buffalo? Caught him from sliding off a roof? She even split a roof beam once, when it was like to fall from fifty feet up and squash him on the floor of a half-built church; she split that beam neat as you please, so it fell on one side of him and the other, with just a space for him to stand there in between. And a hundred other times when she acted so early that nobody ever even guessed his life had been saved, even those times she saved him, using the caul.

How did it work? She hardly knew. Except that it was his own power she was using, the gift born right in him. Over the years he'd learned somewhat about his knack for making things and shaping them and holding them together and splitting them apart. Finally this last year, all caught up in the wars between Red men and White, he'd taken charge of saving his own life, so she hardly had to do a thing to save him anymore. Good thing, too. There wasn't much of that caul left.

She closed the lid of the box. I don't want to see him, thought Peggy. I don't want to know any more about him.

But her fingers opened that lid right back up, cause of course she had to know. She'd lived half her life, it seemed like, touching that caul and searching for his heartfire away far off in the northwest Wobbish country, in the town of Vigor Church, seeing how he was doing, looking up the paths of his future to see what danger lay in ambush. And when she was sure he was safe, she'd look farther ahead, and see him coming back one day to Hatrack River, where he was born, coming back and looking into her face and saying, It was you who saved me all those times, you who saw I was a Maker back afore a living soul thought such a thing was possible. And then she'd watch him learn the great depths of his power, the work he had to do, the crystal city he had to build; she saw him sire babies on her, and saw him touch the nursing infants she held in her arms; she saw the ones they buried and the ones that lived; and last of all she saw him—

Tears came down her face. I don't want to know, she said. I don't want to know all the roads of the future. Other girls can dream of love, the joys of marriage, of being mothers to strong healthy babes; but all my dreams have dying in them, too, and pain, and fear, because my dreams are true dreams, I know more than a body can know and still have any hope inside her soul.

Yet Peggy *did* hope. Yes sir, you can be sure of it—she still clung to a kind of desperate hope, because even knowing what's likely to come down the pathways of a body's life, she still caught her some glimpses, some clear plain visions of certain days, certain hours, certain passing moments of joy so great it was worth the grief just to get there.

Trouble was those glimpses were so rare and small in the spreading futures of Alvin's life that she couldn't find a road that led there. All the pathways she could find easily, the plain ones, the ones most likely to become real, those all led to Alvin wedding her without love, out of gratitude and duty, a miserable marriage. Like the story of Leah in the Bible, whose beautiful husband Jacob hated her even though she loved him dear and bore him more babies than his other wives and would've died for him if he'd as much as asked her.

It's an evil thing God did to women, thought Peggy, to make us hanker after husband and children till it leads us to a life of sacrifice and misery and grief. Was Eve's sin so terrible, that God should curse all women with that mighty curse? You will groan and bear children, said Almighty Merciful God. You will be eager for your husband, and he will rule over you.

That was what was burning in her—eagerness for her husband. Even though he was only an eleven-year-old boy who was looking, not for a wife, but for a teacher. He may be just a boy, thought Peggy, but I'm a woman, and I've seen the man he'll be, and I yearn for him. She pressed one hand against her breast; it felt so large and soft, still somewhat out of place on her body, which used to be all sticks and corners like a shanty cabin, and now was softening, like a calf being fattened up for the return of the prodigal.

She shuddered, thinking what happened to the fatted calf, and once again touched the caul, and *looked*:

In the distant town of Vigor Church, young Alvin was break-fasting his last morning at his mother's table. The pack he was to carry on his journey to Hatrack River lay on the floor beside the table. His mother's tears flowed undisguised across her cheeks. The boy loved his mother, but never for a moment did he feel sorry to be leaving. His home was a dark place now, stained with too much innocent blood for him to hanker to stay. He was eager to be off, to start his life as a prentice boy to the blacksmith of Hatrack River, and to find the torch girl who saved his life when he was born. He couldn't eat another bite. He pushed back from the table, stood up, kissed his mama—

Peggy let go the caul and closed the lid of the box as tight and quick as if she was trying to catch a fly inside.

Coming to find me. Coming to start a life of misery together. Go ahead and cry, Faith Miller, but not because your little boy Alvin's on his way east. You cry for me, the woman whose life your boy will wreck. You shed your tears for one more woman's lonely pain.

Peggy shuddered, shook off the bleak mood of the grey dawn, and dressed herself quickly, ducking her head to avoid the low sloping crossbeams of the attic roof. Over the years she'd learned ways to push thoughts of Alvin Miller Junior clean out of her mind, long enough to do her duty as daughter in her parents' household and as torch for the people of the country hereabouts. She could go hours without thinking about that boy, when she set her mind to it. And though it was harder now, knowing he was about to set his foot on the road toward her that very morning, she still put thoughts of him aside.

Peggy opened the curtain of the south-facing window and sat before it, leaning on the sill. She looked out over the forest that still stretched from the roadhouse, down the Hatrack River and on to the Hio, with only a few pig farms here and there to block the way. Of course she couldn't *see* the Hio, not that many miles from here, not even in the clear cool air of springtime. But what her natural eyes couldn't see, the burning torch in her could find easy enough. To see the Hio, she had only to search for a far-off heartfire, then slip herself inside that fellow's flame, and see out of his eyes as easy as she could see out of her own. And once there, once she had ahold of someone's heartfire, she could see other things, too, not just what he saw, but what he thought and felt and wished for. And even more: Flickering away in the brightest parts of the flame, often hidden by all the noise of the fellow's present thought and wishes, she could see the paths ahead of him, the choices coming to him, the life he'd make for himself if he chose this or that or another way in the hours and days to come.

Peggy could see so much in other people's heartfires that she hardly was acquainted with her own.

She thought of herself sometimes like that lone lookout boy at the tip-top of a ship's mast. Not that she ever saw her a ship in her whole life, except the rafts on the Hio and one time a canal boat on the Irrakwa Canal. But she read some books, as many as ever she could get Doctor Whitley Physicker to bring back to her from his visits to Dekane. So she knew about the lookout on the mast. Clinging to the rigging, arms half-wrapped in the lines so he didn't fall if there was a sudden roll or pitch of the boat, or a gust of wind unlooked-for; froze blue in winter, burnt red in summer; and nothing to do all day, all the long long hours of his watch, but look out onto the empty blue ocean. If it was a pirate ship, the lookout watched for victims' sails. If it was a whaler, he looked for blows and breaches. Most ships, he just looked for land, for shoals, for hidden sand bars; looked for pirates or some sworn enemy of his nation's flag.

Most days he never saw a thing, not a thing, just waves and dipping sea birds and fluffy clouds.

I am on a lookout perch, thought Peggy. Sent up aloft some sixteen years ago the day I was born, and kept here ever since, never once let down below, never once allowed to rest within the narrow bunkspace of the lowest deck, never once allowed to so much as close a hatch over my head or a door behind my back. Always, always I'm on watch, looking far and near. And because it isn't my natural eyes I look through, I can't shut them, not even in sleep.

No escape from it at all. Sitting here in the attic, she could see without trying:

Mother, known to others as Old Peg Guester, known to herself as Margaret, cooking in the kitchen for the slew of guests due in for one of her suppers. Not like she has any particular knack for cooking, either, so kitchen work is hard, she isn't like Gertie Smith who can make salt pork taste a hundred different ways on a hundred different days. Peg Guester's knack is in womenstuff, midwifery and house hexes, but to make a good inn takes good food and now Oldpappy's gone she has to cook, so she thinks only of the kitchen and couldn't hardly stand interruption, least of all from her daughter who mopes around the house and hardly speaks at all and by and large that girl is the most unpleasant, ill-favored child even though she started out so sweet and promising, everything in life turns sour somehow. . . .

Oh, that was such a joy, to know how little your own mama cared for you. Never mind that Peggy also knew the fierce devotion that her mama had. Knowing that a portion of love abides in your mama's heart doesn't take away but half the sting of knowing her dislike for you as well.

And Papa, known to others as Horace Guester, keeper of the Hatrack River Roadhouse. A jolly fellow, Papa was, even now out in the dooryard telling tales to a guest who was having trouble getting away from the inn. He and Papa always seemed to have something more to talk about, and oh, that guest, a circuit lawyer from up Cleveland way, he fancied Horace Guester was just about the finest most upstanding citizen he ever met, if all folks was as good-hearted as old Horace there'd be no more crime and no more lawyering in the upriver Hio country. Everybody felt that way. Everybody loved old Horace Guester.

But his daughter, Peggy the torch, she saw into his heartfire and knew how he felt about it. He saw those folks a-smiling at him and he said to himself, If they knew what I really was they'd spit in the road at my feet and walk away and forget they ever saw my face or knew my name.

Peggy sat there in her attic room and all the heartfires glowed, all of them in town. Her parents' most, cause she knew them best; the lodgers who stayed in the roadhouse; and then the people of the town.

Makepeace Smith and his wife Gertie and their three snot-nose children planning devilment when they weren't puking or piddling—Peggy saw Makepeace's pleasure in the shaping of iron, his loathing for his own children, his disappointment as his wife changed from a fascinating unattainable vision of beauty into a stringy-haired hag who screamed at the children first and then came to use the same voice to scream at Makepeace.

Pauley Wiseman, the sheriff, loving to make folks a-scared of him; Whitley Physicker, angry at himself because his medicine didn't work more than half the time, and every week he saw death he couldn't do a thing about. New folks, old folks, farmers and professionals, she saw through their eyes and into their hearts. She saw the marriage beds that were cold at night and the adulteries kept secret in guilty hearts. She saw the thievery of trusted clerks and friends and servants, and the honorable hearts inside many who were despised and looked down on.

She saw it all, and said nothing. Kept her mouth shut. Talked to no one. Cause she wasn't going to lie. She promised years before that she'd never lie, and kept her word by keeping still.

Other folks didn't have her problem. They could talk and tell the truth. But Peggy couldn't tell the truth. She knew these folks too well. She knew what they all were scared of, what they all wanted, what they all had done that they'd kill her or theirself if they once got a notion that she knew. Even the ones who never done a bad thing, they'd be so ashamed to think she knew their secret dreams or private craziness. So she never could speak frankly to these folks, or something would slip out, not even a word maybe, it might be just the way she turned her head, the way she sidestepped some line of talk, and they'd know that she knew, or just fear that she knew, or just fear. Just fear alone, without even naming what it was, and it could undo them, some of them, the weakest of them.

She was a lookout all the time, alone atop the mast, hanging to the lines, seeing more than she ever wanted to, and never getting even a minute to herself.

When it wasn't some baby being born, so she had to go and do a seeing, then it was some folks in trouble somewhere that had to be helped. It didn't do her no good to sleep, neither. She never slept all the way. Always a part of her was looking, and saw the fire burning, saw it flash.

Like now. Now this very moment, as she looked out over the forest, there it was. A heartfire burning ever so far off.

She swung herself close in—not her body, of course, her flesh stayed right there in the attic—but being a torch she knew how to look *close* at far-off heartfires.

It was a young woman. No, a girl, even younger than herself. And strange inside, so she knew right off this girl first spoke a language that wasn't English, even though she spoke and thought in English now. It made her thoughts all twisty and queer. But some things run deeper than the tracks that words leave in your brain; Little Peggy didn't need no help understanding that baby the girl held in her arms, and the way she stood at the riverbank knowing she would die, and what a horror waited for her back at the plantation, and what she'd done last night to get away.

See the sun there, three fingers over the trees. This runaway Black slave girl and her little bastard half-White boy-baby, see them standing on the shore of the Hio, half hid up in trees and bushes, watching as the White men pole them rafts on down. She a-scared, she know them dogs can't find her but very soon they get them the runaway finder, very worse thing, and how she ever cross that river with this boy-baby?

She cotch her a terrible thought: I leave this boy-baby, I hide him in this rotten log, I swim and steal the boat and I come back to here. That do the job, yes sir.

But then this Black girl who nobody never teach how to be a mama, she know a good mama don't leave this baby who still gots to suck two-hand times a day. She whisper, Good mama don't leave a little boy-baby where old fox or weasel or badger come and nibble off little parts and kill him dead. No ma'am not me.

So she just set down here a-hold of this baby, and watch the river flow on, might as well be the seashore cause she never get across.

Maybe some White folks help her? Here on the Appalachee shore the White folk hang them as help a slavegirl run away. But this runaway Black slavegirl hear stories on the plantation, about Whites who say nobody better be own by nobody else. Who say this Black girl better have that same right like the White lady, she say no to any man be not her true husband. Who say this Black girl better can keep her baby, not let them White boss promise he sell it on weaning day, they send this boy-baby to grow up into a house slave in Drydenshire, kiss a white man's feet if he say boo.

"Oh, your baby is so *lucky*," they say to this slavegirl. "He'll grow up in a fine lord's mansion in the Crown Colonies, where they still have a king—he might even *see* the King someday."

She don't say nothing, but she laugh inside. She don't set no store to see a king. Her pa a king back in Africa, and they shoot him dead. Them Portuguese slavers show her what it mean to be a king—it mean you die quick like everybody, and spill blood red like everybody, and cry out loud in pain and scared—oh, *fine* to be a king, and *fine* to see one. Do them White folk believe this lie?

I don't believe them. I say I believe them but I lie. I never let them take him my boy-baby. A king grandson him, and I tell him every day he growing up. When he the tall king, ain't nobody hit him with the stick or he hit them back, and nobody take his woman, spread her like a slaughterpig and stick this half-White baby in her but he can't do nothing, he sit in his cabin and cry. No ma'am, no sir.

So she do the forbidden evil ugly bad thing. She steal two candles and hot them all soft by the cookfire. She mash them like dough, she mash in milk from her own teat after boy-baby suck, and she mash some of her spit in the wax too, and then she push it and poke it and roll it in ash till she see a poppet shape like Black slavegirl. Her very own self.

Then she hide this Black slavegirl poppet and she go to Fat Fox and beg him feathers off that big old blackbird he cotch him.

"Black slavegirl don't need her no feathers," say Fat Fox.

"I make a boogy for my boy-baby," she say.

Fat Fox laugh, he know she lie. "Ain't no blackfeather boogy. I never heared of such a thing."

Black slavegirl, she say, "My papa king in Umbawana. I know all secret thing."

Fat Fox shake his head, he laugh, he laugh. "What do you know, anyway? You can't even talk English. I'll give you all the blackbird feathers you want, but when that baby stops sucking you come to me and I'll give you another one, all Black this time."

She hate Fat Fox like White Boss, but he got him blackbird feathers so she say, "Yes sir."

Two hands she fill up with feathers. She laugh inside. She far away and dead before Fat Fox never put him no baby in her.

She cover Black slavegirl poppet with feathers till she little girl-shape bird. Very strong thing, this poppet with her own milk and spit in it, blackbird feathers on. Very strong, suck all her life out, but boy-baby, he never kiss no White Boss feet, White Boss never lay no lash on him.

Dark night, moon not showing yet. She slip out her cabin. Boy-baby suck so he make no sound. She tie that baby to her teat so he don't fall. She toss that poppet on the fire. Then all the power of the feather come out, burning, burning, burning. She feel this fire pour into her. She spread her wings, oh so wide, spread them, flap like she see that big old blackbird flap. She rise up into the air, high up in that dark night, she rise and fly, far away north she fly, and when that moon he come up, she keep him at her right hand so she get this boy-baby to land where White say Black girl never slave, half-White boy-baby never slave.

Come morning and the sun and she don't fly no more. Oh, like dying, like dying she think, walking her feet on the ground. That bird with her wing broke, she pray for Fat Fox to find her, she know that now. After you fly, make you sad to walk, hurt you bad to walk, like a slave with chains, that dirt under your feet.

But she walk with that boy-baby all morning and now she come to this wide river. This close I come, say runaway Black slavegirl. I fly this far, yes I fly this river across. But that sun come up and I come down before this river. Now I never cross, old finder find me somehow, whup me half dead, take my boy-baby, sell him south.

Not me. I trick them. I die first.

No, I die second.

Other folks could argue about whether slavery was a mortal sin or just a quaint custom. Other folks could bicker on about how Emancipationists were too crazy to put up with even though slavery was a real bad thing. Other folks could look at Blacks and feel sorry for them but still be somewhat glad they were mostly in Africa or in the Crown Colonies or in Canada or somewhere else far and gone. Peggy couldn't afford the luxury of having opinions on the subject. All she knew was that no heartfire ever was in such pain as the soul of a Black who lived in the thin dark shadow of the lash.

Peggy leaned out the attic window, called out: "Papa!"

He strode out from the front of the house, walked into the road, where he could look up and see her window. "You call me, Peggy?"

She just looked at him, said naught, and that was all the signal that he needed. He good-byed and fare-thee-welled that guest so fast the poor old coot was halfway into the main part of town before he knew what hit him. Pa was already inside and up the stairs.

"A girl with a babe," she told him. "On the far side of the Hio, scared and thinking of killing herself if she's caught."

"How far along the Hio?"

"Just down from the Hatrack Mouth, near as I can guess. Papa, I'm coming with you."

"No you're not."

"Yes I am, Papa. You'll never find her, not you nor ten more like you. She's too scared of White men, and she's got cause."

Papa looked at her, unsure what to do. He'd never let her come before, but usually it was Black men what ran off. But then, usually she found them this side the Hio, lost and scared, so it was safer. Crossing into Appalachee, it was prison for sure if they were caught helping a Black escape. Prison if it wasn't a quick rope on a tree. Emancipationists didn't fare well south of the Hio, and still less the kind of Emancipationist who helped run-off bucks and ewes and pickaninnies get north to French country up in Canada.

"Too dangerous across the river," he said.

"All the more reason you need me. To find her, and to spot if anyone else happens along."

"Your mother would kill me if she knew I was taking you."

"Then I'll leave now, out the back."

"Tell her you're going to visit Mrs. Smith—"

"I'll tell her nothing or I'll tell the truth, Papa."

"Then I'll stay up here and pray the good Lord saves my life by not letting her notice you leaving. We'll meet up at Hatrack Mouth come sundown."

"Can't we—"

"No we can't, not a minute sooner," he said. "Can't cross the river till dark. If they catch her or she dies afore we get there then it's just too bad, cause we can't cross the Hio in the daylight, bet your life on that."

Noise in the forest, this scare Black slavegirl very bad. Trees grab her, owls screech out telling where they find her, this river just laugh at her all along. She can't move cause she fall in the dark, she hurt this baby. She can't stay cause they find her sure.

Flying don't fool them finders, they look far and see her even a hand of hands away off.

A step for sure. Oh, Lord God Jesus save me from this devil in the dark.

A step, and breathing, and branches they brush aside. But no lantern! Whatever come it see me in the dark! Oh, Lord God Moses Savior Abraham.

"Girl."

That voice, I hear that voice, I can't breathe. Can you hear it, little boy-baby? Or do I dream this voice? This lady voice, very soft lady voice. Devil got no lady voice, everybody know, ain't that so?

"Girl, I come to take you across the river and help you and your baby get north and free."

I don't find no words no more, not slave words or Umbawa talk. When I put on feathers do I lose my words?

"We got a good stout rowboat and two strong men to row. I know you understand me and I know you trust me and I know you want to come. So you just set there, girl, you hold my hand, there, that's my hand, you don't have to say a word, you just hold my hand. There's some White men but they're my friends and they won't touch you. Nobody's going to touch you except me, you believe that, girl, you just believe it."

Her hand it touch my skin very cool and soft like this lady voice. This lady angel, this Holy Virgin Mother of God.

Lots of steps, heavy steps, and now lanterns and lights and big old White men but this lady she just hold on my hand.

"Scared plumb to death."

"Look at this girl. She's most wasted away to nothing."

"How many days she been without eating?"

Big men's voices like White Boss who give her this baby.

"She only left her plantation last night," said the Lady.

How this White lady know? She know everything, Eve the mama of all babies. No time to talk, no time to pray, move very quick, lean on this White lady, walk and walk and walk to this boat it lie waiting in the water just like I dream, O! here the boat little boy-baby, boat lift us cross the Jordan to the Promise Land.

They were halfway across the river when the Black girl started shaking and crying and chattering.

"Hush her up," said Horace Guester.

"There's nobody near us," answered Peggy. "No one to hear."

"What's she babbling about?" asked Po Doggly. He was a pig farmer from near Hatrack mouth and for a moment Peggy thought he was talking about *her*. But no, it was the Black girl he meant.

"She's talking in her African tongue, I reckon," said Peggy. "This girl is really something, how she got away."

"With a baby and all," agreed Po.

"Oh, the baby," said Peggy. "I've got to hold the baby."

"Why's that?" asked Papa.

"Because you're both going to have to carry her," she said. "From shore to the wagon, at least. There's no way this child can walk another step."

When they got to shore, they did just that. Po's old wagon was no great shakes for comfort—one old horseblanket was about as soft as it was going to get—but they laid her out and if she minded she didn't say so. Horace held the lantern high and looked at her. "You're plumb right, Peggy."

"What about?" she asked.

"Calling her a child. I swear she couldn't be thirteen. I swear it. And her with a baby. You sure this baby's hers?"

"I'm sure," said Peggy.

Po Doggly chuckled. "Oh, you know them guineas, just like bunny rabbits, the minute they can they do." Then he remembered that Peggy was there. "Begging your pardon, ma'am. We don't never have ladies along till tonight."

"It's *her* pardon you have to beg," said Peggy coldly. "This child is a mixup. Her owner sired this boy without a by-your-leave. I reckon you understand me."

"I won't have you discussing such things," said Horace Guester.

His temper was hot, all right. "Bad enough you coming along on this without you knowing all this kind of thing about this poor girl, it ain't right telling her secrets like that."

Peggy fell silent and stayed that way all the ride home. That was what happened whenever she spoke frankly which is why she almost never did. The girl's suffering made her forget herself and talk too much. Now Papa was thinking on about how much his daughter knew about this Black girl in just a few minutes, and worrying how much she knew about *him*.

Do you want to know what I know, Papa? I know why you do this. You're not like Po Doggly, Papa, who doesn't think much of Blacks but hates seeing any wild thing cooped up. He does this, helping slaves make their way to Canada, cause he's just got that need in him to set them free. But you, Papa, you do it to pay back your secret sin. Your pretty little secret who smiled at you like heartbreak in person and you could've said no but you didn't, you said yes oh yes. While Mama was expecting me, it was, and you were off in Dekane buying supplies, you stayed there a week and had that woman must be ten times in six days, I remember every one of those times as clear as you do, I can feel you dreaming about her in the night. Hot with shame, hotter with desire, I know just how a man feels when he wants a woman so bad his skin itches and he can't hold still. All these years you've hated yourself for what you did and hated yourself all the more for loving that memory, and so you pay for it. You risk going to jail or getting hung up in a tree somewhere for the crows to pick, not because you love the Black man but because you hope maybe doing good for God's children might just set you free of your own secret love of evil.

And here's the funny thing, Papa. If you knew I knew your secret you would probably die, it might just kill you on the spot. And yet if I could tell you, just tell you that I know, then I could tell you something else on top of that, I could say, Papa, don't you see that it's your knack? You who thinks he never had no knack, but you got one. It's the knack for making folks feel loved. They come to your inn and they feel right to home. Well you saw her, and she was hungry, that woman in Dekane, she needed to feel the way you make folks feel, needed you so bad. And it's hard, Papa, hard not to love a body who loves you so powerful, who hangs onto you like clouds hanging onto the moon, knowing you're going to go on, knowing you'll never stay, but hungering, Papa. I looked for that woman, looked for her heartfire, far and wide I searched for her, and I found her. I know where she is. She ain't young now like you remember. But she's still pretty, pretty as you recall her, Papa. And she's a good woman, and you done her no harm. She remembers you fondly, Papa. She knows God forgave her and you both. It's you who won't forgive, Papa.

Such a sad thing, Peggy thought, coming home in that wagon. Papa's doing something that would make him a hero in any other daughter's eyes. A great man. But because I'm a torch, I know the truth. He doesn't come out here like Hector afore the gates of Troy, risking death to save other folks. He comes slinking like a whipped dog, cause he *is* a whipped dog inside. He runs out here to hide from a sin that the good Lord would have forgave long ago if he just allowed forgiveness to be possible.

Soon enough, though, Peggy stopped thinking it was sad about her Papa. It was sad about most *everybody,* wasn't it? But most sad people just kept right on being sad, hanging onto misery like the last keg of water in a drouth. Like the way Peggy kept waiting here for Alvin even though she knew he'd bring no joy to her.

It was that girl in the back of the wagon who was different. She had a terrible misery coming on her, going to lose her boy-baby, but she didn't just set and wait for it to happen so she could grieve. She said no. Plain no, just like that, I won't let you sell this boy south on me, even to a good rich family. A rich man's slave is still a slave, ain't he? And down south means he'll be even farther away from where he can run off and make it north. Peggy could feel those feelings in that girl, even as she tossed and moaned in the back of the wagon.

Something more, though. That girl was more a hero than Papa or Po Doggly either one. Because the only way she could think to get away was to use a witchery so strong that Peggy never even heard of it before. Never dreamed that Black folks had such lore.

But it was no lie, it was no dream neither. That girl flew. Made a wax poppet and feathered it and burnt it up. Burnt it right up. It let her fly all this way, this long hard way till the sun came up, far enough that Peggy saw her and they took her across the Hio. But what a price that runaway had paid for it.

When they got back to the roadhouse, Mama was just as angry as Peggy ever saw her. "It's a crime you should have a whipping for, taking your sixteen-year-old daughter out to commit a crime in the darkness."

But Papa didn't answer. He didn't have to, once he carried that girl inside and laid her on the floor before the fire.

"She can't have ate a thing for days. For weeks!" cried Mama. "And her brow is like to burn my hand off just to touch her. Fetch me a pan of water, Horace, to mop her brow, while I het up the broth for her to sip—"

"No, Mama," said Peggy. "Best you find some milk for the baby."

"The baby won't die, and this girl's likely to, don't you tell me my business, I know physicking for *this*, anyway—"

"No, Mama," said Peggy. "She did a witchery with a wax poppet. It's a Black sort of witchery, but she had the know-how and she had the power, being the daughter of a king in Africa. She knew the price and now she can't help but pay."

"Are you saying this girl's bound to die?" asked Mama.

"She made a poppet of herself, Mama, and put it on the fire. It gave her the wings to fly one whole night. But the cost of it is the rest of her life."

Papa looked sick at heart. "Peggy, that's plain crazy. What good would it do her to escape from slavery if she was just going to die? Why not kill herself there and save the trouble?"

Peggy didn't have to answer. The baby she was a-holding started to cry right then, and that was all the answer there was.

"I'll get milk," said Papa. "Christian Larsson's bound to have a gill or so to spare even this time of the night."

Mama stopped him, though. "Think again, Horace," she said. "It's near midnight now. What'll you tell him you need the milk *for*?"

Horace sighed, laughed at his own foolishness. "For a runaway slavegirl's little pickaninny baby." But then he turned red, getting hot with anger. "What a crazy thing this Black girl done," he said. "She came all this way, knowing that she'd die, and now what does she reckon we'll do with a little pickaninny like that? We sure can't take it north and lay it across the Canadian border and let it bawl till some Frenchman comes to take it."

"I reckon she just figures it's better to die free than live slave," said Peggy. "I reckon she just knew that whatever life that baby found here had to be better than what it was there."

The girl lay there before the fire, breathing soft, her eyes closed.

"She's asleep, isn't she?" asked Mama.

"Not dead yet," said Peggy, "but not hearing us."

"Then I'll tell you plain, this is a bad piece of trouble," said Mama. "We can't have people knowing you bring runaway slaves through here. Word of that would spread so fast we'd have two dozen finders camped here every week of the year, and one of them'd be bound to take a shot at you sometime from ambush."

"Nobody has to know," said Papa.

"What are you going to do, tell folks you happened to trip over her dead body in the woods?"

Peggy wanted to shout at them, She ain't dead yet, so mind how you talk! But the truth was they had to get some things planned, and quick. What if one of the guests woke up in the night and came downstairs? There'd be no keeping this secret then.

"How soon will she die?" Papa asked. "By morning?"

"She'll be dead before sunrise, Papa."

Papa nodded. "Then I better get busy. The girl I can take care of. You women can think of something to do with that pickaninny, I hope."

"Oh, we can, can we?" said Mama.

"Well I know I can't, so you'd better."

"Well then maybe I'll just tell folks it's my own babe."

Papa didn't get mad. Just grinned, he did, and said, "Folks ain't going to believe that even if you dip that boy in cream three times a day."

He went outside and got Po Doggly to help him dig a grave.

"Passing this baby off as born around here ain't such a bad idea," said Mama. "That Black family that lives down in that boggy land—you remember two years back when some slaveowner tried to prove he used to own them? What's their name, Peggy?"

Peggy knew them far better than any other White folks in Hatrack River did; she watched over them the same as everyone else, knew all their children, knew all their names. "They call their name Berry," she said. "Like a noble house, they just keep that family name no matter what job each one of them does."

"Why couldn't we pass this baby off as theirs?"

"They're poor, Mama," said Peggy. "They can't feed another mouth."

"We could help with that," said Mama. "We have extra."

"Just think a minute, Mama, how that'd look. Suddenly the Berrys get them a light-colored baby like this, you *know* he's half-White just to look at him. And then Horace Guester starts bringing gifts down to the Berry house."

Mama's face went red. "What do you know about such things?" she demanded.

"Oh, for heaven's sake, Mama, I'm a torch. And you know people would start to talk, you know they would."

Mama looked at the Black girl lying there. "You got us into a whole lot of trouble, little girl."

The baby started fussing.

Mama stood up and walked to the window, as if she could see out into the night and find some answer writ on the sky. Then, abruptly, she headed for the door, opened it.

"Mama," said Peggy.

"There's more than one way to pluck a goose," said Mama.

Peggy saw what Mama had thought of. If they couldn't take the baby down to the Berry place, they could maybe keep the baby here at the roadhouse and say they were taking care of it for the Berrys cause they were so poor. As long as the Berry family went along with the tale, it would account for a half-Black baby showing

up one day. And nobody'd think the baby was Horace's bastard—
not if his wife brought it right into the house.

"You realize what you're asking them, don't you?" said Peggy.
"Everybody's going to think somebody else has been plowing with
Mr. Berry's heifer."

Mama looked so surprised Peggy almost laughed out loud. "I
didn't think Blacks cared about such things," she said.

Peggy shook her head. "Mama, the Berrys are just about the
best Christians in Hatrack River. They have to be, to keep forgiving
the way White folks treat them and their children."

Mama closed the door again and stood inside, leaning on it.
"How *do* folks treat their children?"

It was a pertinent question, Peggy knew, and Mama had thought
of it only just in time. It was one thing to look at that scrawny
fussing little Black baby and say, I'm going to take care of this
child and save his life. It was something else again to think of him
being five and seven and ten and seventeen years old, a young buck
living right there in the house.

"I don't think you have to fret about that," said Little Peggy,
"not half so much as how *you* plan to treat this boy. Do you plan
to raise him up to be your servant, a lowborn child in your big fine
house? If that's so, then this girl died for nothing, she might as
well have let them sell him south."

"I never hankered for no slave," said Mama. "Don't you go
saying that I did."

"Well, what then? Are you going to treat him as your own son,
and stand with him against all comers, the way you would if you'd
ever borne a son of your own?"

Peggy watched as Mama thought of that, and suddenly she saw
all kinds of new paths open up in Mama's heartfire. A son—that's
what this half-White boy could be. And if folks around here looked
cross-eyed at him on account of him not being all White, they'd
have to reckon with Margaret Guester, they would, and it'd be a
fearsome day for them, they'd have no terror at the thought of hell,
not after what she'd put them through.

Mama hadn't felt such a powerful grim determination in all the years Peggy'd been looking into her heart. It was one of those times when somebody's whole future changed right before her eyes. All the old paths had been pretty much the same; Mama had no choices that would change her life. But now, this dying girl had brought a transformation. Now there were hundreds of new paths open, and all of them had a little boy-child in them, needing her the way her daughter'd never needed her. Set upon by strangers, cruelly treated by the boys of the town, he'd come to her again and again for protection, for teaching, for toughening, the kind of thing that Peggy'd never done.

That's why I disappointed you, wasn't it, Mama? Cause I knew too much, too young. You wanted me to come to you in my confusion, with my questions. But I never had no questions, Mama, cause I knew from childhood up. I knew what it meant to be a woman from the memories in your own head. I knew about married love without you telling me. I never had a tearful night pressed up against your shoulder, crying cause some boy I longed for wouldn't look at me; I never longed for any boy around here. I never did a thing you dreamed your little girl would do, cause I had a torch's knack, and I knew everything and needed nothing that you wanted to give me.

But this half-Black boy, he'll need you no matter what his knack might be. I see down all those paths, that if you take him in, if you raise him up, he'll be more son to you than I ever was your daughter, though your blood is half of mine.

"Daughter," said Mama, "if I go through this door, will it turn out well for the boy? And for us, too?"

"Are you asking me to See for you, Mama?"

"I am, Little Peggy, and I never asked for that before, never on my own behalf."

"Then I'll tell you." Peggy hardly needed to look far down the paths of Mama's life to find how much pleasure she'd have in the boy. "If you take him in, and treat him like your own son, you'll never regret doing it."

"What about your papa? Will he treat him right?"

"Don't you know your own husband?" asked Peggy.

Mama walked a step toward her, her hand all clenched up even though she never laid a hand on Peggy. "Don't get fresh with me," she said.

"I'm talking the way I talk when I See," said Peggy. "You come to me as a torch, I talk as a torch to you."

"Then say what you have to say."

"It's easy enough. If you don't know how your husband will treat this boy, you don't know that man at all."

"So maybe I don't," said Mama. "Maybe I don't know him at all. Or maybe I do, and I want you to tell me if I'm right."

"You're right," said Peggy. "He'll treat him fair, and make him feel loved all the days of his life."

"But will he really love him?"

There wasn't no chance that Peggy'd answer that question. Love wasn't even in the picture for Papa. He'd take care of the boy because he ought to, because he felt a bounden duty, but the boy'd never know the difference, it'd feel like love to him, and it'd be a lot more dependable than love ever was. But to explain that to Mama would mean telling her how Papa did so many things because he felt so bad about his ancient sins, and there'd never be a time in Mama's life when she was ready to hear *that* tale.

So Peggy just looked at Mama and answered her the way she answered other folks who pried too deep into things they didn't really want to know. "That's for him to answer," Peggy said. "All you need to know is that the choice you already made in your heart is a good one. Already just deciding that has changed your life."

"But I haven't even decided yet," said Mama.

In Mama's heart there wasn't a single path left, not a single one, in which she didn't get the Berrys to say it was their boy, and leave him with her to raise.

"Yes you have," said Peggy. "And you're glad of it."

Mama turned and left, closing the door gentle behind her, so as not to wake the traveling preacher who was sleeping in the room upstairs of the door.

Peggy had just one moment's unease, and she wasn't even sure why. If she'd thought about it a minute, she'd have known it was on account of how she cheated her Mama without even knowing it. When Peggy did a Seeing for anybody else, she always took care to look far down the paths of their life, looking for darkness from causes not even guessed at. But Peggy was so sure she knew her Mama and Papa, she didn't even bother looking except at what was coming up right away. That's how it goes within a family. You think you know each other so well, and so you don't bother hardly getting to know each other at all. It wouldn't be years yet till Peggy would think back on this day, and try to figure why she didn't See what was coming. Sometimes she'd even imagine that her knack failed her. But it didn't. She failed her own knack. She wasn't the first to do so, nor the last, nor even the worst, but there's few ever lived to regret it more.

The moment of unease passed, and Peggy forgot it as her thoughts turned to the Black girl on the common-room floor. She was awake, her eyes open. The baby was still mewling. Without the girl saying a thing, Peggy knew she was willing for the babe to suckle, if she had anything in her breasts to suck on out. The girl hadn't even strength to open up her faded cotton shirt. Peggy had to sit beside her, cradling the child against her own thighs while she fumbled the girl's buttons open with her free hand. The girl's chest was so skinny, her ribs so stark and bare, that her breasts looked to be saddlebags tossed onto a rail fence. But the nipple still stood up for the baby to suck, and a white froth soon appeared around the baby's lips, so there was something there, even now, even at the very end of his mama's life.

The girl was far too weak to talk, but she didn't need to; Peggy heard what she wanted to say, and answered her. "My own mama's going to keep your boy," said Peggy. "And no wise is she going to let any man make a slave of him."

That was what the girl wanted most to hear—that and the sound of her greedy boy-baby slurping and humming and squealing at her breast.

But Peggy wanted her to know more than that before she died. "Your boy-baby's going to know about you," she told the girl. "He's going to hear how you gave your life so you could fly away and take him here to freedom. Don't you think he'll ever forget you, cause he won't.''

Then Peggy looked into the child's heartfire, searched there for what he'd be. Oh, that was a painful thing, because the life of a half-White boy in a White town was hard no matter which of the paths of his life he chose. Still, she saw enough to know the nature of the babe whose fingers scratched and clutched at his mama's naked chest. "And he'll be a man worth dying for, too, I promise you that.''

The girl was glad to hear it. It brought her peace enough that she could sleep again. After a time the babe, satisfied, also fell asleep. Peggy picked him up, wrapped him in a blanket, and laid him in the crook of his mama's arm. Every last moment of your mama's life you'll be with her, she told the boychild silently. We'll tell you that, too, that she held you in her arms when she died.

When she died. Papa was out with Po Doggly, digging her grave; Mama was off at the Berrys, to persuade them to help her save the baby's life and freedom; and here was Peggy, thinking as if the girl was already dead.

But she wasn't dead, not yet. And all of a sudden it came to Peggy, with a flash of anger that she was too stupid to think of it before, that there was one soul she knew of who had the knack in him to heal the sick. Hadn't he knelt by Ta-Kumsaw at the battle of Detroit, that great Red man's body riddled with bullet holes, hadn't Alvin knelt there and healed him up? Alvin could save this girl, if he was here.

She cast off in the darkness, searching for the heartfire that burned so bright, the heartfire she knew better than any in the world, better even than her own. And there he was, running in the darkness, traveling the way Red men did, like he was asleep, and the land around him was his soul. He was coming faster than any White could ever come, even with the fastest horse on the best road between the Wobbish and the Hatrack, but he wouldn't be here till noon tomorrow, and by then this runaway slavegirl would be dead and in the ground up in the family graveyard. By twelve hours at most she'd miss the one man in this country who could have saved her life.

Wasn't that the way of it? Alvin could save her, but he'd never know she needed saving. While Peggy, who couldn't do a thing, she knew all that was happening, knew all the things that might happen, knew the one thing that *should* happen if the world was good. It wasn't good. It wouldn't happen.

What a terrible gift it was, to be a torch, to know all these things a-coming, and have so little power to change them. The only power she'd ever had was just the words of her mouth, telling folks, and even then she couldn't be sure what they'd choose to do. Always there'd be some choice they could make that would set them down a path even worse than the one she wanted to save them from— and so many times in their wickedness or cantankerousness or just plain bad luck, they'd make that terrible choice and then things'd be worse for them than if Peggy'd just kept still and never said a thing. I wish I didn't know. I wish I had some hope that Alvin would come in time. I wish I had some hope this girl would live. I wish that I could save her life myself.

And then she thought of the many times she *had* saved a life. Alvin's life, using Alvin's caul. At that moment hope *did* spark up in her heart, for surely, just this once, she could use a bit of the last scrap of Alvin's caul to save this girl, to restore her.

Peggy leapt up and ran clumsily to the stairs, her legs so numb from sitting on the floor that she couldn't hardly feel her own footsteps on the bare wood. She tripped on the stairs and made some noise, but none of the guests woke up, as far as she noticed right off like that. Up the stairs, then up the attic ladderway that Oldpappy made into a proper stairway not three months afore he died. She threaded her way among the trunks and old furniture until she reached her room up against the west end of the house. Moonlight came in through her south-facing window, making a squared-off pattern on the floor. She pried up the floorboard and took the box from the place where she hid it whenever she left the room.

She walked too heavy or this one guest slept too light, but as she came down the ladderway, there he stood, skinny white legs sticking out from under his longshirt, a-gazing down the stairs, then back toward his room, like as if he couldn't make up his mind whether to go in or out, up or down. Peggy looked into his heartfire, just to find

out whether he'd been downstairs and seen the girl and her baby—
if he had, then all their thought and caution had been in vain.

But he hadn't—it was still possible.

"Why are you still dressed for going out?" he asked. "At this time
of the morning, too?"

She gently laid her finger against his lips. To silence him, or at
least that's how the gesture began. But she knew right away that she
was the first woman ever to touch this man upon the face since his
mama all those many years ago. She saw that in that moment his heart
filled, not with lust, but with the vague longings of a lonely man. He
was the minister who'd come day before yesterday morning, a traveling preacher—from Scotland, he said. She'd hardly paid him no
mind, her being so preoccupied with knowing Alvin was on his way
back. But now all that mattered was to send him back into his room,
quick as could be, and she knew one sure way to do it. She put her
hands on his shoulders, getting a strong grip behind his neck, and
pulled him down to where she could kiss him fair on the lips. A good
long buss, like he never had from a woman in all his days.

Just like she expected, he was back into his room almost before
she let go of him. She might've laughed at that, except she knew
from his heartfire it wasn't her kiss sent him back, like she planned.
It was the box she still held in one hand, which she had pressed
up against the back of his neck when she held him. The box with
Alvin's caul inside.

The moment it touched him, he felt what was inside. It wasn't
no knack of his, it was something else—just being so near something
of Alvin's done it to him. She saw the vision of Alvin's face loom
up inside his mind, with such fear and hatred like she never seen
before. Only then did she realize that he wasn't just any minister.
He was Reverend Philadelphia Thrower, who once had been a
preacher back in Vigor Church. Reverend Thrower, who once had
tried to kill the boy, except Alvin's pa prevented him.

The fear of a woman's kiss was nothing to him compared to his
fear of Alvin Junior. The trouble was that now he was *so* afraid he
was already thinking of leaving right this minute and getting out of
this roadhouse. If he did that, he'd have to come downstairs and then

he'd see all, just what she meant to fend off. This was how it went so often—she tried to stave off a bad thing and it turned out worse, something so unlikely she didn't see it. How could she not have re-ckonized who he was? Hadn't she seen him through Alvin's eyes all those many times in years past? But he'd changed this last year, he looked thin and haunted and older. Besides, she wasn't looking for him here, and anyhow it was too late to undo what she already done. All that mattered now was to keep him in his room.

So she opened his door and followed him inside and looked him square in the face and said, "He was born here."

"Who?" he said. His face was white as if he'd just seen the devil himself. He knew who she meant.

"And he's coming back. Right now he's on his way. You're only safe if you stay in your room tonight, and leave in the morning at first light."

"I don't know—know what you're talking about."

Did he really think he could fool a torch? Maybe he didn't know she was—no, he knew, he knew, he just didn't believe in torching and hexing and knacks and suchlike. He was a man of science and higher religion. A blamed fool. So she'd have to prove to him that what he feared most was so. She knew him, and she knew his secrets. "You tried to kill Alvin Junior with a butchery knife," she said.

That did it, right enough. He fell to his knees. "I'm not afraid to die," he said. Then he began to murmur the Lord's prayer.

"Pray all night, if you like," she said, "but stay in your room to do it."

Then she stepped through the door and closed it. She was halfway down the stairs when she heard the bar fall into place across the door. Peggy didn't even have time to care whether she caused him undue misery—he wasn't really a murderer in his heart. All she cared for now was to get the caul down to where she could use it to help the runaway, if by any chance Alvin's power was really hers to use. So much time that minister had cost her. So many of the slavegirl's precious breaths.

She was still breathing, wasn't she? Yes. No. The babe lay sleeping beside her, but her chest didn't move even as much as him, her lips didn't make even so much as a baby's breath on Peggy's hand. But her heartfire still burned! Peggy could see that plain enough, still burned bright because she was so strong-hearted, that slavegirl was. So Peggy opened up the box, took out the scrap of caul, and rubbed a dry corner of it to dust between her fingers, whispering to her, "Live, get strong." She tried to do what Alvin did when he healed, the way he could feel the small broken places in a person's body, set them right. Hadn't she watched him as he did it so many times before? But it was different, doing it herself. It was strange to her, she didn't have the vision for it, and she could feel the life ebbing away from the girl's body, the heart stilled, the lungs slack, the eyes open but unlighted, and at last the heartfire flashed like a shooting star, all sudden and bright, and it was gone.

Too late. If I hadn't stopped in the hall upstairs, hadn't had to deal with the minister—

But no, no, she couldn't blame herself, it wasn't her power anyway, it was too late before she began. The girl had been dying all through her body. Even Alvin himself, if he was here, even he couldn't have done it. It was never more than a slim hope. Never even hope enough that she could see a single pathway where it worked. So she wouldn't do like so many did, she wouldn't endlessly blame herself when after all she'd done her best at a task that had little hope in it from the start.

Now that the girl was dead, she couldn't leave the baby there to feel his mama's arm grow cold. She picked him up. He stirred, but slept on in the way that babies do. Your mama's dead, little half-White boy, but you'll have *my* mama, and my papa too. They got love enough for a little one; you won't starve for it like some children I seen. So you make the best of it, boy-baby. Your mama died to bring you here—you make the best of it, and you'll be something, right enough.

You'll be something, she heard herself whispering. You'll be something, and so will I.

She made her decision even before she realized there was even a decision to be made. She could feel her own future changing even though she couldn't see rightly what it was going to be.

That slave girl guessed at the likeliest future—you don't have to be a torch to see *some* things plain. It was an ugly life ahead, losing her baby, living as a slave till the day she dropped. Yet she saw just the faintest glimmer of hope for her baby, and once she saw it, she didn't hold back, no sir, that glimmer was worth paying her life for.

And now look at me, thought Peggy. Here I look down the paths of Alvin's life and see misery for myself—nowhere near as bad as that slavegirl's, but bad enough. Now and then I catch the shine of a bright chance for happiness, a strange and backward way to have Alvin and have him love me, too. Once I seen it, am I going to sit on my hands and watch that bright hope die, just because I'm not sure how to get to it from here?

If that beat-down child can make her own hope out of wax and ash and feathers and a bit of herself, then I can make my own life, too. Somewhere there's a thread that if I just lay hold on it, it'll lead me to happiness. And even if I never find that particular thread, it'll be better than the despair waiting for me if I stay. Even if I never become a part of Alvin's life when he comes to manhood, well, that's still not as steep a price as that slavegirl paid for freedom.

When Alvin comes tomorrow, I won't be here.

That was her decision, just like that. Why, she could hardly believe she never thought of it before. Of all people in the whole of Hatrack River, she ought to have knowed that there's *always* another choice. Folks talked on about how they were forced into misery and woe, they didn't have no choice at all—but that runaway girl showed that there's always a way out, long as you remember even death can be a straight smooth road sometimes.

I don't even have to get no blackbird feathers to fly, neither.

Peggy sat there holding the baby, making bold and fearsome plans for how she'd leave in the morning afore Alvin could arrive. Whenever she felt a-scared of what she'd set herself to do, she cast her gaze down on that girl, and the sight of her was comfort, it truly was. I might someday end up like you, runaway girl, dead in some stranger's house. But better that unknown future than one I knew all along I'd hate, and then did nothing to avoid.

Will I do it, will I really do it in the morning, when the time's come and no turning back? She touched Alvin's caul with her free hand, just snaking her fingers into the box, and what she saw in Alvin's future made her feel like singing. Used to be most paths showed them meeting up and starting out her life of misery. Now only a few of those paths were there—in most of Alvin's futures, she saw him come to Hatrack River and search for the torch girl and find her gone. Just changing her mind tonight had closed down most of the roads to misery.

Mama came back with the Berrys before Papa came in from gravedigging. Anga Berry was a heavyset woman with laughter lines outnumbering the lines of worry on her face, though both kinds were plain enough. Peggy knew her well and liked her better than most folks in Hatrack River. She had a temper but she also had compassion, and Peggy wasn't surprised at all to see her rush to the body of the girl and take up that cold limp hand and press it to her bosom She murmured words almost like a lullaby, her voice was so low and sweet and kind.

"She's dead," said Mock Berry. "But that baby's strong I see."

Peggy stood up and let Mock see the baby in her arms. She didn't like him half so well as she liked his wife. He was the kind of man who'd slap a child so hard blood flowed, just cause he didn't like what was said or done. It was almost worse cause he didn't rage when he did it. Like he felt nothing at all, to hurt somebody or not hurt somebody made no powerful difference in his mind. But he worked hard, and even though he was poor his family got by; and nobody who knew Mock paid heed to them crude folks what said there wasn't a buck who wouldn't steal or a ewe you couldn't tup.

"Healthy," said Mock. Then he turned to Mama. "When he grow up to be a big old buck, ma'am, you still aim to call him your boy? Or you make him sleep out back in the shed with the animals?"

Well, he wasn't one to pussyfoot around the issue, Peggy saw.

"Shut your mouth, Mock," said his wife. "And you give me that baby, Miss. I just wish I'd knowed he was coming or I'd've kept my youngest on the tit to keep the milk in. Weaned that boy two

months back and he's been nothing but trouble since, but you ain't
no trouble, baby, you ain't no trouble at all.'' She cooed to the baby
just like she cooed to his dead mama, and he didn't wake up either.

"I told you. I'll raise him as my son," said Mama.

"I'm sorry, ma'am, but I just never heard of no White woman
doing such a thing," said Mock.

"What I say," said Mama, "that's what I do."

Mock thought on that a moment. Then he nodded. "I reckon
so," he said. "I reckon I never heard you break your word, not
even to Black folks." He grinned. "Most White folk allow as how
lying to a buck ain't the same as *lying*."

"We'll do like you asked," said Anga Berry. "I'll tell anybody
who ask me this is my boy, only we gave him to you cause we was
too poor."

"But don't you ever go forgetting that it's a lie," said Mock.
"Don't you ever go thinking that if it really was our own baby,
we'd ever give him up. And don't you ever go thinking that my
wife here ever would let some White man put a baby in her, and
her being married to me."

Mama studied Mock for a minute, taking his measure in the way
she had. "Mock Berry, I hope you come and visit me any day you
like while this boy is in my house, and I'll show you how one
White woman keeps her word."

Mock laughed. "I reckon you a regular Mancipationist."

Papa came in then, covered with sweat and dirt. He shook hands
with the Berrys, and in a minute they told him the tale they all
would tell. He made his promises too, to raise the boy like his own
son. He even thought of what never entered Mama's head—he said
a few words to Peggy, to promise her that they wouldn't give no
preference to the boy, neither. Peggy nodded. She didn't want to
say much, cause anything she said would either be a lie or give her
plans away; she knew she had no intention to be in this house for
even a single day of this baby's future here.

"We go on home now, Mrs. Guester," said Anga. She handed
the baby to Mama. "If one of my children wake up with a boogly

dream I best be there or you hear them screams clear up here on the high road.''

''Ain't you going have no preacher say words at her grave?'' said Mock.

Papa hadn't thought of it. ''We do have a minister upstairs,'' he said.

But Peggy didn't let him hold that thought for even a moment. ''No,'' she said, sharp as she could.

Papa looked at her, and knew that she was talking as a torch. Wasn't no arguing that point. He just nodded. ''Not this time, Mock,'' he said. ''Wouldn't be safe.''

Mama fretted Anga Berry clear to the door. ''Is there anything I ought to know?'' said Mama. ''Is there anything different about Black babies?''

''Oh, powerful different,'' said Anga. ''But that baby, he half White I reckon, so you just take care of that White half, and I reckon the Black half take care of hisself.''

''Cow's milk from a pig bladder?'' Mama insisted.

''You know all them things,'' said Anga. ''I learnt everything I know from you, Mrs. Guester. All the women round here do. How come you asking me now? Don't you know I need my sleep?''

Once the Berrys were gone, Papa picked up the girl's body and carried her outside. Not even a coffin, though they would overlay the corpse with stones to keep the dogs off. ''Light as a feather,'' he said when first he hoisted her. ''Like the charred carcass of a burnt log.''

Which was apt enough, Peggy had to admit. That's what she was now. Just ashes. She'd burnt herself right up.

Mama held the pickaninny boy while Peggy went up into the attic and fetched down the cradle. Nobody woke up this time, except that minister. He was *wide* awake behind his door, but he wasn't coming out for any reason. Mama and Peggy made up that little bed in Mama's and Papa's room, and laid the baby in it. ''Tell me if this poor orphan baby's got him a name,'' said Mama.

''She never gave him one,'' said Peggy. ''In her tribe, a woman never got her a name till she married, and a man had no name till he killed him his first animal.''

"That's just awful," said Mama. "That ain't even Christian. Why, she died unbaptized.''

"No," said Peggy. "She was baptized right enough. Her owner's wife saw to that—all the Blacks on their plantation were baptized.''

Mama's face went sour. "I reckon she thought that made her a Christian. Well, I'll have a name for you, little boy.'' She grinned wickedly. "What do you think your papa would do if I named this baby Horace Guester Junior?''

"Die," said Peggy.

"I reckon so," said Mama. "I ain't ready to be a widow yet. So for now we'll name him—oh, I can't think, Peggy. What's a Black man's name? Or should I just name him like any White child?''

"Only Black man's name I know is Othello," said Peggy.

"That's a queer name if I ever heard one," said Mama. "You must've got that out of one of Whitley Physicker's books.''

Peggy said nothing.

"I know," said Mama. "I know his name. Cromwell. The Lord Protector's name.''

"You might better name him Arthur, after the King," said Peggy.

Mama just cackled and laughed at that. "That's your name, little boy. Arthur Stuart! And if the King don't like such a namesake, let him send an army and I still won't change it. His Majesty will have to change his own name first.''

Even though she got to bed so late, Peggy woke early next morning. It was hoofbeats woke her—she didn't have to go to the window to recognize his heartfire as the minister rode away. Ride on, Thrower, she said silently. You won't be the last to run away this morning, fleeing from that eleven-year-old boy.

It was the north-facing window she looked out of. She could see between the trees to the graveyard up the hill. She tried to see where the grave was dug last night, but there wasn't no sign her natural eyes could see, and in a graveyard there wasn't no heartfires neither, nothing to help her. Alvin will see it though, she knew that sure.

He'd head for that graveyard first thing he did, cause his oldest brother's body lay there, the boy Vigor, who got swept away in the Hatrack River saving Alvin's mother's life in the last hour before she gave birth to her seventh son. But Vigor hung on to life just long enough, in spite of the river's strongest pulling at him, hung on just long enough that when Alvin was born he was the seventh of seven living sons. Peggy herself had watched his heartfire flicker and die right after the babe was born. He would've heard that story a thousand times. So he'd come to that graveyard, and *he* could feel his way through the earth and find what lay hidden there. He'd find that unmarked grave, that wasted body so fresh buried there.

Peggy took the box with the caul in it, put it deep in a cloth bag along with her second dress, a petticoat, and the most recent books Whitley Physicker had brought. Just because she didn't want to meet him face to face didn't mean she could forget that boy. She'd touch the caul again tonight, or maybe not till morning, and then she'd stand with him in memory and use his senses to find that nameless Black girl's grave.

Her bag packed, she went downstairs.

Mama had drug the cradle into the kitchen and she was singing to the baby while she kneaded bread, rocking the cradle with one foot, even though Arthur Stuart was fast asleep. Peggy set her bag outside the kitchen door, walked in and touched her Mama's shoulder. She hoped a little that she'd see her Mama grieving something awful when she found out Peggy'd gone off. But it wasn't so. Oh, she'd carry on and rage at first, but in the times to come she'd miss Peggy less than she might've guessed. It was the baby'd take her mind off worrying about her daughter. Besides, Mama knew Peggy could take care of herself. Mama knew Peggy wasn't a one to need to hold a body's hand. While Arthur Stuart needed her.

If this was the first time Peggy noticed how her Mama felt about her, she'd have been hurt deep. But it was the hundredth time, and she was used to it, and looked behind it to the reason, and loved her Mama for being a better soul than most, and forgave her for not loving Peggy more.

"I love you, Mama," said Peggy.

"I love you too, baby," said Mama. She didn't even look up nor guess what Peggy had in mind.

Papa was still asleep. After all, he dug a grave last night and filled it too.

Peggy wrote a note. Sometimes she took care to put in a lot of extra letters in the fancy way they did in books, but this time she wanted to make sure Papa could read it for hisself. That meant putting in no more letters than it took to make the sounds for reading out loud.

> *I lov you Papa and Mama but I got to leav I no its rong to lev Hatrak with out no torch but I bin torch sixtn yr. I seen my fewchr and ile be saf donte you fret on my acown.*

She walked out the front door, carried her bag to the road, and waited only ten minutes before Doctor Whitley Physicker came along in his carriage, bound on the first leg of a trip to Philadelphia.

"You didn't wait on the road like this just to hand me back that Milton I lent you," said Whitley Physicker.

She smiled and shook her head. "No sir, I'd like you take me with you to Dekane. I plan to visit with a friend of my father's, but if you don't mind the company I'd rather not spend the money for a coach."

Peggy watched him consider for a minute, but she knew he'd let her come, and without asking her folks, neither. He was the kind of man thought a girl had as much worth as any boy, and more than that, he plain liked Peggy, thought of her as something like a niece. And he knew that Peggy never lied, so he had no need to check with her folks.

And she hadn't lied to him, no more than she ever lied when she left off without telling all she knew. Papa's old lover, the woman he dreamed of and suffered for, she lived there in Dekane—widowed for the last few years, but her mourning time over so she wouldn't have to turn away company. Peggy knew that lady well, from watching far off for all these years. If I knock on her door, thought Peggy, I don't even have to tell her I'm Horace Guester's girl, she'd take me in as a stranger, she would, and care for me, and help me on my way. But maybe I *will* tell her whose daughter

I am, and how I knew to come to her, and how Papa still lives with the aching memory of his love for her.

The carriage rattled over the covered bridge that Alvin's father and older brothers had built eleven years before, after the river drowned the oldest son. Birds nested in the rafters. It was a mad, musical, happy sound they made, at least to her ears, chirping so loud inside the bridge that it sounded like she imagined grand opera ought to be. They had opera in Camelot, down south. Maybe some-day she'd go and hear it, and see the King himself in his box.

Or maybe not. Because someday she might just find the path that led to that brief but lovely dream, and then she'd have more impor-tant things to do than look at kings or hear the music of the Austrian court played by lacy Virginia musicians in the fancy opera hall in Camelot. Alvin was more important than any of these, if he could only find his way to all his power and what he ought to do with it. And she was born to be part of it. That's how easily she slipped into her dreams of him. Yet why not? Her dreams of him, however brief and hard to find, were true visions of the future, and the greatest joy and the greatest grief she could find for herself both touched this boy who wasn't even a man yet, who had never seen her face to face.

But sitting there in the carriage beside Doctor Whitley Physicker, she forced those thoughts, those visions from her mind. What comes will come, she thought. If I find that path I find it, and if not, then not. For now, at least, I'm free. Free of my watch aloft for the town of Hatrack, and free of building all my plans around that little boy. And what if I end up free of him forever? What if I find another future that doesn't even have him in it? That's the likeliest end of things. Give me time enough, I'll even forget that scrap of a dream I had, and find my own good road to a peaceful end, instead of bending myself to fit his troubled path.

The dancing horses pulled the carriage along so brisk that the wind caught and tossed her hair. She closed her eyes and pretended she was flying, a runaway just learning to be free.

Let him find his path to greatness now without me. Let me have a happy life far from him. Let some other woman stand beside him in his glory. Let another woman kneel a-weeping at his grave.

⋈ 3 ⋈

Lies

ELEVEN-YEAR-OLD Alvin lost half his name when he came to Hatrack River. Back home in the town of Vigor Church, not far from where the Tippy-Canoe poured its waters into the Wobbish, everybody knowed his father was Alvin, miller for the town and the country round about. Alvin Miller. Which made his namesake, his seventh son, Alvin *Junior*. Now, though, he was going to live in a place where there wasn't six folks who so much as ever met his pa. No need for names like Miller and Junior. He was just Alvin, plain Alvin, but hearing that lone name made him feel like only half hisself.

He came to Hatrack River on foot, hundreds of miles across Wobbish and Hio territories. When he set out from home it was with a pair of sturdy broke-in boots on and a pack of supplies on his back. He did five miles that way, before he stopped up at a poor cabin and gave his food to the folk there. After another mile or so he met a poor traveling family, heading on west to the new lands in the Noisy River country. He gave them the tent and blanket in his pack, and because they had a thirteen-year-old boy about

Alvin's size, he pulled off them new boots and gave them straight out, just like that, socks too. He kept only his clothes and the empty pack on his back.

Why, them folks were wide-eyed and silly-faced over it, worrying that Alvin's pa might be mad, him giving stuff away like that, but he allowed as how it was his to give.

"You sure I won't be meeting up with your pa with a musket and a possy-come-and-take-us?" asked the poor man.

"I'm sure you won't, sir," said young Alvin, "on account of I'm from the town of Vigor Church, and the folks there won't see you at all unless you force them."

It took them near ten seconds to realize where they'd heard the name of Vigor Church before. "Them's the folk of the Tippy-Canoe massacre," they said. "Them's the folk what got blood on their hands."

Alvin just nodded. "So you see they'll leave you be."

"Is it true they make every traveler listen to them tell that terrible gory tale of how they killed all them Reds in cold blood?"

"Their blood wasn't cold," said Alvin, "and they only tell travelers who come right on into town. So just stay on the road, leave them be, ride on through. Once you cross the Wobbish, you'll be in open land again, where you'll be glad to meet up with settled folk. Not ten mile on."

Well, they didn't argue no more, nor even ask him how he came not to have to tell the tale hisself. The name of the Massacre of Tippy-Canoe was enough to put a silence on folks like setting in a church, a kind of holy, shameful, reverent attitude. Cause even though most Whites shunned the bloody-handed folk who shed Red men's blood at Tippy-Canoe, they still knew that if they'd stood in the same place, they'd've done the same thing, and it'd be their hands dripping red till they told a stranger about the wretched deed they done. That guilty knowledge didn't make many travelers too keen on stopping in Vigor Church, or any homes in the upper Wobbish country. Them poor folks just took Alvin's boots and gear and moved on down the road, glad of a stretch of canvas over their heads and a slice of leather on their big boy's feet.

Alvin betook him off the road soon after, and plunged into woodland, into the deepest places. If he'd been wearing boots, he would've stumbled and crunched and made more noise than a rutting buffalo in the woods—which is about what most White folks did in the natural forest. But because he was barefoot, his skin touching the forest floor, he was like a different person. He had run behind Ta-Kumsaw through the forests of this whole land, north and south, and in that running young Alvin learned him how the Red man ran, hearing the greensong of the living woodland, moving in perfect harmony to that sweet silent music. When he ran that way, not thinking about where to step, the ground became soft under young Alvin's feet, and he was guided along, no sticks breaking when he stepped, no bushes swishing or twigs snapping off with his onward push. Behind him he left nary a footprint or a broken branch.

Just like a Red man, that was how he moved. And pretty soon his White man's clothing chafed on him, and he stopped and took it off, stuffed it into the pack on his back, and then ran naked as a jaybird, feeling the leaves of the bushes against his body. Soon he was caught up in the rhythm of his own running, forgetting anything about his own body, just part of the living forest, moving onward, faster and stronger, not eating, not drinking. Like a Red man, who could run forever through the deep forest, never needing rest, covering hundreds of miles in a single day.

This was the natural way to travel, Alvin knew it. Not in creaking wooden wagons, rattling over dry ground, sucking along on muddy roads. And not on horseback, a beast sweating and heaving under you, slave to your hurry, not on any errand of its own. Just a man in the woods, bare feet on the ground, bare face in the wind, dreaming as he ran.

All that day and all that night he ran, and well into the morning. How did he find his way? He could feel the slash of the well-traveled road off on his left, like a prickle or an itch, and even though that road led through many a village and many a town, he knew that after a while it'd fetch him up at the town of Hatrack. After all, that was the road his own folks followed, bridging every stream and creek and river on the way, carrying him as a newborn babe in the wagon. Even though he never traveled it before, and wasn't looking at it now, he knew where it led.

So on the second morning he fetched up at the edge of the wood, on the verge of a field of new green maize billowing over rolling ground. There was so many farms in this settled country that the forest was too weak to hold him in his dream much longer anyhow.

It took a while, just standing there, to remember who he was and where he was bound. The music of the greenwood was strong behind him, weak afore. All he could know for sure was a town ahead, and a river maybe five mile on, that's all he could *feel* for sure. But he knew it was the Hatrack River yonder, and so the town could be no other than the one he was bound for.

He had figured to run the forest right up to the edge of town. Now, though, he had no choice but to walk those last miles on White man's feet or not go at all. That was a thought he had never thought of—that there might be places in the world so settled that one farm butted right against the next, with only a row of trees or a rail fence to mark the boundary, farm after farm. Was this what the Prophet saw in his visions of the land? All the forest killed back and these fields put in their place, so a Red man couldn't run no more, nor a deer find cover, nor a bear find him where to sleep come wintertime? If that was so, no wonder he took all the Reds who'd follow him out west, across the Mizzipy. There was no living for a Red man here.

That made Alvin a little sad and a little scared, to leave behind the living lands he'd come to know as well as a man knows his own body. But he wasn't no philosopher. He was a boy of eleven, and he also hankered to see an eastern town, all settled up and civilized. Besides, he had business here, business he'd waited a year to take up, ever since he first learned there was such a body as the torch girl, and how she looked for him to be a Maker.

He pulled his clothes out of his pack and put them on. He walked the edge of the farmland till he came to a road. First time the road crossed a stream, there was proof it was the right road: a covered bridge stood over that little one-jump brooklet. His own pa and older brothers built that bridge, and others like it all the way along that road from Hatrack to Vigor Church. Eleven years ago they built it, when Alvin was a baby sucking on his mama while the wagon rattled west.

He followed the road, and it wasn't awful far. He'd just run hundreds of miles through virgin forest without harm to his feet, but the White man's road had no part of the greensong and it didn't yield to Alvin's feet. Within a couple of miles he was footsore and dusty and thirsty and hungry. Alvin hoped it wasn't too many miles on White man's road, or he'd sure be wishing he'd kept his boots.

The sign beside the road said, Town of Hatrack, Hio.

It was a good-sized town, compared to frontier villages. Of course it didn't compare to the French city of Detroit, but that was a foreign place, and this town was, well, American. The houses and buildings were like the few rough structures in Vigor Church and other new settlements, only smoothed out and growed up to full size. There was four streets that crossed the main road, with a bank and a couple of shops and churches and even a county courthouse and some places with shingles saying Lawyer and Doctor and Alchemist. Why, if there was professional folk here, it was a town *proper,* not just a hopeful place like Vigor Church before the massacre.

Less than a year ago he'd seen a vision of the town of Hatrack. It was when the Prophet, Lolla-Wossiky, caught him up in the tornado that he called down onto Lake Mizogan. The walls of the whirlwind turned to crystal that time, and in the crystal Alvin had seen many things. One of them was the town of Hatrack the way it was when Alvin was born. It was plain that things hadn't stayed the same in these eleven years. He didn't recognize a thing, walking through the town. Why, this place was so big now that not a soul even seemed to notice he was a stranger to give him howdy-do.

He was most of the way through the built-up part of town before he realized that it wasn't the town's bigness that made folks pay him no mind. It was the dust on his face, his bare feet, the empty pack on his back. They looked, they took him in at a glance, and then they looked away, like as if they were halfway scared he'd come up and ask them for bread or a place to stay. It was something Alvin never met up with before, but he knowed it right away for what it was. In the last eleven years, the town of Hatrack, Hio, had learned the difference between rich and poor.

The built-up part was over. He was through the town, and he hadn't seen a single blacksmith's shop, which was what he was supposed to be looking for, nor had he seen the roadhouse where he was born, which was what he was really looking for. All he saw right now was a couple of pig farms, stinking the way pig farms do, and then the road bent a bit south and he couldn't see more.

The smithy had to still be there, didn't it? It was only a year and a half ago that Taleswapper had carried the prentice contract Pa wrote up for Makepeace, the blacksmith of Hatrack River. And less than a year ago that Taleswapper hisself told Alvin that he delivered that letter, and Makepeace Smith was amenable—that was the word he used, *amenable*. Since Taleswapper talked in his halfway English manner, with the *R*s dropped off the ends of words, it sounded to Alvin like old Taleswapper said Makepeace Smith was "a meaner bull," till Taleswapper wrote it down for him. Anyway, the smith was here a year ago. And the torch girl in the roadhouse, the one he visioned in Lolla-Wossiky's crystal tower, she *must* be here. Hadn't she written in Taleswapper's book, "A Maker is born"? When he looked at those words the letters burned with light like as if they been conjured, like the message writ by the hand of God on the wall in that Bible story: "Mean, mean, take all apart, son," and sure enough, it came to pass, Babylon was took all apart. Words of prophecy was what turned letters bright like that. So if that Maker was Alvin himself, and he knowed it was, then she must see more in her torchy way. She must know what a Maker really *is* and how to be one.

Maker. A name folks said with a hush. Or spoke of wistful, saying that the world had done with Makers, there'd be no more. Oh, some said Old Ben Franklin was a Maker, but he denied being so much as a wizard till the day he died. Taleswapper, who knew Old Ben like a father, he said Ben only made one thing in his life, and that was the American Compact, that piece of paper that bound the Dutch and Swedish colonies with the English and German set-tlements of Pennsylvania and Suskwahenny and, most important of all, the Red nation of Irrakwa, altogether forming the United States of America, where Red and White, Dutchman, Swede and Englishman, rich and poor, merchant and laborer, all could vote and all could speak and no one could say, I'm a better man than you. Some folks allowed as how that made Ben as true a Maker as ever lived, but no, said Taleswapper, that made Ben a binder, a knotter, but not a Maker.

I am the Maker that torch girl wrote about. She touched me as I was a-borning, and when she did she saw that I had Maker-stuff in me. I've got to find that girl, growed up to be sixteen years old by now, and she's got to tell me what she saw. Cause the powers I've found inside me, the things that I can do, I know they've got a purpose bigger than just cutting stone without hands and healing the sick and running through the woods like any Red man can but no White man ever could. I've got a work to do in my life and I don't have the first spark of an idea how to get ready for it.

Standing there in the road, with a pig farm on either hand, Alvin heard the sharp *ching ching* of iron striking iron. The smith might as well have called out to him by name. Here I am, said the hammer, find me up ahead along the road.

Before he ever got to the smithy, though, he rounded the bend and saw the very roadhouse where he was born, just as plain as ever in the vision in the crystal tower. Whitewashed shiny and new with only the dust of this summer on it, so it didn't look quite the same, but it was as welcome a sight as any weary traveler could hope for.

Twice welcome, cause inside it, with any decent luck, the torch girl could tell him what his life was supposed to be.

Alvin knocked at the door cause that's what you do, he thought. He'd never stayed in a roadhouse before, and had no notion of a public room. So he knocked once, and then twice, and then hallooed till finally the door opened. It was a woman with flour on her hands and her checked apron, a big woman who looked annoyed beyond belief—but he knew her face. This was the woman in his crystal tower vision, the one what pulled him out of the womb with her own fingers around his neck.

"What in the world are you thinking of, boy, to knock my door like that and start hullaballooing like there was a fire! Why can't you just come on in and set like any other folk, or are you so powerful important that you got to have a servant come and open doors for you?"

"Sorry, ma'am," said Alvin, about as respectful as could be.

"Now what business could you have with us? If you're a beggar then I got to tell you we'll have no scraps till after dinner, but you're welcome to wait till then, and if you got a conscience, why, you can chop some wood for us. Except for look at you, I can't believe you're more than fourteen years old—"

"Eleven, ma'am."

"Well, then, you're right big for your age, but I still can't figure what business you got here. I won't serve you no liquor even if you got money, which I doubt. This is a Christian house, in fact more than mere Christian because we're true-blue Methodist and that means we don't touch a drop nor serve it neither, and even if we did we wouldn't serve children. And I'd stake ten pound of porkfat on a wager that you don't have the price of a night's lodging."

"No ma'am," said Alvin, "but—"

"Well then here you are, dragging me out of my kitchen with the bread half-kneaded and a baby who's bound to cry for milk any minute, and I reckon you don't plan to stand at the head of the table and explain to all my boarders why their dinner is late, on account of a boy who can't open a door his own self, no, you'll leave me to make apologies myself as best I can, which is right uncivil of you if you don't mind my saying, or even if you do."

"Ma'am," said Alvin, "I don't want food and I don't want a room." He knew enough courtesy *not* to add that travelers had always been welcome to stay in his father's house whether they had money or not, and a hungry man didn't get afternoon scraps, he set down at Pa's own table and ate with the family. He was catching on to the idea that things were different here in civilized country.

"Well, all we deal in here is food and rooms," said the roadhouse lady.

"I come here, ma'am, cause I was born in this house almost twelve years ago."

Her whole demeanor changed at once. She wasn't a roadhouse mistress now, she was a midwife. "Born in this house?"

"Born on the day my oldest brother Vigor died in the Hatrack River. I thought as how you might even remember that day, and maybe you could show me the place where my brother lies buried."

Her face changed again. "You," she said. "You're the boy who was born to that family—the seventh son of—"

"Of a seventh son," said Alvin.

"Well what's become of you, tell me! Oh, it was a portentous thing. My daughter stood there and looked afar off and saw that your big brother was still alive as you came out of the womb—"

"Your daughter," said Alvin, forgetting himself so much that he interrupted her clean in the middle of a sentence. "She's a torch."

The lady turned cold as ice. *"Was,"* she said. "She don't torch no more."

But Alvin hardly noticed how the lady changed. "You mean she lost her knack for it? I never heard of a body losing their knack. But if she's here, I'd like to talk to her."

"She ain't here no more," said the lady. Now Alvin finally caught on that she didn't much care to talk about it. "There ain't no torch now in Hatrack River. Babies will be born here without a body touching them to see how they lie in the womb. That's the end of it. I won't say another word about such a girl as that who'd run off, just run right off—"

Something caught in the lady's voice and she turned her back to him.

"I got to finish my bread," said the lady. "The graveyard is up the hill there." She turned around again to face him, with nary a sign of the anger or grief or what-all that she felt a second before. "If my Horace was here I'd have him show you the way, but you'll see it anyhow, there's a kind of path. It's just a family graveyard, with a picket fence around it." Her stern manner softened. "When you're done up there you come on back and I'll serve you better than scraps.'' She hurried on into the kitchen. Alvin followed her.

There was a cradle by the kitchen table, with a babe asleep in it but wiggling somewhat. Something funny about the baby but Alvin couldn't say right off what it was.

''Thank you for your kindness, ma'am, but I don't ask for no handouts. I'll work to pay for anything I eat.''

''That's rightly said, and like a true man—your father was the same, and the bridge he built over the Hatrack is still there, strong as ever. But you just go now, see the graveyard, and then come back by and by.''

She bent over the huge wad of dough on the kneading table. Alvin got the notion for just a moment that she was crying, and maybe he did and maybe he didn't see tears drop from her eyes straight down into the dough. It was plain she wanted to be alone.

He looked again at the baby and realized what was different. ''That's a pickaninny baby, isn't it?'' he said.

She stopped kneading, but left her hands buried to the wrist in dough. ''It's a baby,'' she said, ''and it's *my* baby. I adopted him and he's mine, and if you call him a pickaninny I'll knead your face like dough.''

''Sorry, ma'am, I meant no harm. He just had a sort of cast to his face that gave me that idea, I reckon—''

''Oh, he's half-Black all right. But it's the White half of him I'm raising up, just as if he was my own son. We named him Arthur Stuart.''

Alvin got the joke of that right off. ''Ain't nobody can call the King a pickaninny, I reckon.''

She smiled. ''I reckon not. Now get, boy. You owe a debt to your dead brother, and you best pay it now.''

The graveyard was easy to find, and Alvin was gratified to see that his brother Vigor had a stone, and his grave was as well-tended as any other. Only a few graves here. Two stones with the same name—''Baby Missy''—and dates that told of children dying young. Another stone that said ''Oldpappy'' and then his real name, and dates that told of a long life. And Vigor.

He knelt by his brother's grave and tried to picture what he might have been like. The best he could do was imagine his brother Measure, who was his favorite brother, the one who was captured by Reds along with Alvin. Vigor must have been like Measure. Or maybe Measure was like Vigor. Both willing to die if need be, for their family's sake. Vigor's death saved my life before I was born, thought Alvin, and yet he hung on to the last breath so that when I was born I was still the seventh son of a seventh son, with all my brothers ahead of me alive. The same kind of sacrifice and courage and strength that it took when Measure, who hadn't killed a single Red man, who near died just trying to stop the Tippy-Canoe massacre from happening, took on himself the same curse as his father and his brothers, to have blood on his hands if he failed to tell any stranger the true story of the killing of all them innocent Reds. So when he knelt there at Vigor's grave, it was like he was kneeling at Measure's grave, even though he knew Measure wasn't dead.

Wasn't wholly dead, anyway. But like the rest of the folk of Vigor Church, he'd never leave that place again. He'd live out all his days where he wouldn't have to meet too many strangers, so that for days on end he could forget the slaughter on that day last summer. The whole family, staying together there, with all the folks in the country roundabout, living out their days of life until them as had the curse all died, sharing each other's shame and each other's loneliness like they was all kin, every one of them.

All them together, except for me. I didn't take no curse on me. I left them all behind.

Kneeling there, Alvin felt like an orphan. He might as well be. Sent off to be a prentice here, knowing that whatever he did, whatever he made, his kin could never come on out to see. He could go home to that bleak sad town from time to time, but that was more like a graveyard than this grassy living place, because even with dead folks buried here, there was hope and life in the town nearby, people looking forward instead of back.

Alvin had to look forward, too. Had to find his way to what he was born to be. You died for me, Vigor, my brother that I never met. I just haven't figured out yet why it was so important for me to be alive. When I find out, I hope to make you proud of me. I hope you'll think that I was worth dying for.

When his thoughts was all spent and gone, when his heart had filled up and then emptied out again, Alvin did something he never thought to do. He looked under the ground.

Not by digging, mind you. Alvin's knack was such that he could get the feel of underground without using his eyes. Like the way he looked into stone. Now it might seem to some folk like a kind of grave-robbing, for Al to peek inside the earth where his brother's body lay. But to Al it was the only way he'd ever see the man who died to save him.

So he closed his eyes and gazed under the soil and found the bones inside the rotted wooden box. The size of him—Vigor was a big boy, which is about what it would take to roll and yaw a full-sized tree in a river's current. But the soul of him, that wasn't there, and even though he knowed it wouldn't be Al was somewhat disappointed.

His hidden gaze wandered to the small bodies barely clinging to their own dust, and then to the gnarled old corpse of Oldpappy, whoever that was, fresh in the earth, only a year or so buried.

But not so fresh as the other body. The unmarked body. One day dead at most, she was, all her flesh still on her and the worms hardly working at her yet.

He cried out in the surprise of it, and the grief at the next thought that came to mind. Could it be the torch girl buried there? Her mother said that she run off, but when folks run off it ain't unusual for them to come back dead. Why else was the mother grieving so? The innkeeper's own daughter, buried without a marker—oh, that spoke of terrible bad things. Did she run off and get herself shamed so bad her own folks wouldn't mark her burying place? Why else leave her there without a stone?

"What's wrong with you, boy?"

Alvin stood, turned, faced the man. A stout fellow who was right comfortable to look upon; but his face wasn't too easy right now.

"What are you doing here in this graveyard, boy?"

"Sir," said Alvin, "my brother's buried here."

The man thought a moment, his face easing. "You're one of that family. But I recall all their boys was as old as you even back then—"

"I'm the one what was born here that night."

At that news the man just opened up his arms and folded Alvin up inside. "They named you Alvin, didn't they," said the man, "just like your father. We call him Alvin Bridger around here, he's something of legend. Let me see you, see what you've become. Seventh son of a seventh son, come home to see your birthplace and your brother's grave. Of course you'll stay in my roadhouse. I'm Horace Guester, as you might guess, I'm pleased to meet you, but ain't you somewhat big for—what, ten, eleven years old?"

"Almost twelve. Folks say I'm tall."

"I hope you're proud of the marker we made for your brother. He was admired here, even though we all met him in death and never in life."

"I'm suited," said Alvin. "It's a good stone." And then, because he couldn't help himself, though it wasn't a particularly wise thing to do, he up and asked the question most burning in him. "But I wonder, sir, why one girl got herself buried here yesterday, and no stone nor marker tells her name."

Horace Guester's face turned ashen. "Of course you'd see," he whispered. "Doodlebug or something. Seventh son. God help us all."

"Did she do something shameful, sir, not to have no marker?" asked Alvin.

"Not shame," said Horace. "As God is my witness, boy, this girl was noble in life and died a virtuous death. She stays unmarked so this house can be a shelter to others like her. But oh, lad, say you'll never tell what you found buried here. You'd cause pain to dozens and hundreds of lost souls along the road from slavery to freedom. Can you believe me that much, trust me and be my friend in this? It'd be too much grief, to lose my daughter and have this secret out, all in the same day. Since I can't keep the secret from you, you have to keep it with me, Alvin, lad. Say you will."

"I'll keep a secret if it's honorable, sir," said Alvin, "but what honorable secret leads a man to bury his own daughter without a stone?''

Horace's eyes went wide, and then he laughed like he was calling loony birds. When he got control of hisself, he clapped Alvin on the shoulder. "That ain't my daughter in the ground there, boy, what made you think it was? It's a Black girl, a runaway slave, who died last night on her way north.''

Now Alvin realized for the first time that the body was way too small to be no sixteen-year-old, anyhow. It was a child-size body. "That baby in your kitchen, it's her brother?''

"Her son," said Horace.

"But she's so small," said Alvin.

"That didn't stop her White owner from getting her with child, boy. I don't know how you stand on the question of slavery, or if you even thought about it, but I beg you do some thinking now. Think about how slavery lets a White man steal a girl's virtue and still go to church on Sunday while she groans in shame and bears his bastard child.''

"You're a Mancipationist, ain't you?" said Alvin.

"Reckon I am," said the innkeeper, "but I reckon all good Christian folk are Mancipationists in their hearts.''

"I reckon so," said Alvin.

"I hope *you* are, cause if word gets out that I was helping a slavegirl run off to Canada, there'll be finders and cotchers from Appalachee and the Crown Colonies a-spying on me so I can't help no others get away.''

Alvin looked back at the grave and thought about the babe in the kitchen. "You going to tell that baby where his mama's grave is?''

"When he's old enough to know, and not to tell it," said the man.

"Then I'll keep your secret, if you keep mine.''

The man raised his eyebrows and studied Alvin. "What secret *you* got, Alvin, a boy as young as you?''

"I don't have no partickler wish to have it known I'm a seventh son. I'm here to prentice with Makepeace Smith, which I reckon is the man I hear a-hammering at the forge down yonder.''

"And you don't want folks knowing you can see a body lying in an unmarked grave."

"You caught my drift right enough," said Alvin. "I won't tell your secret, and you won't tell mine."

"You have my word on it," said the man. Then he held out his hand.

Took that hand and shook it, gladly. Most grownup folk wouldn't think of making a bargain like that with a mere child like him. But this man even offered his hand, like they were equals. "You'll see I know how to keep my word, sir," said Alvin.

"And anyone around here can tell you Horace Guester keeps a promise, too." Then Horace told him the story that they were letting out about the baby, how it was the Berrys' youngest, and they gave it up for Old Peg Guester to raise, cause they didn't need another child and she'd always hankered to have her a son. "And that part is true enough," said Horace Guester. "All the more, with Peggy running off."

"Your daughter," said Alvin.

Suddenly Horace Guester's eyes filled up with tears and he shuddered with a sob like Alvin never heard from a growed man in his life. "Just ran off this morning," said Horace Guester.

"Maybe she's just a-calling on somebody in town or something," said Alvin.

Horace shook his head. "I beg your pardon, crying like that, I just beg your pardon, I'm awful tired, truth to tell, up all night last night, and then this morning, her gone like that. She left us a note. She's gone all right."

"Don't you know the man she run off with?" asked Alvin. "Maybe they'll get married, that happened once to a Swede girl out in the Noisy River country—"

Horace turned a bit red with anger. "I reckon you're just a boy so you don't know better than to say such a thing. So I'll tell you now, she didn't run off with no *man*. She's a woman of pure virtue, and no one ever said otherwise. No, she run off alone, boy."

Alvin thought he'd seen all kinds of strange things in his life— a tornado turned into a crystal tower, a bolt of cloth with all the souls of men and women woven in it, murders and tortures, tales and miracles, Alvin knew more of life than most boys at eleven years of age. But this was the strangest thing of all, to think of a girl of sixteen just up and leaving her father's house, without no husband or nothing. In all his life he never saw a woman go *nowhere* by herself beyond her own dooryard.

"Is she—is she *safe?*"

Horace laughed bitterly. "Safe? Of course she's safe. She's a torch, Alvin, the best torch I ever heard of. She can see folks miles off, she knows their hearts, ain't a man born can come near her with evil on his mind without she knows exactly what he's planning and just how to get away. No, I ain't *worried* about her. She can take care of herself better than any man. I just—"

"Miss her," said Alvin.

"I guess it don't take no torch to guess that, am I right, lad? I miss her. And it hurt my feelings somewhat that she up and left with no warning. I could've given her God bless to send her on her way. Her mama could've worked up some good hex, not that Little Peggy'd need it, or anyhow just pack her a cold dinner for on the road. But none of that, no fare-thee-well nor God-be-with-you. It was like as if she was running from some awful boogly monster and had no time to take but one spare dress in a cloth bag and rush on out the door."

Running from some monster—those words stung right to Alvin's soul. She was such a torch that it might well be she saw Alvin coming. Up and ran away the morning he arrived. If she wasn't no torch then maybe it was just chance that took her off the same day he come. But she *was* a torch. She saw him coming. She knew he came all this way a-hoping to meet her and beg her to help him find his way into becoming whatever it was that he was born to be. She saw all that, and ran away.

"I'm right sorry that she's gone," said Alvin.

"I thank you for your pity, friend, it's good of you. I just hope it won't be for long. I just hope she'll do whatever she left to do and come on back in a few days or maybe a couple of weeks." He laughed again, or maybe sobbed, it was about the same sound. "I can't even go ask the Hatrack torch to tell a fortune about her, cause the Hatrack River torch is gone.''

Horace cried outright again, for just a minute. Then he took Alvin by the shoulders and looked him in the eye, not even hiding the tears on his cheeks. "Alvin, you just remember how you seen me crying all unmanlike, and you remember that's how fathers feel about their children when they're gone. That's how your own pa feels right now, having you so far away.''

"I know he does," said Alvin.

"Now if you don't mind," said Horace Guester, "I need to be alone here.''

Alvin touched his arm just a moment and then he went away. Not down to the house to have his noon meal like Old Peg Guester offered. He was too upset to sit and eat with them. How could he explain that he was nigh on to being as heartbroke as them, to have that torch girl gone? No, he'd have to keep silence. The answers he was looking for in Hatrack, they were gone off with a sixteen-year-old girl who didn't want to meet him when he came.

Maybe she seen my future and she hates me. Maybe I'm as bad a boogly monster as anybody ever dreamed of on an evil night.

He followed the sound of the blacksmith's hammer. It led him along a faint path to a springhouse straddling a brook that came straight out of a hillside. And down the stream, along a clear meadow slope, he walked until he came to the smithy. Hot smoke rose from the forge. Around front he walked, and saw the blacksmith inside the big sliding door, hammering a hot iron bar into a curving shape across the throat of his anvil.

Alvin stood and watched him work. He could feel the heat from the forge clear outside; inside must be like the fires of hell. His muscles were like fifty different ropes holding his arm on under the skin. They shifted and rolled across each other as the hammer rose into the air, then bunched all at once as the hammer came down. Close as he was now, Alvin could hardly bear the bell-like crash of iron on iron, with the anvil like a sounding fork to make the sound ring on and on. Sweat dripped off the blacksmith's body, and he was naked to the waist, his white skin ruddy from the heat, streaked with soot from the forge and sweat from his pores. I've been sent here to be prentice to the devil, thought Alvin.

But he knew that was a silly idea even as he thought it. This was a hardworking man, that's all, earning his living with a skill that every town needed if it hoped to thrive. Judging from the size of the corrals for horses waiting to be shod, and the heaps of iron bars waiting to be made into plows and sickles, axes and cleavers, he did a good business, too. If I learn this trade, I'll never be hungry, thought Alvin, and folks will always be glad to have me.

And something more. Something about the hot fire and the ruddy iron. What happened in this place was akin somehow to making. Alvin knew from the way he'd worked with stone in the granite quarry, when he carved the millstone for his father's mill, he knew that with his knack he could probably reach inside the iron and make it go the way he wanted it to go. But he had something to learn from the forge and the hammer, the bellows and the fire and the water in the cooling tubs, something that would help him become what he was born to become.

So now he looked at the blacksmith, not as a powerful stranger, but as Alvin's future self. He saw how the muscles grew on the smith's shoulders and back. Alvin's body was strong from chopping wood and splitting rails and all the hoisting and lifting that he did earning pennies and nickels on neighbors' farms. But in that kind of work, your whole body went into every movement. You rared back with the axe and when it swung it was like your whole body was part of the axhandle, so that legs and hips and back all moved into the chop. But the smith, he held the hot iron in the tongs, held it so smooth and exact against the anvil that while his right arm swung the hammer, the rest of his body couldn't move a twitch, that left arm stayed as smooth and steady as a rock. It shaped the smith's body differently, forced the arms to be much stronger by themselves, muscles rooted to the neck and breastbone standing out in a way they never did on a farmboy's body.

Alvin felt inside himself, the way his own muscles grew, and knew already where the changes would have to come. It was part of his knack, to find his way within living flesh most as easily as he could chart the inner shapes of living stone. So even now he was hunkering down inside, teaching his body to change itself to make way for the new work.

"Boy," said the smith.

"Sir," said Alvin.

"Have you got business for me? I don't know you, do I?"

Alvin stepped forward, held out the note his father writ.

"Read it to me, boy, my eyes are none too good."

Alvin unfolded the paper. "From Alvin Miller of Vigor Church. To Makepeace, Blacksmith of Hatrack River. Here is my boy Alvin what you said could be your prentice till he be seventeen. He'll work hard and do what all you say, and you teach him what all a man needs to be a good smith, like in the articles I signed. He is a good boy."

The smith reached for the paper, held it close to his eyes. His lips moved as he repeated a few phrases. Then he slapped the paper down on the anvil. "This is a fine turn," said the smith. "Don't you know you're about a year late, boy? You was supposed to come last spring. I turned away three offers for prentice cause I had your pa's word you was coming, and here I've been without help this whole year cause he *didn't* keep his word. Now I'm supposed to take you in with a year less on your contract, and not even a by-your-leave or beg-your-pardon."

"I'm sorry, sir," said Alvin. "But we had the war last year. I was on my way here but I got captured by Choc-Taw."

"Captured by—oh, come now, boy, don't tell me tales like that. If the Choc-Taw caught you, you wouldn't have such a dandy head of hair now, would you! And like as not you'd be missing a few fingers."

"Ta-Kumsaw rescued me," said Alvin.

"Oh, and no doubt you met the Prophet hisself and walked on water with him."

As a matter of fact, Alvin done just that. But from the smith's tone of voice, he reckoned that it wouldn't be wise to say so. So Alvin said nothing.

"Where's your horse?" asked the smith.

"Don't have one," said Alvin.

"Your father wrote the date on this letter boy, two days ago! You must've rode a horse."

"I ran." As soon as Alvin said it, he knew it was a mistake.

"*Ran?*" said the smith. "With *bare feet?* It must be nigh four hundred mile or more to the Wobbish from here! Your feet ought to be ripped to rags clear up to your knees! Don't tell me tales, boy! I won't have no liars around me!"

Alvin had a choice, and he knew it. He could explain about how he could run like a Red man. Makepeace Smith wouldn't believe him, and so Alvin would have to show him some of what he could do. It would be easy enough. Bend a bar of iron just by stroking it. Make two stones mash together to form one. But Alvin already made up his mind he didn't want to show his knacks here. How could he be a proper prentice, if folks kept coming around for him to cut them hearthstones or fix a broken wheel or all the other fixing things he had a knack for? Besides, he never done such a thing, showing off just for the sake of proving what he could do. Back home he only used his knack when there was need.

So he stuck with his decision to keep his knack to himself, pretty much. Not tell what he could do. Just learn like any normal boy, working the iron the way the smith himself did, letting the muscles grow slowly on his arms and shoulders, chest and back.

"I was joking," Alvin said. "A man gave me a ride on his spare mount."

"I don't like that kind of joke," said the smith. "I don't like it that you lied to me so easy like that."

What could Alvin say? He couldn't even claim that he hadn't lied—he had, when he told about a man letting him ride. So he was as much a liar as the smith thought. The only confusion was about *which* statement was a lie.

"I'm sorry," said Alvin.

"I'm not taking you, boy. I don't have to take you anyway, a year late. And here you come lying to me the first thing. I won't have it."

"Sir, I'm sorry," said Alvin. "It won't happen again. I'm not known for a liar back home, and you'll see I'll be known for square dealing here, if you give me a chance. Catch me lying or not giving fair work all the time, and you can chuck me, no questions asked. Just give me a chance to prove it, sir.''

"You don't look like you're eleven, neither, boy.''

"But I am, sir. You know I am. You yourself with your own arms pulled my brother Vigor's body from the river on the night that I was born, or so my pa told me.''

The smith's face went distant, as if he was remembering. "Yes, he told you true, I was the one who pulled him out. Clinging to the roots of that tree even in death, so I thought I'd have to cut him free. Come here, boy.''

Alvin walked closer. The smith poked and pushed the muscles of his arms.

"Well, I can see you're not a lazy boy. Lazy boys get soft, but you're strong like a hardworking farmer. Can't lie about *that*, I reckon. Still, you haven't seen what real work is.''

"I'm ready to learn.''

"Oh, I'm sure of that. Many a boy would be glad to learn from me. Other work might come and go, but there's always a need for a blacksmith. That'll never change. Well, you're strong enough in body, I reckon. Let's see about your brain. Look at this anvil. This here's the bick, on the point, you see. Say that.''

"Bick.''

"And then the throat here. And this is the table—it ain't faced with blister steel, so when you ram a cold chisel into it the chisel don't blunt. Then up a notch onto the steel face, where you work the hot metal. And this is the hardie hole, where I rest the butt of the fuller and the flatter and the swage. And this here's the pricking hole, for when I punch holes in strap iron—the hot punch shoots right through into this space. You got all that?''

"I think so, sir.''

"Then name me the parts of the anvil.''

Alvin named them as best he could. Couldn't remember the job each one did, not all of them, anyways, but what he did was good enough, cause the blacksmith nodded and grinned. "Reckon you ain't a half-wit, anyhow, you'll learn quick enough. And big for your age is good. I won't have to keep you on a broom and the bellows for the first four years, the way I do with smaller boys. But your age, that's a sticking point. A term of prentice work is seven year, but my written-up articles with your pa, they only say till you're seventeen.''

"I'm almost twelve now, sir."

"So what I'm saying is, I want to be able to hold you the full seven years, if need be. I don't want you whining off just when I finally get you trained enough to be useful.''

"Seven years, sir. The spring when I'm nigh on nineteen, then my time is up.''

"Seven years is a long time, boy, and I mean to hold you to it. Most boys start when they're nine or ten, or even seven years old, so they can make a living, start looking for a wife at sixteen or seventeen years old. I won't have none of that. I expect you to live like a Christian, and no fooling with any of the girls in town, you understand me?''

"Yes sir."

"All right then. My prentices sleep in the loft over the kitchen, and you eat at table with my wife and children and me, though I'll thank you not to speak until spoken to inside the house—I won't have my prentices thinking they have the same rights as my own children, cause you don't.''

"Yes sir."

"And as for now, I need to het up this strap again. So you start to work the bellows there.''

Alvin walked to the bellows handle. It was T-shaped, for two-handed working. But Alvin twisted the end piece so it was at the same angle as the hammer handle when the smith lifted it into the air. Then he started to work the bellows with one arm.

"What are you doing, boy!" shouted Alvin's new master. "You won't last ten minutes working the bellows with one arm."

"Then in ten minutes I'll switch to my left arm," said Alvin. "But I won't get myself ready for the hammer if I bend over every time I work the bellows.''

The smith looked at him angrily. Then he laughed. "You got a fresh mouth, boy, but you also got sense. Do it your way as long as you can, but see to it you don't slack on wind—I need a hot fire, and that's more important than you working up strength in your arms right now."

Alvin set to pumping. Soon he could feel the pain of this unaccustomed movement gnawing at his neck and chest and back. But he kept going, never breaking the rhythm of the bellows, forcing his body to endure. He could have made the muscles grow right now, teaching them the pattern with his hidden power. But that wasn't what Alvin was here for, he was pretty sure of that. So he let the pain come as it would, and his body change as it would, each new muscle earned by his own effort.

Alvin lasted fifteen minutes with his right hand, ten minutes with his left. He felt the muscles aching and liked the way it felt. Makepeace Smith seemed pleased enough with what he did. Alvin knew that he'd be changed here, that his work would make a strong and skillful man of him.

A man, but not a Maker. Not yet fully on the road to what he was born to be. But since there hadn't been a Maker in the world in a thousand years or more, or so folks said, who was he going to prentice himself to in order to learn *that* trade?

⧖ 4 ⧗

Modesty

WHITLEY PHYSICKER HELPED Peggy down from the carriage in front of a fine-looking house in one of the best neighborhoods of Dekane. "I'd like to see you to the door, Peggy Guester, just to make sure they're home to greet you," said he, but she knew he didn't expect her to allow him to do that. If anybody knew how little she liked to have folks fussing over her, it was Doctor Whitley Physicker. So she thanked him kindly and bid him farewell.

She heard his carriage rolling off, the horse clopping on the cobblestones, as she rapped the knocker on the door. A maid opened the door, a German girl so fresh off the boat she couldn't even speak enough English to ask Peggy's name. She invited her in with a gesture, seated her on a bench in the hall, and then held out a silver plate.

What was the plate *for*? Peggy couldn't hardly make sense at all of what she saw inside this foreign girl's mind. She was expecting something—what? A little slip of paper, but Peggy didn't have a notion why. The girl thrust the salver closer to her, insisting. Peggy couldn't do a thing but shrug.

Finally the German girl gave up and went away. Peggy sat on the bench and waited. She searched for heartfires in the house, and found the one she looked for. Only then did she realize what the plate was for—her calling card. Folks in the city, rich folks anyway, they had little cards they put their name on, to announce theirself when they came to visit. Peggy even remembered reading about it in a book, but it was a book from the Crown Colonies and she never thought folks in free lands kept such formality.

Soon the lady of the house came, the German girl shadowing her, peering from behind her fine day gown. Peggy knew from the lady's heartfire that she didn't think herself dressed in any partickler finery today, but to Peggy she was like the Queen herself.

Peggy looked into her heartfire and found what she had hoped for. The lady wasn't annoyed a bit at seeing Peggy there, merely curious. Oh, the lady was judging her, of course—Peggy never met a soul, least of all herself, what didn't make some judgment of every stranger—but the judgment was kind. When the lady looked at Peggy's plain clothes, she saw a country girl, not a pauper; when the lady looked at Peggy's stern, expressionless face, she saw a child who had known pain, not an ugly girl. And when the lady imagined Peggy's pain, her first thought was to try to heal her. All in all, the lady was *good*. Peggy made no mistake in coming here.

"I don't believe I've had the pleasure to meet you," said the lady. Her voice was sweet and soft and beautiful.

"I reckon not, Mistress Modesty," said Peggy. "My name is Peggy. I think you had some acquaintance with my papa, years ago."

"Perhaps if you told me his name?"

"Horace," said Peggy. "Horace Guester, of Hatrack, Hio."

Peggy saw the turmoil in her heartfire at the very sound of his name—glad memory, and yet a glimmer of fear of what this strange girl might intend. Yet the fear quickly subsided—her husband had died several years ago, and so was beyond hurt. And none of these emotions showed in the lady's face, which held its sweet and friendly expression with perfect grace. Modesty turned to the maid and spoke a few words of fluent German. The maid curtsied and was gone.

"Did your father send you?" asked the lady. Her unspoken

question was: Did your father tell you what I meant to him, and he to me?

"No," said Peggy. "I come here on my own. He'd die if he found out I knew your name. You see I'm a torch, Mistress Modesty. He has no secrets, not from me. Nobody does."

It didn't surprise Peggy one bit how Modesty took that news. Most folks would've thought right off about all the secrets they hoped she wouldn't guess. Instead, the lady thought at once how awful it must be for Peggy, to know things that didn't bear knowing. "How long has it been that way?" she said softly. "Surely not when you were just a little girl. The Lord is too merciful to let such knowledge fill a child's mind."

"I reckon the Lord didn't concern himself much with me," said Peggy.

The lady reached out and touched Peggy's cheek. Peggy knew the lady had noticed she was somewhat dirty from the dust of the road. But what the lady mostly thought of wasn't clothes or cleanliness. A torch, she was thinking. That's why a girl so young wears such a cold, forbidding face. Too much knowledge has made this girl so hard.

"Why have you come to me?" asked Modesty. "Surely you don't mean harm to me or your father, for such an ancient transgression."

"Oh, no ma'am," said Peggy. Never in her life did her own voice sound so harsh to her, but compared to this lady she was squawking like a crow. "If I'm torch enough to know your secret, I'm torch enough to know there was some good in it as well as sin, and as far as the sin goes, Papa's paying for it still, paying double and treble every year of his life."

Tears came into Modesty's eyes. "I had hoped," she murmured, "I had hoped that time would ease the shame of it, and he'd remember it now with joy. Like one of the ancient faded tapestries in England, whose colors are no longer bright, but whose image is the very shadow of beauty itself."

Peggy might've told her that he felt more than joy, that he relived all his feelings for her like it happened yesterday. But that was Papa's secret, and not hers to tell.

Modesty touched a kerchief to her eyes, to take away the tears that trembled there. "All these years I've never spoken to a mortal soul of this. I've poured out my heart only to the Lord, and he's forgiven me; yet I find it somehow exhilarating to speak of this to someone whose face I can see with my eyes, and not just my imagination. Tell me, child, if you didn't come as the avenging angel, have you come perhaps as a forgiving one?"

Mistress Modesty spoke with such elegance that Peggy found herself reaching for the language of the books she read, instead of her natural talking voice. "I'm a—a supplicant," said Peggy. "I come for help. I come to change my life, and I thought, being how you loved my father, you might be willing to do a kindness for his daughter."

The lady smiled at her. "And if you're half the torch you claim to be, you already know my answer. What kind of help do you need? My husband left me a good deal of money when he died, but I think it isn't money that you need."

"No ma'am," said Peggy. But what was it that she wanted, now that she was here? How could she explain why she had come? "I didn't like the life I saw for myself back in Hatrack. I wanted to—"

"Escape?"

"Somewhat like that, I reckon, but not exactly."

"You want to become something other than what you are," said the lady.

"Yes, Mistress Modesty."

"What is it that you wish to be?"

Peggy had never thought of words to describe what she dreamed of, but now, with Mistress Modesty before her, Peggy saw how simply those dreams might be expressed. "You, ma'am."

The lady smiled and touched her own face, her own hair. "Oh, my child, you must have higher aims than that. Much of what is best in me, your father gave me. The way he loved me taught me that perhaps—no, not *perhaps*—that I *was* worth loving. I have learned much more since then, more of what a woman is and ought to be. What a lovely symmetry, if I can give back to his daughter some of the wisdom he brought to me.'' She laughed gently. "I never imagined myself taking a pupil.''

"More like a disciple, I think, Mistress Modesty.''

"Neither pupil nor disciple. Will you stay here as a guest in my home? Will you let me be your friend?''

Even though Peggy couldn't rightly see the paths of her own life, she still felt them open up inside her, all the futures she could hope for, waiting for her in this place. "Oh, ma'am,'' she whispered, "if you will.''

⟐ 5 ⟐

Dowser

HANK DOWSER'D SEEN him prentice boys a-plenty over the years, but never a one as fresh as this. Here was Makepeace Smith bent over old Picklewing's left forehoof, all set to drive in the nail, and up spoke his boy.

"Not that nail," said the blacksmith's prentice boy. "Not there."

Well, that was as fine a moment as Hank ever saw for the master to give his prentice boy a sharp cuff on the ear and send him bawling into the house. But Makepeace Smith just nodded, then looked at the boy.

"You think you can nail this shoe, Alvin?" asked the master. "She's a big one, this mare, but I see you got you some inches since last I looked."

"I can," said the boy.

"Now just hold your horses," said Hank Dowser. "Picklewing's my only animal, and I can't just up and buy me another. I don't want your prentice boy learning to be a farrier and making his mistakes at my poor old nag's expense." And since he was already speaking his mind so frank like, Hank just rattled right on like a plain fool. "Who's the master here, anyway?" said he.

Well, that was the wrong thing to say. Hank knew it the second the words slipped out of his mouth. You don't say Who's the master, not in front of the prentice. And sure enough, Makepeace Smith's ears turned red and he stood up, all six feet of him, with arms like oxlegs and hands that could crush a bear's face, and he said, "I'm the master here, and when I say my prentice is good enough for the job, then he's good enough, or you can take your custom to another smith."

"Now just hold your horses," said Hank Dowser.

"I *am* holding your horse," said Makepeace Smith. "Or at least your horse's leg. In fact, your horse is leaning over on me something heavy. And now you start asking if I'm master of my own smithy."

Anybody whose head don't leak knows that riling the smith who's shoeing your horse is about as smart as provoking the bees on your way in for the honey. Hank Dowser just hoped Makepeace would be somewhat easier to calm down. "Course you are," said Hank. "I meant nothing by it, except I was surprised when your prentice spoke up so smart and all."

"Well that's cause he's got him a knack," said Makepeace Smith. "This boy Alvin, he can tell things about the inside of a horse's hoof—where a nail's going to hold, where it's going into soft hurting flesh, that kind of thing. He's a natural farrier. And if he says to me, Don't drive that nail, well I know by now that's a nail I don't want to drive, cause it'll make the horse crazy or lame."

Hank Dowser grinned and backed off. It was a hot day, that's all, that's why tempers were so high. "I have respect for every man's knack," said Hank. "Just like I expect them to have respect for mine."

"In that case, I've held up your horse long enough," said the smith. "Here, Alvin, nail this shoe."

If the boy had swaggered or simpered or sneered, Hank would've had a reason to be so mad. But Prentice Alvin just hunkered down with nails in his mouth and hooked up the left forehoof. Picklewing leaned on him, but the boy was right tall, even though his face had no sign of beard yet, and he was like a twin of his master, when it come to muscle under his skin. It wasn't one minute, the horse leaning that way, before the shoe was nailed in place. Picklewing didn't so much as shiver, let alone dance the way he usually did when the nails went in. And now that Hank thought about it a little, Picklewing always *did* seem to favor that leg just a little, as if something was a mite sore inside the hoof. But he'd been that way so long Hank hardly noticed it no more.

The prentice boy stepped back out of the way, still not showing any brag at all. He wasn't doing a thing that was the tiniest bit benoctious, but Hank still felt an unreasonable anger at the boy. "How old is he?" asked Hank.

"Fourteen," said Makepeace Smith. "He come to me when he was eleven."

"A mite old for a prentice, wouldn't you say?" asked Hank.

"A year late in arriving, he was, because of the war with the Reds and the French—he's from out in the Wobbish country."

"Them was hard years," said Hank. "Lucky me I was in Irrakwa the whole time. Dowsing wells for windmills the whole way along the railroad they were building. Fourteen, eh? Tall as he is, I reckon he lied about his age even so."

If the boy disliked being named a liar, he didn't show no sign of it. Which made Hank Dowser all the more annoyed. That boy was like a burr under his saddle, just made him mad whatever the boy did.

"No," said the smith. "We know his age well enough. He was born right here in Hatrack River, fourteen years ago, when his folks were passing through on their way west. We buried his oldest brother up on the hill. Big for his age though, ain't he?"

They might've been discussing a horse instead of a boy. But Prentice Alvin didn't seem to mind. He just stood there, staring right through them as if they were made of glass.

"You got four years left of his contract, then?" asked Hank.

"Bit more. Till he's near nineteen."

"Well, if he's already this good, I reckon he'll be buying out early and going journeyman." Hank looked, but the boy didn't brighten up at this idea, neither.

"I reckon not," said Makepeace Smith. "He's good with the horses, but he gets careless with the forge. Any smith can do shoes, but it takes a *real* smith to do a plow blade or a wheel tire, and a knack with horses don't help a bit with that. Why, for my master-piece I done me an anchor! I was in Netticut at the time, mind you. There ain't much call for anchors *here,* I reckon."

Picklewing snorted and stamped—but he didn't dance lively, the way horses do when their new shoes are troublesome. It was a good set of shoes, well shod. Even *that* made Hank mad at the prentice boy. His own anger made no sense to him. The boy had put on Pick-lewing's last shoe, on a leg that might have been lamed in another farrier's hands. The boy had done him *good*. So why this wrath burn-ing just under the surface, getting worse whatever the boy did or said?

Hank shrugged off his feelings. "Well, that's work well done," he said. "And so it's time for me to do my part."

"Now, we both know a dowsing's worth more than a shoeing," said the smith. "So if you need any more work done, you know I owe it to you, free and clear."

"I *will* come back, Makepeace Smith, next time my nag needs shoes." And because Hank Dowser was a Christian man and felt ashamed of how he disliked the boy, he added praise for the lad. "I reckon I'll be sure to come back while this boy's still under prentice bond to you, him having the knack he's got."

The boy might as well not've heard the good words, and the master smith just chuckled. "You ain't the only one who feels like that," he said.

At that moment Hank Dowser understood something that he might've missed otherwise. This boy's knack with hooves was good for trade, and Makepeace Smith was just the kind of man who'd hold that boy to every day of his contract, to profit from the boy's name for clean shoeing with no horses lost by laming. All a greedy master had to do was claim the boy wasn't good at forgework or something like, then use that as a pretext to hold him fast. In the meantime the boy'd make a name for this place as the best farriery in eastern Hio. Money in Makepeace Smith's pocket, and nothing for the boy at all, not money nor freedom.

The law was the law, and the smith wasn't breaking it—he had the right to every day of that boy's service. But the custom was to let a prentice go as soon as he had the skill and had sense enough to make his way in the world. Otherwise, if a boy couldn't hope for early freedom, why should he work hard to learn as quick as he could, work as hard as he could? They said even the slaveowners in the Crown Colonies let their best slaves earn a little pocket money on the side, so's they could buy their freedom sometime before they died.

No, Makepeace Smith wasn't breaking no law, but he was breaking the custom of masters with their prentice boys, and Hank thought ill of him for it; it was a mean sort of master who'd keep a boy who'd already learned everything the master had to teach.

And yet, even knowing that it was the boy who was in the right, and his master in the wrong—even knowing that, he looked at that boy and felt a cold wet hatred in his heart. Hank shuddered, tried to shake it off.

"You say you need a well," said Hank Dowser. "You want it for drinking or for washing or for the smithy?"

"Does it make a difference?" asked the smith.

"Well, I think so," said Hank. "For drinking you need pure water, and for washing you want water that got no disease in it. But for your work in the smithy, I reckon the iron don't give no never mind whether it cools in clear or murky water, am I right?"

"The spring up the hill is giving out, slacking off year by year," said the smith. "I need me a well I can count on. Deep and clean and pure."

"You know why the stream's going slack," said Hank. "Everybody else is digging wells, and sucking out the water before it can seep out the spring. Your well is going to be about the last straw."

"I wouldn't be surprised," said the smith. "But I can't undig their wells, and I got to have my water, too. Reason I settled here was because of the stream, and now they've dried it up on me. I reckon I could move on, but I got me a wife and three brats up at the house, and I like it here, like it well enough. So I figure I'd rather draw water than move."

Hank went on down to the stand of willows by the stream, near where it came out from under an old springhouse, which had fallen into disrepair. "Yours?" asked Hank.

"No, it belongs to old Horace Guester, him who owns the road-house up yonder."

Hank found him a thin willow wand that forked just right, and started cutting it out with his knife. "Springhouse doesn't get much use now, I see."

"Stream's dying, like I said. Half the time in summer there ain't enough water in it to keep the cream jars cool. Springhouse ain't no good if you can't count on it all summer."

Hank made the last slice and the willow rod pulled free. He shaved the thick end to a point and whittled off all the leaf nubs, making it as smooth as ever he could. There was some dowsers who didn't care how smooth the rod was, just broke off the leaves and left the ends all raggedy, but Hank knew that the water didn't always want to be found, and then you needed a good smooth willow wand to find it. There was others used a clean wand, but always the same one, year after year, place after place, but that wasn't no good neither, Hank knew, cause the wand had to be from willow or, sometimes, hickory that grew up sucking the water you were hoping to find. Them other dowsers were mountebanks, though it didn't do no good to say so. They found water most times because in most places if you dig down far enough there's *bound* to be water. But Hank did it right, Hank had the true knack. He could feel the willow wand trembling in his hands, could feel the water singing to him under the ground. He didn't just pick the first sign of water, either. He was looking for clear water, high water, close to the surface and easy to pull. He took *pride* in his work.

But it wasn't like that prentice boy—what was his name?—Alvin. Wasn't like him. Either a man could nail horseshoes without ever laming the horse, or he couldn't. If he *ever* lamed a horse, folks thought twice before they went to that farrier again. But with a dowser, it didn't seem to make no difference if you found water every time or not. If you called yourself a dowser and had you a forked stick, folks would pay you for dowsing wells, without bothering to find out if you had any knack for it at all.

Thinking that, Hank wondered if maybe that was why he hated this boy so much—because the boy already had a name for his good work, while Hank got no fame at all even though he was the only true dowser likely to pass through these parts in a month of Sundays.

Hank set down on the grassy bank of the stream and pulled off his boots. When he leaned to set the second boot on a dry rock where it wouldn't be so like to fill up with bugs, he saw two eyes blinking in the shadows inside a thick stand of bushes. It gave him such a start, cause he thought to see a bear, and then he thought to see a Red man hankering after dowser's scalp, even though both such was gone from these parts for years. No, it was just a little light-skinned pickaninny hiding in the bushes. The boy was a mixup, half-White, half-Black, that was plain to see once Hank got over the surprise. "What're you looking at?" demanded Hank.

The eyes closed and the face was gone. The bushes wiggled and whispered from something crawling fast.

"Never you mind him," said Makepeace Smith. "That's just Arthur Stuart."

Arthur Stuart! Not a soul in New England or the United States but knew that name as sure as if they lived in the Crown Colonies. "Then you'll be glad to hear that I'm the Lord Protector," said Hank Dowser. "Cause if the King be that partickler shade of skin, I got some news that'll get me three free dinners a day in any town in Hio and Suskwahenny till the day I die."

Makepeace laughed brisk at that idea. "No, that's Horace Guester's joke, naming him that way. Horace and Old Peg Guester, they're raising that boy, seeing how his natural ma's too poor to raise him. Course I don't think that's the whole reason. Him being so light-skinned, her husband, Mock Berry, you can't blame him if he don't like seeing that child eat at table with his coal-black children."

Hank Dowser started pulling off his stockings. "You don't suppose old Horace Guester took him in on account of he's the party responsible for causing the boy's skin to be so light."

"Hush your mouth with a pumpkin, Hank, before you say such a thing," said Makepeace. "Horace ain't that kind of a man."

"You'd be surprised who I've known turn out to be that kind of a man," said Hank. "Though I don't think it of Horace Guester, mind."

"Do you think Old Peg Guester'd let a half-Black bastard son of her husband into the house?"

"What if she didn't know?"

"She'd know. Her daughter Peggy used to be torch here in Hatrack River. And everybody knowed that Little Peggy Guester never told a lie."

"I used to hear tell about the Hatrack River torch, afore I ever come here. How come I never seen her?"

"She's gone, that's why," said Makepeace. "Left three years ago. Just run off. You'd be wise never to ask about her up to Guester's roadhouse. They're a mite ticklish on the subject."

Barefoot now, Hank Dowser stood up on the bank of the stream. He happened to glance up, and there off in the trees, just a-watching him, stood that Arthur Stuart boy again. Well, what harm could a little pickaninny do? Not a bit.

Hank stepped into the stream and let the ice-cold water pour over his feet. He spoke silently to the water: I don't mean to block your flow, or slack you down even further. The well I dig ain't meant to do you no harm. It's like giving you another place to flow through, like giving you another face, more hands, another eye. So don't you hide from me, Water. Show me where you're rising up, pushing to reach the sky, and I'll tell them to dig there, and set you free to wash over the earth, you just see if I don't.

"This water pure enough?" Hank asked the smith.

"Pure as it can be," said Makepeace. "Never heard of nobody taking sick from it."

Hank dipped the sharp end of the wand into the water, upstream of his feet. Taste it, he told the wand. Catch the flavor of it, and remember, and find me more just this sweet.

The wand started to buck in his hands. It was ready. He lifted it from the stream; it settled down, calmer, but still shaking just the least bit, to let him know it was alive, alive and searching.

Now there was no more talking, no more thinking. Hank just walked, eyes near closed because he didn't want his vision to distract from the tingling in his hands. The wand never led him astray; to *look* where he was going would be as much as to admit the wand had no power to find.

It took near half an hour. Oh, he found a few places right off, but not good enough, not for Hank Dowser. He could tell by how sharp the wand bucked and dropped whether the water was close enough to the surface to do much good. He was so good at it now that most folks couldn't make no difference between him and a doodlebug, which was about as fine a knack as a dowser could ever have. And since doodlebugs were right scarce, mostly being found among seventh sons or thirteenth children, Hank never wished anymore that he was a doodlebug instead of just a dowser, or not often, anyway.

The wand dropped so hard it buried itself three inches deep in the earth. Couldn't do much better than that. Hank smiled and opened his eyes. He wasn't thirty feet back of the smithy. Couldn't have found a better spot with his eyes open. No doodlebug could've done a nicer job.

The smith thought so, too. "Why, if you'd asked me where I wished the well would be, this is the spot I'd pick."

Hank nodded, accepting the praise without a smile, his eyes half-closed, his whole body still a-tingle with the strength of the water's call to him. "I don't want to lift this wand," said Hank, "till you've dug a trench all round this spot to mark it off."

"Fetch a spade!" cried the smith.

Prentice Alvin jogged off in search of the tool. Hank noticed Arthur Stuart toddling after, running full tilt on them short legs so awkward he was bound to fall. And fall he did, flat down on his face in the grass, moving so fast he slid a yard at least, and came up soaking wet with dew. Didn't pause him none. Just waddled on around the smithy building where Prentice Alvin went.

Hank turned back to Makepeace Smith and kicked at the soil just underfoot. "I can't be sure, not being a doodlebug," said Hank, as modest as he could manage, "but I'd say you won't have to dig ten feet till you strike water here. It's fresh and lively as I ever seen."

"No skin off my nose either way," said Makepeace. "I don't aim to dig it."

"That prentice of yours looks strong enough to dig it hisself, if he doesn't lazy off and sleep when your back is turned."

"He ain't the lazying kind," said Makepeace. "You'll be staying the night at the roadhouse, I reckon."

"I reckon not," said Hank. "I got some folks about six mile west who want me to find them some *dry* ground to dig a good deep cellar."

"Ain't that kind of *anti*-dowsing?"

"It is, Makepeace, and it's a whole lot harder, too, in wettish country like this."

"Well, come back this way, then," said Makepeace, "and I'll save you a sip of the first water pulled up from your well."

"I'll do that," said Hank, "and gladly." That was an honor he wasn't often offered, that first sip from a well. There was power in that, but only if it was freely given, and Hank couldn't keep from smiling now. "I'll be back in a couple of days, sure as shooting."

The prentice boy come back with the spade and set right to digging. Just a shallow trench, but Hank noticed that the boy squared it off without measuring, each side of the hole equal, and as near as Hank could guess, it was true to the compass points as well. Standing there with the wand still rooted into the ground, Hank felt a sudden sickness in his stomach, having the boy so close. Only it wasn't the kind of sickness where you hanker to chuck up what you ate for breakfast. It was the kind of sickness that turns to pain, the sickness that turns to violence; Hank felt himself yearning to snatch the spade out of the boy's hands and smack him across the head with the sharp side of the blade.

Till finally it dawned on him, standing there with the wand a-trembling in his hand. It wasn't *Hank* who hated this boy, no sir. It was the *water* that Hank served so well, the *water* that wanted this boy dead.

The moment that thought entered Hank's head, he fought it down, swallowed back the sickness inside him. It was the plain craziest idea that ever entered his head. Water was water. All it wanted was to come up out of the ground or down out of the clouds and race over the face of the earth. It didn't have no malice in it. No desire to kill. And anyway, Hank Dowser was a Christian, and a Baptist to boot—a natural dowser's religion if there ever was one. When he put folks under the water, it was to baptize them and bring them to Jesus, not to drownd them. Hank didn't have murder in his heart, he had his Savior there, teaching him to love his enemies, teaching him that even to hate a man was like murder.

Hank said a silent prayer to Jesus to take this rage out of his heart and make him stop wishing for this innocent boy's death.

As if in answer, the wand leapt right out of the ground, flew clear out of his hands and landed in the bushes most of two rods off.

That never happened to Hank in all his days of dowsing. A wand taking off like that! Why, it was as if the water had spurned him as sharp as a fine lady spurns a cussing man.

"Trench is all dug," said the boy.

Hank looked sharp at him, to see if he noticed anything funny about the way the wand took off like that. But the boy wasn't even looking at him. Just looking at the ground inside the square he'd just ditched off.

"Good work," said Hank. He tried not to let his voice show the loathing that he felt.

"Won't do no good to dig here," said the boy.

Hank couldn't hardly believe his ears. Bad enough the boy sassing his own master, in the trade he knew, but what in tarnation did this boy know about dowsing?

"What did you say, boy?" asked Hank.

The boy must have seen the menace in Hank's face, or caught the tone of fury in his voice, because he backed right down. "Nothing, sir," he said. "None of my business anyhow."

Such was Hank's built-up anger, though, that he wasn't letting the boy off so easy. "You think you can do my job too, is that it? Maybe your master lets you think you're as good as he is cause you got your knack with *hooves,* but let me tell you, boy, I am a true dowser and my wand tells me there's water here!''

"That's right," said the boy. He spoke mildly, so that Hank didn't really notice that the boy had four inches on him in height and probably more than that in reach. Prentice Alvin wasn't so big you'd call him a giant, but you wouldn't call him no dwarf, neither.

"That's *right*? It ain't for you to say right or wrong to what my wand tells me!''

"I know it, sir, I was out of turn."

The smith came back with a wheelbarrow, a pick, and two stout iron levers. "What's all this?" he asked.

"Your boy here got smart with me," said Hank. He knew as he said it that it wasn't quite fair—the boy had already apologized, hadn't he?

Now at last Makepeace's hand lashed out and caught the boy a blow like a bear's paw alongside his head. Alvin staggered under the cuffing, but he didn't fall. "I'm sorry, sir," said Alvin.

"He said there wasn't no water here, where I said the well should be." Hank just couldn't stop himself. "I had respect for *his* knack. You'd think he'd have respect for mine."

"Knack or no knack," said the smith, "he'll have respect for my customers or he'll learn how long it takes to be a smith, oh sir! he'll learn."

Now the smith had one of the heavy iron levers in his hand, as if he meant to cane the boy across the back with it. That would be sheer murder, and Hank hadn't the heart for it. He held out his hand and caught the end of the lever. "No, Makepeace, wait, it's all right. He did tell me he was sorry."

"And is that enough for you?"

"That and knowing you'll listen to me and not to him," said Hank. "I'm not so old I'm ready to hear boys with hoof-knacks tell me I can't dowse no more."

"Oh, the well's going to be dug right here, you can bet your life. And this boy's going to dig it all himself, and not have a bite to eat until he strikes water."

Hank smiled. "Well, then, he'll be glad to discover that I know what I'm doing—he won't have to dig far, that's for sure."

Makepeace rounded on the boy, who now stood a few yards off, his hands slack at his side, showing no anger on his face, nothing at all, really. "I'm going to escort Mr. Dowser back to his new-shod mare, Alvin. And this is the last I want to see of you until you can bring me a bucket of clean water from this well. You won't eat a bite or have a sip of water until you drink it from here!"

"Oh, now," said Hank, "have a heart. You know it takes a couple of days sometimes for the dirt to settle out of a new well."

"Bring me a bucket of water from the new well, anyway," said Makepeace. "Even if you work all night."

They headed back for the smithy then, to the corral where Pickle-wing waited. There was some chat, some work at saddling up, and then Hank Dowser was on his way, his nag riding smoother and easier under him, just as happy as a clam. He could see the boy working as he rode off. There wasn't no flurry of dirt, just me-thodical lifting and dumping, lifting and dumping. The boy didn't seem to stop to rest, either. There wasn't a single break in the sound of his labor as Hank rode off. The *shuck* sound of the spade dipping into the soil, then the *swish-thump* as the dirt slid off onto the pile.

Hank didn't calm down his anger till he couldn't hear a sound of the boy, or even remember what the sound was like. Whatever power Hank had as a dowser, this boy was the enemy of his knack, that much Hank knew. He had thought his rage was unreasonable before, but now that the boy had spoke up, Hank knew he had been right all along. The boy thought he was a master of water, maybe even a doodlebug, and that made him Hank's enemy.

Jesus said to give your enemy your own cloak, to turn the other cheek—but what about when your enemy aims to take away your livelihood, what then? Do you let him ruin you? Not this Christian, thought Hank. I learned that boy something this time, and if it doesn't take, I'll learn him more later.

❧ 6 ❧

Masquerade

PEGGY WASN'T THE belle of the Governor's Ball, but that was fine
with her. Mistress Modesty had long since taught her that it was a
mistake for women to compete with each other. ''There is no single
prize to be won, which, if one woman attains it, must remain out
of reach for all the others.''

No one else seemed to understand this, however. The other women
eyed each other with jealous eyes, measuring the probable expense
of gowns, guessing at the cost of whatever amulet of beauty the
other woman wore; keeping track of who danced with whom, how
many men arranged to be presented.

Few of them turned a jealous eye toward Peggy—at least not when
she first entered the room in mid-afternoon. Peggy knew the impres-
sion she was making. Instead of an elegant coiffure, her hair was
brushed and shining, pulled up in a style that looked well-tended,
but prone to straying locks here and there. Her gown was simple,
almost plain—but this was by calculation. ''You have a sweet young
body, so your gown must not distract from the natural litheness of
youth.'' Moreover, the gown was unusually modest, showing less

bare flesh than any other woman's dress; yet, more than most, it revealed the free movement of the body underneath it.

She could almost hear Mistress Modesty's voice, saying, "So many girls misunderstand. The corset is not an end in itself. It is meant to allow old and sagging bodies to imitate the body that a healthy young woman naturally has. A corset on *you* must be lightly laced, the stays only for comfort, not containment. Then your body can move freely, and you can breathe. Other girls will marvel that you have the courage to appear in public with a natural waistline. But men don't measure the cut of a woman's clothes. Instead they pleasure in the naturalness of a lady who is comfortable, sure of herself, enjoying life on this day, in this place, in his company."

Most important, though, was the fact that she wore no jewelry. The other ladies all depended on beseemings whenever they went out in public. Unless a girl had a knack for beseemings herself, she had to buy—or her parents or husband had to buy—a hex engraven on a ring or amulet. Amulets were preferred, since they were worn nearer the face, and so one could get by with a much weaker—and therefore cheaper—hex. Such beseemings had no effect from far off, but the closer you came to a woman with a beseeming of beauty, the more you began to feel that her face was particularly beautiful. None of her features was transformed; you still saw what was actually there. It was your judgment that changed. Mistress Modesty laughed at such hexes. "What good does it do to fool someone, when he knows that he's being fooled?" So Peggy wore no such hex.

All the other women at the ball were in disguise. Though no one's face was hidden, this ball was a masquerade. Only Peggy and Mistress Modesty, of all the women here, were not in costume, were not pretending to some unnatural ideal.

She could guess at the other girls' thoughts as they watched her enter the room: Poor thing. How plain. No competition there. And their estimation was true enough—at least at first. No one took particular notice of Peggy.

But Mistress Modesty carefully selected a few of the men who approached her. "I'd like you to meet my young friend Margaret," she would say, and then Peggy would smile the fresh and open smile that was not artificial at all—her natural smile, the one that spoke of her honest gladness at meeting a friend of Mistress Modesty's. They would touch her hand and bow, and her gentle echoing courtesy was graceful and unmeasured, an honest gesture; her hand squeezed his as a friendly reflex, the way one greets a hoped-for friend. "The art of beauty is the art of truth," said Mistress Modesty. "Other women pretend to be someone else; you will be your loveliest self, with the same natural exuberant grace as a bounding deer or a circling hawk." The man would lead her onto the floor, and she would dance with him, not worrying about correct steps or keeping time or showing off her dress, but rather enjoying the dance, their symmetrical movement, the way the music flowed through their bodies together.

The man who met her, who danced with her, remembered. Afterward the other girls seemed stilted, awkward, unfree, artificial. Many men, themselves as artificial as most of the ladies, did not know themselves well enough to know they enjoyed Peggy's company more than any other young lady's. But then, Mistress Modesty did not introduce Peggy to such men. Rather she only allowed Peggy to dance with the kind of man who could respond to her; and Mistress Modesty knew which men *they* were because they were genuinely fond of Mistress Modesty.

So as the hours passed by at the ball, hazy afternoon giving way to bright evening, more and more men were circling Peggy, filling up her dance card, eagerly conversing with her during the lulls, bringing her refreshment—which she ate if she was hungry or thirsty, and kindly refused if she was not—until the other girls began to take note of her. There were plenty of men who took no notice of Peggy, of course; no other girl lacked because of Peggy's plenty. But they didn't see it that way. What they saw was that Peggy was always surrounded, and Peggy could guess at their whispered conversations.

"What kind of spell does she have?"

"She wears an amulet under her bodice—I'm sure I saw its shape pressing against that cheap fabric."

"Why don't they see how thick-waisted she is?"

"Look how her hair is awry, as if she had just come in from the barnyard."

"She must flatter them dreadfully."

"Only a certain *kind* of man is attracted to her, I hope you notice."

Poor things, poor things. Peggy had no power that was not already born within any of these girls. She used no artifice that they would have to buy.

Most important to her was the fact that she did not even use her own knack here. All of Mistress Modesty's other teachings had come easily to her over the years, for they were nothing more than the extension of her natural honesty. The one difficult barrier was Peggy's knack. By habit, the moment she met someone she had always looked into his heartfire to see who he was; and, knowing more about him than she knew about herself, she then had to conceal her knowledge of his darkest secrets. It was this that had made her so reserved, even haughty-seeming.

Mistress Modesty and Peggy both agreed—she could not tell others how much she knew about them. Yet Mistress Modesty assured her that as long as she was concealing something so important, she could not become her most beautiful self—could not become the woman that Alvin would love for herself, and not out of pity.

The answer was simple enough. Since Peggy could not tell what she knew, and could not hide what she knew, the only solution was not to know it in the first place. That was the real struggle of these past three years—to train herself *not* to look into the heartfires around her. Yet by hard work, after many tears of frustration and a thousand different tricks to try to fool herself, she had achieved it. She could enter a crowded ballroom and remain oblivious to the heartfires around her. Oh, she *saw* the heartfires—she could not blind herself—but she paid no attention to them. She did not find herself drawing close to see deeply. And now she was getting skilled enough that she didn't even have to *try* not to see into the heartfire. She could stand this close to someone, conversing, paying attention to their words, and yet see no more of his inner thoughts than any other person would.

Of course, years of torchery had taught her more about human nature—the kinds of thoughts that go behind certain words or tones of voice or expressions or gestures—that she was very good at guessing others' present thoughts. But good people never minded when she seemed to know what was on their mind right at the moment. She did not have to hide that knowledge. It was only their deepest secrets that she could not know—and those secrets were now invisible to her unless she chose to see.

She did not choose to see. For in her new detachment she found a kind of freedom she had never known before in all her life. She could take other people at face value now. She could rejoice in their company, not knowing and therefore not feeling responsible for their hidden hungers or, most terribly, their dangerous futures. It gave a kind of exhilarating madness to her dancing, her laughter, her conversation; no one else at the ball felt so free as Modesty's young friend Margaret, because no one else had ever known such desperate confinement as she had known all her life till now.

So it was that Peggy's evening at the Governor's Ball was glorious. Not a *triumph*, actually, since she vanquished no one—whatever man won her friendship was not conquered, but liberated, even victorious. What she felt was pure joy, and so those who were with her also rejoiced in her company. Such good feelings could not be contained. Even those who gossiped nastily about her behind their fans nevertheless caught the joy of the evening; many told the governor's wife that this was the best ball ever held in Dekane, or for that matter in the whole state of Suskwahenny.

Some even realized who it was who brought such gladness to the evening. Among them were the governor's wife and Mistress Modesty. Peggy saw them talking once, as she turned gracefully on the floor, returning to her partner with a smile that made him laugh with joy to be dancing with her. The governor's wife was smiling and nodding, and she pointed with her fan toward the dance floor, and for a moment Peggy's eyes met hers. Peggy smiled in warm greeting; the governor's wife smiled and nodded back. The gesture did not go unremarked. Peggy would be welcome at any party she wanted to attend in Dekane—two or three a night, if she desired, every night of the year.

Yet Peggy did not glory in this achievement, for she recognized how small it really was. She had won her way into the finest events in Dekane—but Dekane was merely the capital of a state on the edge of the American frontier. If she longed for social victories, she would have to make her way to Camelot, to win the accolades of royalty—and from there to Europe, to be received in Vienna, Paris, Warsaw, or Madrid. Even then, though, even if she had danced with every crowned head, it would mean nothing. She would die, they would die, and how would the world be any better because she had danced?

She had seen true greatness in the heartfire of a newborn baby fourteen years ago. She had protected the child because she loved his future; she had also come to love the boy because of who he was, the kind of soul he had. Most of all, though, more important than her feelings for Prentice Alvin, most of all she loved the work that lay ahead of him. Kings and queens built kingdoms, or lost them; merchants made fortunes, or squandered them; artists made works that time faded or forgot. Only Prentice Alvin had in him the seeds of Making that would stand against time, against the endless wasting of the Unmaker. So as she danced tonight, she danced for him, knowing that if she could win the love of these strangers, she might also win Alvin's love, and earn a place beside him on his pathway to the Crystal City, that place in which all the citizens can see like torches, build like makers, and love with the purity of Christ.

With the thought of Alvin, she cast her attention to his distant heartfire. Though she had schooled herself not to see into nearby heartfires, she never gave up looking into his. Perhaps this made it harder for her to control her knack, but what purpose was it to learn anything, if by learning she lost her connection to that boy? So she did not have to search for him; she knew always, in the back of her mind, where his heartfire burned. In these years she had learned not to see him constantly before her, but still she could see him in an instant. She did so now.

He was digging in the ground behind his smithy. But she hardly noticed the work, for neither did he. What burned strongest in his heartfire was anger. Someone had treated him unfairly—but that could hardly be new, could it? Makepeace, once the most fair-minded of masters, had become steadily more envious of Alvin's skill at ironwork, and in his jealousy he had become unjust, denying Alvin's ability more fervently the further his prentice boy surpassed him. Alvin lived with injustice every day, yet never had Peggy seen such rage in him.

"Is something wrong, Mistress Margaret?" The man who danced with her spoke in concern. Peggy had stopped, there in the middle of the floor. The music still played, and couples still moved through the dance, but near her the dancers had stopped, were watching her.

"I can't—continue," she said. It surprised her to find that she was out of breath with fear. What was she afraid of?

"Would you like to leave the ballroom?" he asked. What was his name? There was only one name in her mind: Alvin.

"Please," she said. She leaned on him as they walked toward the open doors leading onto the porch. The crowd parted; she didn't see them.

It was as if all the anger Alvin had stored up in his years of working under Makepeace Smith now was coming out, and every dig of his shovel was a deep cut of revenge. A dowser, an itinerant water-seeker, that's who had angered him, that's the one he meant to harm. But the dowser was none of Peggy's concern; nor was his provocation, however mean or terrible. It was Alvin. Couldn't he see that when he dug so deep in hatred it was an act of destruction? And didn't he know that when you work to destroy, you invite the Destroyer? When your labor is unmaking, the Unmaker can claim you.

The air outside was cooler in the gathering dusk, the last shred of the sun throwing a ruddy light across the lawns of the Governor's mansion. "Mistress Margaret, I hope I did nothing to cause you to faint."

"No, I'm not even fainting. Will you forgive me? I had a thought, that's all. One that I must think about."

He looked at her strangely. Any time a woman needed to part with a man, she always claimed to be near fainting. But not Mistress Margaret—Peggy knew that he was puzzled, uncertain. The etiquette of fainting was clear. But what was a gentleman's proper manner toward a woman who "had a thought"?

She laid her hand on his arm. "I assure you, my friend—I'm quite well, and I delighted in dancing with you. I hope we'll dance again. But for now, for the moment, I need to be alone."

She could see how her words eased his concern. Calling him "my friend" was a promise to remember him; her hope to dance with him again was so sincere that he could not help but believe her. He took her words at face value, and bowed with a smile. After that she didn't even see him leave.

Her attention was far away, in Hatrack River, where Prentice Alvin was calling to the Unmaker, not guessing what he was doing. Peggy searched and searched in his heartfire, trying to find something she might do to keep him safe. But there was nothing. Now that Alvin was being driven by anger, all paths led to one place, and that place terrified her, for she couldn't see what was there, couldn't see what would happen. And there were no paths out.

What was I doing at this foolish ball, when Alvin needed me? If I had been paying proper attention, I would have seen this coming, would have found some way to help him. Instead I was dancing with these men who mean less than nothing to the future of this world. Yes, they delight in me. But what is that worth, if Alvin falls, if Prentice Alvin is destroyed, if the Crystal City is unmade before its Maker begins to build it?

7

Wells

ALVIN DIDN'T NEED to look up when the dowser left. He could feel where the man was as he moved along, his anger like a black noise in the midst of the sweet green music of the wood. That was the curse of being the only White, man or boy, who could feel the life of the greenwood—it meant that he was also the only White who knew how the land was dying.

Not that the soil wasn't rich—years of forest growth had made the earth so fertile that they said the *shadow* of a seed could take root and grow. There was life in the fields, life in the towns even. But it wasn't part of the land's own song. It was just noise, whispering noise, and the green of the wood, the life of the Red man, the animal, the plant, the soil all living together in harmony, that song was quiet now, intermittent, sad. Alvin heard it dying and he mourned.

Vain little dowser. Why was he so mad? Alvin couldn't figure. But he didn't press it, didn't argue, because almost as soon as the dowser came along, Al could see the Unmaker shadowing the edges of his vision, as if Hank Dowser'd brought him along.

Alvin first saw the Unmaker in his nightmares as a child, a vast nothingness that rolled invisibly toward him, trying to crush him, to get inside him, to grind him into pieces. It was old Taleswapper who first helped Alvin give his empty enemy a name. The Unmaker, which longs to undo the universe, break it all down until everything is flat and cold and smooth and dead.

As soon as he had a name for it and some notion what it *was*, he started seeing the Unmaker in daylight, wide awake. Not right out in the open, of course. Look *at* the Unmaker and most times you can't see him. He goes all invisible behind all the life and growth and up-building in the world. But at the edges of your sight, as if he was sneaking up behind, that's where the sly old snake awaited, that's where Alvin saw him.

When Alvin was a boy he learned a way to make that Unmaker step back a ways and leave him be. All he had to do was use his hands to build something. It could be as simple as weaving grass into a basket, and he'd have some peace. So when the Unmaker showed up around the blacksmith's shop not long after Alvin got there, he wasn't too worried. There was plenty of chance for making things in the smithy. Besides, the smithy was full of fire—fire and iron, the hardest earth. Alvin knew from childhood on that the Unmaker hankered after water. Water was its servant, did most of its work, tearing things down. So it was no wonder that when a water man like Hank Dowser came along, the Unmaker freshened up and got lively.

Now, though, Hank Dowser was on his way, taking his anger and his unfairness with him, but the Unmaker was still there, hiding out in the meadow and the bushes, lurking in the long shadows of the evening.

Dig with the shovel, lever up the earth, hoist it to the lip of the well, dump it aside. A steady rhythm, a careful building of the pile, shaping the sides of the hole. Square the first three feet of the hole, to set the shape of the well house. Then round and gently tapered inward for the stonework of the finished well. Even though you know this well will never draw water, do it careful, dig as if you thought that it would last. Build smooth, as near to perfect as you can, and it'll be enough to hold that sly old spy at bay.

So why didn't Alvin feel a speck more brave about it?

Alvin knew it was getting on toward evening, sure as if he had him a watch in his pocket, cause here came Arthur Stuart, his face just scrubbed after supper, sucking on a horehound and saying not a word. Alvin was used to him by now. Almost ever since the boy could walk, he'd been like Alvin's little shadow, coming every day it didn't rain. Never had much to say, and when he did it wasn't too easy to understand his baby talk—he had trouble with his *R*s and *S*s. Didn't matter. Arthur never wanted nothing and never did no harm, and Alvin usually half-forgot the boy was around.

Digging there with the evening flies out, buzzing in his face, Alvin had nothing to do with his brain but think. Three years he been in Hatrack, and all that time he hadn't got him one inch closer to knowing what his knack was for. He hardly used it, except for the bit he done with the horses, and that was cause he couldn't bear to know how bad they suffered when it was so easy a thing for him to make the shoeing go right. That was a good thing to do, but it didn't amount to much up-building, compared to the ruination of the land all around him.

The White man was the Unmaker's tool in this forest land, Alvin knew that, better even than water at tearing things down. Every tree that fell, every badger, coon, deer, and beaver that got used up without consent, each death was part of the killing of the land. Used to be the Reds kept the balance of things, but now they were gone, either dead or moved west of the Mizzipy—or, like the Irrakwa and the Cherriky, turned White at heart, sleeves rolled up and working hard to unmake the land even faster than the White. No one left to try to keep things whole.

Sometimes Alvin thought he was the only one left who hated the Unmaker and wanted to build against him. And he didn't know how to do it, didn't have any idea what the next step ought to be. The torch who touched him at his birthing, she was the only one who might've taught him how to be a true Maker, but she was gone, run off the very morning that he came. Couldn't be no accident. She just didn't want to teach him aught. He had a destiny, he knew it, and not a soul to help him find the way.

I'm willing, thought Alvin. I got the power in me, when I can figure how to use it straight, and I got the desire to be whatever it is I'm meant to be, but somebody's got to teach me.

Not the blacksmith, that was sure. Profiteering old coot. Alvin knew that Makepeace Smith tried to teach him as little as he could. Even now Alvin reckoned Makepeace didn't know half how much Alvin had learned himself just by watching when his master didn't guess that he was alert. Old Makepeace never meant to let him go if he could help it. Here I got a destiny, a real honest-to-goodness Work to do in my life, just like the old boys in the Bible or Ulysses or Hector, and the only teacher I got is a smith so greedy I have to *steal* learning from him, even though it's mine by right.

Sometimes it burned Alvin up inside, and he got a hankering to do something spetackler to show Makepeace Smith that his prentice wasn't just a boy who didn't know he was being cheated. What would Makepeace Smith do if he saw Alvin split iron with his fingers? What if he saw that Al could straighten a bent nail as strong as before, or heal up brittle iron that shattered under the hammer? What if he saw that Al could beat iron so thin you could see sunlight through it, and yet so strong you couldn't break it?

But that was plain dumb when Alvin thought that way, and he knowed it. Makepeace Smith might gasp the first time, he might even faint dead away, but inside ten minutes he'd be figuring an angle how to make money from it, and Alvin'd be less likely than ever to get free ahead of time. And his fame would spread, yes sir, so that by the time he turned nineteen and Makepeace Smith had to let him go, Alvin would already have too much notice. Folks'd keep him busy healing and doodlebugging and fixing and stone shaping, work that wasn't even halfway toward what he was born for. If they brought him the sick and lame to heal, how would he ever have time to be aught but a physicker? Time enough for healing when he learned the whole way to be a Maker.

The Prophet Lolla-Wossiky showed him a vision of the Crystal City only a week before the massacre at Tippy-Canoe. Alvin knew that someday in the future it was up to him to build them towers of ice and light. That was his destiny, not to be a country fixit man. As long as he was bound to Makepeace Smith's service, he had to keep his real knack secret.

That's why he never ran off, even though he was big enough now that nobody'd take him for a runaway prentice. What good would freedom do? He had to learn first how to be a Maker, or it wouldn't make no difference if he went or stayed.

So he never spoke of what he could do, and scarce used his gifts more than to shoe horses and feel the death of the land around him. But all the time in the back of his brain he recollected what he really was. A Maker. Whatever that is, I'm it, which is why the Unmaker tried to kill me before I was born and in a hundred accidents and almost-murders in my childhood back in Vigor Church. That's why he lurks around now, watching me, waiting for a chance to get me, waiting maybe for a time like tonight, all alone out here in the darkness, just me and the spade and my anger at having to do work that won't amount to nothing.

Hank Dowser. What kind of man won't listen to a good idea from somebody else? Sure the wand went down hard—the water was like to bust up through the earth at that place. But the reason it *hadn't* busted through was on account of a shelf of rock along there, not four feet under the soil. Why else did they think this was a natural meadow here? The big trees couldn't root, because the water that fell here flowed right off the stone, while the roots couldn't punch through the shelf of rock to get to the water underneath it. Hank Dowser could find water, but he sure couldn't find what lay *between* the water and the surface. It wasn't Hank's fault he couldn't see it, but it sure was his fault he wouldn't entertain no notion it might be there.

So here was Alvin, digging as neat a well as you please, and sure enough, no sooner did he have the round side wall of the well defined than *clink, clank, clunk,* the spade rang against stone.

At the new sound, Arthur Stuart ran right up to the edge of the hole and looked in. "Donk donk," he said. Then he clapped his hands.

"Donk donk is right," said Alvin. "I'll be donking on solid rock the whole width of this hole. And I ain't going in to tell Makepeace Smith about it, neither, you can bet on that, Arthur Stuart. He told me I couldn't eat nor drink till I got water, and I ain't about to go in afore dark and start pleading for supper just cause I hit rock, no sir."

"Donk," said the little boy.

"I'm digging every scrap of dirt out of this hole till the rock is bare."

He carefully dug out all the dirt he could, scraping the spade along the bumpy face of the rock. Even so, it was still brown and earthy, and Alvin wasn't satisfied. He wanted that stone to shine white. Nobody was watching but Arthur Stuart, and he was just a baby anyhow. So Alvin used his knack in a way he hadn't done since leaving Vigor Church. He made all the soil flow away from the bare rock, slide right across the stone and fetch up tight against the smooth-edge earthen walls of the hole.

It took almost no time till the stone was so shiny and white you could think it was a pool reflecting the last sunlight of the day. The evening birds sang in the trees. Sweat dripped off Alvin so fast it left little black spots when it fell on the rock.

Arthur stood at the edge of the hole. "Water," he said.

"Now you stand back, Arthur Stuart. Even if this ain't all that deep, you just stand back from holes like this. You can get killed falling in, you know."

A bird flew by, its wings rattling loud as could be. Somewhere another bird gave a frantic cry.

"Snow," said Arthur Stuart.

"It ain't snow, it's rock," said Alvin. Then he clambered up out of the hole and stood there, laughing to himself. "There's your well, Hank Dowser," Alvin said. "You ride on back here and see where your stick drove into the dirt."

He'd be sorry he got Al a blow from his master's hand. It wasn't no joke when a blacksmith hit you, specially one like his master, who didn't go easy even on a little boy, and sure not on a man-size prentice like Alvin.

Now he could go on up to the house and tell Makepeace Smith the well was dug. Then he'd lead his master back down here and show him this hole, with the stone looking up from the bottom, as solid as the heart of the world. Alvin heard himself saying to his master, "You show me how to drink that and I'll drink it." It'd be pure pleasure to hear how Makepeace'd cuss himself blue at the sight of it.

Except now that he could show them how wrong they were to treat him like they did, Alvin knew it didn't matter in the long run whether he taught them a lesson or not. What mattered was Makepeace Smith really did need this well. Needed it bad enough to pay out a dowser's cost in free ironwork. Whether it was dug where Hank Dowser said or somewhere else, Alvin knew he had to dig it.

That would suit Alvin's pride even better, now he thought of it. He'd come in with a bucket, just like Makepeace ordered him to —but from a well of his own choosing.

He looked around in the ruddy evening light, thinking where to start looking for a diggable spot. He heard Arthur Stuart pulling at the meadow grass, and the sound of birds having a church choir practice, they were so loud tonight.

Or maybe they were plain scared. Cause now he was looking around, Alvin could see that the Unmaker was lively tonight. By rights digging the first hole should've been enough to send it head-long, keep it off for days. Instead it followed him just out of sight, ever step he took as he hunted for the place to dig the true well. It was getting more and more like one of his nightmares, where nothing he did could make the Unmaker go away. It was enough to send a thrill of fear right through him, make him shiver in the warm spring air.

Alvin just shrugged off that scare. He knew the Unmaker wasn't going to touch him. For all the years of his life till now, the Unmaker'd tried to kill him by setting up accidents, like water icing up where he was bound to step, or eating away at a riverbank so he slipped in. Now and then the Unmaker even got some man or other to take a few swipes at Alvin, like Reverend Thrower or them Choc-Taw Reds. In all his life, outside his dreams, that Unmaker never did anything direct.

And he won't now either, Alvin told hisself. Just keep searching, so you can dig the *real* well. The false one didn't drive that old deceiver off, but the real one's bound to, and I won't see him shimmering at the edges of my vision for three months after that.

With that thought in mind, Alvin hunkered down and kept his mind on searching for a break in the hidden shelf of stone.

How Alvin searched things out underground wasn't like *seeing*. It was more like he had another hand that skittered through the soil and rock as fast as a waterdrop on a hot griddle. Even though he'd never met him a doodlebug, he figured doodling couldn't be much different than how he done it, sending his bug scouting along under the earth, feeling things out all the way. And if he *was* doodle-bugging, then he had to wonder if folks was right who allowed as how it was the doodlebug's very *soul* that slithered under the ground, and there was tales about doodlebugs whose souls got lost and the doodler never said another word or moved a muscle till he finally died. But Alvin didn't let such tales scare him off from doing what he ought to. If there was a need for stone, he'd find him the natural breaks to make it come away without hardly chipping at it. If there was a need for water, he'd find him a way to dig on down to get it.

Finally he found him a place where the shelf of stone was thin and crumbled. The ground was higher here, the water deeper down, but what counted was he could get through the stone to it.

This new spot was halfway between the house and the smithy—which would be less convenient for Makepeace, but better for his wife Gertie, who had to use the same water. Alvin set to with a will, because it was getting on to dark, and he was determined to take no rest tonight until his work was done. Without even thinking about it he made up his mind to use his power like he used to back on his father's land. He never struck stone with his spade; it was like the earth turned to flour and fair to jumped out of the hole instead of him having to heft it. If any grownup happened to see him right then they'd think they was likkered up or having a conniption fit, he dug so fast. But nobody was looking, except for Arthur Stuart. It was getting nightward, after all, and Al had no lantern, so nobody'd ever even notice he was there. He could use his knack tonight without fear of being found out.

From the house came the sound of shouting, loud but not clear enough for Alvin to make out the words.

"Mad," said Arthur Stuart. He was looking straight at the house, as steady as a dog on point.

"Can you hear what they're saying?" said Alvin. "Old Peg Guester always says you got ears like a dog, perk up at everything."

Arthur Stuart closed his eyes. "You got no right to starve that boy," he said.

Alvin like to laughed outright. Arthur was doing as perfect an imitation of Gertie Smith's voice as he ever heard.

"He's too big to thrash and I got to learn him," said Arthur Stuart.

This time he sounded just like Alvin's master. "I'll be," murmured Alvin.

Little Arthur went right on. "Either Alvin eats this plate of supper Makepeace Smith or you'll wear it on your head. I'd like to see you try it you old hag I'll break your arms."

Alvin couldn't help himself, he just laughed outright. "Consarn it if you ain't a perfect mockingbird, Arthur Stuart."

The little boy looked up at Alvin and a grin stole across his face. Down from the house come the sound of breaking crockery. Arthur Stuart started to laugh and run around in circles. "Break a dish, break a dish, break a dish!" he cried.

"If you don't beat all," said Alvin. "Now you tell me, Arthur, you didn't really understand all them things you just said, did you? I mean, you were just repeating what you heard, ain't that so?"

"Break a dish on his *head*!" Arthur screamed with laughter and fell over backward in the grass. Alvin laughed right along, but he couldn't take his eyes off the little boy. More to him than meets the eye, thought Alvin. Or else he's plain crazy.

From the other direction came another woman's voice, a full-throated call that floated over the moist darkening air. "Ar*thur!* Arthur *Stuart!*"

Arthur sat right up. "Mama," he said.

"That's right, that's Old Peg Guester calling," said Alvin.

"Go to bed," said Arthur.

"Just be careful she don't give you a bath first, boy, you're a mite grimy."

Arthur got up and started trotting off across the meadow, up to the path that led from the springhouse to the roadhouse where he lived. Alvin watched him out of sight, the little boy flapping his arms as he ran, like as if he was flying. Some bird, probably an owl, flew right alongside the boy halfway across the meadow, skimming along the ground like as if to keep him company. Not till Arthur was out of sight behind the springhouse did Alvin turn back to his labor.

In a few more minutes it was full dark, and the deep silence of night came quick after that. Even the dogs were quiet all through town. It'd be hours before the moon came up. Alvin worked on. He didn't have to see; he could feel how the well was going, the earth under his feet. Nor was it the Red man's seeing now, their gift for hearing the greenwood song. It was his own knack he was using, helping him feel his way deeper into the earth.

He knew he'd strike rock twice as deep this time. But when the spade caught up on big chunks of rock, it wasn't a smooth plate like it was at the spot Hank Dowser chose. The stones were crumbly and broke up, and with his knack Al hardly had to press his lever afore the stones flipped up easy as you please, and he tossed them out the well like clods.

Once he dug through that layer, though, the ground got oozy underfoot. If he wasn't who he was, he'd've had to set the work aside and get help to dredge it out in the morning. But for Alvin it was easy enough. He tightened up the earth around the walls of the hole, so water couldn't seep in so fast. It wasn't spadework now. Alvin used a dredge to scoop up the mucky soil, and he didn't need no partner to hoist it out on a rope, either, he just heaved it up and his knack was such that each scoop of ooze clung together and landed neat as you please outside the well, just like he was flinging bunny rabbits out the hole.

Alvin was master here, that was sure, working miracles in this hole in the ground. You tell me I can't eat or drink till the well is dug, thinking you'll have me begging for a cup of water and pleading for you to let me go to bed. Well, you won't see such a thing. You'll have your well, with walls so solid they'll be drawing water here after your house and smithy have crumbled into dust.

But even as he felt the sweet taste of victory, he saw that the Unmaker was closer than it had ever come in years. It flickered and danced, and not just at the edges of his vision anymore. He could see it right in front of him, even in the darkness, he could see it clearer than ever in daylight, cause now he couldn't see nothing real to distract him.

It was scary, all of a sudden, just like the nightmares of his childhood, and for a while Alvin stood in the hole, all froze with fear, as water oozed up from below, making the ground under him turn to slime. Thick slime a hundred feet deep, he was sinking down, and the walls of the well were getting soft, too, they'd cave in on him and bury him, he'd drown trying to breathe muck into his lungs, he knew it, he could feel it cold and wet around his thighs, his crotch; he clenched his fists and felt mud ooze between his fingers, just like the nothingness in all his nightmares—

And then he came to himself, got control. Sure, he was up to his waist in mud, and if he was any other boy in such a case he might have wiggled himself down deeper and smothered hisself, trying to struggle out. But this was Alvin, not some ordinary boy, and he was safe as long as he wasn't booglied up by fear like a child caught in a bad dream. He just made the slime under his feet harden enough to hold his weight, then made the hard place float upward, lifting him out of the mud until he was standing on gravelly mud at the bottom of the well.

Easy as breaking a rat's neck. If that was all the Unmaker could think of doing, it might as well go on home. Alvin was a match for him, just like he was a match for Makepeace Smith and Hank

Dowser both. He dug on, dredged up, hoisted, flung, then bent to dredge again.

He was pretty near deep enough now, a good six feet lower than the stone shelf. Why, if he hadn't firmed up the earthen sides of the well, it'd be full of water over his head already. Alvin took hold of the knotted rope he left dangling and walked up the wall, pulling himself hand over hand up the rope.

The moon was rising now, but the hole was so deep it wouldn't shine into the well until near moon-noon. Never mind. Into the pit Alvin dumped a barrowload of the stones he'd levered out only an hour before. Then he clambered down after it.

He'd been working rock with his knack since he was little, and he was never more sure-handed with it than tonight. With his bare hands he shaped the stone like soft clay, making it into smooth square blocks that he placed all around the walls of the well from the bottom up, braced firm against each other so that the pushing of soil and water wouldn't cave it in. Water would seep easily through the cracks between stones, but the soil wouldn't, so the well would be clean almost from the start.

There wasn't enough stone from the well itself, of course; Alvin made three trips to the stream to load the barrow with water-smoothed rocks. Even though he was using his knack to make the work easier, it was late at night and weariness was coming on him. But he refused to pay attention. Hadn't he learned the Red man's knack for running on long after weariness should have claimed him? A boy who followed Ta-Kumsaw, running without a rest from Detroit to Eight-Face Mound, such a boy had no need to give in to a single night of well-digging, and never mind his thirst or the pain in his back and thighs and shoulders, the ache of his elbows and his knees.

At last, at last, it was done. The moon past zenith, his mouth tasting like a horsehair blanket, but it was done. He climbed on out of the hole, bracing himself against the stone walls he'd just finished building. As he climbed he let go of his hold on the earth around the well, unsealed it, and the water, now tame, began to trickle noisily into the deep stone basin he'd built to hold it.

Still Alvin didn't go inside the house, didn't so much as walk to the stream and drink. His first taste of water would be from this well, just like Makepeace Smith had said. He'd stay here and wait until the well had reached its natural level, and then clear the water and draw up a bucket and carry it inside the house and drink a cup of it in front of his master. Afterward he'd take Makepeace Smith outside and show him the well Hank Dowser called for, the one Makepeace Smith had cuffed him for, and then point out the one where you could drop a bucket and it was splash, not clatter.

He stood there at the lip of the well, imagining how Makepeace Smith would sputter, how he'd cuss. Then he sat down, just to ease his feet, picturing Hank Dowser's face when he saw what Al had done. Then he lay right down to ease his aching back, and closed his eyes for just a minute, so he didn't have to pay no heed to the fluttering shadows of unmaking that kept pestering him out the corners of his eyes.

⚙ 8 ⚙

Unmaker

MISTRESS MODESTY WAS stirring. Peggy heard her breathing change rhythm. Then she came awake and sat up abruptly on her couch. At once Mistress Modesty looked for Peggy in the darkness of the room.

"Here I am," Peggy murmured.

"What has happened, my dear? Haven't you slept at all?"

"I dare not," said Peggy.

Mistress Modesty stepped onto the portico beside her. The breeze from the southwest billowed the damask curtains behind them. The moon was flirting with a cloud; the city of Dekane was a shifting pattern of roofs down the hill below them. "Can you see him?" asked Mistress Modesty.

"Not him," said Peggy. "I see his heartfire; I can see through his eyes, as he sees; I can see his futures. But himself, no, I can't see him."

"My poor dear. On such a marvelous night, to have to leave the Governor's Ball and watch over this faraway child in grave danger." It was Mistress Modesty's way of asking what the danger was without actually *asking*. This way Peggy could answer or not, and neither way would any offense be given or taken.

"I wish I could explain," said Peggy. "It's his enemy, the one with no face—"

Mistress Modesty shuddered. "No face! How ghastly."

"Oh, he has a face for *other* men. There was a minister once, a man who fancied himself a scientist. He saw the Unmaker, but could not see him truly, not as Alvin does. Instead he made up a manshape for him in his mind, and a name—called him 'the Visitor,' and thought he was an angel."

"An angel!"

"I believe that when most of us see the Unmaker, we can't comprehend him, we haven't the strength of intellect for that. So our minds come as close as they can. Whatever shape represents naked destructive power, terrible and irresistible force, that is what we see. Those who *love* such evil power, they make themselves see the Unmaker as beautiful. Others, who hate and fear it, they see the worst thing in the world."

"What does your Alvin see?"

"I could never see it myself, it's so subtle; even looking through his eyes I wouldn't have noticed it, if *he* hadn't noticed it. I saw that he was seeing something, and only then did I understand what it was he saw. Think of it as—the feeling when you think you saw some movement out of the corner of your eye, only when you turn there's nothing there."

"Like someone always sneaking up behind you," said Mistress Modesty.

"Yes, exactly."

"And it's sneaking up on Alvin?"

"Poor boy, he doesn't realize that he's calling to it. He has dug a deep black pit in his heart, just the sort of place where the Unmaker flows."

Mistress Modesty sighed. "Ah, my child, these things are all beyond me. I never had a knack; I can barely comprehend the things you do."

"You? No knack?" Peggy was amazed.

"I know—hardly anyone ever admits to not having one, but surely I'm not the only one."

"You misunderstand me, Mistress Modesty," said Peggy. "I was startled, not that you had no knack, but that you *thought* you had no knack. Of course you have one."

"Oh, but I don't mind not having one, my dear—"

"You have the knack of seeing potential beauty as if it were already there, and by seeing, you let it come to be."

"What a lovely idea," said Mistress Modesty.

"Do you doubt me?"

"I don't doubt that you believe what you say."

There was no point in arguing. Mistress Modesty believed her, but was afraid to believe. It didn't matter, though. What mattered was Alvin, finishing his second well. He had saved himself once; he thought the danger was over. Now he sat at the edge of the well, just to rest a moment; now he lay down. Didn't he see the Unmaker moving close to him? Didn't he realize that his very sleepiness opened himself wide for the Unmaker to enter him?

"No!" whispered Peggy. "Don't sleep!"

"Ah," said Mistress Modesty. "You speak to him. Can he hear you?"

"Never," said Peggy. "Never a word."

"Then what can you do?"

"Nothing. Nothing I can think of."

"You told me you used his caul—"

"It's a part of his power, that's what I use. But even his knack can't send away what came at his own call. I never had the knowledge to fend off the Unmaker itself, anyway, even if I had a yard of his caulflesh, and not just a scrap of it."

Peggy watched in desperate silence as Alvin's eyes closed. "He sleeps."

"If the Unmaker wins, will he die?"

"I don't know. Perhaps. Perhaps he'll disappear, eaten away to nothing. Or perhaps the Unmaker will own him—"

"Can't you see the future, torch girl?"

"All paths lead into darkness, and I see no path emerging."

"Then it's over," whispered Mistress Modesty.

Peggy could feel something cold on her cheeks. Ah, of course: her own tears drying in the cool breeze.

"But if Alvin were awake, *he* could fend off this invisible enemy?" Mistress Modesty asked. "Sorry to bother you with questions, but if I know how it works, perhaps I can help you think of something."

"No, no, it's beyond us, we can only watch—" Yet even as Peggy rejected Mistress Modesty's suggestion, her mind leapt ahead to ways of using it. I must waken him. I don't have to fight the Unmaker, but if I waken him, then he can do his fighting for himself. Weak and weary though he is, he might still find a way to victory. At once Peggy turned and rushed back into her room, scrabbled through her top drawer until she found the carven box that held the caul.

"Should I leave?" Mistress Modesty had followed her.

"Stay with me," said Peggy. "Please, for company. For comfort, if I fail."

"You won't fail," said Mistress Modesty. "*He* won't fail, if he's the man you say he is."

Peggy barely heard her. She sat on the edge of her bed, searching in Alvin's heartfire for some way to waken him. Normally she could use his senses even when he slept, hearing what he heard, seeing his memory of the place around him. But now, with the Unmaker seeping in, his senses were fading. She could not trust them. Desperately she cast about for some other plan. A loud noise? Using what little was left of Alvin's sense of the life around him, she found a tree, then rubbed a tiny bit of the caul and tried—as she had seen Alvin do it—to picture in her mind how the wood in the branch would come apart. It was painfully slow—Alvin did it so quickly!—but at last she made it fall. Too late. He barely heard it. The Unmaker had undone so much of the air around him that the trembling of sound could not pass through it. Perhaps Alvin noticed; perhaps he came a bit closer to wakefulness. Perhaps not.

How can I waken him, when he is so insensible that nothing can disturb him? Once I held this caul as a ridgebeam tumbled toward him; I burned a childsize gap in it, so that the hair of his head wasn't even touched. Once a millstone fell toward his leg; I split it in half. Once his own father stood in a loft, pitchfork in hand, driven by the Unmaker's madness until he had decided to murder his own most-beloved son; I brought Taleswapper down the hill to him, distracting the father from his dark purpose and driving off the Unmaker.

How? How did Taleswapper's coming drive off the Destroyer? Because he would have seen the hateful beast and given the cry against it, that's why the Unmaker left when Taleswapper arrived. Taleswapper isn't anywhere near Alvin now, but surely there's someone I can waken and draw down the hill; someone filled with love and goodness, so that the Unmaker must flee before him.

With agonizing fear she withdrew from Alvin's heartfire even as the blackness of the Unmaker threatened to drown it, and searched in the night for another heartfire, someone she could waken and send to him in time. Yet even as she searched, she could sense in Alvin's heartfire a certain lightening, a hint of shadows within shadows, not the utter emptiness she had seen before where his future ought to be. If Alvin had any chance, it was from her searching. Even if she found someone, she had no notion how to waken them. But she would find a way, or the Crystal City would be swallowed up in the flood that came because of Alvin's foolish, childish rage.

⊱ 9 ⊰

Redbird

ALVIN WOKE UP hours later, the moon low in the west, the first scant light appearing in the east. He hadn't meant to sleep. But he was tired, after all, and his work was done, so of course he couldn't close his eyes and hope to stay awake. There was still time to take a bucketful of water and carry it inside.

Were his eyes open even now? The sky he could see, light grey to the left, light grey to the right. But where were the trees? Shouldn't they have been moving gently in the morning breeze, just at the fringes of his vision? For that matter, there was no breeze; and beyond the sight of his eyes, and touch on his skin, there were other things he could not feel. The green music of the living forest. It was gone; no murmur of life from the sleeping insects in the grass, no rhythm of the heartbeats of the dawn-browsing deer. No birds roosting in the trees, waiting for the sun's heat to bring out the insects.

Dead. Unmade. The forest was gone.

Alvin opened his eyes.

Hadn't they already been open?

Alvin opened his eyes again, and still he couldn't see; without closing them, he opened them still again, and each time the sky seemed darker. No, not darker, simply farther away, rushing up and away from him, like as if he was falling into a pit so deep that the sky itself got lost.

Alvin cried out in fear, and opened his already-open eyes, and saw:

The quivering air of the Unmaker, pressing down on him, poking itself into his nostrils, between his fingers, into his ears.

He couldn't feel it, no sir, except that he knew what *wasn't* there now; the outermost layers of his skin, wherever the Unmaker touched, his own body was breaking apart, the tiniest bits of him dying, drying, flaking away.

"No!" he shouted. The shout didn't make a sound. Instead, the Unmaker whipped inside his mouth, down into his lungs, and he couldn't close his teeth hard enough, his lips tight enough to keep that slimy uncreator from slithering on inside him, eating him away from the inside out.

He tried to heal himself the way he done with his leg that time the millstone broke it clean in half. But it was like the old story Taleswapper told him. He couldn't build things up half so fast as the Unmaker could tear them down. For every place he healed, there was a thousand places wrecked and lost. He was a-going to die, he was half-gone already, and it wouldn't be just death, just losing his flesh and living on in the spirit, the Unmaker meant to eat him body and spirit both alike, his mind and his flesh together.

A splash. He heard a splashing sound. It was the most welcome thing he ever heard in his life, to hear a sound at all. It meant that there *was* something beyond the Unmaker that surrounded and filled him.

Alvin heard the sound echo and ring inside his own memory, and with that to cling to, with that touch of the real world there to hang on to, Alvin opened his eyes.

This time for real, he knew, cause he saw the sky again with its proper fringe of trees. And there was Gertie Smith, Makepeace's missus, standing over him with a bucket in her hands.

"I reckon this is the first water from this well," she said.

Alvin opened his mouth, and felt cool moist air come inside. "Reckon so," he whispered.

"I never would've thought you could dig it all out and line it proper with stones, all in one night," she said. "That mixup boy, Arthur Stuart, he come to the kitchen where I was making breakfast biscuits, and he told me your well was done. I had to come and see."

"He gets up powerful early," said Alvin.

"And you stay up powerful late," said Gertie. "If I was a man your size I'd give my husband a proper licking, Al, prentice or no."

"I just did what he asked."

"I'm certain you did, just like I'm certain he wanted you to excavate that there circle of stone off by the smithy, am I right?" She cackled with delight. "That'll show the old coot. Sets such a store by that dowser, but his own prentice has a better dowsing knack than that old fraud—"

For the first time Alvin realized that the hole he dug in anger was like a signboard telling folks he had more than a hoof-knack in him. "Please, ma'am," he said.

"Please what?"

"My knack ain't dowsing, ma'am, and if you start saying so, I'll never get no peace."

She eyed him cool and steady. "If you ain't got the dowser's knack, boy, tell me how come there's clear water in this well you dug."

Alvin calculated his lie. "The dowser's stick dipped here, too, I saw it, and so when the first well struck stone, I tried here."

Gertie had a suspicious nature. "Do you reckon you'd say the same if Jesus was standing here judging your eternal soul depending on the truth of what you say?"

"Ma'am, I reckon if Jesus was here, I'd be asking forgiveness for my sins, and I wouldn't care two hoots about any old well."

She laughed again, cuffed him lightly on the shoulder. "I like your dowsing story. You just happened to be watching old Hank

Dowser. Oh, that's a good one. I'll tell that tale to everybody, see if I don't.''

"Thank you, ma'am.''

"Here. Drink. You deserve first swallow from the first bucket of clear water from this well.''

Alvin knew that the custom was for the owner to get first drinks. But she was offering, and he was so dry he couldn't have spit two bits' worth even if you paid him five bucks an ounce. So he set the bucket to his lips and drank, letting it splash out onto his shirt.

"I'd wager you're hungry, too,'' she said.

"More tired than hungry, I think,'' said Alvin.

"Then come inside to sleep.''

He knew he should, but he could see the Unmaker not far off, and he was afeared to sleep again, that was the truth. "Thank you kindly, Ma'am, but anyhow, I'd like to be off by myself a few minutes.''

"Suit yourself,'' she said, and went on inside.

The morning breeze chilled him as it dried off the water he spilled on his shirt. Was his ravishment by the Unmaker only a dream? He didn't think so. He was awake right enough, and it was real, and if Gertie Smith hadn't come along and dunked that bucket in the well, he would've been unmade. The Unmaker wasn't hiding out no more. He wasn't sneaking in backways nor roundabout. No matter where he looked, there it was, shimmering in the greyish morning light.

For some reason the Unmaker picked this morning for a face-to-face. Only Alvin didn't know how he was supposed to fight. If digging a well and building it up so fine wasn't making enough to drive off his enemy, he didn't know what else to do. The Unmaker wasn't like the men he wrestled with in town. The Unmaker had nothing he could take ahold of.

One thing was sure. Alvin'd never have a night of sleep again if he didn't take this Unmaker down somehow and wrestle him into the dirt.

I'm supposed to be your master, Alvin said to the Unmaker. So tell me, Unmaker, how do I undo *you,* when all you are is Undoing?

Who's going to teach me how to win this battle, when you can sneak up on me in my sleep, and I don't have the faintest idea how to get to you?

As he spoke these words inside his head, Alvin walked to the edge of the woods. The Unmaker backed away from him, always out of reach. Al knew without looking that it also closed up behind him, so it had him on all sides.

This is the middle of the uncut wood where I ought to feel most at home, but the greensong, it's gone silent here, and all around me is my enemy from birth, and me here with no plan at all.

The Unmaker, though, he had a plan. He didn't need to waste no time a-dithering about what to do, Alvin found that out real quick.

Cause while Alvin was a-standing there in the cool heavy breeze of a summer morning, the air suddenly went chill, and blamed if snowflakes didn't start to fall. Right down on the green-leaf trees they came, settling on the tall thick grass between them. Thick and cold it piled up, not the wet heavy flakes of a warm snow, but the tiny icy crystals of a deep winter blizzard blow. Alvin shivered.

"You can't do this," he said.

But his eyes weren't closed *now*, he knew that. This wasn't no half-asleep dream. This was real snow, and it was so thick and cold that the branches of summer-green trees were snapping, the leaves were tearing off and falling to the ground in a tinkle of broken ice. And Alvin himself was like to freeze himself clear to death if he didn't get out of there somehow.

He started to walk back the way he came, but the snow was coming down so thick he couldn't see more than five or six feet ahead of him, and he couldn't feel his way because the Unmaker had deadened the greensong of the living woods. Pretty soon he wasn't walking, he was running. Only he didn't run surefooted like Ta-Kumsaw taught him; he ran as noisy and stupid as any oaf of a White man, and like most Whites would've, he slipped on a patch of ice-covered stone and sprawled out face down across a reach of snow.

Snow that caught up in his mouth and nose and into his ears, snow that clung between his fingers, just like the slime last night, just like the Unmaker in his dream, and he choked and sputtered and cried out—

"I know it's a lie!"

His voice was swallowed up in the wall of snow.

"It's summer!" he shouted.

His jaw ached from the cold and he knew it'd hurt too much to speak again, but still he screamed through numb lips, "I'll make you stop!"

And then he realized that he could never make anything out of the Unmaker, could never make the Unmaker do or be anything because it was only Undoing and Unbeing. It wasn't the Unmaker he needed to call to, it was all the living things around him, the trees, the grass, the earth, the air itself. It was the greensong that he needed to restore.

He grabbed ahold of that idea and used it, spoke again, his voice scarce more than a whisper now, but he called to them, and not in anger.

"Summer," he whispered.

"Warm air!" he said.

"Leaves green!" he shouted. "Hot wind out of the southwest. Thunderheads in the afternoon, mist in the morning, sunlight hotting it up, burning off the fog!"

Did it change, just a little? Did the snowfall slacken? Did the drifts on the ground melt lower, the heaps on the treelimbs tumble off, baring more of the branch?

"It's a hot morning, dry!" he cried. "Rain may drift in later like the gift of the Wise Men, coming from a long way off, but for now sunlight beating on the leaves, waking you up, you're *growing*, putting out leaves, that's right! That's right!"

There was gladness in his voice because the snowfall was just a spatter of rain now, the snow on the ground was melted back to patches here and there, the broke-off leaves were sprouting on the branch again as quick as militia in a doubletime march.

And in the silence after his last shout, he heard birdsong.

Song like he'd never heard before. He didn't know this bird, this sweet melody that changed with every whistle and never played the same tune again. It was a weaving song, but one whose pattern you couldn't find, so you couldn't ever sing it again, but you also couldn't ravel it, spin it out and break it down. It was all of one piece, all of one single Making, and Alvin knew that if he could just find the bird with that song in his throat he'd be safe. His victory would be complete.

He ran, and now the greensong of the forest was with him, and his feet found the right places to step without him looking. He followed that song until he came to the clearing where the singing was.

Perched on an old log with a patch of snow still in the northwest shadow—a redbird. And sitting in front of that log, almost nose to nose as he listened to it sing—Arthur Stuart.

Alvin walked around the two of them real slow, walking a clean circle before he come much closer. Arthur Stuart like to never noticed he was there, he never took his eyes off that bird. The sunlight dazzled on the two of them, but neither bird nor boy so much as blinked. Alvin didn't say nothing, either. Just like Arthur Stuart, he was all caught up in the redbird song.

It wasn't no different from all the other redbirds, the thousand scarlet songbirds Alvin had seen since he was little. Except that from its throat came music that no other bird had ever sung before. This wasn't *a* redbird. Nor was it *the* redbird. There was no single bird had some gift the other redbirds lacked. It was just Redbird, the one picked for this moment to speak in the voice of all the birds, to sing the song of all the singers, so that this boy could hear.

Alvin knelt down on the new-grown grass not three feet from Redbird, and listened to its song. He knew from what Lolla-Wossiky once told him that Redbird's song was all the stories of the Red man, everything they ever done that was worth doing. Alvin halfway hoped to understand that ancient tale, or at least to hear how Redbird told of things that he took part in. The Prophet Lolla-Wossiky walking on water; Tippy-Canoe River all scarlet with Red folks' blood; Ta-Kumsaw standing with a dozen musketballs in him, still crying out for his men to stand, to fight, to drive the White thieves back.

But the sense of the song eluded him no matter how he listened. He might run the forest with a Red man's legs and hear the greensong with a Red man's ears, but Redbird's song wasn't meant for him. The saying told the truth: No one girl gets all the suitors, and no boy gets all the knacks. There was much that Alvin could do already, and much ahead of him to learn, but there'd be far more that was always out of his ken, and Redbird's song was part of that.

Yet Alvin was sure as shucks that Redbird wasn't here by accident. Come like this at the end of his first face-to-face with the Unmaker, Redbird had to have some purpose. He had to get some answers out of Redbird's song.

Alvin was just about to speak, just about to ask the question burning in him ever since he first learned what his destiny might be. But it wasn't his voice that broke into Redbird's song. It was Arthur Stuart's.

"I don't know days coming up," said the mixup boy. His voice was like music and the words were clearer than any Alvin ever heard that three-year-old say before. "I only know days gone."

It took a second for Alvin to hitch himself to what was going on here. What Arthur said was the answer to Alvin's question. Will I ever be a Maker like the torch girl said? That was what Alvin would've asked, and Arthur's words were the answer.

But not Arthur Stuart's own answer, that was plain. The little boy no more understood what he was saying than he did when he was mimicking Makepeace's and Gertie's quarrel last night. He was giving Redbird's answer. Translating from birdsong into speech that Alvin's ears were fit to understand.

Alvin knew now that he'd asked the wrong question. He didn't need Redbird to tell him he was supposed to be a Maker—he knowed that firm and sure years ago, and knew it still in spite of all doubts. The real question wasn't whether, it was *how* to be a Maker.

Tell me how.

Redbird changed his song to a soft and simple tune, more like normal birdsong, quite different from the thousand-year-old Red man's tale that he'd been singing up to now. Alvin didn't understand the sense of it, but he knew all the same what it was about. It was the song of Making. Over and over, the same tune repeating, only a few moments of it—but they were blinding in their brightness, a song so true that Alvin saw it with his eyes, felt it from his lips to his groin, tasted it and smelled it. The song of Making, and it was his own song, he knew it from how sweet it tasted on his tongue.

And when the song was at its peak, Arthur Stuart spoke again in a voice that was hardly human it piped so sharp, it sang so clear.

"The Maker is the one who is part of what he makes," said the mixup boy.

Alvin wrote the words in his heart, even though he didn't understand them. Because he knew that someday he *would* understand them, and when he did, he would have the power of the ancient Makers who built the Crystal City. He would understand, and use his power, and find the Crystal City and build it once again.

The Maker is the one who is part of what he makes.

Redbird fell silent. Stood still, head cocked; and then became, not Redbird, but any old bird with scarlet feathers. Off it flew.

Arthur Stuart watched the bird out of sight. Then he called out after it in his own true childish voice, "Bird! Fly bird!" Alvin knelt beside the boy, weak from the night's work, the grey dawn's fear, this bright day's birdsong.

"I flied," said Arthur Stuart. For the first time, it seemed, he took notice Alvin was there, and turned to him.

"Did you now?" whispered Alvin, reluctant to destroy the child's dream by telling him that folks don't fly.

"Big blackbird tote me," said Arthur. "Fly and fly." Then Arthur reached up his hands and pressed in on Alvin's cheeks. "Maker," he said. Then he laughed and laughed with joy.

So Arthur wasn't just a mimic. He really understood Redbird's song, some of it, at least. Enough to know the name of Alvin's destiny.

"Don't you tell nobody," Alvin said. "I won't tell nobody you can talk to birds, and you don't tell nobody I'm a Maker. Promise?"

Arthur's face grew serious. "Don't talk birds," he said. "Birds talk *me*." And then: "I *flied*."

"I believe you," Alvin said.

"I beeve *you*," said Arthur. Then he laughed again.

Alvin stood up and so did Arthur. Al took him by the hand. "Let's go on home," he said.

He took Arthur to the roadhouse, where Old Peg Guester was full of scold at the mixup boy for running off and bothering folks all morning. But it was a loving scold, and Arthur grinned like an idiot at the voice of the woman he called Mama. As the door closed with Arthur Stuart on the other side, Alvin told himself, I'm going to tell that boy what he done for me. Someday I'll tell him what this meant.

Alvin came home by way of the springhouse path and headed on down toward the smithy, where Makepeace was no doubt angry at him for not being ready for work, even though he dug a well all night.

The well. Alvin found himself standing by the hole that he had dug as a monument to Hank Dowser, with the white stone bright in the sunlight, bright and cruel as scornful laughter.

In that moment Alvin knew why the Unmaker came to him that night. Not because of the true well that he dug. Not because he had used his knack to hold the water back, not because he had softened the stone and bent it to his need. It was because he had dug that first hole down to the stone for one reason only—to make Hank Dowser look the fool.

To punish him? Yes sir, to make him a laughingstock to any man who saw the stone-bottomed well on the spot that Hank had marked. It would destroy him, take away his name as a dowser—and unfairly so, because he *was* a good dowser who got hisself fooled by the lay of the land. Hank made an honest mistake, and Al had got all set to punish him as if he was a fool, which surely he was not.

Tired as he was, weak from labor and the battle with the Unmaker, Alvin didn't waste a minute. He fetched the spade from where it lay by the working well, then stripped off his shirt and set to work. When he dug this false well, it was a work of evil, to unmake an honest man for no reason better than spite. Filling it in, though, was a Maker's work. Since it was daylight, Alvin couldn't even use his knack to help—he did full labor on it till he thought he was so tired he might just die.

It was noon, and him without supper or breakfast either one, but the well was filled right up, the turves set back on so they'd grow back, and if you didn't look close you'd never know there'd been a hole at all. Alvin *did* use his knack a little, since no one was about, to weave the grassroots back together, knit them into the ground, so there'd be no dead patches to mark the spot.

All the time, though, what burned worse than the sun on his back or the hunger in his belly was his own shame. He was so busy last night being angry and thinking how to make a fool of Hank Dowser that it never once occurred to him to do the right thing and use his knack to break right through the shelf of stone in the very spot Hank picked. No one ever would've known save Alvin hisself that there'd been aught wrong with the place. That would've been the Christian thing, the charitable thing to do. When a man slaps your face, you answer by shaking his hand, that's what Jesus said to do, and Alvin just plain wasn't listening, Alvin was too cussed proud.

That's what called the Unmaker to me, thought Alvin. I could've used my knack to build up, and I used it to tear down. Well, never again, never again, never again. He made that promise three times, and even though it was a silent promise and no one'd ever know, he'd keep it better than any oath he might take before a judge or even a minister.

Well, too late now. If he'd thought of this before Gertie ever saw the false well or drew water from the true, he might've filled up the other well and made this one good after all. But now she'd seen the stone, and if he dug through it then all his secrets would be out. And once you've drunk water from a good new well, you can't never fill it up till it runs dry on its own. To fill up a living well is to beg for drouth and cholera to dog you all the days of your life.

He'd undone all he could. You can be sorry, and you can be forgiven, but you can't call back the futures that your bad decisions lost. He didn't need no philosopher to tell him that.

Makepeace wasn't a-hammering in the forge, and there wasn't no smoke from the smithy chimney, either. Must be Makepeace was up at the house, doing some chores there, Alvin figured. So he put the spade away back in the smithy and then headed on toward the house.

Halfway there, he come to the good well, and there was Makepeace Smith setting on the low wall of footing stones Al had laid down to be foundation for the wellhouse.

"Morning, Alvin," said the master.

"Morning, sir," said Alvin.

"Dropped me the tin and copper bucket right down to the bottom here. You must've dug like the devil hisself, boy, to get it so deep."

"Didn't want it to run dry."

"And lined it with stone already," said the smith. "It's a wonderment, I say."

"I worked hard and fast."

"You also dug in the right place, I see."

Alvin took a deep breath. "The way I figure, sir, I dug right where the dowser said to dig."

"I saw another hole just yonder," said Makepeace Smith. "Stone as thick and hard as the devil's hoof all along the bottom. You telling me you don't aim for folks to guess why you dug there?"

"I filled that old hole up," said Alvin. "I wish I'd never dug such a well. I don't want nobody telling stories on Hank Dowser. There was water there, right enough, and no dowser in the world could've guessed about the stone."

"Except you," said Makepeace.

"I ain't no dowser, sir," said Alvin. And he told the lie again: "I just saw that his wand dipped over here, too."

Makepeace Smith shook his head, a grin just creeping out across his face. "My wife told me that tale already, and I like to died a-laughing at it. I cuffed your head for saying he was wrong. You telling me now you want him to get the credit?"

"He's a true dowser," said Alvin. "And I *ain't* no dowser, sir, so I reckon since he *is* one, he ought to get the name for it."

Makepeace Smith drew up the copper bucket, put it to his lips, and drank a few swallows. Then he tipped back his head and poured the rest of the water straight onto his face and laughed out loud. "That's the sweetest water I ever drunk in my life, I swear."

It wasn't the same as promising to go along with his story and let Hank Dowser think it was his well, but Al knew it was the best he'd get from his master. "If it's all right, sir," said Al, "I'm a mite hungry."

"Yes, go eat, you've earned it."

Alvin walked by him. The smell of new water rose up from the well as he passed.

Makepeace Smith spoke again behind him. "Gertie tells me you took first swallow from the well."

Al turned around, fearing trouble now. "I did, sir, but not till she give it to me."

Makepeace studied on that notion awhile, as if he was deciding whether to make it reason for punishing Al or not. "Well," he finally said, "well, that's just like her, but I don't mind. There's still enough of that first dip in the wooden bucket for me to save a few swallows for Hank Dowser. I promised him a drink from the first bucket, and I'll keep my word when he comes back around."

"When he comes, sir," said Alvin, "and I hope you won't mind, but I think I'd like it best and so would he if I just didn't happen to be at home, if you see what I mean. I don't think he cottoned to me much."

The smith eyed him narrowly. "If this is just a way for you to get a few hours off work when that dowser comes on back, why"—he broke into a grin—"why, I reckon that you've earned it with last night's labor."

"Thank you sir," said Alvin.

"You heading back to the house?"

"Yes sir."

"Well, I'll take those tools and put them away—you carry this bucket to the missus. She's expecting it. A lot less way to tote the water than the stream. I got to thank Hank Dowser special for choosing this very exact spot.'' The smith was still chuckling to himself at his wit when Alvin reached the house.

Gertie Smith took the bucket, set Alvin down, and near filled him to the brim with hot fried bacon and good greasy biscuits. It was so much food that Al had to beg her to stop. ''We've already finished one pig,'' said Alvin. ''No need to kill another just for my breakfast.''

''Pigs are just corn on the hoof,'' said Gertie Smith, ''and you worked two hogs' worth last night, I'll say that.''

Belly full and belching, Alvin climbed the ladder into the loft over the kitchen, stripped off his clothes, and burrowed into the blankets on his bed.

The Maker is the one who is part of what he makes.

Over and over he whispered the words to himself as he went to sleep. He had no dreams or troubles, and slept clear through till suppertime, and then again all night till dawn.

When he woke up in the morning, just before dawn, there was a faint grey scarce brighter than moonlight sifting into the house through the windows. Hardly none of it got up into the loft where Alvin lay, and instead of springing up bright like he did most mornings, he felt logey from sleep and a little sore from his labors. So he lay there quiet, a faint sort of birdsong chirping in the back of his mind. He didn't think on the phrase Arthur Stuart told him from Redbird's song. Instead he got to wondering how things happened yesterday. Why did hard winter turn to summertime again, just from him shouting?

''Summer,'' he whispered. ''Warm air, leaves green.'' What was it about Alvin that when he said *summer,* summer came? Didn't always work that way, for sure—never when he was a-working the iron or slipping through stone to mend or break it. Then he had to hold the shape of it firm in his mind, understand the way things lined up, find the natural cracks and creases, the threads of the metal or the grain of the rock. And when he was a-healing, that was so hard it took his whole mind to find how the body ought to be, and mend it. Things were so small, so hard to see—well, not *see,* but whatever it was he did. Sometimes he had to work so hard to understand the way things were inside.

Inside, down deep, so small and fine, and always the deepest secrets of the way things worked skittered away like roaches when you bring a lamp into the room, always getting smaller, forming themselves up in strange new ways. Was there some particle that was smallest of all? Some place at the heart of things where what he saw was real, instead of just being made up out of lots of smaller pieces, and them out of smaller pieces still?

Yet he hadn't understood how the Unmaker made winter. So how did his desperate cries make the summer come back?

How can I be a Maker if I can't even guess how I do what I do?

The light came stronger from outside, shining through the wavering glass of the windows, and for a moment Alvin thought he saw the light like little balls flying so *fast,* like they was hit with a stick or shot from a gun, only even faster than that, bouncing around, most of them getting stuck in the tiny cracks of the wooden walls or the floor or the ceiling, so only a precious few got up into the loft where they got captured by Alvin's eyes.

Then that moment passed, and the light was just fire, pure fire, drifting into the room like the gentle waves washing against the shore of Lake Mizogan, and wherever they passed, the waves turned things warm—the wood of the walls, the massive kitchen table, the iron of the stove—so that they all quivered, they all danced with life. Only Alvin could see it, only Alvin knew how the whole room awoke with the day.

That fire from the sun, that's what the Unmaker hates most. The life it makes. Put that fire out, that's what the Unmaker says inside himself. Put all fires out, turn all water into ice, the whole world smooth with ice, the whole sky black and cold like night. And to oppose the Unmaker's desire, one lone Maker who can't do right even when he's digging a well.

The Maker is the one who is part of—part of what? What do I make? How am I part of it? When I work the iron, am I part of the iron? When I shiver stone, am I part of the stone? It makes no sense, but I got to make sense of it or I'll lose my war with the

Unmaker. I could fight him all my days, every way I know how, and when I died the world would be farther along his downhill road than it was when I got born. There's got to be some secret, some key to everything, so I can build it all at once. Got to find that key, that's all, find the secret, and then I can speak a word and the Unmaker will shy back and cower and give up and die, maybe even die, so that life and light go on forever and don't fade.

Alvin heard Gertie begin to stir in the bedroom, and one of the children uttered a soft cry, the last noise before waking. Alvin flexed and stretched and felt the sweet delicious pain of sore muscles waking up, getting set for a day at the forge, a day at the fire.

❧ 10 ❧

Goodwife

PEGGY DID NOT sleep as long or as well as Alvin. His battle was over; he could sleep a victor's sleep. For her, though, it was the end of peace.

It was still midafternoon when Peggy tossed herself awake on the smooth linen sheets of her bed in Mistress Modesty's house. She felt exhausted; her head hurt. She wore only her shift, though she didn't remember undressing. She remembered hearing Redbird singing, watching Arthur Stuart interpret the song. She remembered looking into Alvin's heartfire, seeing all his futures restored to him—but still did not find herself in any of them. Then her memory stopped. Mistress Modesty must have undressed her, put her to bed with the sun already nearing noon.

She rolled over; the sheet clung to her, and then her back went cold from sweat. Alvin's victory was won; the lesson was learned; the Unmaker would not find another such opening again. She saw no danger in Alvin's future, not soon. The Unmaker would doubtless lie in wait for another time, or return to working through his human servants. Perhaps the Visitor would return to Reverend Thrower, or some other soul with a secret hunger for evil would receive the Unmaker as a welcome teacher. But that wasn't the danger, not the immediate danger, Peggy knew.

For as long as Alvin had no notion how to be a Maker or what to do with his power, then it made no difference how long they kept the Unmaker at bay. The Crystal City would never be built. And it must be built, or Alvin's life—and Peggy's life, devoted to helping him—both would be in vain.

It seemed so clear now to Peggy, coming out of a feverish exhausted sleep. Alvin's labor was to prepare himself, to master his own human frailties. If there was some knowledge somewhere in the world about the art of Making, or the science of it, Alvin would have no chance to learn it. The smithy was his school, the forge his master, teaching him—what?—to change other men only by persuasion and long-suffering, gentleness and meekness, unfeigned love and kindness. Someone else, then, would have to acquire that pure knowledge which would raise Alvin up to greatness.

I am done with all my schooling in Dekane.

So many lessons, and I have learned them all, Mistress Modesty. All so I would be ready to bear the title you taught me was the finest any lady could aspire to.

Goodwife.

As her mother had been called Goody Guester all these years, and other women Goody this or Goody that, any woman could have the name. But few deserved it. Few there were who inspired others to call her by the name in full: Goodwife, not just Goody; the way that Mistress Modesty was never called Missus. It would demean her name to be touched by a diminished, a common title.

Peggy got up from the bed. Her head swam for a moment; she waited, then got up. Her feet padded on the wooden floor. She walked softly, but she knew she would be heard; already Mistress Modesty would be coming up the stairs.

Peggy stopped at the mirror and looked at herself. Her hair was tousled by sleep, stringy with sweat. Her face was imprinted, red and white, with the creases in the pillowcase. Yet she saw there the face that Mistress Modesty had taught her how to see.

"Our handiwork," said Mistress Modesty.

Peggy did not turn. She knew her mentor would be there.

"A woman should know that she is beautiful," said Mistress Modesty. "Surely God gave Eve a single piece of glass, or flat polished silver, or at least a still pool to show her what it was that Adam saw."

Peggy turned and kissed Mistress Modesty on the cheek. "I love what you've made of me," she said.

Mistress Modesty kissed her in return, but when they drew apart, there were tears in the older woman's eyes. "And now I shall lose your company."

Peggy wasn't used to others guessing what *she* felt, especially when she didn't realize that she had already made the decision.

"Will you?" asked Peggy.

"I've taught you all I can," said Mistress Modesty, "but I know after last night that you need things that I never dreamed of, because you have work to do that I never thought that anyone could do."

"I meant only to be Goodwife to Alvin's Goodman."

"For me that was the beginning and the end," said Mistress Modesty.

Peggy chose her words to be true, and therefore beautiful, and therefore good. "Perhaps all that some men need from a woman is for her to be loving and wise and careful, like a field of flowers where he can play the butterfly, drawing sweetness from her blossoms."

Mistress Modesty smiled. "How kindly you describe me."

"But Alvin has a sturdier work to do, and what he needs is not a beautiful woman to be fresh and loving for him when his work is done. What he needs is a woman who can heft the other end of his burden."

"Where will you go?"

Peggy answered before she realized that she knew the answer. "Philadelphia, I think."

Mistress Modesty looked at her in surprise, as if to say, You've already decided? Tears welled in her eyes.

Peggy rushed to explain. "The best universities are there—free ones, that teach all there is to know, not the crabbed religious schools of New England or the effete schools for lordlings in the South.''

"This isn't sudden," said Mistress Modesty. "You've been planning this for long enough to find out where to go.''

"It *is* sudden, but perhaps I *was* planning, without knowing it. I've listened to others talk, and now there it is already in my mind, all sorted out, the decision made. There's a school for women there, but what matters is the libraries. I have no formal schooling, but somehow I'll persuade them to let me in.''

"It won't take much persuasion," Mistress Modesty said, "if you arrive with a letter from the governor of Suskwahenny. And letters from other men who trust my judgment well enough.''

Peggy was not surprised that Mistress Modesty still intended to help her, even though Peggy had determined so suddenly, so ungracefully to leave. And Peggy had no foolish notion of pridefully trying to do without such help. "Thank you, Mistress Modesty!''

"I've never known a woman—or a man, for that matter—with such ability as yours. Not your knack, remarkable as it is; I don't measure a person by such things. But I fear that you are wasting yourself on this boy in Hatrack River. How could any man deserve all that you've sacrificed for him?''

"Deserving it—that's his labor. Mine is to have the knowledge when he's ready to learn it.''

Mistress Modesty was crying in earnest now. She still smiled— for she had taught herself that love must always smile, even in grief—but the tears flowed down her cheeks. "Oh, Peggy, how could you have learned so well, and yet make such a mistake?''

A mistake? Didn't Mistress Modesty trust her judgment, even now? " 'A woman's wisdom is her gift to women,' " Peggy quoted. " 'Her beauty is her gift to men. Her love is her gift to God.' ''

Mistress Modesty shook her head as she listened to her own maxim from Peggy's lips. "So why do you intend to inflict your wisdom on this poor unfortunate man you say you love?''

"Because some men are great enough that they can love a whole woman, and not just a part of her.''

"Is *he* such a man?"

How could Peggy answer? "He will be, or he won't have me."

Mistress Modesty paused for a moment, as if trying to find a beautiful way to tell a painful truth. "I always taught you that if you become completely and perfectly yourself, then good men will be drawn to you and love you. Peggy, let us say this man has great needs—but if you must become something that is *not* you in order to supply him, then you will not be perfectly yourself, and he will *not* love you. Isn't that why you left Hatrack River in the first place, so he would love you for yourself, and not for what you did for him?"

"Mistress Modesty, I want him to love me, yes. But I love the work he must accomplish even more than that. What I am today would be enough for the man. What I will go and do tomorrow is not for the man, it is for his work."

"But—" began Mistress Modesty.

Peggy raised an eyebrow and smiled slightly. Mistress Modesty nodded and did not interrupt.

"If I love his work more than I love the man, then to be perfectly myself, I must do what his work requires of me. Won't I, then, be even more beautiful?"

"To me, perhaps," said Mistress Modesty. "Few men have vision clear enough for *that* subtle beauty."

"He loves his work more than he loves his life. Won't he, then, love the woman who shares in it more than a woman who is merely beautiful?"

"You may be right," said Mistress Modesty, "for I have never loved work more than I have loved the person doing it, and I have never known a man who truly loved his work more than his own life. All that I have taught you is true in the world I know. If you pass from my world into another one, I can no longer teach you anything."

"Maybe I can't be a perfect woman and also live my life as it must be lived."

"Or perhaps, Mistress Margaret, even the best of the world is not fit to recognize a perfect woman, and so will accept me as a fair counterfeit, while you pass by unknown."

That was more than Peggy could bear. She cast aside decorum and threw her arms around Mistress Modesty and kissed her and cried, assuring her that there was nothing counterfeit about her. But when all the weeping was done, nothing had changed. Peggy was finished in Dekane, and by next morning her trunk was packed.

Everything she had in the world was a gift from Mistress Modesty, except for the box Oldpappy gave her long ago. Yet what was in that box was a heavier burden by far than any other thing that Peggy carried.

She sat in the northbound train, watching the mountains drift by outside her east-facing window. It wasn't all that long ago that Whitley Physicker had brought her to Dekane in his carriage. Dekane had seemed the grandest place at first; at the time it seemed to her that she was discovering the world by coming here. Now she knew that the world was far too large for one person to discover it. She was leaving a very small place and going to another very small place, and perhaps from there to other small places. The same size heartfires blazed in every city, no brighter for having so much company.

I left Hatrack River to be free of you, Prentice Alvin. Instead I found a larger, far more entangling net outside. Your work is larger than yourself, larger than me, and because I know of it I'm bound to help. If I didn't, I'd be a vile person in my own eyes.

So if you end up loving me or not, that doesn't matter all that much. Oh, yes, to *me* it matters, but the course of the world won't change one way or the other. What matters is that we both prepare you to do your work. Then if love comes, then if you can play Goodman to my Goodwife, we'll take that as an unlooked-for blessing and be glad of it as long as we can.

❧ 11 ❧

Wand

IT WAS A week before Hank Dowser found his way back to Hatrack
River. A miserable week with no profit in it, because try as he
would he couldn't find decent dry ground for them folks west of
town to dig their cellar. "It's all wet ground," he said. "I can't
help it if it's all watery."

But they held him responsible just the same. Folks are like that.
They act like they thought the dowser *put* the water where it sets,
instead of just pointing to it. Same way with torches—blamed them
half the time for *causing* what they saw, when all they did was see
it. There was no gratitude or even simple understanding in most
folks.

So it was a relief to be back with somebody half-decent like
Makepeace Smith. Even if Hank wasn't too proud of the way Makepeace was dealing with his prentice boy. How could Hank criticize
him? He himself hadn't done much better—oh, he was pure embarrassed now to think how he railed on that boy and got him a
cuffing, and for nothing, really, just a little affront to Hank Dowser's
pride. Jesus stood and took whippings and a crown of thorns in

silence, but I lash out when a prentice mumbles a few silly words. Oh, thoughts like that put Hank Dowser in a dark mood, and he was aching for a chance to apologize to the boy.

But the boy wasn't there, which was too bad, though Hank didn't have long to brood about it. Gertie Smith took Hank Dowser up to the house and near jammed the food down his throat with a ramrod, just to get in an extra half-loaf of bread, it felt like. "I can't hardly walk," said Hank, which was true; but it was also true that Gertie Smith cooked just as good as her husband forged and that prentice boy shod and Hank dowsed, which is to say, with a true knack. Everybody has his talent, everybody has his gift from God, and we go about sharing gifts with each other, that's the way of the world, the best way.

So it was with pleasure and pride that Hank drank the swallows of water from the first clear bucket drawn from the well. Oh, it was fine water, sweet water, and he loved the way they thanked him from their hearts. It wasn't till he was out getting mounted on his Picklewing again that he realized he hadn't seen the well. Surely he should've seen the well—

He rounded the smithy on horseback and looked where he thought he had dowsed the spot, but the ground didn't appear like it had been troubled in a hundred years. Not even the trench the prentice dug while he was standing there. It took him a minute to find where the well actually was, sort of halfway between smithy and house, a fine little roof over the windlass, the whole thing finished with smooth-worked stone. But surely he hadn't been so near the house when the wand dipped—

"Oh, Hank!" called Makepeace Smith. "Hank, I'm glad you ain't gone yet!"

Where was the man? Oh, there, back in the meadow just up from the smithy, near where Hank had first looked for the well. Waving a stick in his hand—a forked stick—

"Your wand, the one you used to dowse this well—you want it back?"

"No, Makepeace, no thanks. I never use the same wand twice. Doesn't work proper when it isn't fresh."

Makepeace Smith pitched the wand back over his head, walked back down the slope and stood exactly in the place where Hank *thought* he had dowsed the well to be. "What do you think of the well house we built?"

Hank glanced back toward the well. "Fine stonework. If you ever give up the forge, I bet there's a living for you in stonecutting."

"Why, thank you, Hank! But it was my prentice boy did it all."

"That's some boy you got," said Hank. But it left a bad taste in his mouth, to say those words. There was something made him uneasy about this whole conversation. Makepeace Smith meant something sly, and Hank didn't know rightly what it was. Never mind. Time to be on his way. "Good-bye, Makepeace!" he said, walking his nag back toward the road. "I'll be back for shoes, remember!"

Makepeace laughed and waved. "I'll be glad to see your ugly old face when you come!"

With that, Hank nudged old Picklewing and headed off right brisk for the road that led to the covered bridge over the river. That was one of the nicest things about the westbound road out of Hatrack. From there to the Wobbish the track was as sweet as you please, with covered bridges over every river, every stream, every rush and every rivulet. Folks were known to camp at night on the bridges, they were so tight and dry.

There must've been three dozen redbird nests in the eaves of the Hatrack Bridge. The birds were making such a racket that Hank allowed as how it was a miracle they didn't wake the dead. Too bad redbirds were too scrawny for eating. There'd be a banquet on that bridge, if it was worth the trouble.

"Ho there, Picklewing, my girl, ho," he said. He sat astride his horse, a-standing in the middle of the bridge, listening to the redbird song. Remembering now as clear as could be how the wand had leapt clean out of his hands and flung itself up into the meadow grass. Flung itself northeast of the spot he dowsed. And that's just where Makepeace Smith picked it up when he was saying good-bye.

Their fine new well wasn't on the spot he dowsed at all. The whole time he was there, they all were lying to him, pretending he dowsed them a well, but the water they drank was from another place.

Hank knew, oh yes, he knew who chose the spot they used. Hadn't the wand as much as told him when it flew off like that? Flew off because the boy spoke up, that smart-mouth prentice. And now they made mock of him behind his back, not saying a thing to his face, of course, but he knew that Makepeace was laughing the whole time, figuring he wasn't even smart enough to notice the switch.

Well, I noticed, yes sir. You made a fool of me, Makepeace Smith, you and that prentice boy of yours. But I noticed. A man can forgive seven times, or even seven times seven. But then there comes the fiftieth time, and even a good Christian can't forget.

"Gee-ap," he said angrily. Picklewing's ears twitched and she started forward in a gentle walk, new shoes clopping loud on the floorboards of the bridge, echoing from the walls and ceiling. "Alvin," whispered Hank Dowser. "Prentice Alvin. Got no respect for any man's knack except his own."

⚹ 12 ⚹

School Board

WHEN THE CARRIAGE pulled up in front of the inn, Old Peg Guester was upstairs hanging mattresses half out the windows to let them air, so she saw. She recognized Whitley Physicker's rig, a new-fangled closed car that kept the weather and most of the dust out; Physicker could use a carriage like that, now that he could afford to pay a man just to drive for him. It was things like that carriage that had most folks calling him *Dr. Physicker* now, instead of just Whitley.

The driver was Po Doggly, who used to have a farm of his own till he got to likkering up after his wife died. It was a good thing, Physicker hiring him when other folks just thought of old Po as a drunk. Things like that made most plain folks think well of Dr. Physicker, even if he did show off his money more than was seemly among Christians.

Anyway, Po hopped down from his seat and swung around to open the door of the carriage. But it wasn't Whitley Physicker got out first—it was Pauley Wiseman, the sheriff. If ever a man didn't deserve his last name, it was Pauley Wiseman. Old Peg felt herself wrinkle up inside just seeing him. It was like her husband Horace always said—any man who *wants* the job of sheriff is plainly unfit for the office. Pauley Wiseman wanted his job, wanted it more than most folks wanted to breathe. You could see it in the way he wore his stupid silver star right out in the open, on the outside of his coat, so nobody'd forget they was talking to the man who had the keys to the town jail. As if Hatrack River needed a jail!

Then Whitley Physicker got out of the carriage, and Old Peg knew exactly what business they were here for. The school board had made its decision, and these two were come to make sure she settled for it without making any noise about it in public. Old Peg tossed the mattress she was holding, tossed it so hard it near to flew clean out the window; she caught it by a corner and pulled it back so it'd hang proper and get a good airing. Then she ran down the stairs—she wasn't so old yet she couldn't run a flight of stairs when she wanted. Downward, anyways.

She looked around a bit for Arthur Stuart, but of course he wasn't in the house. He was just old enough for chores, and he did them, right enough, but after that he was always off by himself, over in town sometimes, or sometimes bothering around that blacksmith boy, Prentice Alvin. "What you do that for, boy?" Old Peg asked him once. "What you always have to be with Prentice Alvin for?" Arthur just grinned and then put his arms out like a street rassler all set to grab and said, "Got to learn how to throw a man twice my size." What made it funny was he said it just exactly in Alvin's own voice, complete with the way Alvin would've said it—with a joke in his voice, so you'd know he didn't take himself all that serious. Arthur had that knack, to mimic folks like as if he knew them right to the soul. Sometimes it made her wonder if he didn't have something of the torchy knack, like her runaway daughter Little Peggy; but no, it didn't seem like Arthur actually understood what he was doing. He was just a mimic. Still, he was smart as a whip, and that's why Old Peg knew the boy deserved to be in school, probably more than any other child in Hatrack River.

She got to the front door just as they started in to knock. She stood there, panting a little from her run down the stairs, waiting to open it even though she saw their shadows through the lace-curtain windows on the door. They were kind of shifting their weight back and forth, like they was nervous—as well they should be. Let 'em sweat.

It was just like them folks on the school board, to send Whitley Physicker of all people. It made Old Peg Guester mad just to see his shadow at her door. Wasn't he the one who took Little Peggy off six years ago, and then wouldn't tell her where the girl went? Dekane was all he said, to folks she seemed to know. And then Peg's husband Horace reading the note over and over, saying, If a torch can't see her own future safe, none of us can look out for her any better. Why, if it hadn't been for Arthur Stuart needing her so bad, Old Peg would have up and left. Just up and left, and see how they liked that! Take her daughter away and tell her it's all for the best—such a thing to tell a mother! Let's see what they think when *I* leave. If she hadn't had Arthur to look after, she would have gone so fast her shadow would've been stuck in the door.

And now they send Whitley Physicker to do it again, to set her grieving over another child, just like before. Only worse this time, because Little Peggy really *could* take care of herself, while Arthur Stuart couldn't, he was just a six-year-old boy, a boy with no future at all unless Old Peg fought for it tooth and nail.

They knocked again. She opened the door. There was Whitley Physicker, looking all cheerful and dignified, and behind him Pauley Wiseman, looking all important and dignified. Like two masts on the same ship, with sails all puffed out and bossy-looking. All full of wind. Coming to tell me what's right and proper, are you? We'll see.

"Goody Guester," said Dr. Physicker. He doffed his hat proper, like a gentleman. That's what's wrong with Hatrack River these days, thought Old Peg. Too many folks putting on like gentlemen and ladies. Don't they know this is Hio? All the high-toned folks are down in the Crown Colonies with His Majesty, the other Arthur Stuart. The long-haired White king, as opposed to her own short-haired Black boy Arthur. Anybody in the state of Hio who thinks he's a gentleman is just fooling himself and nobody but the other fools.

"I suppose you want to come in," said Old Peg.

"I hoped you'd invite us," said Physicker. "We come from the school board."

"You can turn me down on the porch as easy as you can inside my house."

"Now see here," said Sheriff Pauley. He wasn't used to folks leaving him standing on porches.

"We didn't come to turn you down, Goody Guester," said the doctor.

Old Peg didn't believe it for a minute. "You telling me that stiff-necked bunch of high-collar hypocrites is going to let a Black child into the new school?"

That set Sheriff Pauley off like gunpowder in a bucket. "Well, if you're so all-fired sure you know the answer, Old Peg, why'd you bother asking the question?"

"Cause I wanted you all down on record as being Black-hating slavers in your hearts! Then someday when the Emancipationists have their way and Black people have all their rights everywhere, you'll have to wear your shame in public like you deserve."

Old Peg didn't even hear her husband coming up behind her, she was talking so loud.

"Margaret," said Horace Guester. "No man stands on my porch without a welcome."

"*You* welcome them yourself, then," said Old Peg. She turned her back on Dr. Physicker and Sheriff Pauley and walked on into the kitchen. "I wash my hands of it," she shouted over her shoulder.

But once she was in the kitchen she realized that she wasn't cooking yet this morning, she was doing the upstairs beds. And as she stood there, kind of confused for a second, she got to thinking it was Pontius Pilate who did that first famous hand-washing. Why, she'd confessed herself unrighteous with her own words. God wouldn't look kindly on her if she once started in imitating someone as killed the Lord Jesus, like Pilate did. So she turned around and walked back into the common room and sat down near the hearth. It being August there wasn't no fire in it, which made it a cool place to sit. Not like the kitchen hearth, which was hot as the devil's privy on summer days like this. No reason she should sweat her heart out in the kitchen while these two decided the fate of Arthur Stuart in the coolest spot in the house.

Her husband and the two visitors looked at her but didn't say a thing about her storming out and then storming back in. Old Peg knew what was said behind her back—that you might as well try to set a trap for a cyclone as to tangle with Old Peg Guester—but she didn't mind a bit if men like Whitley Physicker and Pauley Wiseman walked a little wary around her. After a second or two, waiting for her to settle down, they went right on with their talk.

"As I was saying, Horace, we looked at your proposal seriously," Physicker said. "It would be a great convenience to us if the new teacher could be housed in your roadhouse instead of being boarded here and there the way it usually happens. But we wouldn't consider having you do it for free. We have enough students enrolled and enough basis in the property tax to pay you a small stipend for the service."

"How much does a sty pen come to in money?" asked Horace.

"The details remain to be worked out, but the sum of twenty dollars for the year was mentioned."

"Well," said Horace, "that's a mite low, if you're thinking you're paying the actual cost."

"On the contrary, Horace, we know that we're underpaying you by considerable. But since you offered to do it free, we hoped this would be an improvement on the original offer."

Horace was all set to agree, but Peg wouldn't stand for all this pretending. "I know what it is, Dr. Physicker, and it's no improvement. We didn't offer to put up the schoolteacher for *free*. We offered to put up *Arthur Stuart*'s teacher for free. And if you figure twenty dollars is going to make me change my mind about that, you better go back and do your figuring again."

Dr. Physicker got a pained look on his face. "Now, Goody Guester. Don't get ahead of yourself on this. There was not a man on the school board who had any personal objection to having Arthur Stuart attend the new school.''

When Physicker said that, Old Peg took a sharp look at Pauley Wiseman. Sure enough, he squirmed in his chair like he had a bad itch in a place where a gentleman doesn't scratch. That's right, Pauley Wiseman. Dr. Physicker can say what he likes, but *I* know *you*, and there was one, at least, who had all kinds of objections to Arthur Stuart.

Whitley Physicker went on talking, of course. Since he was pretending that everybody loved Arthur Stuart dearly, he couldn't very well take notice of how uncomfortable Sheriff Pauley was. ''We know Arthur has been raised by the two oldest settlers and finest citizens of Hatrack River, and the whole town loves him for his own self. We just can't think what benefit a school education would give the boy.''

''It'll give him the same benefit it gives any other boy or girl,'' said Old Peg.

''Will it? Will his knowing how to read and write get him a place in a counting house? Can you imagine that even if they let him take the bar, any jury would listen to a Black lawyer plead? Society has decreed that a Black child will grow up to be a Black man, and a Black man, like ancient Adam, will earn his bread by the sweat of his body, not by the labors of his mind.''

''Arthur Stuart is smarter than any child who'll be in that school and you know it.''

''All the more reason we shouldn't build up young Arthur's hopes, only to have them dashed when he's older. I'm talking about the way of the world, Goody Guester, not the way of the heart.''

''Well why don't you wise men of the school board just say, To hell with the way of the world, we'll do what's right! I can't make you do what you don't want to do, but I'll be damned if I let you pretend it's for Arthur's own good!''

Horace winced. He didn't like it to hear Old Peg swear. She'd only taken it up lately, beginning with the time she cussed Millicent Mercer right in public for insisting on being called ''Mistress

Mercher" instead of "Goody Mercher." It didn't sit well with Horace, her using those words, especially since she didn't seem to ken the time and place for it like a man would, or at least so he said. But Old Peg figured if you can't cuss at a lying hypocrite, then what was cussing invented for?

Pauley Wiseman started turning red, barely controlling a stream of his own favorite cusswords. But Whitley Physicker was now a gentleman, so he merely bowed his head for a moment, like as if he was saying a prayer—but Old Peg figured it was more likely he was waiting till he calmed down enough for his words to come out civil. "Goody Guester, you're right. We didn't think up that story about it being for Arthur's own good till after the decision was made."

His frankness left her without a word, at least for the moment. Even Sheriff Pauley could only give out a kind of squeak. Whitley Physicker wasn't sticking to what they all agreed to say; he sounded espiciously close to telling the truth, and Sheriff Pauley didn't know what to do when people started throwing the truth around loose and dangerous. Old Peg enjoyed watching Pauley Wiseman look like a fool, it being something for which old Pauley had a particular knack.

"You see, Goody Guester, we want this school to work proper, we truly do," said Dr. Physicker. "The whole idea of public schools is a little strange. The way they do schools in the Crown Colonies, it's all the people with titles and money who get to attend, so that the poor have no chance to learn or rise. In New England all the schools are religious, so you don't come out with bright minds, you come out with perfect little Puritans who all stay in their place like God meant them to. But the public schools in the Dutch states and Pennsylvania are making people see that in America we can do it different. We can teach every child in every wildwood cabin to read and write and cipher, so that we have a whole population educated enough to be fit to vote and hold office and govern ourselves."

"All this is well and good," said Old Peg, "and I recollect hearing you give this exact speech in our common room not three

months ago before we voted on the school tax. What I can't figure, Whitley Physicker, is why you figure my son should be the
exception.''

At this, Sheriff Pauley decided it was time to put an oar in. And
since the truth was being used so recklessly, he lost control of
himself and spoke truthfully himself. It was a new experience, and
it went to his head a little. ''Begging your pardon, Old Peg, but
there isn't a drop of your blood in that boy, so he's no-wise your
son, and if Horace here has some part of him, it isn't enough to
turn him White.''

Horace slowly got to his feet, as if he was preparing to invite
Sheriff Pauley outside to punch some caution into him. Pauley
Wiseman must have known he was in trouble the second he accused
Horace of maybe being the father of a half-Black bastard. And when
Horace stood up so tall like that, Pauley remembered he wasn't no
match for Horace Guester. Horace wasn't exactly a small man and
Pauley wasn't exactly a large one. So old Pauley did what he always
did when things got out of hand. He turned kind of sideways so
his badge was facing straight at Horace Guester. Take a lick at me,
that badge said, and you'll be facing a trial for assaulting an officer
of the law.

Still, Old Peg knew that Horace wouldn't hit a man over a word;
he hadn't even knocked down that river rat who accused Horace of
unspeakable crimes with barnyard animals. Horace just wasn't the
kind to lose control of himself in anger. In fact, Old Peg could see
that as Horace stood there, he'd already forgotten about his anger
at Pauley Wiseman and was thinking over an idea.

Sure enough, Horace turned to Old Peg as if Wiseman didn't
even exist. ''Maybe we should give it up, Peg. It was fine when
Arthur was a sweet little baby, but . . .''

Horace, who was looking right at Old Peg's face, he knew better
than to finish his sentence. Sheriff Pauley wasn't half so bright.
''He just gets blacker every day, Goody Guester.''

Well, what do you say to that kind of thing, anyway? At least
now it was plain what was going on—that it was Arthur Stuart's

color and nothing else that was keeping him out of the new Hatrack River School.

Whitley Physicker sighed into the silence. Nothing that happened with Sheriff Pauley there ever went according to plan. "Don't you see?" said Physicker. He sounded mild and reasonable, which he was good at. "There's some ignorant and backward folks"—and at this he took a cool look at Sheriff Pauley—"who can't abide the thought of a Black child getting the same education as their own boys and girls. What's the advantage of schooling, they figure, if a Black has it the same as a White? Why, the next thing you know, Blacks would be wanting to vote or hold office."

Old Peg hadn't thought of that. It just never entered her mind. She tried to imagine Mock Berry being governor, and trying to give orders to the militia. There wasn't a soldier in Hio who'd take orders from a Black man. It'd be as unnatural as a fish jumping out of the river to kill him a bear.

But Old Peg wasn't going to give up so easy, just because Whitley Physicker made one point like that. "Arthur Stuart's a good boy," she said. "He wouldn't no more try to vote than I would."

"I know that," said Physicker. "The whole school board knows that. But it's the backwoods people who won't know it. They're the ones who'll hear there's a Black child in the school and they'll keep their children home. And here we'll be paying for a school that won't be doing its job of educating the citizenry of our republic. We're asking Arthur to forgo an education that will do him no good anyway, in order to allow others to receive an education that will do them and our nation a great deal of good."

It all sounded so logical. After all, Whitley Physicker was a doctor, wasn't he? He'd even been to college back in Philadelphia, so he had a deeper understanding than Old Peg would ever have. Why did she think even for a moment that she could disagree with a man like Physicker and not be wrong?

Yet even though she couldn't think of a single argument against him, she couldn't get rid of a feeling deep in her guts that if she said yes to Whitley Physicker, she'd be stabbing a knife right into little Arthur's heart. She could imagine him asking her, "Mama, why can't I go to school like all my friends?" And then all these fine words from Dr. Physicker would fly away like she'd never heard them, and she'd just sit there and say, "It's because you're Black, Arthur Stuart Guester."

Whitley Physicker seemed to take her silence as surrender, which it nearly was. "You'll see," said Physicker. "Arthur won't mind not going to school. Why, the White boys'll all be jealous of *him,* when he can be outside in the sun while they're cooped up in a classroom."

Old Peg Guester knew there was something wrong with all this, that it wasn't as sensible as it sounded, but she couldn't think what it was.

"And someday things might be different," said Physicker. "Someday maybe society will change. Maybe they'll stop keeping Blacks as slaves in the Crown Colonies and Appalachee. Maybe there'll be a time when . . ." His voice trailed off. Then he shook himself. "I get to wondering sometimes, that's all," he said. "Silly things. The world is the way the world is. It just isn't natural for a Black man to grow up like a White."

Old Peg felt a bitter hatred inside her when he said those words. But it wasn't a hot rage, to make her shout at him. It was a cold, despairing hate, that said, Maybe I *am* unnatural, but Arthur Stuart is my true son, and I won't betray him. No I won't.

Again, though, her silence was taken to mean consent. The men all got up, looking relieved, Horace most of all. It was plain they never figured Old Peg would listen to reason so fast. The visitors' relief was to be expected, but why was Horace looking so happy? Old Peg had a nasty suspicion and she knew at once that it had to be the truth—Horace Guester and Dr. Physicker and Sheriff Pauley had already worked things out between them before they ever come a-calling today. This whole conversation was pretend. Just a show put on to make Old Peg Guester happy.

Horace didn't want Arthur Stuart in school any more than Whitley Physicker or anybody else in Hatrack River.

Old Peg's anger turned hot, but now it was too late. Physicker and Pauley was out the door, Horace following on out after them. No doubt they'd all pat each other on the back and share a smile out of Old Peg's sight. But Old Peg wasn't smiling. She remembered all too clear how Little Peggy had done a Seeing for her that last night before she run off, a Seeing about Arthur Stuart's future. Old Peg had asked Little Peggy if Horace would ever love little Arthur, and the girl refused to answer. That *was* an answer, sure enough. Horace might go through the motions of treating Arthur like his own son, but in fact he thought of him as just a Black boy that his wife had taken a notion to care for. Horace was no papa to Arthur Stuart.

So Arthur's an orphan all over again. Lost his father. Or, rightly speaking, never had a father. Well, so be it. He's got two mothers: the one who died for him when he was born, and me. I can't get him in the school. I knew I couldn't, knew it from the start. But I can get him an education all the same. A plan for it sprung into her head all at once. It all depended on the schoolmistress they hired, this teacher lady from Philadelphia. With luck she'd be a Quaker, with no hate for Blacks and so the plan would work out just fine. But even if the schoolmistress hated Blacks as bad as a finder watching a slave stand free on the Canadian shore, it wouldn't make a bit of difference. Old Peg would find a way. Arthur Stuart was the only family she had left in the world, the only person she loved who didn't lie to her or fool her or do things behind her back. She wasn't going to let him be cheated out of anything that might do him good.

❖ 13 ❖

Springhouse

ALVIN FIRST KNEW something was up when he heard Horace and Old Peg Guester yelling at each other up at the old springhouse. It was so loud for a minute there that he could hear them clear over the sound of the forgefire and his own hammering. Then they quietened themselves down a mite, but by then Alvin was so curious he kind of laid off the hammer. Laid it right down, in fact, and stepped outside to hear better.

No, no, he wasn't *listening*. He was just going to the well to fetch more water, some to drink and some for the cooling barrel. If he happened to hear them somewhat, he couldn't be blamed, now, could he?

"Folks'll say I'm a bad innkeeper, making the teacher live in the springhouse instead of putting her up proper."

"It's just an empty building, Horace, and we'll put it to use. And it'll leave us the rooms in the inn for paying customers."

"I won't have that schoolmistress living off alone by herself. It ain't decent!"

"Why, Horace? Are you planning to make advances?"

Alvin could hardly believe his ears. Married people just didn't say such things to each other. Alvin half expected to hear the sound of a slap. But instead Horace must've just took it. Everybody said he was henpecked, and this was about all the proof a body'd need, to have his wife accuse him of hankering after adultery and him not hit her or even say boo.

"It doesn't matter, anyway," said Old Peg. "Maybe you'll have your way and she'll say no. But we'll fix it up, anyway, and offer it to her."

Horace mumbled something that Alvin couldn't hear.

"I don't care if Little Peggy *built* this springhouse. She's gone of her own free will, left without so much as a word to me, and I'm not about to keep this springhouse like a monument just because she used to come here when she was little. Do you hear me?"

Again Alvin couldn't hear what Horace said.

On the other hand, he could hear Old Peg right fine. Her voice just sailed right out like a crack of thunder. "You're telling *me* who loved who? Well let me tell you, Horace Guester, all your love for Little Peggy didn't keep her here, *did* it? But my love for Arthur Stuart is going to get him an education, do you understand me? And when it's all said and done, Horace Guester, we'll just see who does better at loving their children!"

There wasn't exactly a slap or nothing, but there was a slammed door which like to took the door of the springhouse off its hinges. Alvin couldn't help craning his neck a little to see who did the slamming. Sure enough, it was Old Peg stalking away.

A minute later, maybe even more, the door opened real slow. Alvin could barely make it out through the brush and leaves that had grown up between the well and the springhouse. Horace Guester came out even slower, his face downcast in a way Alvin had never seen him before. He stood there awhile, his hand on the door. Then he pushed it closed, as gentle as if he was tucking a baby into bed. Alvin always wondered why they hadn't tore down that springhouse years ago, when Alvin dug the well that finally killed the stream that used to go through it. Or at least why they never put it to some use. But now Alvin knew it had something to do with Peggy, that torch girl who left right before Alvin showed up in Hatrack River. The way Horace touched that door, the way he closed it, it made Alvin see for the first time how much a man might dote on a child of his, so that even when she was gone, the places that she loved were like holy ground to her old dad. For the first time Alvin wondered if he'd ever love a child of his own like that. And then he wondered who the mother of that child might be, and if she'd ever scream at him the way Old Peg screamed at Horace, and if he'd ever have at her the way Makepeace Smith had at his wife Gertie, him flailing with his belt and her throwing the crockery.

"Alvin," said Horace.

Well, Alvin like to died with embarrassment, to be caught staring at Horace like that. "I beg pardon, sir," said Alvin. "I shouldn't ought to've been listening."

Horace smiled wanly. "I reckon as you'd have to be a deaf mute not to hear that last bit."

"It got a mite loud," said Alvin, "but I didn't exactly go out of my way not to hear, neither."

"Well, I know you're a good boy, and I never heard of no one carrying tales from you."

The words "good boy" rankled a bit. Alvin was eighteen now, less than a year to being nineteen, long since ready to be a journeyman smith out on his own. Just because Makepeace Smith wouldn't release him early from his prenticeship didn't make it right for Horace Guester to call him a *boy*. I may be Prentice Alvin, and not a man yet afore the law, but no woman yells *me* to shame.

"Alvin," said Horace, "you might tell your master we'll be needing new hinges and fittings for the springhouse doors. I reckon we're fixing it up for the new schoolteacher to live here, if she wants."

So that was the way of it. Horace had lost the battle with Old Peg. He was giving in. Was that the way of marriage, then? A man either had to be willing to hit his wife, like Makepeace Smith, or he'd be bossed around like poor Horace Guester. Well, if that's the choices, I'll have none of it, thought Alvin. Oh, Alvin had an eye for girls in town. He'd see them flouncing along the street, their breasts all pushed up high by their corsets and stays, their waists so small he could wrap his great strong hands right around and toss them every which way, only he never thought of tossing or grabbing, they just made him feel shy and hot at the same time, so he looked down when they happened to look at him, or got busy loading or unloading or whatever business brought him into town.

Alvin knew what they saw when they looked at him, those town girls. They saw a man with no coat on, just in his shirt-sleeves, stained and wet from his labor. They saw a poor man who'd never keep them in a fine white clapboard house like their papa, who was no doubt a lawyer or a judge or a merchant. They saw him *low,* a mere prentice still, and him already more than eighteen years old. If by some miracle he ever married one such girl, he knew how it would be, her always looking down at him, always expecting him to give way for her because she was a lady.

And if he married a girl who was as low as himself, it would be like Gertie Smith or Old Peg Guester, a good cook or a hard worker or whatever, but a hellion when she didn't get her way. There was no woman in Alvin Smith's life, that was sure. He'd never let himself be showed up like Horace Guester.

"Did you hear me, Alvin?"

"I did, Mr. Horace, and I'll tell Makepeace Smith first off when I see him. All the fittings for the springhouse."

"And nice work, too," said Horace. "It's for the schoolmistress to live there." But Horace wasn't so whipped that he couldn't get a curl to his lip and a nasty tone to his voice as he said, "So she can give *private* lessons."

The way he said "private lessons" made it sound like it'd be a whorehouse or something, but Alvin knew right off, by putting things together, exactly who would be getting private lessons. Didn't everybody know how Old Peg had asked to have Arthur Stuart accepted at the school?

"Well, so long," said Horace.

Alvin waved him good-bye, and Horace ambled away along the path to the inn.

Makepeace Smith didn't come in that afternoon. Alvin wasn't

surprised. Now that Alvin had his full mansize on him, he could do the whole work of the smithy, and faster and better than Makepeace. Nobody said aught about it, but Alvin noticed back last year that folks took to dropping in during the times when Makepeace *wasn't* at the forge. They'd ask Alvin to do their ironwork quick-like, while they was there waiting. "Just a little job," they'd say, only sometimes the job wasn't all that little. And pretty soon Alvin realized that it wasn't just chance brought them by. They wanted *Alvin* to do the work they needed.

It wasn't because Alvin did anything peculiar to the iron, either, except a hex or two where it was called for, and every smith did that. Alvin knew it wouldn't be right to best his master using some secret knack—it'd be like slipping a knife into a rassling match. It'd just bring him trouble anyway, if he used his knack to give *his* iron any peculiar strength. So he did his work natural, with his own strong arm and good eye. He'd earned every inch of muscle in his back and shoulders and arms. And if people liked his work better than Makepeace Smith's, why, it was because Alvin was a better blacksmith, not because his knack gave him the advantage.

Anyhow, Makepeace must've caught on to what was happening, and he took to staying away from the forge more and more. Maybe it was because he knew it was better for business, and Makepeace was humble enough to give way before his prentice's skill—but Alvin never quite believed that. More likely Makepeace stayed away so folks wouldn't see how he snuck a look over Alvin's shoulder now and then, trying to figure out what Al did better than his master. Or maybe Makepeace was plain jealous, and couldn't bear to watch his prentice at work. Could be, though, that Makepeace was just lazy, and since his prentice boy was doing the work just fine, why *shouldn't* Makepeace go out to drink himself silly with the river rats down at Hatrack Mouth?

Or perhaps, by some strange twist of chance, Makepeace was actually ashamed of how he kept Alvin to his prentice contract even though Alvin was plainly ready to take to the road as a journeyman. It was a low thing for a master to hold a prentice after he knew his trade, just to get the benefit of his labor without having to pay him a fair wage. Alvin brought good money into Makepeace Smith's household, everybody knew that, and all the while Alvin stayed dirt poor, sleeping in a loft and never two coins in his pocket to make a jingle when he walked to town. Sure, Gertie fed him proper—best food in town, Al knew well, having eaten a bite now and then with one of the town boys. But good food wasn't the same thing as a good wage. Food you ate and it was gone. Money you could use to buy things, or to do things—to have *freedom*. That contract Makepeace Smith kept in the cupboard up to the house, the one signed by Alvin's father, it made Alvin a slave as sure any Black in the Crown Colonies.

Except for one difference. Alvin could count the days till freedom. It was August. Not even a year left. Next spring he'd be free. No slave in the South ever knew such a thing; nary such a hope would ever enter their heads. Alvin had thought on that often enough over the years, when he was feeling most put upon; he'd think, if they can keep on living and working, having no hope of freedom, then I can hold out for another five years, three years, one year, knowing that it'll come to an end someday.

Anyway, Makepeace Smith didn't show up that afternoon, and when Alvin finished his assigned work, instead of doing chores and cleaning up, instead of getting ahead, he went on up to the springhouse and took the measure of the doors and windows. It was a place built to keep in the cool of the stream, so the windows didn't open, but the schoolmistress wouldn't cotton to *that,* never having a breath of air, so Alvin took the measure there, too. Not that he exactly decided to make the new window frames himself, seeing how he wasn't no carpenter particularly, except what woodworking skill any man learns. He was just taking the measure of the place, and when he got to the windows he kept going.

He took the measure of a lot of things. Where a little pot-bellied stove would have to go, if the place was going to be warm in the winter; and figuring that, he also figured how to lay in the right foundation under the heavy stove, and how to put the flaring around the chimney, all the things it'd take to make the springhouse into a tight little cabin, fit for a lady to live in.

Alvin didn't write down the measures. He never did. He just knew them, now that he'd put his fingers and hands and arms into all the places; and if he forgot, and took the measure wrong somehow, he knew that in a pinch he could make it fit even so. It was a kind of laziness, he knew, but he got precious little advantage from his knack these days, and there was no shame in such small fidging.

Arthur Stuart wandered along when Al was just about done at the springhouse. Alvin didn't say nothing, nor did Arthur; you don't greet somebody who belongs where you are, you hardly notice them. But when Alvin needed to get the measure of the roof, he just said so and then tossed Arthur up onto the roof as easy as Peg Guester tossed the feather mattresses from the inn beds.

Arthur walked like a cat on top of the roof, paying no heed to being up so high. He paced off the roof and kept his own count, and when he was done he didn't even wait to make sure Alvin was ready to catch him, he just took a leap into the air. It was like Arthur believed he could fly. And with Alvin there to catch him below, why, it might as well be true, since Alvin had such arms on him that he could catch Arthur easy and let him down as gentle as a mallard settling onto a pond.

When Al and Arthur was done with measuring, they went back to the smithy. Alvin took a few bars of iron from the pile, het up the forge, and set to work. Arthur set in to pumping the bellows and fetching tools—they'd been doing this so long that it was like Arthur was Alvin's own prentice, and it never occurred to either of them that there was anything wrong with it. They just did this together, so smooth that to other folks it looked like a kind of dance.

A couple of hours later, Alvin had all the fittings. It should've taken less time by half, only for some reason Alvin got it into his head that he ought to make a lock for the door, and then he got it into his head that it ought to be a real lock, the kind that a few rich folks in town ordered from back east in Philadelphia—with a proper key and all, and a catch that shut all by itself when you closed the door, so you'd never forget to lock the door behind you.

What's more, he put secret hexes on all the fittings, perfect six-point figures that spoke of safety, and no one with harm in his heart being about to turn the lock. Once the lock was closed and fastened in place on the door, nobody'd see those hexes, but they'd do the work sure, since when Alvin made a hex the measure was so perfect it cast a network of hexes like a wall for many yards on every side.

It occurred to Alvin to wonder why a hex should work at all. Of course he knew why it was such a magical shape, being twice three; and he knew how you could lay hexes down on a table and they'd fit snug together, as perfect as squares, only stronger, woven not with warp and weft, but with warp and weft and hax. It wasn't like squares, which were hardly ever found in nature, being too simple and weak; there was hexes in snowflakes and crystals and honeycombs. Making a single hex was the same as making a whole fabric of hexes, so that the perfect hexes he hid up inside the lock would wrap all the way around the house, sealing it from outside harm as surely as if he forged a net of iron and wove it right in place.

But that didn't answer the question *why* it worked. Why his hidden hexes should bar a man's hand, turn a man's mind away from entering. Why the hex should invisibly repeat itself as far as it could, and the more perfect the hex, the farther the net it threw. All these years of puzzling things out, and he still knew so little. Knew so near to nothing that he despaired, and even now, holding the springhouse fittings in his hands, he wondered if in fact he shouldn't content himself to be a good smith and forget these tales of Makering.

With all his wondering and questioning, Alvin never did ask himself what should have been the plainest question of all. Why would a schoolmistress need such a perfectly hexed, powerful lock? Alvin didn't even try to guess. He wasn't thinking like that. Instead he just knew that such a lock was something fine, and this little house had to be as fine as he could make it. Later on he'd wonder about it, wonder if he knew even then, before he met her, what this schoolmistress would mean to him. Maybe he already had a plan in the back of his mind, just like Old Peg Guester did. But he sure didn't know about it yet, and that was the truth. When he made all those fancy fittings, with patterns cut in them so the door would look pretty, he most likely was doing it for Arthur Stuart; maybe he was halfway thinking that if the schoolmistress had a right pretty little place to live, she'd be more inclined to give Arthur Stuart his private lessons.

It was time to quit for the day, but Alvin didn't quit. He pushed all the fittings up to the springhouse in a wheelbarrow, along with a couple of other tools he figured to need, and some scrap tin for the flaring of the chimney. He worked fast, and without quite meaning to, he used his knack to smooth the labor. Everything fit first time; the doors rehung as nice as could be, and the lock fitted exactly to the inside face of the door, bolted on so tight that it'd never come off. This was a door no man could force—easier to chop through the split-log wall than attack this door. And with the hexes inside, a man wouldn't dare to lift his axe against the house, or if he did, he'd be too weak to strike a telling blow—these were hexes that even a Red might not laugh at.

Al took another trip back to the shed outside the smithy and chose the best of the old broke-down pot-belly stoves that Makepeace had bought for the iron in them. Carrying a whole stove wasn't easy even for a man strong as a blacksmith, but it was sure the wheelbarrow couldn't handle such a load. So Alvin hefted it up the hill by main strength. He left it outside while he brought stones from the old streambed to make a foundation under the floor at the place where the stove would go. The floor of the springhouse was set on beams running the length of the house inside, but they hadn't planked over the strip where the stream used to go—it wouldn't have been much of a springhouse if they covered over the cold water. Anyway he put a tight stone foundation under an upstream corner where the floor was done but not too high off the ground, and then bolted sheets of thin-beat iron on top of the planks to make a fireproof floor. Then he hefted the stove into place and piped it up to the hole he knocked in the roof.

He set Arthur Stuart to work with a rasp, tearing the dead moss off the inside of the walls. It came off easy, but it mostly kept Arthur distracted so he didn't notice that Alvin was fixing things on that brokedown stove that couldn't be fixed by a natural man. Good as new, and all fittings tight.

"I'm hungry," said Arthur Stuart.

"Get on up to Gertie and tell her I'm working late and please send food down for both of us, since you're helping."

Arthur Stuart took off running. Alvin knew that he'd deliver the message word for word, and in Alvin's own voice, so that Gertie'd laugh out loud and give him a good supper in a basket. Probably such a good supper that Arthur'd have to stop and rest three or four times on the way back, it'd be so heavy.

All this time Makepeace Smith never so much as showed his face.

When Arthur Stuart finally got back, Alvin was on the roof putting the final touch on the flaring, and fixing some of the shingles while he was up there. The flaring fit so tight water'd never get into the house, he saw to that. Arthur Stuart stood below, waiting and watching, not asking if he could go ahead and eat, not even asking how long till Alvin'd come down; he wasn't the type of child to whine or complain. When Alvin was done, he dropped over the edge of the roof, caught himself on the lip of the eaves, then dropped to the ground.

"Cold chicken be mighty good after a hot day's work," said Arthur Stuart, in a voice that was exactly Gertie Smith's, except pitched in a child's high voice.

Alvin grinned at him and opened the basket. They fell to eating like sailors who'd been on short rations for half the voyage, and in no time they was both lying there on their backs, bellies packed full, belching now and then, watching the white clouds move like placid cattle grazing across the sky.

The sun was getting low toward the west now. Definitely time to pack in for the day, but Alvin just couldn't feel good about that. "Best you get home," he said. "Maybe if you just run that empty basket back up to Gertie Smith's, you can get in without your Ma gets too upset at you."

"What you doing now?"

"Got windows to frame and re-hang."

"Well I got walls to finish rasping down," said Arthur Stuart.

Alvin grinned, but he also knew that what he planned to do to the windows wasn't a thing he wanted witnesses for. He had no intention of actually doing a lot of carpentry, and he didn't ever let anybody watch him do something *obvious* with his knack. "Best you go home now," said Alvin.

Arthur sighed.

"You been a good help to me, but I don't want you getting in trouble."

To Alvin's surprise, Arthur just returned his own words back to him in his own voice. "You been a good help to me, but I don't want you getting in trouble."

"I mean it," said Alvin.

Arthur Stuart rolled over, got up, came over and sat down astride of Alvin's belly—which Arthur often did, but it didn't feel none too comfortable at the moment, there being about a chicken and a half inside that belly.

"Come on, Arthur Stuart," said Alvin.

"I never told nobody bout no redbird," said Arthur Stuart.

Well, that just sent a chill right through Alvin. Somehow he'd figured that Arthur Stuart was just too young that day more than three years ago to even remember that anything happened. But Alvin should've knowed that just because Arthur Stuart didn't talk about something didn't mean that he forgot. Arthur never forgot so much as a caterpillar crawling on a leaf.

If Arthur Stuart remembered the redbird, then he no doubt remembered that day when it was winter out of season, when Alvin's knack dug a well and made the stone come clean of dirt without using his hands. And if Arthur Stuart knew all about Alvin's knack, then what point was there in trying to sneak around and make it secret?

"All right then," said Alvin. "Help me hang the windows." Alvin almost added, "as long as you don't tell a soul what you see." But Arthur Stuart already understood that. It was just one of the things that Arthur Stuart understood.

They finished before dark, Alvin cutting into the wood of the window frames with his bare fingers, shaping what was just wood nailed into wood until it was windows that could slide free, up and down. He made little holes in the sides of the window frames and whittled plugs of wood to fit them, so the window would stay up as far as a body might want. Of course, he didn't quite whittle like a natural man, since each stroke of the knife took off a perfect arc. Each plug was done in about six passes of the knife.

Meantime Arthur Stuart finished the rasping, and then they swept out the house, using a broom of course, but Alvin helped with his knack so that every scrap of sawdust and iron filings and flakes of moss and ancient dust ended up outside the house. Only thing they didn't do was try to cover the strip of open dirt down the middle of the springhouse, where once the stream flowed. That'd take felling a tree to get the planks, and anyway Alvin was starting to get a little scared, seeing how much he'd done and how fast he'd done it. What if somebody came *tonight* and realized that all this work was done in a single long afternoon? There'd be questions. There'd be guesses.

"Don't tell anybody that we did this all in a day," said Alvin.

Arthur Stuart just grinned. He'd lost one of his front teeth recently, so there was a spot where his pink gums showed up. Pink as a White person's gums, Alvin thought. Inside his mouth he's no different from a White. Then Alvin had this crazy idea of God taking all the people in the world who ever died and flaying them and hanging up their bodies like pigs in the butcher's shop, just meat and bones hanging there by the heel, even the guts and the head gone, just meat. And then God would ask folks like the Hatrack River School Board to come in and pick out which was Black folks and which was Red and which was White. They couldn't do it. Then God would say, "Well why in hell did you say that this one and this one and this one couldn't go to school with this one and this one and this one?" What answer would they have then? Then God would say, "You people, you're all the same rare meat under the skin. But I tell you, I don't like your flavor. I'm going to toss your beefsteaks to the dogs."

Well, that was such a funny idea that Alvin couldn't help but tell it to Arthur Stuart, and Arthur Stuart laughed just as hard as Alvin. Only after it was all said and the laughing was done did Alvin remember that maybe nobody'd told Arthur Stuart about how his ma tried to get him into the school and the school board said no. "You know what this is all about?"

Arthur Stuart didn't understand the question, or maybe he understood it even better than Alvin did. Anyways, he answered, "Ma's hoping the teacher lady'll learn me to read and write here in this springhouse."

"Right," said Alvin. No point in explaining about the school, then. Either Arthur Stuart already knew how some White folks felt about Blacks, or else he'd find out soon enough without Alvin telling him now.

"We're all the same rare meat," said Arthur Stuart. He used a funny voice that Alvin had never heard before.

"Whose voice was that?" asked Alvin.

"God, of course," said Arthur Stuart.

"Good imitation," said Alvin. He was being funny.

"Sure is," said Arthur Stuart. He wasn't.

Turned out nobody came to the springhouse for a couple of days and more. It was Monday of the next week when Horace ambled into the smithy. He came early in the morning, at a time when Makepeace was most likely to be there, ostentatiously "teaching" Alvin to do something that Alvin already knew how to do.

"*My* masterpiece was a ship's anchor," said Makepeace. "Course, that was back in Newport, afore I come west. Them ships, them whaling ships, they weren't like little bitty houses and wagons. They needed *real* ironwork. A boy like you, you do well enough out here where they don't know better, but you'd never make a go of it *there*, where a smith has to be a *man*."

Alvin was used to such talk. He let it roll right off him. But he was grateful anyway when Horace came in, putting an end to Makepeace's brag.

After all the *good-morning*s and *howdy-do*s, Horace got right to business. "I just come by to see when you'll have a chance to get started on the springhouse."

Makepeace raised an eyebrow and looked at Alvin. Only then did Alvin realize that he'd never mentioned the job to Makepeace.

"It's already done, sir," Alvin said to Makepeace—for all the world as if Makepeace's unspoken question had been, "Are you finished yet?" and not, "What is this springhouse job the man's talking about?"

"Done?" said Horace.

Alvin turned to him. "I thought you must've noticed. I thought you were in a hurry, so I did it right off in my free time."

"Well, let's go see it," said Horace. "I didn't even think to look on my way down here."

"Yes, I'm dying to look at it myself," said the smith.

"I'll just stay here and keep working," said Alvin.

"No," said Makepeace. "You come along and show off this work you done in your *free time*." Alvin didn't hardly notice how Makepeace emphasized the last two words, he was so nervous to show off what he done at the springhouse. He only barely had sense enough to drop the keys he made into his pocket.

They made their way up the hill to the springhouse. Horace was the kind of man who could tell when somebody did real good work, and wasn't shy to say so. He fingered the fancy new hingework and admired the lock afore he put in the key. To Alvin's pride it turned smooth and easy. The door swung open quiet as a leaf in autumn. If Horace noticed the hexes, he didn't let on. It was other things he noticed, not hexery.

"Why, you cleaned off the walls," said Horace.

"Arthur Stuart did that," said Alvin. "Rasped it off neat as you please."

"And this stove—I tell you, Makepeace, I didn't figure the price of a new stove in this."

"It isn't a new stove," said Alvin. "I mean, begging your pardon, but it was a brokedown stove we kept for the scrap, only when I looked it over I saw we could fix it up, so why not put it here?"

Makepeace gave Alvin a cool look, then turned back to Horace. "That don't mean it's free, of course."

"Course not," said Horace. "If you bought it for scrap, though . . ."

"Oh, the price won't be too terrible high."

Horace admired how it joined to the roof. "Perfect work," he said. He turned around. To Alvin he looked a little sad, or maybe just resigned. "Have to cover the rest of the floor, of course."

"Not our line of work," said Makepeace Smith.

"Just talking to myself, don't mind me." Horace went over to the east window, pushed against it with his fingers, then raised it. He found the pegs on the sill and put them into the third hole on each side, then let the window fall back down to rest against the pegs. He looked at the pegs, then out the window, then back at the pegs, for a long time. Alvin dreaded having to explain how he, not trained as a fine carpenter, managed to hang such a fine window. Worse yet, what if Horace guessed that this was the original window, not a new one? That could only be explained by Alvin's knack—no carpenter could get inside the wood to cut out a sliding window like that.

But all Horace said was, "You did some extra work."

"Just figured it needed doing," said Alvin. If Horace wasn't going to ask about how he did it, Alvin was just as happy not to explain.

"I didn't reckon to have it done so fast," said Horace. "Nor to have so much done. The lock looks to be an expensive one, and the stove—I hope I don't have to pay for all at once."

Alvin almost said, You don't have to pay for any of it, but of course that wouldn't do. It was up to Makepeace Smith to decide things like that.

But when Horace turned around, looking for an answer, he didn't face Makepeace Smith, he stood square on to Alvin. "Makepeace Smith here's been charging full price for your work, so I reckon I shouldn't pay you any less."

Only then did Alvin realize that he made a mistake when he said he did the work in his free time, since work a prentice did in his official free time was paid for direct to the prentice, and not the master. Makepeace Smith never gave Alvin free time—whatever work anyone wanted done, Makepeace would hire Alvin out to do, which was his right under the prentice contract. By calling it free time, Alvin seemed to be saying that Makepeace had given him time off to earn money for himself.

"Sir, I—"

Makepeace spoke up before Alvin could explain the mistake. "Full price wouldn't be right," said Makepeace. "Alvin getting so close to the end of his contract, I thought he should start trying things on his own, see how to handle money. But even though the work looks right to you, to me it definitely looks second rate. So half price is right. I figure it took at least twenty hours to do all this—right, Alvin?"

It was more like ten, but Alvin just nodded. He didn't know what to say, anyway, since his master was obviously not committed to telling the plain truth about this job. And the job he did would have been at least twenty hours—two full days' labor—for a smith without Alvin's knack.

"So," said Makepeace, "between Al's labor at half price and the cost of the stove and the iron and all, it comes to fifteen dollars."

Horace whistled and rocked back on his heels.

"You can have my labor free, for the experience," Alvin said.

Makepeace glared at him.

"Wouldn't dream of it," said Horace. "The Savior said the laborer is worthy of his hire. It's the sudden high price of iron I'm a little skeptical about."

"It's a *stove,*" said Makepeace Smith.

Wasn't till I fixed it, Alvin said silently.

"You bought it as scrap iron," said Horace. "As you said about Al's labor, full price wouldn't be right."

Makepeace sighed. "For old times' sake, Horace, cause you brought me here and helped set me up on my own when I came west eighteen years ago. Nine dollars."

Horace didn't smile, but he nodded. "Fair enough. And since you usually charge four dollars a day for Alvin's hire, I guess his twenty hours at *half* price comes to four bucks. You come by the house this afternoon, Alvin, I'll have it for you. And Makepeace, I'll pay you the rest when the inn fills up at harvest time.''

''Fair enough,'' said Makepeace.

''Glad to see that you're giving Alvin free time now,'' said Horace. ''There's been a lot of folks criticizing you for being so tight with a good prentice, but I always told them, Makepeace is just biding his time, you'll see.''

''That's right,'' said Makepeace. ''I was biding my time.''

''You don't mind if I tell other folks that the biding's done?''

''Alvin still has to do his work for me,'' said Makepeace.

Horace nodded wisely. ''Reckon so,'' he said. ''He works for you mornings, for himself afternoons—is that right? That's the way most fair-minded masters do it, when a prentice gets so near to journeyman.''

Makepeace began to turn a little red. Alvin wasn't surprised. He could see what was happening—Horace Guester was being like a lawyer for him, seizing on this chance to shame Makepeace into treating Alvin fair for the first time in more than six years of prenticing. When Makepeace decided to pretend that Alvin really *did* have free time, why, that was a crack in the door, and Horace was muscling his way through by main force. Pushing Makepeace to give Alvin half days, no less! That was surely too much for Makepeace to swallow.

But Makepeace swallowed. ''Half days is fine with me. Been meaning to do that for some time.''

''So you'll be working afternoons yourself now, right, Makepeace?''

Oh, Alvin had to gaze at Horace with pure admiration. He wasn't going to let Makepeace get away with lazing around and forcing Alvin to do all the work at the smithy.

''When I work's my own business, Horace.''

''Just want to tell folks when they can be sure to find the master in, and when the prentice.''

''I'll be in *all day.*''

''Why, glad to hear it,'' said Horace. ''Well, fine work, I must say, Alvin. Your master done a good job teaching you, and you been carefuler than I ever seen before. You make sure to come by this evening for your four dollars.''

"Yes sir. Thank you, sir.''

"I'll just let you two get back to work now,'' said Horace. "Are these the only two keys to the door?''

"Yes sir,'' said Alvin. "I oiled them up so they won't rust.''

"I'll keep them oiled myself. Thanks for the reminder.''

Horace opened the door and pointedly held it open till Makepeace and Alvin came on out. Horace carefully locked the door, as they watched. He turned and grinned at Alvin. "Maybe first thing I'll have you do is make a lock this fine for *my* front door.'' Then he laughed out loud and shook his head. "No, I reckon not. I'm an innkeeper. My business is to let people in, not lock them out. But there's others in town who'll like the look of this lock.''

"Hope so, sir. Thank you.''

Horace nodded again, then took a cool gaze at Makepeace as if to say, Don't forget all you promised to do here today. Then he ambled off up the path to the roadhouse.

Alvin started down the hill to the smithy. He could hear Makepeace following him, but Alvin wasn't exactly hoping for a conversation with his master just now. As long as Makepeace said nothing, that was good enough for Alvin.

That lasted only till they were both inside the smithy.

"That stove was broke to hell and back,'' said Makepeace.

That was the last thing Alvin expected to hear, and the most fearful. No chewing-out for claiming free time; no attempt to take back what he'd promised in the way of work schedule. Makepeace Smith had remembered that stove better than Alvin expected.

"Looked real bad, all right,'' said Alvin.

"No way to fix it without recasting,'' said Makepeace. "If I didn't know it was impossible, I would've fixed it myself.''

"I thought so, too,'' said Alvin. "But when I looked it over—''

The look on Makepeace Smith's face silenced him. He knew. There was no doubt in Alvin's mind. The master knew what his prentice boy could do. Alvin felt the fear of being found out right down to his bones; it felt just like hide-and-go-find with his brothers and sisters when he was little, back in Vigor Church. The worst was when you were the last one still hid and unfound, all the waiting and waiting, and then you hear the footsteps coming, and you tingle all over, you feel it in every part of your body, like as if your whole self was awake and itching to move. It gets so bad you want to jump out and scream, "Here I am! I'm here!" and then run like a rabbit, not to the haven tree, but just anywhere, just run full out until every muscle of your body was wore out and you fell down on the earth. It was crazy—no good came of such craziness. But that's how it felt playing with his brothers and sisters, and that's how it felt now on the verge of being found out.

To Alvin's surprise, a slow smile spread across his master's face. "So that's it," said Makepeace. "That's it. Ain't you full of surprises. I see it now. Your pa said when you was born, he's the seventh son of a seventh son. Your way with horses, sure, I knew about that. And what you done finding that well, sense like a doodlebug, I could see *that*, too. But now." Makepeace grinned. "Here I thought you were a smith like never was born, and all the time you was fiddling with it like an alchemist."

"No sir," said Alvin.

"Oh, I'll keep your secret," said Makepeace. "I won't tell a soul." But he was laughing in the way he had, and Alvin knew that while Makepeace wouldn't tell straight out, he'd be dropping hints from here to the Hio. But that wasn't what bothered Alvin most.

"Sir," said Alvin, "all the work I ever done for *you*, I done honest, with my own arms and skill."

Makepeace nodded wisely, like he understood some secret meaning in Alvin's words. "I get it," he said. "Secret's safe with me. But I knew it all along. Knew you couldn't be as good a smith as you seemed."

Makepeace Smith had no idea how close he was to death. Alvin wasn't a murderous soul—any lust for blood that might have been born in him was driven out of him on a certain day inside Eight-

Face Mound near seven years ago. But during all the years of his prenticeship, he had never heard one word of praise from this man, nothing but complaints about how lazy Alvin was, and how second-rate his work was, and all the time Makepeace Smith was lying, all the time he knew Alvin was good. Not till Makepeace was convinced Alvin had used hidden knackery to do his smithwork, not till now did Makepeace ever let Alvin know that he was, in fact, a good smith. Better than good. Alvin knew it, of course, knew he was a natural smith, but never having it said out loud hurt him deeper than he guessed. Didn't his master know how much a word might have meant, even half an hour ago, just a word like, "You've got some skill at this, boy," or, "You have a right good hand with that sort of work"? But Makepeace couldn't do it, had to lie and pretend Alvin had no skill until now, when Makepeace believed that he didn't have a smith's skill after all.

Alvin wanted to reach out and take hold of Makepeace's head and ram it into the anvil, ram it so hard that the truth would be driven right through Makepeace's skull and into his brain. I never used my Maker's knack in any of my smithwork, not since I got strong enough to do it with my own strength and skill, so don't smirk at me like I'm just a trickster, and no real smith. Besides, even if I used my Maker's art, do you think that's easy, either? Do you think I haven't paid a price for that as well?

All the fury of Alvin's life, all these years of slavery, all these years of rage at the unfairness of his master, all these years of secrecy and disguise, all his desperate longing to know what to do with his life and having no one in the world to ask, all this was burning inside Alvin hotter than the forge fire. Now the itching and tingling inside him wasn't a longing to run. No, it was a longing to do violence, to stop that smile on Makepeace Smith's face, to stop it forever against the anvil's beak.

But somehow Alvin held himself motionless, speechless, as still as an animal trying to be invisible, trying not to be where he is. And in that stillness Alvin heard the greensong all around him, and he let the life of the woodland come into him, fill his heart, bring him peace. The greensong wasn't loud as it used to be, farther west in wilder times, when the Red man still sang along with the green-wood music. It was weak, and sometimes got near drowned out by the unharmonious noise of town life or the monotones of well-tended fields. But Alvin could still find the song at need, and sing silently along with it, and let it take over and calm his heart.

Did Makepeace Smith know how close he came to death? For it was sure he'd be no match for Alvin rassling, not with Al so young and tall and so much terrible righteous fire in his heart. Whether he guessed or not, the smile faded from Makepeace Smith's face, and he nodded solemnly. "I'll keep all I said, up there, when Horace pushed me so hard. I know you probably put him up to it, but I'm a fair man, so I'll forgive you, long as you still pull some weight here for me, till your contract's up."

Makepeace's accusation that Alvin conspired with Horace should have made Alvin angrier, but by now the greensong owned him, and Alvin wasn't hardly even in the smithy. He was in the kind of trance he learned when he ran with Ta-Kumsaw's Reds, where you forget who and where you are, and your body's just a far-off creature running through the woods.

Makepeace waited for an answer, but it didn't come. So he just nodded wisely and turned to leave. "I got business in town," he said. "Keep at it." He stopped at the wide doorway and turned back into the smithy. "While you're at it, you might as well fix those other brokedown stoves in the shed."

Then he was gone.

Alvin stood there a long time, not moving, not hardly even knowing he had a body to move. It was full noon before he came to himself and took a step. His heart was utterly at peace then, with not a spot of rage left in it. If he'd thought about it, he probably would've knowed that the anger was sure to come back, that he wasn't so much healed as soothed. But soothing was enough for now, it'd do. His contract would be up this spring, and then he'd be out of this place, a free man at last.

One thing, though. It never did occur to him to do what Make-peace Smith asked, and fix those other brokedown stoves. And as for Makepeace, he never brought it up again, neither. Alvin's knack wasn't a part of his prenticeship, and Makepeace Smith must've knowed that, deep down, must've knowed he didn't have the right to tell young Al what to do when he was a-Making.

A few days later Alvin was one of the men who helped lay the new floor in the springhouse. Horace took him aside and asked him why he never came by for his four dollars.

Alvin couldn't very well tell him the truth, that he'd never take money for work he did as a Maker. "Call it my share of the teacher's salary," said Alvin.

"You got no property to pay tax on," said Horace, "nor any children to go to the school, neither."

"Then say I'm paying you for my share of the land my brother's body sleeps in up behind the roadhouse," said Alvin.

Horace nodded solemnly. "That debt, if there *was* a debt, was paid in full by your father's and brothers' labor seventeen year gone, young Alvin, but I respect your wish to pay your share. So this time I'll consider you paid in full. But any other work you do for me, you take full wages, you hear me?"

"I will, sir," said Alvin. "Thank you sir."

"Call me Horace, boy. When a growed man calls me sir it just makes me feel old."

They went back to work then, and said nary another word about Alvin's work on the springhouse. But something stuck in Alvin's mind all the same: what Horace said when Alvin offered to let his wages be a share of the teacher's salary. "You got no property, nor any children to go to the school." There it was, right there, in just a few words. That was why even though Alvin had his full growth on him, even though Horace called him a growed man, he wasn't really a man yet, not even in his own eyes. Because he had no family. Because he had no property. Till he had those, he was just a big old boy. Just a child like Arthur Stuart, only taller, with some beard showing when he didn't shave.

And just like Arthur Stuart, he had no share in the school. He was too old. It wasn't built for the likes of him. So why did he wait so anxious for the schoolmistress to come? Why did he think of her with so all-fired much hope? She wasn't coming here for him, and yet he knew that he had done his work on the springhouse for her, as if to put her in his debt, or perhaps to thank her in advance for what he wanted her, so desperately, to do for him.

Teach me, he said silently. I got a Work to do in this world, but nobody knows what it is or how it's done. Teach me. That's what I want from you, Lady, to help me find my way to the root of the world or the root of myself or the throne of God or the Unmaker's heart, wherever the secret of Making lies, so that I can build against the snow of winter, or make a light to shine against the fall of night.

❧ 14 ❧

River Rat

ALVIN WAS IN Hatrack Mouth the afternoon the teacher came. Makepeace had sent him with the wagon, to fetch a load of new iron that come down the Hio. Hatrack Mouth used to be just a single wharf, a stop for riverboats unloading stuff for the town of Hatrack River. Now, though, as river traffic got thicker and more folks were settling out in the western lands on both sides of the Hio, there was a need for a couple of inns and shops, where farmers could sell provender to passing boats, and river travelers could stay the night. Hatrack Mouth and the town of Hatrack River were getting more important all the time, since this was the last place where the Hio was close to the great Wobbish Road—the very road that Al's own father and brothers cut through the wilderness west to Vigor Church. Folks would come downriver and unship their wagons and horses here, and then move west overland.

There was also things that folks wouldn't tolerate in Hatrack River itself: gaming houses, where poker and other games got played and money changed hands, the law not being inclined to venture much into the dens of river rats and other such scum. And upstairs of such houses, it was said there was women who wasn't ladies, plying a trade that decent folks scarcely whispered about and boys of Alvin's age talked of in low voices with lots of nervous laughter.

It wasn't the thought of raised skirts and naked thighs that made Alvin look forward to his trips to Hatrack Mouth. Alvin scarce noticed those buildings, knowing he had no business there. It was the wharf that drew him, and the porthouse, and the river itself, with boats and rafts going by all the time, ten going downstream for every one coming up. His favorite boats were the steamboats, whistling and spitting their way along at unnatural speeds. With heavy engines built in Irrakwa, these riverboats were wide and long, and yet they moved upstream against the current faster than rafts could float downstream. There was eight of them on the Hio now, going from Dekane down to Sphinx and back again. No farther than Sphinx, though, since the Mizzipy was thick with fog, and nary a boat dared navigate there.

Someday, thought Alvin, someday a body could get on such a boat as *Pride of the Hio* and just float away. Out to the West, to the wild lands, and maybe catch a glimpse of the place where Ta-Kumsaw and Tenskwa-Tawa live now. Or upriver to Dekane, and thence by the new steam train that rode on rails up to Irrakwa and the canal. From there a body could travel the whole world, oceans across. Or maybe he could stand on this bank and the whole world would someday pass him by.

But Alvin wasn't lazy. He didn't linger long at riverside, though he might want to. Soon enough he went into the porthouse and turned in Makepeace Smith's chit to redeem the iron packed in nine crates on the dock.

"Don't want you using my hand trucks to tote those, now," said the portmaster. Alvin nodded—it was always the same. Folks wanted iron bad enough, the portmaster included, and he'd be up to the smithy soon enough asking for this or that. But in the meantime, he'd let Alvin heft the iron all himself, and not let him wear out the portmaster's trucks moving such a heavy load. Nor did Makepeace ever give Alvin money enough to hire one of the river rats to help with the toting. Truth to tell, Alvin was glad enough of that. He didn't much like the sort of man who lived the river life. Even though the day of brigands and pirates was pretty much over, there being too much traffic on the water now for much to happen in secret, still there was thievery enough, and crooked dealing, and Alvin looked down hard on the men who did such things. To his way of thinking, such men counted on the trust of honest folks, and then betrayed them; and what could that do, except make it so folks would stop trusting each other at all? I'd rather face a man with raw fighting in him, and match him arm for arm, than face a man who's full of lies.

So wouldn't you know it, Alvin met the new teacher and matched himself with a river rat all in the same hour.

The river rat he fought was one of a gang of them lolling under the eaves of the porthouse, probably waiting for a gaming house to open. Each time Alvin came out of the porthouse with a crate of iron bars, they'd call out to him, taunting him. At first it was sort of good-natured, saying things like, "Why are you taking so many trips, boy? Just tuck one of those crates under each arm!" Alvin just grinned at remarks like that, since he knew that they knew just how heavy a load of iron was. Why, when they unloaded the iron from the boat yesterday, the boatmen no doubt hefted two men to a crate. So in a way, teasing him about being lazy or weak was a kind of compliment, since it was only a joke because the iron was heavy and Alvin was really very strong.

Then Alvin went on to the grocer's, to buy the spices Gertie had asked him to bring home for her kitchen, along with a couple of Irrakwa and New England kitchen tools whose purpose Al could only half guess at.

When he came back, both arms full, he found the river rats still loitering in the shade, only they had somebody new to taunt, and their mockery was a little ugly now. It was a middle-aged woman, some forty years old by Alvin's guess, her hair tied up severe in a bun and a plain hat atop it, her dark dress right up to the neck and down the wrist as if she was afraid sunlight on her skin might kill her. She was staring stonily ahead while the river rats had words at her.

"You reckon that dress is sewed on, boys?"

They reckoned so.

"Probably never comes up for no man."

"Why no, boys, there's nothing *under* that skirt, she's just a doll's head and hands sewed onto a stuffed dress, don't you think?"

"No way could she be a *real* woman."

"I can tell a real woman when I see one, anyway. The minute they lay eyes on me, *real* women just naturally start spreading their legs and raising their skirts."

"Maybe if you helped her out a little, you could turn her into a real woman."

"This one? This one's carved out of wood. I'd get splinters in my oar, trying to row in such waters."

Well, that was about all Alvin could stand to hear. It was bad enough for a man to think such thoughts about a woman who invited it—the girls from the gaming houses, who opened their necklines down to where you could count their breasts as plain as a cow's teats and flounced along the streets kicking up their skirts till you could see their knees. But this woman was plainly a lady, and by rights oughtn't to have to hear the dirty thoughts of these low men. Alvin figured she must be waiting for somebody to fetch her—the stagecoach to Hatrack River was due, but not for a couple of hours yet. She didn't look fearful—she probably knew these men was more brag than action, so her virtue was safe enough. And from her face Alvin couldn't guess whether she was even listening, her expression was so cold and faraway. But the river rats' words embarrassed *him* so much he couldn't stand it, and couldn't feel right about just driving his wagon off and leaving her there. So he put the parcels he got from the port grocer into the wagon and then walked up to the river rats and spoke to the loudest and crudest talker among them.

"Maybe you'd best speak to her like a lady," said Alvin. "Or perhaps not speak to her at all."

Alvin wasn't surprised to see the glint these boys all got in their eyes the minute he spoke. Provoking a lady was one kind of fun, but he knew they were sizing him up now to see how easy he'd be to whup. They always loved a chance to teach a lesson to a town boy, even one built up as strong as Alvin was, him being a blacksmith.

"Maybe you'd best not speak to us at all," said the loud one. "Maybe you already said more than you ought."

One of the river rats didn't understand, and thought the game was still talking dirty about the lady. "He's just jealous. He wants to pole her muddy river himself."

"I haven't said enough," said Alvin, "not while you still don't have the manners to know how to speak to a lady."

Only now did the lady speak for the first time. "I don't need protection, young man," she said. "Just go along, please." Her voice was strange-sounding. Cultured, like Reverend Thrower, with all the words clear. Like people who went to school in the East.

It would have been better for her not to speak, since the sound of her voice only encouraged the river rats.

"Oh, she's sweet on this boy!"

"She's making a move on him!"

"He wants to row our boat!"

"Let's show her who the real man is!"

"If she wants his little mast, let's cut it off and give it to him."

A knife appeared, then another. Didn't she know enough to keep her mouth shut? If they dealt with Alvin alone, they'd set up to have a single fight, one to one. But if they got to showing off for her, they'd be happy enough to gang up on him and cut him bad, maybe kill him, certainly take an ear or his nose or, like they said, geld him.

Alvin glared at her for a moment, silently telling her to shut her mouth. Whether she understood his look or just figured things out for herself or got plain scared to say more, she didn't offer any more conversation, and Alvin set to turning things in a direction he could handle.

"Knives," said Alvin, with all the contempt he could muster. "So you're afraid to face a blacksmith with bare hands?"

They laughed at him, but the knives got pulled back and put away.

"Blacksmith's *nothing* compared to the muscles we get poling the river."

"You don't pole the river no more, boys, and everybody knows that," said Alvin. "You just set back and get fat, watching the paddlewheel push the boat along."

The loudest talker got up and stepped out, pulling his filthy shirt off over his head. He was strongly muscled, all right, with more than a few scars making white and red marks here and there on his chest and arms. He was also missing an ear.

"From the look of you," said Alvin, "you've fought a lot of men."

"Damn straight," said the river rat.

"And from the look of you, I'd say most of them was better than you."

The man turned red, blushing under his tan clear down to his chest.

"Can't you give me somebody who's worth rassling? Somebody who mostly *wins* his fights?"

"I win my fights!" shouted the man—getting mad, so he'd be easy to lick, which was Al's plan. But the others, they started pulling him back.

"The blacksmith boy's right, you're no great shakes at rassling."

"Give him what he wants."

"Mike, you take this boy."

"He's yours, Mike."

From the back—the shadiest spot, where he'd been sitting on the only chair with a back to it—a man stood up and stepped forward.

"I'll take this boy," he said.

At once the loud one backed off and got out of the way. This wasn't what Alvin wanted at all. The man they called Mike was bigger and stronger than any of the others, and as he stripped his shirt off, Al saw that while he had a scar or two, he was mostly clean, and he had both his ears, a sure sign that if he ever lost a rassling match, he sure never lost *bad*.

He had muscles like a buffalo.

"My name is Mike Fink!" he bellowed. "And I'm the meanest, toughest son-of-a-bitch ever to walk on the water! I can orphan baby alligators with my bare hands! I can throw a live buffalo up onto a wagon and slap him upside the head until he's dead! If I don't like the bend of a river, I grab ahold of the end of it and give it a shake to straighten it out! Every woman I ever put down come up with triplets, if she come up at all! When I'm done with you, boy, your hair will hang down straight on both sides cause you won't have no more ears. You'll have to sit down to piss, and you'll never have to shave again!"

All the time Mike Fink was making his brag, Alvin was taking off his shirt and his knife belt and laying them on the wagon seat. Then he marked a big circle in the dirt, making sure he looked as calm and relaxed as if Mike Fink was a spunky seven-year-old boy, and not a man with murder in his eyes.

So when Fink was shut of boasting, the circle was marked. Fink walked to the circle, then rubbed it out with his foot, raising a dust. He walked all around the circle, rubbing it out. "I don't know who taught you how to rassle, boy," he said, "but when you rassle *me*, there ain't no lines and there ain't no rules."

Once again the lady spoke up. "Obviously there are no rules when you speak, either, or you'd know that the word *ain't* is a sure sign of ignorance and stupidity."

Fink turned to the woman and made as if to speak. But it was like he knew he had nothing to say, or maybe he figured that whatever he said would make him sound more ignorant. The contempt in her voice enraged him, but it also made him doubt himself. At first Alvin thought the lady was making it more dangerous for him, meddling again. But then he realized that she was doing to Fink what Alvin had tried to do to the loudmouth—make him mad enough to fight stupid. Trouble was, as Alvin sized up the river man, he suspected that Fink didn't fight stupid when he was mad —it just made him fight meaner. Fight to kill. Act out his brag about taking off parts of Alvin's body. This wasn't going to be a friendly match like the ones Alvin had in town, where the game was just to throw the other man, or if they was fighting on grass, to pin him down.

"You're not so much," Alvin said, "and you know it, or you wouldn't have a knife hid in your boot."

Fink looked startled, then grinned. He pulled up his pantleg and took a long knife out of his boot, tossed it to the men behind him. "I won't need a knife to fight *you*," he said.

"Then why don't you take the knife out of the *other* boot?" asked Alvin.

Fink frowned and raised the other pantleg. "Ain't no knife here," he said.

Alvin knew better, of course, and it pleased him that Fink was worried enough about this fight not to part with his most secret knife. Besides which, probably nobody else knew about that knife but Alvin, with his ability to see what others couldn't see. Fink didn't want to let on to the others that he had such a knife, or word would spread fast along the river and he'd get no advantage from it.

Still, Alvin couldn't afford to let Fink fight with the knife on him. "Then take off the boots and we'll fight barefoot," Alvin said. It was a good idea anyway, knife or no knife. Alvin knew that when the river rats fought, they kicked like mules with their boots. Fighting barefoot might take some of the spunk out of Mike Fink.

But if Fink lost any spunk, he didn't show it. Just sat down in the dust of the road and pulled off his boots. Alvin did the same, and his socks too—Fink didn't wear socks. So now the two of them had on nothing but their trousers, and already out in the sunlight there was enough dust and sweat that their bodies were looking a little streaked and cakey with clay.

Not so caked up, though, that Alvin couldn't feel a hex of protection drawn over Mike Fink's whole body. How could such a thing be? Did he have a hex on some amulet in his pocket? The pattern was strongest near his backside, but when Alvin sent his bug to search that pocket, there was nothing but the rough cotton canvas of Fink's trousers. He wasn't carrying so much as a coin.

By now a crowd was gathered. Not just the river rats who'd been resting in the porthouse shade, but a whole slew of others, and it was plain they all expected Mike Fink to win. He must be something of a legend on the river, Alvin realized, and no surprise, with this mysterious hex he had. Alvin could imagine folks poking a knife at Fink, only to twist at the last moment, or lose their grip, or somehow keep the knife from doing harm. It was a lot easier to win all your wrassling if no man's teeth could bite into you, and if a knife couldn't do much more than graze your skin.

Fink tried all the obvious stuff first, of course, because it made the best show: Roaring, rushing at Alvin like a buffalo, trying to get a bear hug on him, trying to grab onto Alvin and give him a swing like a rock on a string. But Alvin wouldn't have none of that. He didn't even have to use knackery to get away, neither. He was younger and quicker than Fink, and the river man hardly so much as laid a hand on him, Al dodged away so sudden. At first the crowd hooted and called Alvin coward. But after a while of this, they began to laugh at Fink, since he looked so silly, rushing and roaring and coming up empty all the time.

In the meantime, Alvin was exploring to find the source of Fink's hex, for there was no hope of winning this fight if he couldn't get rid of that strong web. He found it soon enough—a pattern of dye embedded deep in the skin of Fink's buttock. It wasn't a perfect hex anymore, since the skin had changed shape somewhat as Fink grew over the years, but it was a clever pattern, with strong locks and links—good enough to cast a strong net over him, even if it was misshapen.

If he hadn't been in the middle of a rassling match with Fink, Alvin might have been more subtle, might have just weakened the hex a little, for he had no will to deprive Fink of the hex that had protected him for so long. Why, Fink might die of it, losing his hex, especially if he had let himself get careless, counting on it to protect him. But what choice did Alvin have? So he made the dyes in Fink's skin start to flow, seeping into his bloodstream and getting carried away. Alvin could do without full concentration—just set it to happening and let it glide on, while he worked on dodging out of Fink's way.

Soon enough Al could sense the hex weakening, fading, finally collapsing completely. Fink wouldn't know it, but Alvin did—he could now be hurt like any other man.

By this time, though, Fink was no longer making those rough and stupid rushes at him. He was circling, feinting, looking to grapple in a square, then use his greater bulk to throw Alvin. But Alvin had a longer reach, and there was no doubt his arms were stronger, so whenever Fink reached to grab, Alvin batted the river man's arms out of the way.

With the hex gone, however, Alvin didn't slap him away. Instead, he reached inside Fink's arms, so that as Fink grasped his arms, Alvin got his hands hooked behind Fink's neck.

Alvin pulled down hard, bowing Fink down so his head was even with Alvin's chest. It was too easy—Fink was letting him, and Alvin guessed why. Sure enough, Fink pulled Alvin closer and brought his head up fast, expecting to catch Alvin on the chin with the back of his head. He was so strong he might've broke Alvin's neck doing that—only Alvin's chin wasn't where Fink thought it would be. In fact, Alvin had already rared his own head back, and when Fink came up hard and out of control, Alvin rammed forward and smashed his forehead into Fink's face. He could feel Fink's nose crumple under the blow, and blood erupted down both their faces.

It wasn't all that surprising, for a man's nose to get broke during a rassle like this. It hurt like blazes, of course, and it would've stopped a friendly match—though of course a friendly match wouldn't have included head butts. Any other river rat would've shook his head, roared a couple of times, and charged back into the fight.

Instead, Fink backed away, a look of real surprise on his face, his hands gripping his nose. Then he let out a howl like a whupped dog.

Everybody else fell silent. It was such a funny thing to happen, a river rat like Mike Fink howling at a broke-up nose. No, it wasn't rightly funny, but it was strange. It wasn't how a river rat was supposed to act.

"Come on, Mike," somebody murmured.

"You can take him, Mike."

But it was a half-hearted sort of encouragement. They'd never seen Mike Fink act hurt or scared before. He wasn't good at hiding it, either. Only Al knew why. Only Al knew that Mike Fink had never in his life felt such a pain, that Fink had never once shed his own blood in a fight. So many times he'd broke the other fellow's nose and laughed at the pain—it was easy to laugh, because he didn't know how it felt. Now he knew. Trouble was, he was learning what others learned at six years old, and so he was acting like a six-year-old. Not crying, exactly, but howling.

For a minute Alvin thought that maybe the match was over. But Fink's fear and pain soon turned to rage, and he waded back into the fight. Maybe he'd learned pain, but he hadn't learned caution from it.

So it took a few more holds, a few more wrenches and twists, before Alvin got Fink down onto the ground. Even as frightened and surprised as Fink was, he was the strongest man Alvin had ever rassled. Till this fight with Fink, Alvin had never really had occasion to find out just how strong he was; he'd never been pushed to his limit. Now he was, and he found himself rolling over and over in the dust, hardly able to breathe it was so thick, Fink's own hot panting breath now above him, now below, knees ramming, arms pounding and gripping, feet scrabbling in the dust, searching for purchase enough to get leverage.

In the end it came down to Fink's inexperience with weakness. Since no man could ever break a bone of his, Fink had never learned to tuck his legs, never learned not to expose them to where a man could stomp them. When Alvin broke free and scrambled to his feet, Fink rolled over quick and, for just a moment, lying there on the ground, he drew one leg across the other like a pure invitation. Alvin didn't even think, he just jumped into the air and came down with both feet onto Fink's top leg, jamming downward with all his weight, so the bones of the top leg were bowed over the lower one. So sharp and hard was the blow that it wasn't just the top leg that shattered, but the bottom one, too. Fink screamed like a child in the fire.

Only now did Alvin realize what he'd done. Oh, yes, of course he'd ended the fight—nobody's tough enough to fight on with two broken legs. But Alvin could tell at once, without looking—or at least without looking with his *eyes*—that these were not clean breaks, not the kind that can heal easy. Besides, Fink wasn't a young man now, and sure he wasn't a boy. If these breaks healed at all, they'd leave him lame at best, outright crippled at the worst. His livelihood would be gone. Besides, he must have made a lot of enemies over the years. What would they do now, with him broken and halt? How long would he live?

So Alvin knelt on the ground beside where Mike Fink writhed —or rather, the upper half of him writhed, while he tried to keep his legs from moving at all—and touched the legs. With his hands in contact with Fink's body, even through the cloth of his pants, Alvin could find his way easier, work faster, and in just a few moments, he had knitted the bones together. That was all he tried to do, no more—the bruise, the torn muscle, the bleeding, he had to leave that or Fink might get up and attack him again.

He pulled his hands away, and stepped back from Fink. At once the river rats gathered around their fallen hero.

"Is his legs broke?" asked the loudmouth river rat.

"No," said Alvin.

"They're broke to pieces!" howled Fink.

By then, another man had slit right up the pantleg. Sure enough he found the bruise, but as he felt along the bone, Fink screeched and pulled away. "Don't touch it!"

"Didn't feel broke to me," said the man.

"Look how he's moving his legs. They ain't broke."

It was true enough—Fink was no longer writhing with just the top half of his body, his legs were wiggling now as much as any other part of him.

One man helped Fink to his feet. Fink staggered, almost fell, caught himself by leaning against the loudmouth, smearing blood from his nose on the man's shirt. The others pulled away from him.

"Just a boy," muttered one.

"Howling like a puppydog."

"Big old baby."

"Mike *Fink*." And then a chuckle.

Alvin stood by the wagon, putting on his shirt, then sat up on the wagon seat to pull on his shoes and socks. He glanced up to find the lady watching him. She stood not six feet off, since the smith's wagon was pulled right up against the loading dock. She had a look of sour distaste. Alvin realized she was probably disgusted at how dirty he was. Maybe he shouldn't have put his shirt right back on, but then, it was also impolite to go shirtless in front of a lady. In fact, the town men, especially the doctors and lawyers, they acted ashamed to be out in public without a proper coat and waistcoat and cravat. Poor folks usually didn't have such clothes, and a prentice would be putting on airs to dress like that. But a shirt—he had to have his shirt on, whether he was filthy with dust or not.

"Beg pardon, Ma'am," he said. "I'll wash when I get home."

"Wash?" she asked. "And when you do, will your brutality also wash away?"

"I reckon I don't know, since I never heard that word."

"I daresay you haven't," she said. "Brutality. From the word *brute*. Meaning beast."

Alvin felt himself redden with anger. "Maybe so. Maybe I should've let them go on talking to you however they liked."

"I paid no attention to them. They didn't bother me. You had no need to protect me, especially not that way. Stripping naked and rolling around in the dirt. You're covered with blood."

Alvin hardly knew what to answer, she was so snooty and boneheaded. "I wasn't naked," Alvin said. Then he grinned. "And it was *his* blood."

"And are you proud of that?"

Yes, he was. But he knew that if he said so, it would diminish him in her sight. Well, what of that? What did he care what she thought of him? Still, he said nothing.

In the silence between them, he could hear the river rats behind him, hooting at Fink, who wasn't howling anymore, but wasn't saying much, either. It wasn't just Fink they were thinking about now, though.

"Town boy thinks he's tough."

"Maybe we ought to show him a *real* fight."

"Then we'll see how uppity his ladyfriend is."

Alvin couldn't rightly tell the future, but it didn't take no torch to guess at what was going to happen. Al's boots were on, his horse was full-hitched, and it was time to go. But snooty as she was, he couldn't leave the lady behind. He knew she'd be the river rats' target now, and however little she thought she needed protection, he knew that these river men had just watched their best man get whupped and humbled, and all on account of her, which meant she'd likely end up lying in the dirt with her bags all dumped in the river, if not worse.

"Best you get in," Alvin said.

"I wonder that you dare to give me instructions like a common—What are you doing?"

Alvin was tossing her trunk and bags into the back of the wagon. It seemed so obvious to him that he didn't bother answering her.

"I think you're robbing me, sir!"

"I am if you don't get in," said Alvin.

By now the river rats were gathering near the wagon, and one of them had hold of the horse's harness. She glanced around, and her angry expression changed. Just a little. She stepped from the dock onto the wagon seat. Alvin took her hand and helped her arrange herself on the seat. By now, the loudmouth river rat was standing beside him, leaning on the wagon, grinning wickedly. "You beat one of us, blacksmith, but can you beat us all?"

Alvin just stared at him. He was concentrating on the man holding the horse, making his hand suddenly tingle with pain, like he was being punctured with a hundred pins. The man cried out and let go the horse. The loudmouth looked away from Alvin, toward the sound of the cry, and in the moment Alvin kicked him in the ear with his boot. It wasn't much of a kick, but then, it wasn't much of an ear, either, and the man ended up sitting in the dirt, holding his head.

"Gee-yap!" shouted Alvin.

The horse obediently lunged forward—and the wagon moved about an inch. Then another inch. Hard to get a wagonload of iron moving fast, at least all of a sudden. Alvin made the wheels turn smooth and easy, but he couldn't do a thing about the weight of the wagon or the strength of the horse. By the time the horse got moving, the wagon was a good deal heavier, with the weight of river rats hanging on it, pulling back, climbing aboard.

Alvin turned around and swung his whip at them. The whip was for show—it didn't hit a one. Still, they all fell off or let go of the wagon as if it *had* hit them, or scared them anyway. What really happened was that all of a sudden the wood of the wagon got as slick as if it was greased. There was no way for them to hold onto it. So the wagon lurched forward as they collapsed back into the dust of the road.

They weren't done, though. After all, Alvin had to turn around and head back *up* the road right past them in order to get to Hatrack River. He was trying to figure what to do next when he heard a musket go off, loud as a cannonshot, the sound hanging on in the heavy summer air. When he got the wagon turned around, he saw the portmaster standing on the dock, his wife behind him. He was holding one musket, and she was reloading the one he had just fired.

"I reckon we get along well enough most of the time, boys," said the portmaster. "But today you just don't seem to know when you been beat fair and square. So I guess it's about time you settled down in the shade, cause if you make another move toward that wagon, them as don't die from buckshot'll be standing trial in Hatrack River, and if you think you won't pay dear for assaulting a local boy and the new schoolteacher, then you really are as dumb as you look."

It was quite a little speech, and it worked better than most speeches Alvin had heard in his life. Those river rats just settled right down in the shade, taking a couple of long pulls from a jug and watching Al and the lady with a real sullen look. The portmaster went back inside before the wagon even turned the corner onto the town road.

"You don't suppose the portmaster is in danger from having helped us, do you?" asked the lady. Alvin was pleased to hear that the arrogance was gone from her voice, though she still spoke as clear and even as the ringing of a hammer on iron.

"No," said Alvin. "They all know that if ever a portmaster got harmed, them as did it would never work again on the river, or if they did, they wouldn't live through a night ashore."

"What about you?"

"Oh, I got no such guarantee. So I reckon I won't come back to Hatrack Mouth for a couple of weeks. By then all those boys'll have jobs and be a hundred miles up or downstream from here." Then he remembered what the portmaster had said. "You're the new schoolteacher?"

She didn't answer. Not directly, anyway. "I suppose there are men like that in the East, but one doesn't meet them in the open like this."

"Well, it's a whole lot better to meet them in the open than it is to meet them in private!" Al said, laughing.

She didn't laugh.

"I was waiting for Dr. Whitley Physicker to meet me. He expected my boat later in the afternoon, but he may be on his way."

"This is the only road, Ma'am," Alvin said.

"Miss," she said. "Not madame. That title is properly reserved for married women."

"Like I said, it's the only road. So if he's on his way, we won't *miss* him. Miss."

This time Alvin didn't laugh at his own joke. On the other hand, he thought, looking out of the corner of his eye, that he just might have caught a glimpse of her smiling. So maybe she wasn't as hoity-toity as she seemed, Alvin thought. Maybe she's almost human. Maybe she'll even consent to give private schooling to a certain little half-Black boy. Maybe she'll be worth the work I went to fixing up the springhouse.

Because he was facing forward, driving the wagon, it wouldn't be natural, let alone good manners, for him to turn and stare right at her like he wanted to. So he sent out his bug, his spark, that part of him that "saw" what no man or woman could rightly with their own eyes see. For Alvin this was near second nature by now, to explore people under the skin so to speak. Keep in mind, though, that it wasn't like he could see with his eyes. Sure enough he could tell what was under a body's clothes, but he still didn't see folks naked. Instead he just got a close-in experience of the surface of their skin, almost like he'd took up residence in one of their pores. So he didn't think of it like he was peeping in windows or nothing. It was just another way of looking at folks and understanding them; he wouldn't see a body's shape or color, but he'd see whether they was sweating or hot or healthy or tensed-up. He'd see bruises and old healed-up injuries. He'd see hidden money or secret papers— but if he was to read the papers, he had to discover the feel of the ink on the surface and then trace it until he could build up a picture of the letters in his mind. It was very slow. Not like seeing, no sir.

Anyhow, he sent his bug to "see" this high-toned lady that he couldn't exactly look at. And what he found caught him by surprise. Cause she was every bit as hexed-up as Mike Fink had been.

No, more. She was layers deep in it, from hexy amulets hanging around her neck to hexes stitched into her clothes, even a wire hex embedded in the bun of her hair. Only one of them was for protection, and it wasn't half so strong as Mike Fink's had been. The rest were all—for what? Alvin hadn't seen such work before, and it took some thought and exploration to figure out what these hexwork webs that covered her were doing. The best he could get, riding along in the wagon, keeping his eyes on the road ahead, was that somehow these hexes were doing a powerful beseeming, making her look to be something that she wasn't.

The first thought he had, as I suppose was natural, was to try to discover what she really was, under her disguise. The clothes she wore were real enough—the hexery was only changing the sound of her voice, the hue and texture of the surface of her skin. But Alvin had little practice with beseemings, and none at all with beseemings wove from hexes. Most folks did a beseeming with a word and a gesture, tied up with a drawing of what they wanted to seem to be. It was a working on other folks' minds, and once you saw through it, it didn't fool you at all. Since Alvin always saw through it, such beseemings had no hold on him.

But hers was different. The hex changed the way light hit her and bounced off, so that you weren't fooled into thinking you saw what wasn't there. Instead you really saw her different, the light actually struck your eyes that way. Since it wasn't a change made on Alvin's mind, knowing the trickery didn't help him see the truth. And using his bug, he couldn't tell much about what was hidden away behind the hexes, except that she wasn't quite so wrinkled-up and bony as she looked, which made him guess she might be younger.

It was only when he gave up trying to guess at what lay under the disguise that he came to the real question: Why, if a woman had the power to disguise herself and seem to be anything she wanted, why would she choose to look like *that*? Cold, severe, getting old, bony, unsmiling, pinched-up, angry, aloof. All the things a woman ought to hope she never was, this teacher lady *chose* to be.

Maybe she was a fugitive in disguise. But she was definitely a woman underneath the hexes, and Alvin never heard of a woman outlaw, so it couldn't be that. Maybe she was just young, and figured other folks wouldn't take her serious if she didn't look older. Alvin knew about *that* right enough. Or maybe she was pretty, and men kept thinking of her the wrong way—Alvin tried to conjure up in his mind what might've happened with those river rats if she'd been real beautiful. But truth to tell, the rivermen probably would've been polite as they knew how, if she was pretty. It was only ugly women they felt free to taunt, since ugly women probably reminded them of their mothers. So her plainness wasn't exactly protection. And it wasn't designed to hide a scar, neither, cause Alvin could see her skin wasn't pocked or blemished or marred.

Truth was he couldn't guess at why she was all hid up under so many layers of lies. She could be anything or anybody. He couldn't even ask her, since to tell her he saw through her disguise was the same as to tell her of his knack, and how could he know she could be trusted with such a secret as *that,* when he didn't even know who she really was or why she chose to live inside a lie?

He wondered if he ought to tell somebody. Shouldn't the school board know, before putting the town's children into her care, that she wasn't exactly what she seemed to be? But he couldn't tell them, either, without giving himself away; and besides, maybe her secret was her own business and no harm to anyone. Then if he told the truth on her, it would ruin both him and her, with no good done for anybody.

No, best to watch her, real careful, and learn who she was the only way a body can ever truly know other folks: by seeing what they do. That's the best plan Alvin could think of, and the truth is, now that he knew she had such a secret, how could he *keep* from paying special attention to her? Using his bug to explore around him was such a habit for him that he'd have to work *not* to check up on her, especially if she was living up at the springhouse. He half hoped she wouldn't, so he wouldn't be bothered so much by this mystery; but he just as much hoped she would, so he could keep watch and make sure she was a rightful sort of person.

And I could watch her even better if I studied from her. I could watch her with her own eyes, ask her questions, listen to her answers, and judge what kind of person she might be. Maybe if she taught me long enough, she'd come to trust me, and I her, and then I'd tell her I'm to be a Maker and she'd tell her deep secrets to me and we'd help each other, we'd be true friends the way I haven't had no true friend since I left my brother Measure behind me in Vigor Church.

He wasn't pushing the horse too hard, the load being so heavy, what with her trunk and bags on top of the iron—and herself, to boot. So after all their talk, and then all this silence as he tried to figure out who she really was, they were still only about a half a mile out of Hatrack Mouth when Dr. Physicker's fancy carriage came along. Alvin recognized the carriage right off, and hailed Po Doggly, who was driving. It took all of a couple of minutes to move the teacher and her things from wagon to carriage. Po and Alvin did all the lifting—Dr. Physicker used all his efforts to help the teacher lady into the carriage. Alvin had never seen the doctor act so elegant.

"I'm terribly sorry you had to suffer the discomforts of a ride in that wagon," said the doctor. "I didn't think that I was late."

"In fact you're early," she said. And then, turning graciously to Alvin, she added, "And the wagon ride was surprisingly pleasant."

Since Alvin hadn't said a word for most of the journey, he didn't rightly know whether she meant it as a compliment for him being good company, or as gratitude that he kept his mouth shut and didn't bother her. Either way, though, it made him feel a kind of burning in his face, and not from anger.

As Dr. Physicker was climbing into the carriage, the teacher asked him, "What is this young man's name?" Since she spoke to the doctor, Alvin didn't answer.

"Alvin," said the doctor, settling into his seat. "He was born here. He's the smith's apprentice."

"Alvin," she said, now directing herself to him through the carriage window. "I thank you for your gallantry today, and I hope you'll forgive the ungraciousness of my first response. I had underestimated the villainous nature of our unwelcome companions."

Her words were so elegant-sounding it was like music hearing her talk, even though Alvin could only half-guess what she was saying. Her expression, though, was about as kindly as her forbidding face could look, he reckoned. He wondered what her real visage might look like underneath.

"My pleasure, Ma'am," he said. "I mean Miss."

From the driver's bench, Po Doggly gee-ed the pair of mares and the carriage took off, still heading toward Hatrack Mouth, of course. It wasn't easy for Po to find a place on that road to turn around, either, so Alvin was well on his way before the carriage came back and passed him. Po slowed the carriage, and Dr. Physicker leaned over and tossed a dollar coin into the air. Alvin caught it, more by reflex than by thought.

"For your help for Miss Larner," said Dr. Physicker. Then Po gee-ed the horses again and they went on, leaving Alvin to chew on the dust in the road.

He felt the weight of the coin in his hand, and for a moment he wanted to throw it after the carriage. But that wouldn't do no good at all. No, he'd give it back to Physicker some other time, in some way that wouldn't get nobody riled up. But still it hurt, it stung deep, to be paid for helping a lady, like as if he was a servant or a child or something. And what hurt worst was wondering if maybe it was her idea to pay him. As if she thought he had earned a quarter-day's wages when he fought for her honor. It was sure that if he'd been wearing a coat and cravat instead of one filthy shirt, she'd have thought he done the service due a lady from any Christian gentleman, and she'd know she owed him gratitude instead of payment.

Payment. The coin burned in his hand. Why, for a few minutes there he'd almost thought she liked him. Almost he had hoped that maybe she'd agree to teach him, to help him work out some understanding of how the world works, of what he could do to be a true Maker and tame the Unmaker's terrible power. But now that it was plain she despised him, how could he even ask? How could he even pretend to be worthy of teaching, when he knew that all she saw about him was filth and blood and stupid poverty? She knew he meant well, but he was still a brute in her eyes, like she said first off. It was still in her heart. Brutality.

Miss Larner. That's what the doctor called her. He tasted the name as he said it. Dust in his mouth. You don't take animals to school.

☙ 15 ❧

Teacher

Miss Larner had no intention of giving an inch to these people. She had heard enough horror stories about frontier school boards to know that they would try to get out of keeping most of the promises they made in their letters. It was beginning already.

"In your letters you represented to me that I would have a residence provided as part of my salary. I do not regard an inn as a private residence."

"You'll have you own private room," said Dr. Physicker.

"And take all my meals at a common table? This is not acceptable. If I stay, I will be spending all my days in the company of the children of this town, and when that day's work is over, I expect to be able to prepare my own meals in private and eat them in solitude, and then spend the evening in the company of books, without distraction or annoyance. That is not possible in a roadhouse, gentlemen, and so a room in a roadhouse does *not* constitute a private residence."

She could see them sizing her up. Some were abashed by the mere precision of her speech—she knew perfectly well that country lawyers put on airs in their own towns, but they were no match for someone of real education. The only real trouble was going to come from the sheriff, Pauley Wiseman. How absurd, for a grown man still to use a child's nickname.

"Now see here, young lady," said the sheriff.

She raised an eyebrow. It was typical of such a man that, even though Miss Larner seemed to be on the greying side of forty, he would assume that her unmarried status gave him the right to call her "young lady," as one addresses a recalcitrant girlchild.

"What is 'here' that I am failing to see?"

"Well, Horace and Peg Guester *did* plan to offer you a small house off by yourself, but we said no to it, plain and simple, we said no to them, and we say no to you."

"Very well, then. I see that you do not, after all, intend to keep your word to me. Fortunately, gentlemen, I am not a common schoolteacher, grateful to take whatever is offered. I had a good position at the Penn School, and I assure you that I can return there at will. Good day."

She rose to her feet. So did all the men except the sheriff—but they weren't rising out of courtesy.

"Please."

"Sit down."

"Let's talk about this."

"Don't be hasty."

It was Dr. Physicker, the perfect conciliator, who took the floor now, after giving the sheriff a steady look to quell him. The sheriff, however, did not seem particularly quelled.

"Miss Larner, our decision on the private house was not an irrevocable one. But please consider the problems that worried us. First, we were concerned that the house would not be suitable. It's not really a house at all, but a mere room, made out of an abandoned springhouse—"

The old springhouse. "Is it heated?"

"Yes."

"Has it windows? A door that can be secured? A bed and table and chair?"

"All of that, yes."

"Has it a wooden floor?"

"A nice one."

"Then I doubt that its former service as a springhouse will bother me. Had you any other objections?"

"We damn well do!" cried Sheriff Wiseman. Then, seeing the horrified looks around the room, he added, "Begging the lady's pardon for my rough language."

"I am interested in hearing those objections," said Miss Larner.

"A woman alone, in a solitary house in the woods! It ain't proper!"

"It is the word *ain't* which is not proper, Mr. Wiseman," said Miss Larner. "As to the propriety of my living in a house to myself, I assure you that I have done so for many years, and have managed to pass that entire time quite unmolested. Is there another house within hailing distance?"

"The roadhouse to one side and the smith's place to the other," said Dr. Physicker.

"Then if I am under some duress or provocation, I can assure you that I will make myself heard, and I expect those who hear will come to my aid. Or are you afraid, Mr. Wiseman, that I may enter into some improper activity *voluntarily*?"

Of course that was exactly what he was thinking, and his reddening face showed it.

"I believe you have adequate references concerning my moral character," said Miss Larner. "But if you have any doubts on that score, it would be better for me to return to Philadelphia at once, for if at my age I cannot be trusted to live an upright life without supervision, how can you possibly trust me to supervise your young children?"

"It just ain't decent!" cried the sheriff. "Aren't."

"Isn't." She smiled benignly at Pauley Wiseman. "It has been my experience, Mr. Wiseman, that when a person assumes that others are eager to commit indecent acts whenever given the opportunity, he is merely confessing his own private struggle."

Pauley Wiseman didn't understand that she had just accused him, not until several of the lawyers started in laughing behind their hands.

"As I see it, gentlemen of the school board, you have only two alternatives. First, you can pay my boat passage back to Dekane and my overland passage to Philadelphia, plus the salary for the month that I will have expended in traveling."

"If you don't teach, you get no salary," said the sheriff.

"You speak hastily, Mr. Wiseman," said Miss Larner. "I believe the lawyers present will inform you that the school board's letters constitute a contract, of which you are in breach, and that I would therefore be entitled to collect, not just a month's salary, but the entire year's."

"Well, that's not *certain*, Miss Larner," began one of the lawyers.

"Hio is one of the United States now, sir," she answered, "and there is ample precedent in other state courts, precedent which is binding until and unless the government of Hio makes specific legislation to the contrary."

"Is she a schoolteacher or a lawyer?" asked another lawyer, and they all laughed.

"Your second alternative is to allow me to inspect this—this springhouse—and determine whether I find it acceptable, and if I do, to allow me to live there. If you ever find me engaging in morally reprehensible behavior, it is within the terms of our contract that you may discharge me forthwith."

"We can put you in *jail*, that's what we can do," said Wiseman.

"Why, Mr. Wiseman, aren't we getting ahead of ourselves, talking of jail when I have yet to select which morally hideous act I shall perform?"

"Shut up, Pauley," said one of the lawyers.

"Which alternative do you choose, gentlemen?" she asked.

Dr. Physicker was not about to let Pauley Wiseman have at the more weak-willed members of the board. He'd see to it there was no further debate. "We don't need to retire to consider this, do we, gentlemen? We may not be Quakers here in Hatrack River, so we aren't used to thinking of ladies as wanting to live by themselves and engage in business and preach and whatnot, but we're open-minded and willing to learn new ways. We want your services, and we'll keep to the contract. All in favor?''

"Aye."

"Opposed? The ayes have it."

"Nay," said Wiseman.

"The voting's over, Pauley."

"You called it too damn fast!"

"Your negative vote has been recorded, Pauley."

Miss Larner smiled coldly. "You may be sure *I* won't forget it, Sheriff Wiseman."

Dr. Physicker tapped the table with his gavel. "This meeting is adjourned until next Tuesday afternoon at three. And now, Miss Larner, I'd be delighted to escort you to the Guesters' springhouse, if this is a convenient hour. Not knowing when you would arrive, they have given me the key and asked me to open the cottage for you; they'll greet you later."

Miss Larner was aware, as they all were, that it was odd, to say the least, for the landlord not to greet his guest in person.

"You see, Miss Larner, it wasn't certain whether you'd accept the cottage. They wanted you to make your decision when you saw the place—and not in their presence, lest you feel embarrassed to decline it."

"Then they have acted graciously," said Miss Larner, "and I will thank them when I meet them."

It was humiliating, Old Peg having to walk out to the springhouse all by herself to plead with this stuck-up snooty old Philadelphia spinster. Horace ought to be going out there with her. Talk man to man with her—that's what this woman seemed to think she was, not a lady but a lord. Might as well come from Camelot, she might, thinks she's a princess giving orders to the common folk. Well, they took care of it in France, old Napoleon did, put old Louis the Seventeenth right in his place. But lordly women like this teacher lady, Miss Larner, they never got their comeuppance, just went on through life thinking folks what didn't talk perfect was too low to take much account of.

So where was Horace, to put this teacher lady in her place? Setting by the fire. Pouting. Just like a four-year-old. Even Arthur Stuart never got such a pout on him.

"I don't like her," says Horace.

"Well like her or not, if Arthur's to get an education it's going to be from her or nobody," says Old Peg, talking plain sense as usual, but does Horace listen? I should laugh.

"She can live there and she can teach Arthur if she pleases, or not if she don't please, but I don't like her and I don't think she belongs in that springhouse."

"Why, is it holy ground?" says Old Peg. "Is there some curse on it? Should we have built a palace for her royal highness?" Oh, when Horace gets a notion on him it's no use talking, so why did she keep on trying?

"None of that, Peg," said Horace.

"Then what? Or don't you need reasons anymore? Do you just decide and then other folks better make way?"

"Because it's Little Peggy's place, that's why, and I don't like having that benoctious woman living there!"

Wouldn't you know? It was just like Horace, to bring up their runaway daughter, the one who never so much as wrote to them once she ran away, leaving Hatrack River without a torch and Horace without the love of his life. Yes ma'am, that's what Little Peggy was to him, the love of his life. If I ran off, Horace, or, God forbid, if I died, would you treasure my memory and not let no other woman take my place? I reckon not. I reckon there wouldn't be time for my spot on the sheet to get cold afore you'd have some other woman lying there. Me you could replace in a hot minute, but Little Peggy, we have to treat the springhouse as a *shrine* and make me come out here all by myself to face this high-falutin old maid and beg her to teach a little black child. Why, I'll be lucky if she doesn't try to buy him from me.

Miss Larner took her time about answering the door, too, and when she did, she had a handkerchief to her face—probably a perfumed one, so she wouldn't have to smell the odor of honest country folks.

"If you don't mind I've got a thing or two I'd like to discuss with you," said Old Peg.

Miss Larner looked away, off over Old Peg's head, as if studying some bird in a far-off tree. "If it's about the school, I was told I'd have a week to prepare before we actually registered students and began the autumn session."

From down below, Old Peg could hear the *ching-ching-ching* of one of the smiths a-working at the forge. Against her will she couldn't help thinking of Little Peggy, who purely hated that sound. Maybe Horace was right in his foolishness. Maybe Little Peggy haunted this springhouse.

Still, it was Miss Larner standing in the doorway now, and Miss Larner that Old Peg had to deal with. "Miss Larner, I'm Margaret Guester. My husband and I own this springhouse."

"Oh. I beg your pardon. You're my landlady, and I'm being ungracious. Please come in."

That was a bit more like it. Old Peg stepped up through the open door and stood there a moment to take in the room. Only yesterday it had seemed bare but clean, a place full of promise. Now it was almost homey, what with a doily and a dozen books on the armoire, a small woven rug on the floor, and two dresses hanging from hooks on the wall. The trunks and bags filled a corner. It looked a bit like somebody lived there. Old Peg didn't know what she'd expected. Of course Miss Larner had more dresses than this dark traveling outfit. It's just Old Peg hadn't thought of her doing something so ordinary as changing clothes. Why, when she's got one dress off and before she puts on another, she probably stands there in her underwear, just like anybody.

"Do sit down, Mrs. Guester."

"Around here we ain't much with Mr. and Mrs., except them lawyers, Miss Larner. I'm Goody Guester, mostly, except when folks call me Old Peg."

"Old Peg. What a—what an interesting name."

She thought of spelling out why she was called "Old" Peg— how she had a daughter what run off, that sort of thing. But it was going to be hard enough to explain to this teacher lady how she come to have a Black son. Why make her family life seem even more strange?

"Miss Larner, I won't beat around the bush. You got something that I need."

"Oh?"

"That is, not me, to say it proper, but my son, Arthur Stuart."

If she recognized that it was the King's proper name, she gave no sign. "And what might he need from me, Goody Guester?"

"Book-learning."

"That's what I've come to provide to all the children in Hatrack River, Goody Guester."

"Not Arthur Stuart. Not if those pin-headed cowards on the school board have their way."

"Why should they exclude your son? Is he over-age, perhaps?"

"He's the right age, Miss Larner. What he ain't is the right color."

Miss Larner waited, no expression on her face.

"He's Black, Miss Larner."

"Half-Black, surely," offered the teacher.

Naturally the teacher was trying to figure how the innkeeper's wife came to have her a half-Black boy-baby. Old Peg got some pleasure out of watching the teacher act polite while she must surely be cringing in horror inside herself. But it wouldn't do to let such a thought linger too long, would it? "He's adopted, Miss Larner," said Old Peg. "Let's just say that his Black mama got herself embarrassed with a half-White baby."

"And you, out of the goodness of your heart—"

Was there a nasty edge to Miss Larner's voice? "I wanted me a child. I ain't taking care of Arthur Stuart for pity. He's *my* boy now."

"I see," said Miss Larner. "And the good people of Hatrack

River have determined that their children's education will suffer if half-Black ears should hear my words at the same time as pure White ears.''

Miss Larner sounded nasty again, only now Old Peg dared to let herself rejoice inside, hearing the way Miss Larner said those words. ''Will you teach him, Miss Larner?''

''I confess, Goody Guester, that I have lived in the City of Quakers too long. I had forgotten that there were places in this world where people of small minds would be so shameless as to punish a mere child for the sin of being born with skin of a tropical hue. I can assure you that I will refuse to open school at all if your adopted son is not one of my pupils.''

''No!'' cried Old Peg. ''No, Miss Larner, that's going too far.''

''I am a committed Emancipationist, Goody Guester. I will not join in a conspiracy to deprive any Black child of his or her intellectual heritage.''

Old Peg didn't know what in the world an intellectual heritage was, but she knew that Miss Larner was in too much sympathy. If she kept up this way, she'd be like to ruin everything. ''You got to hear me out, Miss Larner. They'll just get another teacher, and I'll be worse off, and so will Arthur Stuart. No, I just ask that you give him an hour in the evening, a few days a week. I'll make him study somewhat in the daytime, to learn proper what you teach him quick. He's a bright boy, you'll see that. He already knows his letters—he can A it and Z it better than my Horace. That's my husband, Horace Guester. So I'm not asking more than a few hours a week, if you can spare it. That's why we worked up this spring-house, so you could do it and none the wiser.''

Miss Larner arose from where she sat on the edge of her bed, and walked to the window. ''This is not what I ever imagined— to teach a child in secret, as if I were committing a crime.''

''In *some* folks' eyes, Miss Larner—''

''Oh, I have no doubt of that.''

''Don't you Quakers have silent meetings? All I ask is a kind of quiet meeting, don't you know—''

''I am not a Quaker, Goody Guester. I am merely a human being who refuses to deny the humanity of others, unless their own acts prove them unworthy of that noble kinship.''

''Then you'll teach him?''

''After hours, yes. Here in my home, which you and your husband so kindly provided, yes. But in secret? Never! I shall proclaim to all in this place that I am teaching Arthur Stuart, and not just a few nights a week, but daily. I am free to tutor such pupils as I desire—my contract is quite specific on that point—and as long as I do not violate the contract, they must endure me for at least a year. Will that do?''

Old Peg looked at the woman in pure admiration. ''I'll be jig- gered,'' she said, ''you're mean as a cat with a burr in its behind.''

''I regret that I've never seen a cat in such an unfortunate situ- ation, Goody Guester, so that I cannot estimate the accuracy of your simile.''

Old Peg couldn't make no sense of the words Miss Larner said, but she caught something like a twinkle in the lady's eye, so it was all right.

''When should I send Arthur to you?'' she asked.

''As I said when I first opened the door, I'll need a week to prepare. When school opens for the White children, it opens for Arthur Stuart as well. There remains only the question of payment.''

Old Peg was taken aback for a moment. She'd come here prepared to offer money, but after the way Miss Larner talked, she thought there'd be no cost after all. Still, teaching was Miss Larner's live- lihood, so it was only fair. ''We thought to offer you a dollar a month, that being most convenient for us, Miss Larner, but if you need more—''

''Oh, not cash, Goody Guester. I merely thought to ask if you might indulge me by allowing me to hold a weekly reading of poetry in your roadhouse on Sunday evenings, inviting all in Hatrack River who aspire to improve their acquaintance with the best literature in the English language.''

''I don't know as how there's all that many who hanker after poetry, Miss Larner, but you're welcome to have a go of it.''

''I think you'll be pleasantly surprised at the number of people who wish to be thought educated, Goody Guester. We shall have difficulty finding seats for all the ladies of Hatrack River who compel their husbands to bring them to hear the immortal words of Pope and Dryden, Donne and Milton, Shakespeare and Gray and—oh, I shall be daring—Wordsworth and Coleridge, and perhaps even an American poet, a wandering spinner of strange tales named Blake."

"You don't mean old Taleswapper, do you?"

"I believe that is his most common sobriquet."

"You've got some of his poems wrote down?"

"Written? Hardly necessary, for that dear friend of mine. I have committed many of his verses to memory."

"Well, don't that old boy get around. Philadelphia, no less."

"He has brightened many a parlor in that city, Goody Guester. Shall we hold our first soiree this Sunday?"

"What's a swore raid?"

"Soiree. An evening gathering, perhaps with ginger punch—"

"Oh, you don't have to teach me nothing about hospitality, Miss Larner. And if that's the price for Arthur Stuart's education, Miss Larner, I'm sore afraid I'm cheating you, because it seems to me you're doing *us* the favor both ways."

"You're most kind, Goody Guester. But I must ask you one question."

"Ask away. Can't promise I'm too good at answers."

"Goody Guester," said Miss Larner. "Are you aware of the Fugitive Slave Treaty?"

Fear and anger stabbed right through Old Peg's heart, even to hear it mentioned. "A devilish piece of work!"

"Slavery is a devilish work indeed, but the treaty was signed to bring Appalachee into the Compact, and to keep our fragile nation from war with the Crown Colonies. Peace is hardly to be labeled devilish."

"It is when it's a peace that says they can send their damned finders into the free states and bring back captive Black people to be slaves!"

"Perhaps you're right, Goody Guester. Indeed, one could say

that the Fugitive Slave Treaty is not so much a treaty of peace as it is an article of surrender. Nevertheless, it is the law of the land.''

Only now did Old Peg realize what this teacher just done. What could it mean, her bringing up the Fugitive Slave Treaty, excepting to make sure Old Peg knew that Arthur Stuart wasn't safe here, that finders could still come from the Crown Colonies and claim him as the property of some family of White so-called Christians? And that also meant that Miss Larner didn't believe a speck of her story about where Arthur Stuart come from. And if she saw through the lie so easy-like, why was Old Peg fool enough to think everybody else believed it? Why, as far as Old Peg knew, the whole town of Hatrack River had long since guessed that Arthur Stuart was a slave boy what somehow run off and got hisself a White mama.

And if everybody knew, what was to stop somebody from giving report on Arthur Stuart, sending word to the Crown Colonies about a runaway slavechild living in a certain roadhouse near the Hatrack River? The Fugitive Slave Treaty made her adoption of Arthur Stuart plain illegal. They could take the boy right out of her arms and she'd never have the right to see him again. In fact, if she ever went south they could arrest her and hang her under the slave-poaching laws of King Arthur. And thinking of that monstrous King in his lair in Camelot made her remember the unkindest thing of all—that if they ever took Arthur Stuart south, they'd change his name. Why, it'd be high treason in the Crown Colonies, having a slavechild named with the same name as the King. So all of a sudden poor Arthur would find hisself with some other name he never heard of afore. She couldn't help thinking of the boy all confused, somebody calling him and calling him, and whipping him for not coming, but how could he know to come, since nobody called him by his right name?

Her face must've painted a plain picture of all the thoughts going through her head, because Miss Larner walked behind her and put her hands on Old Peg's shoulders.

"You've nought to fear from me, Goody Guester. I come from Philadelphia, where people speak openly of defying that treaty. A young New Englander named Thoreau has made quite a nuisance of himself, preaching that a bad law must be defied, that good citizens must be prepared to go to jail themselves rather than submit to it. It would do your heart good to hear him speak.''

Old Peg doubted that. It only froze her to the heart to think of the treaty at all. Go to jail? What good would that do, if Arthur was being whipped south in chains? No matter what, it was none of Miss Larner's business. "I don't know why you're saying all this, Miss Larner. Arthur Stuart is the freeborn son of a free Black woman, even if she got him on the wrong side of the sheets. The Fugitive Slave Treaty means nothing to me.''

"Then I shall think no more of it, Goody Guester. And now, if you'll forgive me, I'm somewhat weary from traveling, and I had hoped to retire early, though it's still light outside.''

Old Peg sprang to her feet, mighty relieved at not talking anymore about Arthur and the Treaty. "Why, of course. But you ain't hopping into bed without taking a bath, are you? Nothing like a bath for a traveler.''

"I quite agree, Goody Guester. However, I fear my luggage was not copious enough for me to bring my tub along.''

"I'll send Horace over with my spare tub the second I get back, and if you don't mind hotting up your stove there, we can get water from Gertie's well yonder and set it to steaming in no time.''

"Oh, Goody Guester, I fear you'll convince me before the evening's out that I'm in Philadelphia after all. It shall be almost disappointing, for I had steeled myself to endure the rigors of primitive life in the wilderness, and now I find that you are prepared to offer all the convivial blessings of civilization.''

"I'll take it that what you said mostly means thank you, and so I say you're welcome, and I'll be back in no time with Horace and the tub. And don't you dare fetch your own water, at least not today. You just set there and read or philosophate or whatever an educated person does instead of dozing off.''

With that Old Peg was out of the springhouse. She like to flew along the path to the inn. Why, this teacher lady wasn't half so bad as she seemed at first. She might talk a language that Old Peg couldn't hardly understand half the time, but at least she was willing to talk to folks—and she'd teach Arthur at no cost and hold poetry readings in the roadhouse to boot. Best of all, though, best of all she might even be willing to talk to Old Peg sometimes and maybe some of that smartness might rub off on her. Not that smartness was all that much good to a woman like Old Peg, but then, what good was a jewel on a rich lady's finger, either? And if being around this educated eastern spinster gave Old Peg even a jigger more understanding of the great world outside Hatrack River, it was more than Old Peg had dared to hope for in her life. Like daubing just a spot of color on a drab moth's wing. It don't make the moth into a butterfly, but maybe now the moth won't despair and fly into the fire.

Miss Larner watched Old Peg walk away. Mother, she whispered. No, didn't even whisper. Didn't even open her mouth. But her lips pressed together a bit tighter with the *M,* and her tongue shaped the other sounds inside her mouth.

It hurt her, to deceive. She had promised never to lie, and in a sense she wasn't lying even now. The name she had taken, *Larner,* meant nothing more than *teacher,* and since she *was* a teacher, it was as truly her name as Father's name was Guester and Makepeace's name was Smith. And when people asked her questions, she never lied to them, though she did refuse to answer questions that might tell them more than they ought to know, that might set them wondering.

Still, despite her elaborate avoidance of an open lie, she feared that she merely deceived herself. How could she believe that her presence here, so disguised, was anything but a lie?

And yet surely even that deception was the truth, at its root. She was no longer the same person she had been when she was torch of Hatrack River. She was no longer connected to these people in the former ways. If she claimed to be Little Peggy, that would be a deeper lie than her disguise, for they would suppose that she was the girl they once knew, and treat her accordingly. In that sense, her disguise was a reflection of who she really was, at least here and now—educated, aloof, a deliberate spinster, and sexually unavailable to men.

So her disguise was not a lie, surely it was not; it was merely a way to keep a secret, the secret of who she used to be, but was no longer. Her vow was still unbroken.

Mother was long since out of sight in the woods between the springhouse and the inn, but still Peggy looked after her. And if she wanted, Peggy could have seen her even yet, not with her eyes, but with her torch sight, finding Mother's heartfire and moving close, looking tight. Mother, don't you know you have no secrets from your daughter Peggy?

But the fact was that Mother could keep all the secrets she desired. Peggy would not look into her heart. Peggy hadn't come home to be the torch of Hatrack River again. After all these years of study, in which Peggy had read so many books so rapidly that she feared once that she might run out, that there might not be books enough in America to satisfy her—after all these years, there was only one skill she was certain of. She had finally mastered the ability *not* to see inside the hearts of other people unless she wanted to. She had finally tamed her torchy sight.

Oh, she still looked inside other people when she needed to, but she rarely did. Even with the school board, when she had to tame them, it took no more than her knowledge of human nature to guess their present thoughts and deal with them. And as for the futures revealed in the heartfire, she no longer noticed them.

I am not responsible for your futures, none of you. Least of all you, Mother. I have meddled enough in your life, in everyone's lives. If I know all your futures, all you people in Hatrack River, then I have a moral imperative to shape my own actions to help you achieve the happiest possible tomorrow. Yet in so doing, I cease to exist myself. My own future becomes the only one with no hope, and why should that be? By shutting my eyes to what *will* happen, I become like you, able to live my life according to my guesses at what *may* happen. I couldn't guarantee you happiness anyway, and this way at least I also have a chance of it myself.

Even as she justified herself, she felt the same sour guilt well up inside her. By rejecting her knack, she was sinning against the God that gave it to her. That great magister Erasmus, he had taught as much: Your knack is your destiny. You'll never know joy except through following the path laid out before you by what is inside you. But Peggy refused to submit to that cruel discipline. Her childhood had already been stolen from her, and to what end? Her mother disliked her, the people of Hatrack River feared her, often hated her, even as they came to her again and again, seeking answers to their selfish, petty questions, blaming her if any seeming ill came into their lives, but never thanking her for saving them from dire events, for they never knew how she had saved them because the evils never happened.

It wasn't gratitude she wanted. It was freedom. It was a lightening of her burden. She had started bearing it too young, and they had shown her no mercy in their exploitation. Their own fears always outweighed her need for a carefree girlhood. Did any of them understand that? Did any of them know how gratefully she left them all behind?

Now Peggy the torch was back, but they'd never know it. I did not come back for *you*, people of Hatrack River, nor did I come to serve your children. I came back for one pupil only, the man who stands even now at the forge, his heartfire burning so brightly that I can see it even in my sleep, even in my dreams. I came back having learned all that the world can teach, so I in turn can help that young man achieve a labor that means more than any one of us. *That* is my destiny, if I have one.

Along the way I'll do what other good I can—I'll teach Arthur Stuart, I'll try to fulfill the dreams his brave young mother died for; I'll teach all the other children as much as they're willing to learn, during those certain hours of the day that I've contracted for; I'll bring such poetry and learning into the town of Hatrack River as you're willing to receive.

Perhaps you don't desire poetry as much as you would like to have my torchy knowledge of your possible futures, but I daresay poetry will do you far more good. For knowing the future only makes you timid and complacent by turns, while poetry can shape you into the kind of souls who can face any future with boldness and wisdom and nobility, so that you need not know the future at all, so that any future will be an opportunity for greatness, if you have greatness in you. Can I teach you to see in yourselves what Gray saw?

> *Some heart once pregnant with celestial fire,*
> *Hands that the rod of empire might have swayed,*
> *Or waked to ecstasy the living lyre.*

But she doubted that any of these ordinary souls in Hatrack River were really mute, inglorious Miltons. Pauley Wiseman was no secret Caesar. He might wish for it, but he lacked the wit and self-control. Whitley Physicker was no Hippocrates, however much he tried to be a healer and conciliator—his love of luxury undid him, and like many other well-meaning physician he had come to work for what the fee could buy, and not for joy of the work itself.

She picked up the water bucket that stood by the door. Weary as she was, she would not allow herself to seem helpless even for a moment. Father and Mother would come and find Miss Larner had already done for herself all that she could do before the tub arrived.

Ching-ching-ching. Didn't Alvin rest? Didn't he know the sun was boiling the western sky, turning it red before sinking out of sight behind the trees? As she walked down the hill toward the smithy, she felt as if she might suddenly begin to run, to fly down the hill to the smithy as she had flown the day that Alvin was born. It was raining that day, and Alvin's mother was stuck in a wagon in the river. It was Peggy who saw them all, their heartfires off in the blackness of the rain and the flooding river. It was Peggy who gave alarm, and then Peggy who stood watch over the birthing, seeing Alvin's futures in his heartfire, the brightest heartfire she had ever seen or would ever see in all her life. It was Peggy who saved his life then by peeling the caul away from his face; and, by using bits of that caul, Peggy who had saved his life so many times over the years. She might turn her back on being torch of Hatrack River, but she'd never turn her back on *him*.

But she stopped herself halfway down the hill. What was she thinking of? She could not go to him, not now, not yet. He had to come to *her*. Only that way could she become his teacher; only that way was there a chance of becoming anything more than that.

She turned and walked across the face of the hill, slanting down and eastward toward the well. She had watched Alvin dig the well—both wells—and for once she was helpless to help him when the Unmaker came. Alvin's own anger and destructiveness had called his enemy, and there was nothing Peggy could do with the caul to save him that time. She could only watch as he purged the unmaking that was inside himself, and so defeated, for a time, the Unmaker who stalked him on the outside. Now this well stood as a monument both to Alvin's power and to his frailty.

She dropped the copper bucket into the well, and the windlass clattered as the rope unwound. A muffled splash. She waited a moment for the bucket to fill, then wound it upward. It arrived brimming. She meant to pour it out into the wooden bucket she brought with her, but instead she brought the copper bucket to her lips and drank from the cold heavy load of water that it bore. So many years she had waited to taste that water, the water that Alvin tamed the night he tamed himself. She had been so afraid, watching him all night, and when at last in the morning he filled up the first vengeful hole he dug, she wept in relief. This water wasn't salty, but still it tasted to her like her own tears.

The hammer was silent. As always, she found Alvin's heartfire at once, without even trying. He was leaving the smithy, coming outside. Did he know she was there? No. He always came for water when he finished his work for the day. Of course she could not turn to him, not yet, not until she actually heard his step. Yet, though she knew he was coming and listened for him, she couldn't hear him; he moved as silently as a squirrel on a limb. Not until he spoke did he make a sound.

"Pretty good water, ain't it?"

She turned around to face him. Turned too quickly, too eagerly—the rope still held the bucket, so it lurched out of her hands, splashed her with water, and clattered back down into the well.

"I'm Alvin, you remember? Didn't mean to frighten you, Ma'am. Miss Larner."

"I foolishly forgot the bucket was tied," she said. "I'm used to pumps and taps, I'm afraid. Open wells are not common in Philadelphia."

She turned back to the well to draw the bucket up again.

"Here, let me," he said.

"There's no need. I can wind it well enough."

"But why should you, Miss Larner, when I'm glad to do it for you?"

She stepped aside and watched as he cranked the windlass with one hand, as easily as a child might swing a rope. The bucket fairly flew to the top of the well. She looked into his heartfire, just dipped in, to see if he was showing off for her. He was not. He could not see how massive his own shoulders were, how his muscles danced under the skin as his arm moved. He could not even see the peacefulness of his own face, the same quiet repose that one might see in the face of a fearless stag. There was no watchfulness in him. Some people had darting eyes, as if they had to be alert for danger, or perhaps for prey. Others looked intently at the task at hand, concentrating on what they were doing. But Alvin had a quiet distance, as if he had no particular concern about what anyone else or he himself might be doing, but instead dwelt on inward thoughts that no one else could hear. Again the words of Gray's *Elegy* played out in her mind.

> *Far from the madding crowd's ignoble strife,*
> *Their sober wishes never learned to stray;*
> *Along the cool, sequestered vale of life*
> *They kept the noiseless tenor of their way.*

Poor Alvin. When I'm done with you, there'll be no cool sequestered vale. You'll look back on your prenticeship as the last peaceful days of your life.

He gripped the full, heavy bucket with one hand on the rim, and easily tipped it to pour it out into the bucket she had brought, which he held in his other hand; he did it as lightly and easily as a housewife pours cream from one cup into another. What if those hands as lightly and easily held my arms? Would he break me without meaning to, being so strong? Would I feel manacled in his irresistible grasp? Or would he burn me up in the white heat of his heartfire?

She reached out for her bucket.

"Please let me carry it, Ma'am. Miss Larner."

"There's no need."

"I know I'm dirtied up, Miss Larner, but I can carry it to your door and set it inside without messing anything."

Is my disguise so monstrously aloof that you think I refuse your help out of excessive cleanliness? "I only meant that I didn't want to make you work anymore today. You've helped me enough already for one day."

He looked straight into her eyes, and now he lost that peaceful expression. There was even a bit of anger in his eyes. "If you're afraid I'll want you to pay me, you needn't have no fear of that. If this is your dollar, you can have it back. I never wanted it." He held out to her the coin that Whitley Physicker had tossed him from the carriage.

"I reproved Dr. Physicker at the time. I thought it insulting that *he* should presume to pay you for the service you did me out of pure gallantry. It cheapened both of us, I thought, for him to act as if the events of this morning were worth exactly one dollar."

His eyes had softened now.

Peggy went on in her Miss Larner voice. "But you must forgive Dr. Physicker. He is uncomfortable with wealth, and looks for opportunities to share it with others. He has not yet learned how to do it with perfect tact."

"Oh, it's no never mind now, Miss Larner, seeing how it didn't come from you." He put the coin back in his pocket and started to carry the full bucket up the hill toward the house.

It was plain he was unaccustomed to walking with a lady. His strides were far too long, his pace too quick, for her to keep up with him. She couldn't even walk the same route he took—he seemed oblivious to the degree of slope. He was like a child, not an adult, taking the most direct route even if it meant unnecessary clambering over obstacles.

And yet I'm barely five years older than he is. Have I come to believe my own disguise? At twenty-three, am I already thinking and acting and living like a woman of twice that age? Didn't I once love to walk just as he does, over the most difficult ground, for the sheer love of the exertion and accomplishment?

Nevertheless, she walked the easier path, skirting the hill and then climbing up where the slope was longer and gentler. He was already there, waiting at the door.

"Why didn't you open the door and set the bucket inside? The door isn't locked," she said.

"Begging your pardon, Miss Larner, but this is a door that asks not to be opened, whether it's locked or not."

So, she thought, he wants to make sure I know about the hidden hexes he put in the locks. Not many people could see a hidden hex—nor could she, for that matter. She wouldn't have known about them if she hadn't watched him put the hexes in the lock. But of course she couldn't very well tell him *that*. So she asked, "Oh, is there some protection here that I can't see?"

"I just put a couple of hexes into the lock. Nothing much, but it should make it fairly safe here. And there's a hex in the top of the stove, so I don't think you have to worry much about sparks getting free."

"You have a great deal of confidence in your hexery, Alvin."

"I do them pretty good. Most folks knows a few hexes, anyway, Miss Larner. But not many smiths can put them into the iron. I just wanted you to know."

He wanted her to know more than that, of course. So she gave him the response he hoped for. "I take it, then, that you did some of the work on this springhouse."

"I done the windows, Miss Larner. They glide up and down sweet as you please, and there's pegs to hold them in place. And the stove, and the locks, and all the iron fittings. And my helper, Arthur Stuart, he scraped down the walls."

For a young man who seemed artless, he was steering the conversation rather well. For a moment she thought of toying with him, of pretending not to make the connections he was counting on, just to see how he handled it. But no—he was only planning to ask her to do what she came here to do. There was no reason to make it hard for him. The teaching itself would be hard enough. "Arthur Stuart," she said. "He must be the same boy that Goody Guester asked me to teach privately."

"Oh, did she already ask you? Or shouldn't I ask?"

"I have no intention of keeping it a secret, Alvin. Yes, I'll be teaching Arthur Stuart."

"I'm glad of that, Miss Larner. He's the smartest boy you ever knew. And a mimic! Why, he can hear anything once and say it back to you in your own voice. You'll hardly believe it even when he's a-doing it."

"I only hope he doesn't choose to play such a game when I'm teaching him."

Alvin frowned. "Well, it isn't rightly a game, Miss Larner. It's just something he does without meaning to in particular. I mean to say, if he starts talking back to you in your own voice, he isn't making fun or nothing. It's just that when he hears something he remembers it voice and all, if you know what I mean. He can't split them up and remember the words without the voice that gave them."

"I'll keep that in mind."

In the distance, Peggy heard a door slam closed. She cast out and looked, finding Father's and Mother's heartfires coming toward her. They were quarreling, of course, but if Alvin was to ask her, he'd have to do it quickly.

"Was there something else you wanted to say to me, Alvin?"

This was the moment he'd been leading up to, but now he was turning shy on her. "Well, I had some idea of asking you—but you got to understand, I didn't carry the water for you so you'd feel obliged or nothing. I would've done that anyway, for anybody, and as for what happened today, I didn't rightly know that you were the teacher. I mean maybe I might've guessed, but I just didn't think of it. So what I done was just itself, and you don't owe me nothing."

"I think I'll decide how much gratitude I owe, Alvin. What did you want to ask me?"

"Of course you'll be busy with Arthur Stuart, so I can't expect you to have much time free, maybe just one day a week, just an hour even. It could be on Saturdays, and you could charge whatever you want, my master's been giving me free time and I've saved up some of my own earnings, and—''

''Are you asking me to tutor you, Alvin?''

Alvin didn't know what the word meant.

''Tutor you. Teach you privately.''

''Yes, Miss Larner.''

''The charge is fifty cents a week, Alvin. And I wish you to come at the same time as Arthur Stuart. Arrive when he does, and leave when he does.''

''But how can you teach us both at once?''

''I daresay you could benefit from some of the lessons I'll be giving him, Alvin. And when I have him writing or ciphering, I can converse with you.''

''I just don't want to cheat him out of his lesson time.''

''Think clearly, Alvin. It would not be proper for you to take lessons with me alone. I may be somewhat older than you, but there are those who will search for fault in me, and giving private instruction to a young bachelor would certainly give cause for tongues to wag. Arthur Stuart will be present at all your lessons, and the door of the springhouse will stand open.''

''We could go up and you could teach me at the roadhouse.''

''Alvin. I have told you the terms. Do you wish to engage me as your tutor?''

''Yes, Miss Larner.'' He dug into his pocket and pulled out a coin. ''Here's a dollar for the first two weeks.''

Peggy looked at the coin. ''I thought you meant to give this dollar back to Dr. Physicker.''

''I wouldn't want to make him uncomfortable about having so much money, Miss Larner.'' He grinned.

Shy he may be, but he can't stay serious for long. There'll always be a tease in him, just below the surface, and eventually it will always come out.

''No, I imagine not,'' said Miss Larner. ''Lessons will begin next week. Thank you for your help.''

At that moment, Father and Mother came up the path. Father

carried a large tub over his head, and he staggered under the weight. Alvin immediately ran to help—or, rather, to simply take the tub and carry it himself.

That was how Peggy saw her father's face for the first time in more than six years—red, sweating, as he puffed from the labor of carrying the tub. And angry, too, or at least sullen. Even though Mother had no doubt assured him that the teacher lady wasn't half so arrogant as she seemed at first, still Father was resentful of this stranger living in the springhouse, a place that belonged only to his long-lost daughter.

Peggy longed to call out to him, call him Father, and assure him that it *was* his daughter who dwelt here now, that all his labor to make a home of this old place was really a gift of love to her. How it comforted her to know how much he loved her, that he had not forgotten her after all these years; yet it also made her heart break for him, that she couldn't name herself to him truly, not yet, not if she was to accomplish all she needed to. She would have to do with him what she was already trying to do with Alvin and with Mother—not reclaim old loves and debts, but win new love and friendship.

She could not come home as a daughter of this place, not even to Father, who alone would purely rejoice at her coming. She had to come home as a stranger. For surely that's what she was, even if she had no disguise, for after three years of one kind of learning in Dekane and another three of schooling and study, she was no longer Little Peggy, the quiet, sharp-tongued torch; she had long since become something else. She had learned many graces under the tutelage of Mistress Modesty; she had learned many other things from books and teachers. She was not who she had been. It would be as much a lie to say, Father, I am your daughter Little Peggy, as it was to say what she said now: "Mr. Guester, I am your new tenant, Miss Larner. I'm very glad to meet you."

He huffed up to her and put out his hand. Despite his misgivings, despite the way he had avoided meeting her when first she arrived at the roadhouse an hour or so past, he was too much the consummate innkeeper to refuse to greet her with courtesy—or at least the rough country manners that passed for courtesy in this frontier town.

"Pleased to meet you, Miss Larner. I trust your accommodation is satisfactory?"

It made her a little sad, to hear him trying fancy language on her, the way he talked to those customers he thought of as "dignitaries," meaning that he believed their station in life to be above his. *I've learned much, Father, and this above all: that no station in life is above any other, if it's occupied by someone with a good heart.*

As to whether Father's heart was good, Peggy believed it but refused to look. She had known his heartfire far too well in years past. If she looked too closely now, she might find things a daughter had no right to see. She'd been too young to control herself when she explored his heartfire all those years ago; in the innocence of childhood she had learned things that made both innocence and childhood impossible. Now, though, with her knack better tamed, she could at last give him privacy in his own heart. She owed him and Mother that.

Not to mention that she owed it to herself not to know *exactly* what they thought and felt about everything.

They set up the tub in her little house. Mother had brought another bucket and a kettle, and now Father and Alvin both set to toting water up from the well, while Mother boiled some on the stove. When the bath was ready, she sent the men away; then Peggy sent Mother away as well, though not without considerable argument. "I am grateful for your solicitude," Peggy said, "but it is my custom to bathe in utter privacy. You have been exceptionally kind, and as I now take my bath, alone, you may be sure I will think of you gratefully every moment."

The stream of high-sounding language was more than even Mother could resist. At last the door was closed and locked, the curtains drawn. Peggy removed her traveling gown, which was heavy with dust and sweat, and then peeled away her chemise and her pantalets, which clung hotly to her skin. It was one of the benefits of her disguise, that she need not trouble herself with corsetry. No one expected a spinster of her supposed age to have the perversely slender waist of those poor young victims of fashion who bound themselves until they could not breathe.

Last of all she removed her amulets, the three that hung around her neck and the one enwrapped with her hair. The amulets were hard-won, and not just because they were the new, expensive ones that acted on what others actually saw, and not just on their opinion of it. It had taken four visits before the hexman believed that she really did want to appear ugly. "A girl so lovely as you, you don't need my art," he said it over and over again, until she finally took him by the shoulders and said, "That's why I need it! To make me *stop* being beautiful." He gave in, but kept muttering that it was a sin to cover what God created well.

God or Mistress Modesty, thought Peggy. I *was* beautiful in Mistress Modesty's house. Am I beautiful now, when no one sees me but myself, I who am least likely to admire?

Naked at last, herself at last, she knelt beside the tub and ducked her head to begin the washing of her hair. Immersed in water, hot as it was, she felt the same old freedom she had felt so long ago in the springhouse, the wet isolation in which no heartfires intruded, so she was truly herself alone, and had a chance of knowing what her self might actually be.

There was no mirror in the springhouse. Nor had she brought one. Nevertheless, she knew when her bath was done and she toweled herself before the stove, already sweating in the steamy room, in the early August evening—she knew that she *was* beautiful, as Mistress Modesty had taught her how to be; knew that if Alvin could see her as she really was, he would desire her, not for wisdom, but for the more casual and shallow love that any man feels for a woman who delights his eyes. So, just as she had once hidden from him so he wouldn't marry her for pity, now she hid from him so he wouldn't marry her for boyish love. This self, the smooth and youthful body, would remain invisible to him, so that her truer self, the sharp and well-filled mind, might entice the finest man in him, the man that would be, not a lover, but a Maker.

If only she could somehow disguise his body from her own eyes, so that she would not have to imagine his touch, as gentle as the touch of air on her skin as she moved across the room.

✤ 16 ✤

Property

THE BLACKS STARTED in a-howling before the roosters got up. Cavil Planter didn't get up right away; the sound of it sort of fit into his dream. Howling Blacks figured in his dreams pretty common these days. Anyway it finally woke him, and he bounded up out of bed. Barely light outside; he had to open the curtain to get light enough to find his trousers. He could make out shadows moving down near the slave quarters, but couldn't see what all was going on. He thought the worst, of course, and pulled his shotgun down from the rack on his bedroom wall. Slaveowners, in case you didn't guess, always keep their firearms in the same room where they sleep.

Out in the hall, he nearly bumped into somebody. She screeched. It took Cavil a moment to realize it was his wife, Dolores. Sometimes he forgot she knew how to walk, seeing how she only left her room at certain times. He just wasn't used to seeing her out of bed, moving around the house without a slave or two to lean on.

"Hush now, Dolores, it's me, Cavil."

"Oh, what is it, Cavil! What's happening out there!" She was clinging to his arm, so he couldn't move on.

"Don't you think I can tell you better if you let me go find out?"

She hung on tighter. "Don't do it, Cavil! Don't go out there alone! They might kill you!"

"Why would they kill me? Am I not a righteous master? Will the Lord not protect me?" All the same, he felt a thrill of fear. Could this be the slave revolt that every master feared but none spoke of? He realized now that this very thought had been lingering at the back of his mind since he first woke up. Now Dolores had put it into words. "I have my shotgun," said Cavil. "Don't worry about me."

"I'm afraid," said Dolores.

"You know what *I'm* afraid of? That you'll stumble in the dark and really hurt yourself. Go back to bed, so I don't have to worry about you while I'm outside."

Somebody started pounding at the door.

"Master! Master!" cried a slave. "We need you, Master!"

"Now see? That's Fat Fox," said Cavil. "If it was a revolt, my love, they'd strangle him first off, before they ever came after me."

"Is that supposed to make me feel better?" she asked.

"Master! Master!"

"To bed," said Cavil.

For a moment her hand rested on the hard cold barrel of the shotgun. Then she turned and, like a pale grey ghost in the darkness of the hall, she disappeared into the shadows toward her room.

Fat Fox was near to jumping up and down he was so agitated. Cavil looked at him, as always, with disgust. Even though Cavil depended on Fat Fox to let him know which slaves talked ugly behind his back, Cavil didn't have to like him. There wasn't a hope in heaven of saving the soul of any full-blood Black. They were all born in deep corruption, like as if they embraced original sin and sucked more of it with their mother's milk. It's a wonder their milk wasn't black with all the foulness that must be in it. I wish it wasn't such a slow process, turning the Black race White enough to be worth trying to save their souls.

"It's that Salamandy girl, Master," said Fat Fox.

"Is her baby coming early?" said Cavil.

"Oh no," said Fat Fox. "No, no, it ain't coming, no Master. Oh please come on down. It ain't that gun you needing, Master. It's your big old buck knife I think."

"I'll decide that," said Cavil. If a Black suggests you ought to put your gun away, that's when you hang onto it tightest of all.

He strode toward the slave women's quarters. It was getting light enough by now that he could see the ground, could see the Blacks all slinking here and there in the dark, watching him, white eyes watching. That was a mercy from the Lord God, making their eyes white, else you couldn't see them at all in the shadows.

There was a passel of women all outside the door to the cabin where Salamandy slept. Her being so close to her time, she didn't have to do any field work these days, and she got a bed with a fine mattress. Nobody could say Cavil Planter didn't take care of his breeding stock.

One of the women—in the darkness he couldn't tell who, but from the voice he thought it was maybe Coppy, the one baptized as Agnes but who chose to call herself after the copperhead rattler—anyway she cried out, "Oh, Master, you got to let us bleed a chicken on this one!"

"No heathen abominations shall be practiced on my plantation," said Cavil sternly. But he knew now that Salamandy was dead. Only a month from delivery, and she was dead. It stabbed his heart deep. One child less. One breeding ewe gone. O God have mercy on me! How can I serve thee aright if you take away my best concubine?

It smelled like a sick horse in the room, from her bowel opening up as she died. She'd hung herself with the bedsheet. Cavil damned himself for a fool, giving her such a thing. Here he meant it as a sign of special favor, her being on her sixth half-White baby, to let her have a sheet on her mattress, and now she turned around and answered him like this.

Her feet dangled not three inches from the floor. She must have stood on the bed and then stepped off. Even now, as she swayed slightly in the breeze of his movement in the room, her feet bumped into the bedstead. It took a second or two for Cavil to realize what that meant. Since her neck wasn't broke, she must have been a long time strangling, and the whole time the bed was inches away, and she *knew* it. The whole time, she could have stopped strangling at any time. Could have changed her mind. This was a woman who wanted to die. No, wanted to *kill*. Murder that baby she was carrying.

Proof again how strong these Blacks were in their wickedness. Rather than give birth to a half-White child with a hope of salvation, she'd strangle to death herself. Was there no limit to their perversity? How could a godly man save such creatures?

"She kill herself, Master!" cried the woman who had spoke before. He turned to look at her, and now it was light enough to see for sure that it was Coppy talking. "She waiting for tomorrow night to kill somebody else, less we bleed a chicken on her!"

"It makes me ill, to think you'd use this poor woman's death as an excuse to roast a chicken out of turn. She'll have a decent burial, and her soul will *not* hurt anyone, though as a suicide she will surely burn in hell forever."

At his words Coppy wailed in grief. The other women joined in her keening. Cavil had Fat Fox set a group of young bucks digging a grave—not in the regular slaveyard, of course, since as a suicide she couldn't lie in consecrated ground. Out among the trees, with no marker, as befit a beast that took the life of her own young.

She was in the ground before nightfall. Since she was a suicide, Cavil couldn't very well ask the Baptist preacher or the Catholic priest to come help with it. In fact, he figured to say the words himself, only it happened that tonight was the night he'd already invited a traveling preacher to supper. That preacher showed up early, and the house slaves sent him around back where he found the burial in progress and offered to help.

"Oh, you don't need to do that," said Cavil.

"Let it never be said that Reverend Philadelphia Thrower did not extend Christian love to all the children of God—White or Black, male or female, saint or sinner."

The slaves perked up at that, and so did Cavil—for the opposite reason. That was Emancipationist talk, and Cavil felt a sudden fear that he had invited the devil into his own house by bringing this Presbyterian preacher. Nevertheless, it would probably do much to quiet the Blacks' superstitious fears if he allowed the rites to be administered by a real preacher. And sure enough, when the words were said and the grave was covered, they all seemed right quiet —none of that ghastly howling.

At dinner, the preacher—Thrower, that was his name—eased Cavil's fears considerably. "I believe that it is part of God's great plan for the Black people to be brought to America in chains. Like the children of Israel, who had to suffer years of bondage to the Egyptians, these Blacks souls are under the Lord's own lash, shaping them to His own purposes. The Emancipationists understand one truth—that God loves his Black children—but they misunderstand everything else. Why, if they had their way and freed all the slaves at once, it would accomplish the devil's purpose, not God's, for without slavery the Blacks have no hope of rising out of their savagery."

"Now, that sounds downright theological," said Cavil.

"Don't the Emancipationists understand that every Black who escapes from his rightful master into the North is doomed to eternal damnation, him and all his children? Why, they might as well have remained in Africa as go north. The Whites up north hate Blacks, as well they should, since only the most evil and proud and stiff-necked dare to offend God by leaving their masters. But you here in Appalachee and in the Crown Colonies, you are the ones who truly love the Black man, for only you are willing to take responsibility for these wayward children and help them progress on the road to full humanity."

"You may be a Presbyterian, Reverend Thrower, but you know the true religion."

"I'm glad to know I'm in the home of a godly man, Brother Cavil."

"I hope I am your brother, Reverend Thrower."

And that's how the talk went on, the two of them liking each other better and better as the evening wore. By nightfall, when they sat on the porch cooling off, Cavil began to think he had met the first man to whom he might tell some part of his great secret.

Cavil tried to bring it up casual. "Reverend Thrower, do you think the Lord God speaks to any men today?"

Thrower's voice got all solemn. "I know He does."

"Do you think He might even speak to a common man like me?"

"You mustn't hope for it, Brother Cavil," said Thrower, "for the Lord goes where He will, and not where we wish. Yet I do know that it's possible for even the humblest man to have a—visitor."

Cavil felt a trembling in his belly. Why, Thrower sounded like he already knew Cavil's secret. But still he didn't blurt it out all at once. "You know what I think?" said Cavil. "I think that the Lord God can't appear in his true form, because his glory would kill a natural man."

"Oh, indeed," said Thrower. "As when Moses craved a vision of the Lord, and the Lord covered his eyes with His hand, only letting Moses see His back parts as he passed by."

"I mean, what if a man like me saw the Lord Jesus himself, only not looking like any painting of him, but instead looking like an overseer. I reckon that a man sees only what will make him understand the power of God, not the true majesty of the Lord."

Thrower nodded wisely. "It may well be," he said. "That's a plausible explanation. Or it might be that you only saw an angel."

There it was—that simple. From "what if a man like me" to Thrower saying "you saw an angel." That's how much alike these two men were. So Cavil told the whole story, for the first time ever, near seven years after it happened.

When he was done, Thrower took his hand and held it in a brotherly grip, looking him in the eye with a fierce-looking kind of expression. "To think of your sacrifice, mingling your flesh with that of these Black women, in order to serve the Lord. How many children?"

"Twenty-five that got born alive. You helped me bury the twenty-sixth inside Salamandy's belly this evening."

"Where are all these hopeful half-White youngsters?"

"Oh, that's half the labor I'm doing," said Cavil. "Till the Fugitive Slave Treaty, I used to sell them all south as soon as I could, so they'd grow up there and spread White blood throughout the Crown Colonies. Each one will be a missionary through his seed. Of course, the last few I've kept here. It ain't the safest thing, neither, Reverend Thrower. All my breeding-age stock is pure Black, and folks are bound to wonder where these mixup children come from. So far, though, my overseer, Lashman, he keeps his mouth shut if he notices, and nobody else ever sees them.''

Thrower nodded, but it was plain his mind was on something else. ''Only twenty-*five* of these children?''

''It's the best I could do,'' said Cavil. ''Even a Black woman can't make a baby right off after a birthing.''

''I meant—you see, I also had a—visitation. It's the reason why I came here, came touring through Appalachee. I was told that I would meet a farmer who also knew my Visitor, and who had produced twenty-six living gifts to God.''

''Twenty-*six*.''

''Living.''

''Well, you see—well, ain't that just the way of it. You see, I wasn't including in my tally the very first one born, because his mother run off and stole him from me a few days before he was due to be sold. I had to refund the money in cash to the buyer, and it was no good tracking, the dogs couldn't pick up her scent. Word among the slaves was that she turned into a blackbird and *flew,* but you know the tales they tell.''

''So—twenty-six then. And tell me this—is there some reason why the name 'Hagar' should mean anything to you?''

Cavil gasped. ''No one knows I called the mother by that name!''

''My Visitor told me that Hagar had stolen away your first gift.''

''It's Him. You've seen Him, too.''

''To me he comes as—not an overseer. More like a scientist—a man of unguessable wisdom. Because *I* am a scientist, I imagine, besides my vocation as a minister. I have always supposed that He was a mere angel—listen to me, a *mere* angel—because I dared not hope that He was—was the Master himself. But now what you tell me— could it be that we have both entertained the presence of our Lord? Oh, Cavil, how can I doubt it? Why else would the Lord have brought us together like this? It means that I—that I'm forgiven.''

''Forgiven?''

At Cavil's question, Thrower's face darkened.

Cavil hastened to reassure him. ''No, you don't need to tell me if you don't want.''

''I—it is almost unbearable to think of it. But now that I am clearly deemed acceptable—or at least, now that I've been given another chance—Brother Cavil, once I was given a mission to perform, one as dark and difficult and secret as your own. Except that where you have had the courage and strength to prevail, I failed. I tried, but I had not wit or vigor enough to overcome the power of the devil. I thought I was rejected, cast off. That's why I became a traveling preacher, for I felt myself unworthy to take a pulpit of my own. But now—''

Cavil nodded, holding the man's hands as tears flowed down his cheek.

At last Thrower looked up at him. ''How do you suppose our— Friend—meant me to help you in your work?''

''I can't say,'' said Cavil. ''But there's only one way I can think of, offhand.''

''Brother Cavil, I'm not sure if I can take upon myself that loathsome duty.''

''In my experience, the Lord strengthens a man, and makes it— bearable.''

''But in my case, Brother Cavil—you see, I've never known a woman, as the Bible speaks of it. Only once have my lips touched a woman's, and that was against my will.''

''Then I'll do my best to help you. How if we pray together good and long, and then I show you once?''

Well, that seemed like the best idea either of them could think of right offhand, and so they did it, and it turned out Reverend Thrower was a quick learner. Cavil felt a great sense of relief to have someone else join in, not to mention a kind of peculiar pleasure at having somebody watch him and then watching the other fellow in turn. It was a powerful sort of brotherhood, to have their seed mingled in the same vessel, so to speak. Like Reverend Thrower said, ''When this field comes to harvest, Brother Cavil, we shall not guess whose seed came unto ripeness, for the Lord gave us this field together, for this time.''

Oh, and then Reverend Thrower asked the girl's name. "Well, we baptized her as 'Hepzibah,' but she goes by the name 'Roach.' "

"Roach!"

"They all take animal names. I reckon she doesn't have too high an opinion of herself."

At that, Thrower just reached over and took Roach's hand and patted it, as kindly a gesture as if Thrower and Roach was man and wife, an idea that made Cavil almost laugh right out. "Now, Hepzibah, you must use your Christian name," said Thrower, "and not such a debasing animal name."

Roach just looked at him wide-eyed, lying there curled up on the mattress.

"Why doesn't she answer me, Brother Cavil?"

"Oh, they never talk during this. I beat that out of them early—they always tried to talk me out of doing it. I figure better to have no words than have them say what the devil wants me to hear."

Thrower turned back to the woman. "But now I ask you to speak to me, Roach. You won't say devil words, will you?"

In answer, Roach's eyes wandered upward to where part of a bedsheet was still knotted around a rafter. It had been raggedly hacked off below the knot.

Thrower's face got kind of sick-looking. "You mean this is the room where—the girl we buried—"

"This room has the best bed," said Cavil. "I didn't want us doing this on a straw pallet if we didn't have to."

Thrower said nothing. He just left the room, pretty quick, plunging outside into the darkness. Cavil sighed, picked up the lantern, and followed him. He found Thrower leaning over the pump. He could hear Roach skittering out of the room where Salamandy died, heading for her own quarters, but he didn't give no never mind to her. It was Thrower—surely the man wasn't so beside himself that he'd throw up on the drinking water!

"I'm all right," whispered Thrower. "I just—the same room—I'm not at all superstitious, you understand. It just seemed disrespectful to the dead."

These northerners. Even when they understood somewhat about

slavery, they couldn't get rid of their notion of Blacks as if they was people. Would you stop using a room just because a mouse died there, or you once killed a spider on the wall? Do you burn down your stable just because your favorite horse died there?

Anyway, Thrower got himself together, hitched up his trousers and buttoned them up proper, and they went back into the house. Brother Cavil put Thrower in their guest room, which wasn't all that much used, so there was a cloud of dust when Cavil slapped the blanket. "Should have known the house slaves'd be slacking in this room," said Brother Cavil.

"No matter," said Thrower. "On a night this warm, I'll need no blanket."

On the way down the hall to his own bedroom, Cavil paused a moment to listen for his wife's breathing. As sometimes happened, he could hear her whimpering softly in her bedroom. The pain must be bad indeed. Oh Lord, thought Cavil, how many more times must I do Thy bidding before You'll have mercy and heal my Dolores? But he didn't go in to her—there was nothing he could do to help her, besides prayer, and he'd need his sleep. This had been a late night, and tomorrow had work enough.

Sure enough, Dolores had had a bad night—she was still asleep at breakfast time. So Cavil ended up eating with Thrower. The preacher put away an astonishingly large portion of sausage and grits. When his plate was clean for the third time, he looked at Cavil and smiled. "The Lord's service can give a man quite an appetite!" They both had a good laugh at that.

After breakfast, they walked outside. It happened they went near the woods where Salamandy had been buried. Thrower suggested looking at the grave, or else Cavil probably never would have known what the Blacks did in the night. There were footprints all over the grave itself, which was churned into mud. Now the drying mud was covered with ants.

"Ants!" said Thrower. "They can't possibly smell the body under the ground."

"No," said Cavil. "What they're finding is fresher and right on top. Look at that—cut-up entrails."

"They didn't—exhume her body and—"

"Not *her* guts, Reverend Thrower. Probably a squirrel or black-bird or something. They did a devil sacrifice last night."

Thrower immediately began murmuring a prayer.

"They know I forbid such things," said Cavil. "By evening, the proof of it would no doubt be gone. They're disobeying me behind my back. I won't have it."

"Now I understand the magnitude of the work you slaveowners have. The devil has an iron grip upon their souls."

"Well, never you mind. They'll pay for it today. They want blood dropped on her grave? It'll be their own. Mr. Lashman! Where are you! Mr. Lashman!"

The overseer had only just arrived for the day's work.

"A little half-holiday for the Blacks this morning, Mr. Lash-man," said Cavil.

Lashman didn't ask why. "Which ones you want whipped?"

"All of them. Ten lashes each. Except the pregnant women, of course. But even they—one lash for each of them, across the thighs. And all to watch."

"They get a bit unruly, watching it, sir," said Lashman.

"Reverend Thrower and I will watch also," said Cavil.

While Lashman was off assembling the slaves, Thrower mur-mured something about not really wanting to watch.

"It's the Lord's work," said Cavil. "I have stomach enough to watch any act of righteousness. I thought after last night that you did too."

So they watched together as each slave in turn was whipped, the blood dripping down onto Salamandy's grave. After a while Thrower didn't even flinch. Cavil was glad to see it—the man wasn't weak, after all, just a little soft from his upbringing in Scotland and his life in the North.

Afterward, as Reverend Thrower prepared to be on his way—he had promised to preach in a town a half-day's ride south—he happened to ask Cavil a question.

"I noticed that all your slaves seem—not old, you understand, but not young, either."

Cavil shrugged. "It's the Fugitive Slave Treaty. Even though my farm's prospering, I can't buy or sell any slaves—we're part of the United States now. Most folks keep up by breeding, but you know all my pickaninnies ended up south, till lately. And now I've lost me another breeder, so I'm down to five women now. Salamandy was the best. The others don't have so many years of babies left in them."

"It occurs to me," said Thrower. He paused in thought.

"What occurs to you?"

"I've traveled a lot in the North, Brother Cavil, and in most every town in Hio and Suskwahenny and Irrakwa and Wobbish, there's a family or two of Blacks. Now, you know and I know that they didn't grow on northern trees."

"All runaways."

"Some, no doubt, have their freedom legally. But many— certainly there are many runaways. Now, I understand that it's a custom for every slaveowner to keep a cachet of hair and nail clippings and—"

"Oh, yes, we take them from the minute they're born or the minute we buy them. For the Finders."

"Exactly."

"But we can't exactly send the Finders to walk every foot of ground in the whole North, hoping to run into one particular runaway buck. It'd cost more than the price of the slave."

"It seems to me that the price of slaves has gone up lately."

"If you mean that we can't buy one at any price—"

"That's what I mean, Brother Cavil. And what if the Finders don't have to go blindly through the North, relying on chance? What if you arranged to hire people in the North to scour the papers and take note of the name and age of every Black they see there? Then the Finders could go armed with information."

Well, that idea was so good that it stopped Cavil right short. "There's got to be something wrong with that idea, or somebody'd already be doing it."

"Oh, I'll tell you why nobody's done it so far. There's a good deal of ill-feeling toward slaveowners in the North. Even though northerners hate their Black neighbors, their misguided consciences

won't let them cooperate in any kind of slave search. So any south-
erner who ever went north searching for a runaway soon learned
that if he didn't have his Finder right with him, or if the trail was
cold, then there was no use searching.''

"That's the truth of it. Like a bunch of thieves up North, con-
spiring to keep a man from recovering his run-off stock.''

"But what if you had northerners doing the searching for you?
What if you had an agent in the North, a minister perhaps, who
could enlist others in the cause, who could find people who could
be trusted? Such an endeavor would be expensive, but given the
impossibility of *buying* new slaves in Appalachee, don't you imagine people would be willing to pay enough to finance the work of
recovering their runaways?''

"Pay? They'd pay double what you ask. They'd pay up front on
the chance of you doing it.''

"Suppose I charged twenty dollars to register their runaway—
birthdate, name, description, time and circumstances of escape—
and then charged a thousand dollars if I provide them with
information leading to recovery?''

"Fifty dollars to register, or they won't believe you're serious.
And another fifty whenever you send them information, even if it
doesn't turn out to be the right one. And *three* thousand for runaways
recovered healthy.''

Thrower smiled slightly. "I don't wish to make an unfair profit
from the work of righteousness.''

"Profit! You got a lot of folks up there to pay if you're going to
do a good job. I tell you, Thrower, you write up a contract, and then
get the printer in town to run you off a thousand copies. Then you
just go around and tell what you plan to one slaveowner in each town
you come to in Appalachee. I reckon you'll have to get a new print-
ing done within a week. We're not talking profit here, we're talking
a valuable service. Why, I'll bet you get contributions from folks what
never had a runaway. If you can make it so the Hio River stops being
the last barrier before they get away clean, it'll not only return old
runaways, it'll make the other slaves lose hope and stay home!''

Not half an hour later, Thrower was back outside and on his

horse—but now he had notes written up for the contract and letters of introduction from Cavil to his lawyer and to the printer, along with letters of credit to the tune of five hundred dollars. When Thrower protested that it was too much, Cavil wouldn't even hear him out. "To get you started," said Cavil. "We both know whose work we're doing. It takes money. I have it and you don't, so take it and get busy."

"That's a Christian attitude," said Thrower. "Like the saints in the early Church, who had all things in common."

Cavil patted Thrower's thigh, where he sat stiff in the saddle—northerners just didn't know how to sit a horse. "We've had more in common than any other two men alive," said Cavil. "We've had the same visions and done the same works, and if that don't make us two peas in a pod, I don't know what will."

"When next I see the Visitor, if I should be so fortunate, I know that he'll be pleased."

"Amen," said Cavil.

Then he slapped Thrower's horse and watched him out of sight. My Hagar. He's going to find my Hagar and her little boy. Nigh on seven years since she stole my firstborn child from me. Now she'll come back, and this time she'll stay in chains and give me more children until she can't have no more. And as for the boy, he'll be my Ishmael. That's what I'll call him, too. Ishmael. I'll keep him right here, and raise him up to be strong and obedient and a true Christian. When he's old enough I'll hire him out to other plantations, and during the nights he'll go and carry on my work, spreading the chosen seed throughout Appalachee. Then my children will surely be as numberless as the sands of the sea, just like Abraham.

And who knows? Maybe then the miracle will happen, and my own dear wife will be healed, and she'll conceive and bear me a pure White child, my Isaac, to inherit all my land and all my work. Lord my Overseer, be merciful to me.

❧ 17 ❧

Spelling Bee

EARLY JANUARY, WITH deep snow, and a wind sharp enough to slice your nose off—so of course that was a day for Makepeace Smith to decide *he* had to work in the forge all day, while Alvin went into town to buy supplies and deliver finished work. In the summer, the choice of jobs tended to go the other way.

Never mind, thought Alvin. He *is* the master here. But if I'm ever master of my own forge, and if I have me a prentice, you can bet he'll be treated fairer than I've been. A master and prentice ought to share the work alike, except for when the prentice plain don't know how, and then the master ought to teach him. That's the bargain, not to have a slave, not to always have the prentice take the wagon into town through the snow.

Truth to tell, though, Alvin knew he wouldn't have to take the wagon. Horace Guester's sleigh-and-two would do the job, and he knew Horace wouldn't mind him taking it, as long as Alvin did whatever errands the roadhouse needed doing in town.

Alvin bundled himself tight and pushed out into the wind—it was right in his face, from the west, the whole way up to the roadhouse. He took the path up by Miss Larner's house, it being the closest way with the most trees to break the wind. Course she wasn't in. It being school hours, she was with the children in the schoolhouse in town. But the old springhouse, it was Alvin's school-house, and just passing by the door got him to thinking about his studies.

She had him learning things he never thought to learn. He was expecting more of ciphering and reading and writing, and in a way that's what she had him doing, right enough. But she didn't have him reading out of those primers like the children—like Arthur Stuart, who plugged away at his studies by lamplight every night in the springhouse. No, she talked to Alvin about ideas he never would've thought of, and all his writing and calculating was about such things.

Yesterday:

"The smallest particle is an atom," she said. "According to the theory of Demosthenes, everything is made out of smaller things, until you come to the atom, which is smallest of all and cannot be divided."

"What's it look like?" Alvin asked her.

"I don't know. It's too small to see. Do *you* know?"

"I reckon not. Never saw anything so small but what you could cut it in half."

"But can't you *imagine* anything smaller?"

"Yeah, but I can split that too."

She sighed. "Well, now, Alvin, think again. If there *were* a thing so small it couldn't be divided, what would it be like?"

"*Real* small, I reckon."

But he was joking. It was a problem, and he set out to answer it the way he answered any practical problem. He sent his bug out into the floor. Being wood, the floor was a jumble of things, the broke-up once-alive hearts of living trees, so Alvin quickly sent his bug on into the iron of the stove, which was mostly all one thing inside. Being hot, the bits of it, the tiniest parts he ever saw clear, they were a blur of movement; while the fire inside, it made its own outward rush of light and heat, each bit of it so small and fine that he could barely hold the idea of it in his mind. He never really *saw* the bits of fire. He only knew that they had just passed by.

"Light," he said. "And heat. They can't be cut up."

"True. Fire isn't like earth—it can't be cut. But it can be changed, can't it? It can be extinguished. It can cease to be itself. And therefore the parts of it must become something else, and so they were not the unchangeable and indivisible atoms."

"Well, there's nothing smaller than those bits of fire, so I reckon there's no such thing as an atom."

"Alvin, you've got to stop being so empirical about things."

"If I knowed what that was, I'd stop being it."

"If I knew."

"Whatever."

"You can't always answer every question by sitting back and doodlebugging your way through the rocks outside or whatever."

Alvin sighed. "Sometimes I wish I never told you what I do."

"Do you want me to teach you what it means to be a Maker or not?"

"That's just *what* I want! And instead you talk about atoms and gravity and—I don't care what that old humbug Newton said, nor anybody else! I want to know how to make the—*place*." He remembered only just in time that there was Arthur Stuart in the corner, memorizing every word they said, complete with tone of voice. No sense filling Arthur's head with the Crystal City.

"Don't you understand, Alvin? It's been so long—thousands of years—that no one knows what a Maker really is, or what he does. Only that there were such men, and a few of the tasks that they could do. Changing lead or iron into gold, for instance. Water into wine. That sort of thing."

"I expect iron to gold'd be easier," said Alvin. "Those metals are pretty much all one thing inside. But wine—that's such a mess of different stuff inside that you'd have to be a—a—" He couldn't think of a word for the most power a man could have.

"Maker."

That was the word, right enough. "I reckon."

"I'm telling you, Alvin, if you want to learn how to do the things that Makers once did, you have to understand the nature of things. You can't change what you don't understand.''

''And I can't understand what I don't see.''

''Wrong! Absolutely false, Alvin Smith! It is what you *can* see that remains impossible to understand. The world you actually see is nothing more than an example, a special case. But the underlying principles, the order that holds it all together, *that* is forever invisible. It can only be discovered in the imagination, which is precisely the aspect of your mind that is most neglected.''

Well, last night Alvin just got mad, which she said would only guarantee that he'd stay stupid, which he said was just fine with him as he'd stayed alive against long odds by being as pure stupid as he was without any help from *her*. Then he stormed on outside and walked around watching the first flakes of this storm start coming down.

He'd only been walking a little while when he realized that she was right, and he knowed it all along. Knew it. He always sent out his bug to see what was *there,* but then when he got set to make a change, he first had to think up what he *wanted* it to be. He had to think of something that wasn't there, and hold a picture of it in his mind, and then, in that way he was born with and still didn't understand, he'd say, See this? This is how you ought to be! And then, sometimes fast, sometimes slow, the bits of it would move around until they lined up right. That's how he always did it: separating a piece off of living rock; joining together two bits of wood; making the iron line up strong and true; spreading the heat of the fire smooth and even along the bottom of the crucible. So I do see what isn't there, in my mind, and that's what makes it *come* to be there.

For a terrible dizzying moment he wondered if maybe the whole world was maybe no more than what he imagined it to be, and if that was true then if he stopped imagining, it'd just go away. Of course, once he got his sense together he knew that if he'd been thinking it up, there wouldn't be so many strange things in the world that he never could've thought of himself.

So maybe the world was all dreamed up in the mind of God. But no, can't be that neither, because if God dreamed up men like White Murderer Harrison then God wasn't too good. No, the best Alvin could think of was that God worked pretty much the way Alvin did—told the rocks of the earth and the fire of the sun and stuff like that, told it all how it was supposed to be and then let it be that way. But when God told *people* how to be, why, they just thumbed their noses and laughed at him, mostly, or else they pretended to obey while they still went on and did what they pleased. The planets and the stars and the elements, they all might be thought up from the mind of God, but people were just too cantankerous to blame them on anybody but their own self.

Which was about the limit of Alvin's thinking last night, in the snow—wondering about what he could never know. Things like I wonder what God dreams about if he ever sleeps, and if all his dreams come true, so that every night he makes up a whole new world full of people. Questions that couldn't never get him a speck closer to being a Maker.

So today, slogging through the snow, pushing against the wind toward the roadhouse, he started thinking again about the original question—what an atom would be like. He tried to picture something so tiny that he couldn't cut it. But whenever he imagined something like that—a little box or a little ball or something— why, then he'd just up and imagine it splitting right in half.

The only way he couldn't split something in half was if it was so thin nothing could be thinner. He thought of it squished so flat it was thinner than paper, so thin that in that direction it didn't even *exist,* if you looked at it edge-on it would just plain not be there. But even then, he might not be able to split it along the edge, but he could still imagine turning it and slicing it across, just like paper.

So—what if it was squished up in another direction, too, so it was all edge, going on like the thinnest thread you ever dreamed of? Nobody could see it, but it would still be there, because it would stretch from here to there. He sure couldn't split that along the edge, and it didn't have any flat surface like paper had. Yet as long as it stretched like invisible thread from one spot to another, no matter how short the distance was, he could still imagine snipping it right in half, and each half in half again.

No, the only way something could be small enough to be an atom is if it had no size at all in any direction, not length nor breadth nor depth. That would be an atom all right—only it wouldn't even *exist,* it'd just be *nothing.* Just a place without anything in it.

He stood on the porch of the roadhouse, stamping snow off his feet, which did better than knocking for telling folks he was there. He could hear Arthur Stuart's feet running to open the door, but all he was thinking about was atoms. Because even though he'd just figured out that there couldn't be no atoms, he was beginning to realize it might be even crazier to imagine there *not* being atoms, so things could always get cut into smaller bits and *those* things into smaller bits, and those into even *smaller* bits, forever and ever. And when you think about it, it's got to be one or the other. Either you get to the bit that can't be split, and it's an atom, or you never do, and so it goes on *forever,* which is more than Alvin's head could hold.

Alvin found himself in the roadhouse kitchen, with Arthur Stuart piggyback, playing with Alvin's hat and scarf. Horace Guester was out in the barn stuffing straw into new bedticks, so Alvin asked Old Peg for use of the sleigh. It was hot in the kitchen, and Goody Guester didn't look to be in good temper. She allowed as how he could take the sled, but there was a price to pay.

"Save the life of a certain child, Alvin, and take Arthur Stuart with you," she said, "or I swear he'll do one more thing to rile me and end up in the pudding tonight."

It was true that Arthur Stuart seemed to be in a mood to make trouble—he was strangling Alvin with his own scarf and laughing like a fool.

"Let's do some lessons, Arthur," said Alvin. "Spell 'choking to death.' "

"C-H-O-K-I-N-G," said Arthur Stuart. "T-W-O. D-E-A-T-H."

Mad as she was, Goody Guester just had to break up laughing —not because he spelled "to" wrong, but because he'd spelled out the words in the most perfect imitation of Miss Larner's voice. "I swear, Arthur Stuart," she said, "you best never let Miss Larner hear you go on like that or your schooling days are over."

"Good! I hate school!" said Arthur.

"You don't hate school so much as you'd hate working with me in the kitchen every day." said Goody Guester. "All day every day, summer and winter, even swimming days."

"I might as well be a slave in Appalachee!" shouted Arthur Stuart.

Goody Guester stopped teasing and being mad, both, and turned solemn. "Don't even joke like that, Arthur. Somebody died once just to keep you from being such a thing."

"I know," said Arthur.

"No you don't, but you'd better just think before you—"

"It was my mama," said Arthur.

Now Old Peg started looking scared. She took a glance at Alvin and then said, "Never mind about that, anyway."

"My mama was a blackbird," said Arthur. "She flew so high, but then the ground caught her and she got stuck and died."

Alvin saw how Goody Guester looked at him, even more nervous-like. So maybe there was something to Arthur's story of flying after all. Maybe somehow that girl buried up beside Vigor, maybe somehow she got a blackbird to carry her baby somehow. Or maybe it was just some vision. Anyway, Goody Guester had decided to act like it was nothing after all—too late to fool Alvin, of course, but she wouldn't know that. "Well, that's a pretty story, Arthur," said Old Peg.

"It's true," said Arthur. "I remember."

Goody Guester started looking even more upset. But Alvin knew better than to argue with Arthur about this blackbird idea he had, and about him flying once. The only way to stop Arthur talking about it was to get his mind on something else. "Better come with me, Arthur Stuart," said Alvin. "Maybe you got a blackbird mama sometime in your past, but I have a feeling your mama here in this kitchen is about to knead you like dough."

"Don't forget what I need you to buy for me," said Old Peg.

"Oh, don't worry. I got a list," said Alvin.

"I didn't see you write a thing!"

"Arthur Stuart's my list. Show her, Arthur."

Arthur leaned close to Alvin's ear and shouted so loud it like to split Alvin's eardrums right down to his ankles. "A keg of wheat flour and two cones of sugar and a pound of pepper and a dozen sheets of paper and a couple of yards of cloth that might do for a shirt for Arthur Stuart."

Even though he was shouting, it was his mama's own voice.

She purely hated it when he mimicked her, and so here she came with the stirring fork in one hand and a big old cleaver in the other. "Hold still, Alvin, so I can stick the fork in his mouth and shave off a couple of ears!"

"Save me!" cried Arthur Stuart.

Alvin saved him by running away, at least till he got to the back door. Then Old Peg set down her instruments of boy-butchery and helped Alvin bundle Arthur Stuart up in coats and leggings and boots and scarves till he was about as big around as he was tall. Then Alvin pitched him out the door into the snow and rolled him with his foot till he was covered with snow.

Old Peg barked at him from the kitchen door. "That's right. Alvin Junior, freeze him to death right before his own mother's eyes, you irresponsible prentice boy you!"

Alvin and Arthur Stuart just laughed. Old Peg told them to be careful and get home before dark and then she slammed the door tight.

They hitched up the sleigh, then swept out the new snow that had blown in while they were hitching it and got in and pulled up the lap robe. They first went on down to the forge again to pick up the work Alvin had to deliver—mostly hinges and fittings and tools for carpenters and leatherworkers in town, who were all in the midst of their busiest season of the year. Then they headed out for town.

They didn't get far before they caught up to a man trudging townward—and none too well dressed, either, for weather like this. When they were beside him and could see his face, Alvin wasn't surprised to see it was Mock Berry.

"Get on this sleigh, Mock Berry, so I won't have your death on my conscience," said Alvin.

Mock looked at Alvin like his words was the first Mock even noticed somebody was there on the road, even though he'd just been passed by the horses, snorting and stamping through the snow. "Thank you, Alvin," said the man. Alvin slid over on the seat to make room. Mock climbed up beside him—clumsy, cause his hands were cold. Only when he was sitting down did he seem to notice Arthur Stuart sitting on the bench. And then it was like somebody slapped him—he started to get right back down off the sleigh.

"Now hold on!" said Alvin. "Don't tell me you're just as stupid as the White folks in town, refusing to sit next to a mixup boy! Shame on you!"

Mock looked at Alvin real steady for a long couple of seconds before he decided how to answer. "Look here, Alvin Smith, you know me better than that. I know how such mixup children come to be, and I don't hold against them what some White man done to their mama. But there's a story in town about who's the real mama of this child, and it does me no good to be seen coming into town with this child nearby."

Alvin knew the story well enough—how Arthur Stuart was supposedly the child of Mock's wife Anga, and how, since Arthur was plainly fathered by some White man, Mock refused even to have the boy in his own house, which led to Goody Guester taking Arthur in. Alvin also knew the story wasn't true. But in a town like this it was better to have such a story believed than to have the true story guessed at. Alvin wouldn't put it past some folks to try to get Arthur Stuart declared a slave and shipped on south just to be rid of him so there'd be no more trouble about schools and such.

"Never mind about that," said Alvin. "Nobody's going to see you on a day like this, and even if they do, Arthur looks like a wad of cloth, and not a boy at all. You can hop off soon as we get into town." Alvin leaned out and took Mock's arm and pulled him onto the seat. "Now pull up the lap robe and snuggle close so I don't have to take you to the undertaker on account of having froze to death."

"Thank you kindly, you persnickety uppity prentice boy." Mock pulled the lap robe up so high that it covered Arthur Stuart completely. Arthur yelled and pulled it down again so he could see over the top. Then he gave Mock Berry such a glare that it might have burnt him to a cinder, if he hadn't been so cold and wet.

When they got into town, there was sleighs a-plenty, but none of the merriment of the first heavy snowfall. Folks just went about their business, and the horses stood and waited, stamping their feet and snorting and steaming in the cold wind. The lazier sort of folks—the lawyers and clerks and such—they were all staying at home on a day like this. But the people with real work to do, they had their fires hot, their workshops busy, their stores open for business. Alvin made his rounds a-dropping off ironwork with the folks who'd called for it. They all put their signature on Makepeace's delivery book—one more slight, that he wouldn't trust Alvin to take cash, like he was a nine-year-old prentice boy and not more than twice that age.

On those quick errands, Arthur Stuart stayed bundled up on the sleigh—Alvin never stayed indoors long enough to warm up from the walk between sleigh and front door. It wasn't till they got to Pieter Vanderwoort's general store that it was worth going inside and warming up for a spell. Pieter had his stove going right hot, and Alvin and Arthur wasn't the first to think of warming up there. A couple of boys from town were there warming their feet and sipping tea with a nip or two from a flask in order to keep warm. They weren't any of the boys Alvin spent much time with. He'd thrown them once or twice, but that was true of every male creature in town who was willing to rassle. Alvin knew that these two— Martin, that was the one with pimples, and the other one was Daisy—I know that sounds like a crazy name for anyone but a cow, but that was his name all right—anyway, Alvin knew that these two boys were the kind who like to set cats afire and make nasty jokes about girls behind their back. Not the kind that Alvin spent much time with, but not any that he had any partickler dislike for, neither. So he nodded them good afternoon, and they nodded him back. One of them held up his flask to share, but Alvin said no thanks and that was that.

At the counter, Alvin pulled off some of his scarves, which felt good because he was so sweaty underneath; then he set to unwinding Arthur Stuart, who spun around like a top while Alvin pulled on the end of each scarf. Arthur's laughing brought Mr. Vanderwoort out from the back, and he set to laughing, too.

"They're so cute when they're little, aren't they," said Mr. Vanderwoort.

"He's just my shopping list today, aren't you, Arthur?"

Arthur Stuart spouted out his list right off, using his Mama's voice again. "A keg of wheat flour and two cones of sugar and a pound of pepper and a dozen sheets of paper and a couple of yards of cloth that might do for a shirt for Arthur Stuart."

Mr. Vanderwoort like to died laughing. "I get such a kick out of that boy, the way he talks like his mama."

One of the boys by the stove gave a whoop.

"I mean his adopted mama, of course," said Vanderwoort.

"Oh, she's probably his mama all right!" said Daisy. "I hear Mock Berry does a *lot* of work up to the roadhouse!"

Alvin just set his jaw against the answer that sprang to mind. Instead he hotted up the flask in Daisy's hand, so Daisy whooped again and dropped it.

"You come on back with me, Arthur Stuart," said Vanderwoort.

"Like to burned my hand off!" muttered Daisy.

"You just say the list over again, bit by bit, and I'll get what's wanted," said Vanderwoort. Alvin lifted Arthur over the counter and Vanderwoort set him down on the other side.

"You must've set it on the stove like the blamed fool you are, Daisy," said Martin. "What is it, whiskey don't warm you up less it's boiled?"

Vanderwoort led Arthur into the back room. Alvin took a couple of soda crackers from the barrel and pulled up a stool near the fire.

"I didn't set it anywheres near the stove," said Daisy.

"Howdy, Alvin," said Martin.

"Howdy, Martin, Daisy," said Alvin. "Good day for stoves."

"Good day for nothing," muttered Daisy. "Smart-mouth pickaninnies and burnt fingers."

"What brings you to town, Alvin?" asked Martin. "And how come you got that baby buck with you? Or did you buy him off Old Peg Guester?"

Alvin just munched on his cracker. It was a mistake to punish Daisy for what he said before, and a worse mistake to do it again. Wasn't it trying to punish folks that brought the Unmaker down on him last summer? No, Alvin was working on curbing his temper, so he said nothing. Just broke off pieces of the cracker with his mouth.

"That boy ain't for sale," said Daisy. "Everybody knows it. Why, she's even trying to educate him, I hear."

"I'm educating my dog, too," said Martin. "You think that boy's learnt him how to beg or point game or anything useful?"

"But you got yourself the advantage there, Marty," said Daisy. "A dog's got him enough brains to know he's a dog, so he don't try to learn how to read. But you get one of these hairless monkeys, they get to thinking they're people, you know what I mean?"

Alvin got up and walked to the counter. Vanderwoort was coming back now, arms full of stuff. Arthur was tagging along behind.

"Come on behind the counter with me, Al," said Vanderwoort. "Best if you pick out the cloth for Arthur's shirt."

"I don't know a thing about cloth," said Alvin.

"Well, I know about cloth but I don't know about what Old Peg Guester likes, and if she ain't happy with what you come home with, I'd rather it be your fault than mine."

Alvin hitched his butt up onto the counter and swung his legs over. Vanderwoort led him back and they spent a few minutes picking out a plaid flannel that looked suitable enough and might also be tough enough to make patches on old trousers out of the leftover scraps. When they came back, Arthur Stuart was over by the fire with Daisy and Martin.

"Spell 'sassafras,' " said Daisy.

"Sassafras," said Arthur Stuart, doing Miss Larner's voice as perfect as ever. "S-A-S-S-A-F-R-A-S."

"Was he right?" asked Martin.

"Beats hell out of me."

"Now don't be using words like that around a child," said Vanderwoort.

"Oh, never you mind," said Martin. "He's our pet pickaninny. We won't do him no harm."

"I'm not a pickaninny," said Arthur Stuart. "I'm a mixup boy."

"Well, ain't that the truth!" Daisy's voice went so loud and high that his voice cracked.

Alvin was just about fed up with them. He spoke real soft, so only Vanderwoort could hear him. "One more whoop and I'll fill that boy's ears with snow."

"Now don't get riled," said Vanderwoort. "They're harmless enough."

"That's why I won't kill him." But Alvin was smiling, and so was Vanderwoort. Daisy and Martin were just playing, and since Arthur Stuart was enjoying it, why not?

Martin picked something off a shelf and brought it over to Vanderwoort. "What's this word?" he asked.

"Eucalyptus," said Vanderwoort.

"Spell 'eucalipidus,' mixup boy."

"Eucalyptus," said Arthur. "E-U-C-A-L-Y-P-T-U-S."

"Listen to that!" cried Daisy. "That teacher lady won't give time of day to us, but here we got her own voice spelling whatever we say."

"Spell 'bosoms,' " said Martin.

"Now that's going too far," said Vanderwoort. "He's just a boy."

"I just wanted to hear the teacher lady's voice saying it," said Martin.

"I know what you wanted, but that's behind-the-barn talk, not in my general store."

The door opened and, after a blast of cold wind, Mock Berry came in, looking tired and half-froze, which of course he was.

The boys took no notice. "Behind the barn don't got a stove," said Daisy.

"Then keep that in mind when you decide how to talk," said Vanderwoort.

Alvin watched how Mock Berry took sidelong glances at the stove, but made no move to go over there. No man in his right mind would choose not to go to the stove on a day like this—but Mock Berry knew there was worse things than being cold. So instead he just walked up to the counter.

Vanderwoort must've known he was there, but for a while he just kept on watching Martin and Daisy play spelling games with Arthur Stuart, paying no mind to Mock Berry.

"Suskwahenny," said Daisy.

"S-U-S-K-W-A-H-E-N-N-Y," said Arthur.

"I bet that boy could win any spelling bee he ever entered," said Vanderwoort.

"You got a customer," said Alvin.

Vanderwoort turned real slow and looked at Mock Berry without expression. Then, still moving slow, he walked over and stood in front of Mock without a word.

"Just need me two pounds of flour and twelve feet of that half-inch rope," said Mock.

"Hear that?" said Daisy. "He's a-fixing to powder his face white and then hang himself, I'll bet."

"Spell 'suicide,' boy," said Martin.

"S-U-I-C-I-D-E," said Arthur Stuart.

"No credit," said Vanderwoort.

Mock laid down some coins on the counter. Vanderwoort looked at it a minute. "Six feet of rope."

Mock just stood there.

Vanderwoort just stood there.

Alvin knew it was more than enough money for what Mock wanted to buy. He couldn't hardly believe Vanderwoort was raising his price for a man about as poor but hard-working as any in town. In fact, Alvin began to understand a little about why Mock stayed so poor. Now, Alvin knew there wasn't much he could do about it—but he could at least do what Horace Guester had once done for him with his master Makepeace—make Vanderwoort put things

· *251* ·

out in the open and stop pretending he wasn't being as unfair as he was being. So Alvin laid down the paper Vanderwoort had just written out for him. "I'm sorry to hear there's no credit," Alvin said. "I'll go fetch the money from Goody Guester."

Vanderwoort looked at Alvin. Now he could either make Alvin go fetch the money or say right out that there was credit for the *Guesters,* just not for Mock Berry.

Of course he chose another course. Without a word he went into the back and weighed out the flour. Then he measured out twelve feet of half-inch rope. Vanderwoort was known for giving honest measure. But then, he was also known for giving a fair price, which is why it took Alvin aback to see him do otherwise with Mock Berry.

Mock took his rope and his flour and started out.

"You got change," said Vanderwoort.

Mock turned around, looking surprised though he tried not to. He came back and watched as Vanderwoort counted out a dime and three pennies onto the counter. Then, hesitating a moment, Mock scooped them off the counter and dropped them into his pocket. "Thank you sir," he said. Then he went back out into the cold.

Vanderwoort turned to Alvin, looking angry or maybe just resentful. "I can't give credit to everybody."

Now, Alvin could've said something about at least he could give the same price to Blacks as Whites, but he didn't want to make an enemy out of Mr. Vanderwoort, who was after all a mostly good man. So Alvin grinned real friendly and said, "Oh, I know you can't. Them Berrys, they're almost as poor as me."

Vanderwoort relaxed, which meant it was Alvin's good opinion he wanted more than to get even for Alvin embarrassing him. "You got to understand, Alvin, it ain't good for trade if they come in here all the time. Nobody minds that mixup boy of yours—they're cute when they're little—but it makes folks stay away if they think they might run into one of them here."

"I always knowed Mock Berry to keep his word," said Alvin. "And nobody ever said he stole or slacked or any such thing."

"No, nobody ever told such a tale on him."

"I'm glad to know you count us both among your customers," said Alvin.

"Well, lookit here, Daisy," said Martin. "I think *Prentice* Alvin's gone and turned preacher on us. Spell 'reverend,' boy."

"R-E-V-E-R-E-N-D."

Vanderwoort saw things maybe turning ugly, so of course he tried to change the subject. "Like I said, Alvin, that mixup boy's bound to be the best speller in the county, don't you think? What I want to know is, why don't he go on and get into the county spelling bee next week? I think he'd bring Hatrack River the championship. He might even get the *state* championship, if you want my opinion."

"Spell 'championship,' " said Daisy.

"Miss Larner never said me that word," said Arthur Stuart.

"Well figure it out," said Alvin.

"C-H-A-M-P," said Arthur. "E-U-N-S-H-I-P."

"Sounds right to me," said Daisy.

"Shows what *you* know," said Martin.

"Can you do better?" asked Vanderwoort.

"*I'm* not going to be in the county spelling bee," said Martin.

"What's a spelling bee?" asked Arthur Stuart.

"Time to go," said Alvin, for he knew full well that Arthur Stuart wasn't a regular admitted student in the Hatrack River Grammar School, and so it was a sure thing he wouldn't be in no spelling bee. "Oh, Mr. Vanderwoort, I owe you for two crackers I ate."

"I don't charge my friends for a couple of crackers," said Vanderwoort.

"I'm proud to know you count me one of your friends," said Alvin. Alvin meant it, too—it took a good man to get caught out doing something wrong, and then turn around and treat the one that caught him as a friend.

Alvin wound Arthur Stuart back into his scarves, and then wrapped himself up again, and plunged back into the snow, this time carrying all that he bought from Vanderwoort in a burlap sack. He tucked the sack under the seat of the sleigh so it wouldn't get snowed on. Then he lifted Arthur Stuart into place and climbed up after. The horses looked happy enough to get moving again—they only got colder and colder, standing in the snow.

On the way back to the roadhouse they found Mock Berry on the road and took him on home. Not a word did he say about what happened in the store, but Alvin knew it wasn't cause he didn't appreciate it. He figured Mock Berry was plain ashamed of the fact that it took an eighteen-year-old prentice boy to get him honest measure and fair price in Vanderwoort's general store—only cause the boy was White. Not the kind of thing a man loves to talk about.

"Give a howdy to Goody Berry," said Alvin, as Mock hopped off the sleigh up the lane from his house.

"I'll say you said so," said Mock. "And thanks for the ride." In six steps he was clean gone in the blowing snow. The storm was getting worse and worse.

Once everything was dropped off at the roadhouse, it was near time for Alvin's and Arthur's schooling at Miss Larner's house, so they headed on down there and threw snowballs at each other all the way. Alvin stopped in at the forge to give the delivery book to Makepeace. But Makepeace must've laid off early cause he wasn't there; Alvin tucked the book onto the shelf by the door, where Makepeace would know to look for it. Then he and Arthur went back to snowballs till Miss Larner came back.

Dr. Whitley Physicker drove her in his covered sleigh and walked her right up to her door. When he took note of Alvin and Arthur waiting around, he looked a bit annoyed. "Don't you boys think Miss Larner shouldn't have to do any more teaching on a day like this?"

Miss Larner laid a hand on Dr. Physicker's arm. "Thank you for bringing me home, Dr. Physicker," she said.

"I wish you'd call me Whitley."

"You're kind to me, Dr. Physicker, but I think your honored title suits me best. As for these pupils of mine, it's in bad weather that I do my best teaching, I've found, for they aren't wishing to be at the swimming hole."

"Not me!" shouted Arthur Stuart. "How do you spell 'championship'?"

"C-H-A-M-P-I-O-N-S-H-I-P, " said Miss Larner. "Wherever did you hear that word?"

"C-H-A-M-P-I-O-N-S-H-I-P," said Arthur Stuart—in Miss Larner's voice.

"That boy is certainly remarkable," said Physicker. "A mockingbird, I'd say."

"A mockingbird copies the song," said Miss Larner, "but makes no sense of it. Arthur Stuart may speak back the spellings in my voice, but he truly knows the word and can read it or write it whenever he wishes."

"I'm not a mockingbird," said Arthur Stuart. "I'm a spelling bee championship."

Dr. Physicker and Miss Larner exchanged a look that plainly meant more than Alvin could understand just from watching.

"Very well," said Dr. Physicker. "Since I did in fact enroll him as a special student—at your insistence—he *can* compete in the county spelling bee. But don't expect to take him any farther, Miss Larner!"

"Your reasons were all excellent, Dr. Physicker, and so I agree. But *my* reasons—"

"Your reasons were overwhelming, Miss Larner. And I can't help but relish in advance the consternation of the people who fought to keep him out of school, when they watch him do as well as children twice his age."

"Consternation, Arthur Stuart," said Miss Larner.

"Consternation," said Arthur. "C-O-N-S-T-E-R-N-A-T-I-O-N."

"Good evening, Dr. Physicker. Come inside, boys. Time for school."

Arthur Stuart won the county spelling bee, with the word "celebratory." Then Miss Larner immediately withdrew him from further competition; another child would take his place at the state competition. As a result there was little note taken, except among the locals. Along with a brief notice in the Hatrack River newspaper.

Sheriff Pauley Wiseman folded up that page of the newspaper with a short note and put them in an envelope addressed to Reverend

Philadelphia Thrower, The Property Rights Crusade, 44 Harrison Street, Carthage City, Wobbish. It took two weeks for that newspaper page to be spread open on Thrower's desk, along with the note, which said simply:

> *Boy turned up here summer 1811, only a few weeks old best guess. Lives in Horace Guester's roadhouse, Hatrack River. Adoption don't hold water I reckon if the boy's a runaway.*

No signature—but Thrower was used to that, though he didn't understand it. Why should people try to conceal their identity when they were taking part in works of righteousness? He wrote his own letter and sent it south.

A month later, Cavil Planter read Thrower's letter to a couple of Finders. Then he handed them the cachets he'd saved all these years, those belonging to Hagar and her stole-away Ishmael-child. "We'll be back before summer," said the black-haired Finder. "If he's yourn, we'll have him."

"Then you'll have earned your fee and a fine bonus as well," said Cavil Planter.

"Don't need no bonus," said the white-haired Finder. "Fee and costs is plenty."

"Well, then, as you wish," said Cavil. "I know God will bless your journey."

✥ 18 ✥

Manacles

IT WAS EARLY spring, a couple of months before Alvin's nineteenth birthday, when Makepeace Smith come to him and said, "About time you start working on a journeyman piece, Al, don't you think?"

The words sang like redbird song in Alvin's ears, so he couldn't hardly speak back except to nod.

"Well, what do you think you'll make?" asked the master.

"I been thinking maybe a plow," said Alvin.

"That's a lot of iron. Takes a perfect mold, and no easy one, neither. You're asking me to put a good bit of iron at risk, boy."

"If I fail, you can always melt it back."

Since they both knew that Alvin had about as much chance of failing as he did of flying, this was pretty much empty talk—just the last rags of Makepeace's old pretense about how Alvin wasn't much good at smithing.

"Reckon so," said Makepeace. "You just do your best, boy. Hard but not too brittle. Heavy enough to bite deep, but light enough to pull. Sharp enough to cut the earth, and strong enough to cast all stones aside."

"Yes sir." Alvin had memorized the rules of the tools back when he was twelve years old.

There were some other rules that Alvin meant to follow. He had to prove to himself that he was a good smith, and not just a half-baked Maker, which meant that he'd use none of his knack, only the skills that any smith has—a good eye, knowledge of the black metal, the vigor of his arms and the skill of his hands.

Working on his journeyman piece meant he had no other duties till it was done. He started from scratch on this one, as a good journeyman always does. No common clay for the mold—he went upriver on the Hatrack to the best white clay, so the face of the mold would be pure and smooth and hold its shape. Making a mold meant seeing things all inside-out, but Alvin had a good mind for shapes. He patted and stroked the clay into place on the wooden frame, all the time seeing how the different pieces of the mold would give the cooling iron its plow shape. Then he baked the mold dry and hard, ready to receive the iron.

For the metal, he took from the pile of scrap iron and then carefully filed the iron clean, getting rid of all dirt and rust. He scoured the crucible, too. Only then was he ready to melt and cast. He hotted up the coal fire, running the bellows himself, raising and lowering the bellows handle just like he done when he was a new prentice. At last the iron was white in the crucible—and the fire so hot he could scarce bear to come near it. But he came near it anyway, tongs in hand, and hoisted the crucible from the fire, then carried it to the mold and poured. The iron sparked and dazzled, but the mold held true, no buckling or breaking in the heat.

Set the crucible back in the fire. Push the other parts of the mold into place. Gently, evenly, getting no splash. He had judged the amount of liquid iron just right—when the last part of the form slipped into place, just a bit of iron squeezed out evenly all around the edges, showing there was just enough, and scarce any waste.

And it was done. Nothing for it but to wait for the iron to cool and harden. Tomorrow he'd know what he'd wrought.

Tomorrow Makepeace Smith would see his plow and call him a

man—a journey man, free to practice at any forge, though not yet
ready to take on his own prentices. But to Alvin—well, he'd reached
that point of readiness years ago. Makepeace would have only a
few weeks short of the full seven years of Alvin's service—that's
what he'd been waiting for, not for this plow.

No, Alvin's real journeyman work was yet to come. After Makepeace declared the plow good enough, then Alvin had yet another
work to perform.

"I'm going to turn it gold," said Alvin.

Miss Larner raised an eyebrow. "And what then? What will you
tell people about a golden plow? That you found it somewhere?
That you happened to have some gold lying about, and thought—
this is just enough to make a plow?"

"You're the one what told me a Maker was the one who could
turn iron to gold."

"Yes, but that doesn't mean it's wise to do it." Miss Larner
walked out of the hot forge into the stagnant air of late afternoon.
It was cooler, but not much—the first hot night of spring.

"More than gold," said Alvin. "Or at least not normal gold."

"Regular gold isn't good enough for you?"

"Gold is dead. Like iron."

"It isn't dead. It's simply—earth without fire. It never *was* alive,
so it can't be dead."

"You're the one who told me that if I can imagine it, then maybe
I can make it come to be."

"And you can imagine living gold?"

"A plow that cuts the earth with no ox to draw it."

She said nothing, but her eyes sparkled.

"If I could make such a thing, Miss Larner, would you consider
as how I'd graduated from your school for Makers?"

"I'd say you were no longer a prentice Maker."

"Just what I thought, Miss Larner. A journeyman blacksmith
and a journeyman Maker, both, if I can do it."

"And can you?"

Alvin nodded, then shrugged. "I think so. It's what you said about atoms, back in January."

"I thought you gave up on that."

"No ma'am. I just kept thinking—what is it you can't cut into smaller pieces? And then I thought—why, if it's got any size at all, it can be cut. So an atom, it's nothing more than just a place, one exact place, with no width at all."

"Euclid's geometric point."

"Well, yes ma'am, except that you said his geometry was all imaginary, and this is real."

"But if it has no size, Alvin—"

"That's what I thought—if it's got no size, then it's nothing. But it *isn't* nothing. It's a place. Only then I thought, it *isn't* a place—it just *has* a place. If you see the difference. An atom can be in one place, one pure geometric point like you said, but then it can *move*. It can be somewhere else. So, you see, it not only has place, it has a past and a future. Yesterday it was there, today it's here, and tomorrow over yonder."

"But it isn't *anything*, Alvin."

"No, I know that, it isn't any*thing*. But it ain't *nothing*, neither."

"Isn't. Either."

"I know all that grammar, Miss Larner, but I'm not thinking about that right now."

"You won't have good grammar unless you use it even when you're not thinking about it. But never mind."

"See, I start thinking, if this atom's got no size, how can anybody tell where it is? It's not giving off any light, because it's got no fire in it to give off. So here's what I come up with: Just suppose this atom's got no *size,* but it's still got some kind of mind. Some kind of tiny little wit, just enough to know where it is. And the only power it has is to move somewhere else, and know where it is *then.*"

"How could that be, a memory in something that doesn't exist?"

"Just suppose it! Say you got thousands of them just lying around, just going any which way. How can any of them tell where they are? Since all the others are moving any which way, nothing around it stays the same. But then suppose somebody comes along—and I'm thinking about God here—somebody who can show them a pattern. Show them some way to set still. Like he says—you, there, you're the center, and all the rest of you, you just stay the same distance away from him all the time. Then what have you got?''

Miss Larner thought for a moment. ''A hollow sphere. A ball. But still composed of nothing, Alvin.''

''But don't you see? That's why I knew that this was true. I mean, if there's one thing I know from doodlebugging, it's that everything's mostly empty. That anvil, it looks solid, don't it? But I tell you it's mostly empty. Just little bits of ironstuff, hanging a certain distance from each other, all patterned there. But most of the anvil is the empty space between. Don't you see? Those bits are acting just like the atoms I'm talking about. So let's say the anvil is like a mountain, only when you get real close you see it's made of gravel. And then when you pick up the gravel, it crumbles in your hand, and you see it's made of dust. And if you could pick up a single fleck of dust you'd see that it was just like the mountain, made of even tinier gravel all over again.''

''You're saying that what we see as solid objects are really nothing but illusion. Little nothings making tiny spheres that are put together to make your bits, and pieces made from bits, and the anvil made from pieces—''

''Only there's a lot more steps between, I reckon. Don't you see, this explains everything? Why it is that all I have to do is imagine a new shape or a new pattern or a new order, and show it in my mind, and if I think it clear and strong enough, and command the bits to change, why—they do. Because they're *alive*. They may be small and none too bright, but if I show them clear enough, they can do it.''

''This is too strange for me, Alvin. To think that everything is really nothing.''

''No, Miss Larner, you're missing the point. The point is that everything is *alive*. That everything is made out of living atoms, all obeying the commands that God gave them. And just following those commands, why, some of them get turned into light and heat, and some of them become iron, and some water, and some air, and some of them our own skin and bones. All those things are real— and so those atoms are real.''

"Alvin, I told you about atoms because they were an interesting theory. The best thinkers of our time believe there are no such things."

"Begging your pardon, Miss Larner, but the best thinkers never saw the things I saw, so they don't know diddly. I'm telling you that this is the only idea I can think of that explains it all—what I see and what I do."

"But where did these atoms come from?"

"They don't come from anywhere. Or rather, maybe they come from everywhere. Maybe these atoms, they're just there. Always been there, always will be there. You can't cut them up. They can't die. You can't make them and you can't break them. They're forever."

"Then God didn't create the world."

"Of course he did. The atoms were nothing, just places that didn't even know where they were. It's God who put them all into places so he'd know where they were, and so *they'd* know where they were—and everything in the whole universe is made out of them."

Miss Larner thought about it for the longest time. Alvin stood there watching her, waiting. He knew it was true, or at least truer than anything else he'd ever heard of or thought of. Unless she could think of something wrong with it. So many times this year she'd done that, point out something he forgot, some reason why his idea wouldn't work. So he waited for her to come up with something. Something wrong.

Maybe she would've. Only while she was standing there outside the forge, thinking, they heard the sound of horses cantering up the road from town. Of course they looked to see who was coming in such a rush.

It was Sheriff Pauley Wiseman and two men that Alvin never saw before. Behind them was Dr. Physicker's carriage, with old

Po Doggly driving. And they didn't just pass by. They stopped right there at the curve by the forge.

"Miss Larner," said Pauley Wiseman. "Arthur Stuart around here?"

"Why do you ask?" said Miss Larner. "Who are these men?"

"He's here," said one of the men. The white-haired one. He held up a tiny box between his thumb and forefinger. Both the strangers looked at it, then looked up the hill toward the springhouse. "In there," said the white-haired man.

"You need any more proof than that?" asked Pauley Wiseman. He was talking to Dr. Physicker, who was now out of his carriage and standing there looking furious and helpless and altogether terrible.

"Finders," whispered Miss Larner.

"That's us," said the white-haired one. "You got a runaway slave up there, Ma'am."

"He is not," she said. "He is a pupil of mine, legally adopted by Horace and Margaret Guester—"

"We got a letter from his owner, giving his birthdate, and we got his cachet here, and he's the very one. We're sworn and certified, Ma'am. What we Find is found. That's the law, and if you interfere, you're obstructing." The man spoke real nice and quiet and polite.

"Don't worry, Miss Larner," said Dr. Physicker. "I already have a writ from the mayor, and that'll hold him till the judge gets back tomorrow."

"Hold him in *jail,* of course," said Pauley Wiseman. "Wouldn't want anybody to try to run off with him, now, would we?"

"Wouldn't do much good if they tried," said the white-haired Finder. "We'd just follow. And then we'll probably shoot them dead, seeing how they was thieves escaping with stolen property."

"You haven't even told the Guesters, have you!" said Miss Larner.

"How could I?" said Dr. Physicker. "I had to stay with *them,* to make sure they didn't just take him."

"We obey the law," said the white-haired Finder.

"There he is," said the black-haired Finder.

Arthur Stuart stood in the open door of the springhouse.

"Just stay where you are, boy!" shouted Pauley Wiseman. "If you move a muscle I'll whip you to jelly!"

"You don't have to threaten him," said Miss Larner, but there wasn't nobody to listen, since they were all running up the hill.

"Don't hurt him!" cried Dr. Physicker.

"If he don't run, he won't get hurt," said the white-haired Finder.

"Alvin," said Miss Larner. "Don't do it."

"They ain't taking Arthur Stuart."

"Don't use your power like that. Not to hurt someone."

"I tell you—"

"Think, Alvin. We have until tomorrow. Maybe the judge—"

"Putting him in jail!"

"If anything happens to these Finders, then the nationals will be in it, to enforce the Fugitive Slave Treaty. Do you understand me? It's not a local crime like murder. You'd be taken off to Appalachee to be tried."

"I can't do *nothing*."

"Run and tell the Guesters."

Alvin waited just a moment. If it was up to him, he'd burn their hands right off before he let them take Arthur. But already the boy was between them, their fingers digging into Arthur's arms. Miss Larner was right. What they needed was a way to win Arthur's freedom for sure, not some stupid blunder that would end up making things worse.

Alvin ran for the Guesters' house. It surprised him how they took it—like they'd been expecting it all the time for the last seven years. Old Peg and Horace just looked at each other, and without a word Old Peg started in packing—her clothes *and* Arthur Stuart's.

"What's she packing *her* things for?" asked Alvin.

Horace smiled, a real tight smile. "She ain't going to let Arthur spend a night in jail alone. So she'll have them lock her up right alongside him."

It made sense—but it was strange to think of people like Arthur Stuart and Old Peg Guester in jail.

"What are *you* going to do?" asked Alvin.

"Load my guns," said Horace. "And when they're gone, I'll follow."

Alvin told him what Miss Larner had said about the nationals coming if somebody laid hand on a Finder.

"What's the worst they can do to me? Hang me. I tell you, I'd rather be hanged than live in this house a single day if they take Arthur Stuart away and I done nothing to stop them. And I can do it, Alvin. Hell, boy, I must've saved fifty runaway slaves in my time. Po Doggly and me, we used to pick them up this side of the river and send them on to safety in Canada. Did it all the time."

Alvin wasn't a bit surprised to hear of Horace Guester being an Emancipationist—and not a talker, neither.

"I'm telling you this, Alvin, cause I need your help. I'm just one man and there's two of them. I got no one I can trust—Po Doggly ain't gone with me on something like this in a week of Christmases, and I don't know where he stands no more. But you—I know you can keep a secret, and I know you love Arthur Stuart near as much as my wife does."

The way he said it gave Alvin pause. "Don't *you* love him, sir?"

Horace looked at Alvin like he was crazy. "They ain't taking a mixup boy right out from under my roof, Al."

Goody Guester come downstairs then, with two bundles in home-spun bags under her arms. "Take me into town, Horace Guester."

They heard the horses riding by on the road outside.

"That's probably them," said Alvin.

"Don't worry, Peg," said Horace.

"Don't *worry*?" Old Peg turned on him in fury. "Only two things are likely to happen out of this, Horace. Either I lose my son to slavery in the South, or my fool husband gets himself probably killed trying to rescue him. Of course I won't worry." Then she burst into tears and hugged Horace so tight it near broke Alvin's heart to see it.

It was Alvin drove Goody Guester into town on the roadhouse wagon. He was standing there when she finally wore down Pauley Wiseman so he'd let her spend the night in the cell—though he made her take a terrible oath about not trying to sneak Arthur Stuart out of jail before he'd do it.

As he led the way to the jail cell, Pauley Wiseman said, "You shouldn't fret none, Goody Guester. His master's no doubt a good man. Folks here got the wrong idea of slavery, I reckon."

She whirled on him. "Then you'll go in his place, Pauley? Seeing how it's so fine?"

"Me?" He was no more than amused at the idea. "I'm *White*, Goody Guester. Slavery ain't my natural state."

Alvin made the keys slide right out of Pauley's fingers.

"I'm sure getting clumsy," said Pauley Wiseman.

Goody Guester's foot just naturally ended up right on top of the key ring.

"Just lift up your foot, Goody Guester," said the sheriff, "or I'll charge you with aiding and abetting, not to mention resisting."

She moved her foot. The sheriff opened the door. Old Peg stepped through and gathered Arthur Stuart into her arms. Alvin watched as Pauley Wiseman closed and locked the door behind them. Then he went on home.

Alvin broke open the mold and rubbed away the clay that still clung to the face of the plow. The iron was smooth and hard, as good a plow as Alvin ever saw cast till then. He searched inside it and found no flaws, not big enough to mar the plow, anyway. He filed and rubbed, rubbed and filed till it was smooth, the blade sharp as if he meant to use it in a butcher shop instead of some field somewhere. He set it on top of the workbench. Then he sat there waiting while the sun rose and the rest of the world came awake.

In due time Makepeace came down from the house and looked at the plow. But Alvin didn't see him, being asleep. Makepeace woke him up enough to get him to walk back up to the house.

"Poor boy," said Gertie. "I bet he never even went to sleep last

night. I bet he went on down and worked on that fool plow all
night.''

"Plow looks fair.''

"Plow looks perfect, I'll bet, knowing Alvin.''

Makepeace grimaced. "What do you know about ironwork?''

"I know Alvin and I know you.''

"Strange boy. Ain't it the truth though? He does his best work
when he stays up all night.'' Makepeace even had some affection
in his voice, saying that. But Alvin was asleep in his bed by then
and didn't hear.

"Sets such store by that mixup child,'' said Gertie. "No wonder
he couldn't sleep.''

"Sleeping now,'' said Makepeace.

"Imagine sending Arthur Stuart into slavery at his age.''

"Law's the law,'' said Makepeace. "Can't say I like it, but a
fellow has to live by the law or what then?''

"You and the law,'' said Gertie. "I'm glad we don't live on the
other side of the Hio, Makepeace, or I swear you'd be wanting
slaves instead of prentices—if you know the difference.''

That was as pure a declaration of war as they ever gave each
other, and they were all set for one of their rip-snorting knock-
about break-dish fights, only Alvin was snoring up in the loft and
Gertie and Makepeace just glared at each other and let this one go.
Since all their quarrels came out the same, with all the same cruel
things said and all the same hurts and harms done, it was like they
just got tired and said, Pretend I just said all the things you hate
worst in all the world to hear, and I'll pretend you said the things
I hate worst back to me, and then let be.

Alvin didn't sleep all that long, nor all too well, neither. Fear
and anger and eagerness all played through his body till he could
hardly hold still, let alone keep his brain drifting with the currents
of his dreams. He woke up dreaming of a black plow turned to
gold. He woke up dreaming of Arthur Stuart being whipped. He
woke up again thinking of aiming a gun at one of them Finders and
pulling the trigger. He woke up again thinking of aiming at a Finder

and *not* pulling the trigger, and then watching them go away drag-ging Arthur after them, him screaming all the time, Alvin, where are you! Alvin, don't let them take me.

"Wake up or hush up!" shouted Gertie. "You're scaring the children."

Alvin opened his eyes and leaned over the edge of the loft. "Your children ain't even here."

"Then you're scaring *me*. I don't know what you was dreaming, boy, but I hope that dream never comes even to my worst enemy —which happens to be my husband this morning, if you want to know the truth."

Her mentioning Makepeace made Alvin alert, yes sir. He pulled on his trousers, wondering when and how he got up to this loft and who pulled his pants and boots off. In just that little amount of time, Gertie somehow got food on the table—cornbread and cheese and a dollop of molasses. "I don't have time to eat, Ma'am," said Alvin. "I'm sorry, but I got to—"

"You got time."

"No Ma'am, I'm sorry—"

"Take the bread, then, you plain fool. You plan to work all day with an empty belly? After only a morning's sleep? Why, it ain't even noon yet."

So he was chewing on bread when he come down the hill to the forge. There was Dr. Physicker's carriage again, and the Finders' horses. For a second Alvin thought—they come here cause Arthur Stuart got away somehow, and the Finders lost him, and—

No. They had Arthur Stuart with them.

"Good morning, Alvin," said Makepeace. He turned to the other men. "I must be about the softest master I ever heard of, letting my prentice boy sleep till near noon."

Alvin didn't even notice how Makepeace was criticizing him and calling him a prentice *boy* when his journeyman piece stood there finished on the workbench. He just squatted down in front of Arthur Stuart and looked him in the eyes.

"Stand back now," said the white-haired Finder.

Alvin didn't hardly notice him. He wasn't really seeing Arthur

Stuart, not with his eyes, anyhow. He was searching his body for some sign of harm. None. Not yet anyway. Just the fear in the boy.

"You haven't told us yet," said Pauley Wiseman. "Will you make them or not?"

Makepeace coughed. "Gentlemen, I once made a pair of manacles, back in New England. For a man convicted of treason, being shipped back to England in irons. I hope I never make a manacle for a seven-year-old boy who done no harm to a living soul, a boy who played around my forge and—"

"Makepeace," said Pauley Wiseman. "I told them that if you made the manacles, they wouldn't have to use this."

Wiseman held up the heavy iron-and-wood collar that he'd left leaning against his leg.

"It's the law," said the white-haired Finder. "We bring runaway slaves back home in that collar, to show the others what happens. But him being just a boy, and seeing how it was his mama what run away and not him, we agreed to manacles. But it don't make no difference to me. We get paid either way."

"You and your damned Fugitive Slave Treaty!" cried Makepeace. "You use that law to make slavers out of us, too."

"I'll make them," said Alvin.

Makepeace looked at him in horror. "You!"

"Better than that collar," said Alvin. What he didn't say was, I don't intend for Arthur Stuart to wear those manacles a minute longer than tonight. He looked at Arthur Stuart. "I'll make you some manacles as don't hurt much, Arthur Stuart."

"Wisely done," said Pauley Wiseman.

"Good to see somebody with sense here," said the white-haired Finder.

Alvin looked at him and tried to hold all his hatred in. He couldn't quite do it. So his spittle ended up spattering the dust at the Finder's feet.

The black-haired Finder looked ready to throw a punch at him for that, and Alvin wouldn't've minded a bit to grapple with him and maybe rub his face in the dirt a minute or two. But Pauley Wiseman jumped right between them and he had sense enough to do his talking to the black-haired Finder, and not to Alvin. "You got to be a blame fool, setting to rassle with a blacksmith. Look at his arms."

"I could take him," said the Finder.

"You folks got to understand," said the white-haired Finder. "It's our knack. We can no more help being Finders than—"

"There's some knacks," said Makepeace, "where it'd be better to die at birth than grow up and use it." He turned to Alvin. "I don't want you using my forge for this."

"Don't make a nuisance of yourself, Makepeace," said Pauley Wiseman.

"Please," said Dr. Physicker. "You're doing the boy more harm than good."

Makepeace backed off, but none too graciously.

"Give me your hands, Arthur Stuart," Alvin said.

Alvin made a show of measuring Arthur's wrists with a string. Truth was, he could see the measure of him in his mind, every inch of him, and he'd shape the iron to fit smooth and perfect, with rounded edges and no more weight than needed. Arthur wouldn't feel no pain from these manacles. Not with his body, anyhow.

They all stood and watched Alvin work. It was the smoothest, purest job they'd ever see. Alvin used his knack this time, but not so it'd show. He hammered and bent the strap iron, cutting it exactly right. The two halves of each manacle fit snug, so they wouldn't shift and pinch the skin. And all the time he was thinking how Arthur used to pump the bellows for him, or just stand there and talk to him while he worked. Never again. Even after they saved him tonight, they'd have to take him to Canada or hide him somehow—as if you could hide from a Finder.

"Good work," said the white-haired Finder. "I never saw me a better blacksmith."

Makepeace piped up from the dark corner of the forge. "You should be proud of yourself, Alvin. Why, let's make those manacles your journeyman piece, all right?"

Alvin turned and faced him. "My journeyman piece is that plow setting on the workbench, Makepeace."

It was the first time Alvin ever called his master by his first name. It was as clear as Alvin could let him know that the days of Makepeace talking to him like that were over now.

Makepeace didn't want to understand him. "Watch how you talk to me, boy! Your journeyman piece is what I say it is, and—"

"Come on, boy, let's get these on you." The white-haired Finder wasn't interested in Makepeace's talk, it seemed.

"Not yet," said Alvin.

"They're ready," said the Finder.

"Too hot," said Alvin.

"Well dip them in that bucket there and cool them off."

"If I do that, they'll change shape just a little, and then they'll cut the boy's arms so they bleed."

The black-haired Finder rolled his eyes. What did he care about a little blood from a mixup boy?

But the white-haired Finder knew that nobody'd stand for it if he didn't wait. "No hurry," he said. "Can't take too long."

They sat around waiting without a word. Then Pauley started in talking about nothing, and so did the Finders, and even Dr. Physicker, just jawing away like as if the Finders were any old visitors. Maybe they thought they were making the Finders feel more kindly so they wouldn't take it out on the boy once they had him across the river. Alvin had to figure that so he wouldn't hate them.

Besides, an idea was growing in his mind. It wasn't enough to get Arthur Stuart away tonight—what if Alvin could make it so even the Finders couldn't find him again?

"What's in that cachet you Finders use?" he asked.

"Don't you wish you knew," said the black-haired Finder.

"It's no secret," said the white-haired Finder. "Every slaveowner makes up a box like this for each slave, soon as he's bought or born. Scrapings from his skin, hair from his head, a drop of blood, things like that. Parts of his own flesh."

"You get his scent from that?"

"Oh, it ain't a scent. We ain't *bloodhounds,* Mr. Smith."

Alvin knew that calling him Mr. Smith was pure flattery. He smiled a little, pretending that it pleased him.

"Well then how does it help?"

"Well, it's our *knack*," said the white-haired Finder. "Who knows how it works? We just look at it, and we—it's like we see the shape of the person we're looking for."

"It ain't like that," said the black-haired Finder.

"Well that's how it is for *me*."

"I just know where he is. Like I can see his soul. If I'm close enough, anyway. Glowing like a fire, the soul of the slave I'm searching for." The black-haired Finder grinned. "I can see from a long way off."

"Can you show me?" asked Alvin.

"Nothing to see," said the white-haired Finder.

"I'll show you, boy," said the black-haired Finder. "I'll turn my back and y'all move that boy around in the forge. I'll point to him over my shoulder, perfect all the time."

"Come on now," said the white-haired Finder.

"We got nothing to do anyway till the iron cools. Give me the cachet."

The black-haired Finder did what he bragged—pointed at Arthur Stuart the whole time. But Alvin hardly saw that. He was busy watching from the inside of that Finder, trying to understand what he was doing, what he was *seeing*, and what it had to do with the cachet. He couldn't see how seven-year-old dried-up bits of Arthur Stuart's newborn body could show them where he was *now*.

Then he remembered that for a moment right at first the Finder hadn't pointed at all. His finger had wandered a little, and only after just that pause had he started pointing right at Arthur Stuart. Like as if he'd been trying to sort out which of the people behind him in the smithy was Arthur. The cachet wasn't for Finding—it was for recognizing. The Finders saw everybody, but they couldn't tell who was who without a cachet.

So what they were seeing wasn't Arthur's mind, or Arthur's soul. They were just seeing a body, like every other body unless they could sort it out. And what they were sorting was plain enough to Alvin—hadn't he healed enough people in his life to know that

people were pretty much the same, except for some bits at the center
of each living piece of their flesh? Those bits were different for
every single person, yet the same in every part of that person's
flesh. Like it was God's way of naming them right in their flesh.
Or maybe it was the mark of the beast, like in the book of Revelation.
Didn't matter. Alvin knew that the only thing in that cachet that
was the same as Arthur Stuart's body was that signature that lived
in every part of his body, even the dead and cast-off parts in the
cachet.

I can change those bits, thought Alvin. Surely I can change them,
change them in every part of his body. Like turning iron into gold.
Like turning water into wine. And then their cachet wouldn't work
at all. Wouldn't help them at all. They could search for Arthur
Stuart all they liked, but as long as they didn't actually see his face
and recognize him the regular way, they'd never find him.

Best of all, they wouldn't even realize what happened. They'd
still have the cachet, same as ever, and they'd know it hadn't been
changed a bit because Alvin wouldn't change it. But they could
search the whole world over and never find a body just like those
specks in their cachet, and they'd never guess why.

I'll do it, thought Alvin. Somehow I'll figure a way to change
him. Even though there must be millions of those signatures all
through his body, I'll find a way to change every one. Tonight I'll
do it, and tomorrow he'll be safe forever.

The iron was cool. Alvin knelt before Arthur Stuart and gently
put the manacles in place. They fit his flesh so perfectly he might
have cast them in a mold taken from Arthur's own body. When
they were locked into place, with a length of light chain strung
between them, Alvin looked Arthur Stuart in the eye. "Don't be
afraid," he said.

Arthur Stuart didn't say a thing.

"I won't forget you," said Alvin.

"Sure," said the black-haired Finder. "But just in case you get
ideas about remembering him while he's on his way home to his
rightful master, I ought to tell you square—we never both of us

sleep at the same time. And part of being a Finder is, we know if anybody's coming. You can't sneak up on us. Least of all you, smith boy. I could see *you* ten miles away.''

Alvin just looked at him. Eventually the Finder sneered and turned away. They put Arthur Stuart onto the horse in front of the white-haired Finder. But Alvin figured that as soon as they got across the Hio, they'd have Arthur walking. Not out of meanness, maybe— but it wouldn't do no good for Finders to show themselves being kindly to a runaway. Besides, they had to set an example for the other slaves, didn't they? Let them see a boy seven years old walking along, feet bleeding, head bowed, and they'd think twice about trying to run off with their children. They'd know that Finders have no mercy.

Pauley and Dr. Physicker rode away with them. They were seeing the Finders to the Hio River and watching them cross the river, to make sure they did no hurt to Arthur Stuart while he was in free territory. It was the best they could do.

Makepeace didn't have much to say, but what he said, he said plain. ''A real man would never put manacles on his own friend,'' said Makepeace. ''I'll go up to the house and sign your journeyman papers. I don't want you in my smithy or my house another night.'' He left Alvin alone by the forge.

He'd been gone no more than five minutes when Horace Guester got to the smithy.

''Let's go,'' he said.

''No,'' said Alvin. ''Not yet. They can see us coming. They'll tell the sheriff if they're being followed.''

''We got no choice. Can't lose their trail.''

''You know something about what I am and what I can do,'' said Alvin. ''I've got them even now. They won't get more than a mile from the Hio shore before they fall asleep.''

''You can do that?''

''I know what goes on inside people when they're sleepy. I can make that stuff start happening inside them the minute they're in Appalachee.''

''While you're at it, why don't you kill them?''

"I can't."

"They aren't men! It wouldn't be murder, killing them!"

"They *are* men," said Alvin. "Besides, if I kill them, then it's a violation of the Fugitive Slave Treaty."

"Are you a lawyer now?"

"Miss Larner explained it to me. I mean she explained it to Arthur Stuart while I was there. He wanted to know. Back last fall. He said, 'Why don't my pa just kill them if some Finders come for me?' And Miss Larner, she told him how there'd just be more Finders coming, only this time they'd hang you and take Arthur Stuart anyway."

Horace's face had turned red. Alvin didn't understand why for a minute, not till Horace Guester explained. "He shouldn't call me his pa. I never wanted him in my house." He swallowed. "But he's right. I'd kill them Finders if I thought it'd do good."

"No killing," said Alvin. "I think I can fix it so they'll never find Arthur again."

"I know. I'm going to ride him to Canada. Get to the lake and sail across."

"No sir," said Alvin. "I think I can fix it so they'll never find him *anywhere*. We just got to hide him till they go away."

"Where?"

"Springhouse, if Miss Larner'll let us."

"Why there?"

"I got it hexed up every which way from Tuesday. I thought I was doing it for the teacher lady. But now I reckon I was really doing it for Arthur Stuart."

Horace grinned. "You're really something, Alvin. You know that?"

"Maybe. Sure wish I knew *what*."

"I'll go ask Miss Larner if we can make use of her house."

"If I know Miss Larner, she'll say yes before you finish asking."

"When do we start, then?"

It took Alvin by surprise, having a grown man ask *him* when they should start. "Soon as it's dark, I reckon. Soon as those two Finders are asleep."

"You can really *do* that?"

"I can if I keep watching them. I mean sort of watching. Keeping track of where they are. So I don't go putting the wrong people to sleep."

"Well, are you watching them now?"

"I know where they are."

"Keep watching, then." Horace looked a little scared, almost as bad as he did near seven years ago, when Alvin told him he knew about the girl buried there. Scared because he knew Alvin could do something strange, something beyond any hexings or knacks in Horace's ken.

Don't you know me, Horace? Don't you know that I'm still Alvin, the boy you liked and trusted and helped so many times? Finding out that I'm stronger than you thought, in ways you didn't think of, that don't mean I'm a whit more dangerous to you. No reason to be a-scared.

As if Horace could hear his words, the fear eased away from his face. "I just mean—Old Peg and I are counting on you. Thank God you ended up in this place, right at this time when we needed you so bad. The good Lord's looking out for us." Horace smiled, then turned and left the smithy.

What Horace said, it left Alvin feeling good, feeling sure of himself. But then, that was Horace's knack, wasn't it—to give folks the view of theirselves they most needed to see.

Alvin turned his thoughts at once to the Finders, and sent out his bug to stay with them, to keep track of the way their bodies moved like small black storms through the greensong around them, with Arthur Stuart's small song bright and clear between them. Black and White don't have nothing to do with bright and dark at heart, I reckon, thought Alvin. His hands stayed busy doing work at the forge, but for the life of him he couldn't pay real attention to it. He'd never watched somebody so far off before—except for that time he got helped by powers he didn't understand, inside Eight-Face Mound.

And the worst thing of all would be if he lost them, if they got away with Arthur Stuart, all because Alvin didn't pay attention close enough and lost that boy among all the beat-down souls of slaves in Appalachee and on beyond, in the deep South where all White men were servants to the other Arthur Stuart, King of England, and so all Blacks were slaves of slaves. Ain't going to lose Arthur in a place so bad. Going to hold on tight to him, like as if he got a thread to connect him to me.

Almost as soon as he thought of it, almost as soon as he imagined a thin invisible thread connecting him and that mixup boy, why, there it was. There was a thread in the air, a thread about as thin as what he imagined once trying to understand what an atom might be. A thread that only had size in one direction—the direction that led toward Arthur Stuart, connecting them heart to heart. Stay with him, Alvin told the thread, like as if it really was alive. And in answer it seemed to grow brighter, thicker, till Alvin was sure anybody who come along could see it.

But when he looked with his eyes, he couldn't see the thread at all; it only appeared to him again when he looked without eyes. It plain astonished him, that such a thing could come to be, created —not out of nothing—but created without pattern except the pattern found in Alvin's own mind. This is a Making. My first, thin, invisible Making—but it's real, and it's going to lead me to Arthur Stuart tonight, so I can set him free.

In her little house, Peggy watched Alvin and Arthur Stuart both, looking back and forth from one to the other, trying to find some pathway that led for Arthur's freedom without costing Alvin's death or capture. No matter how closely and carefully she looked, there was no such path. The Finders were too skilled with their terrible knack; on some paths, Alvin and Horace might carry Arthur off, but he'd only be found again and recaptured—at the cost of Alvin's blood or Alvin's freedom.

So she watched despairing as Alvin spun his almost nonexistent thread. Only then, for the first time, did she see some glimmer of a possibility of freedom in Arthur Stuart's heartfire. It came, not from the fact that the thread would lead Alvin to the boy—on many paths before he spun the thread, she had seen Alvin finding the

Finders and putting them to sleep. No, the difference now was that Alvin could make the thread at all. The possibility of it had been so small that there had been no path that showed it. Or perhaps— something she hadn't thought of before—the very act of Making was such a violation of the natural order that her own knack couldn't see paths that relied on it, not until it was actually accomplished.

Yet even at the moment of Alvin's birth, hadn't she seen his glorious future? Hadn't she seen him building a city made of the purest glass or ice? Hadn't she seen his city filled with people who spoke with the tongues of angels and saw with the eyes of God? The fact that Alvin would Make, that was always probable, provided he stayed alive. But any one particular act of Making, that was never likely, never natural enough for a torch—even an extraordinary torch like Peggy—to see it.

She saw Alvin put the Finders to sleep almost as soon as it was dark and they could find a stopping place on the far side of the Hio. She saw Alvin and Horace meet in the smithy, preparing to set out through the woods to the Hio, avoiding the road so they wouldn't meet the sheriff and Dr. Physicker coming back from Hatrack Mouth. But she paid little heed to them. Now that there was new hope, she gave her full attention to Arthur's future, studying how and where his slender new paths of freedom were rooted to the present action. She could not find the clear moment of choice and change. To her that fact was proof that all depended on Alvin becoming a Maker, truly, on this night.

"O God," she whispered, "if thou didst cause this boy to be born with such a gift, I pray thee teach him Making now, tonight."

Alvin stood beside Horace, masked by shadows at the riverbank, waiting for a well-lighted riverboat to pass. Out on the boat, musicians were playing, and people danced a fancy quadrille on the decks. It made Alvin angry, to see them playing like children when a real child was being carried off to slavery tonight. Still, he knew they meant no harm, and knew it wasn't fair to blame others for being happy while somebody they don't even know might be grieving. By that measure there'd be no happiness in all the world, Alvin figured. Life being how it is, Alvin thought, there's not a moment in the day when there ain't at least a few hundred people grieving about something.

The ship had no sooner passed around a bend than they heard a crashing in the woods behind them. Or rather, Alvin heard the sound, and it only seemed like crashing to *him* because of his sense of the right order of things in the greenwood song. It took more than a few minutes before Horace heard it at all. Whoever it was sneaking up on them, he was right stealthy for a White man.

"Now I'm wishing for a gun," whispered Horace.

Alvin shook his head. "Wait and watch," he whispered—so faint his lips barely moved.

They waited. After a while, they saw a man step out of the woods and slither down the bank to the muddy edge of the water, where the boat rocked on the water. Seeing nobody there, he looked around, then sighed and stepped out into the boat, turned around and sat down in the stern, glumly resting his chin on his hands.

Suddenly Horace started chuckling. "Play fetch with my bones when I'm dead, but I do think that's old Po Doggly."

At once the man in the boat leaned back and Alvin could finally see him clear in the moonlight. It *was* Dr. Physicker's driver, sure enough. But this didn't seem to bother Horace none. He was already slipping down the riverbank, to splash out to the boat, climb aboard, and give Po Doggly such a violent hug the boat took on water. In only a second they both noticed that the boat was rocking out of kilter, and without a word they both shifted exactly right to balance the load, and then again without a word Po got the oars into the locks while Horace took a flat tin baling cup out from under his bench and commenced to dipping it and pouring it out overboard, again and again.

Alvin marveled for a moment at how smooth the two of them fit together. He didn't even have to ask—he knew from how they acted that they'd done this sort of thing a good many times before. Each knew what the other was going to do, so they didn't even have to think about it anymore. One man did his part, and the other his, and neither even had to check to make sure both parts were getting done.

Like the bits and pieces that made up everything in the world; like the dance of atoms Alvin had imagined in his mind. He'd never realized it before, but people could be like those atoms, too. Most of the time people were all disorganized, nobody knowing who anybody else was, nobody holding still long enough to trust or be trusted, just like Alvin imagined atoms might have been before God taught them who they were and gave them work to do. But here were two men, men that nobody'd ever figure even knew each other hardly, except as how everybody in a town like Hatrack River knows everybody else. Po Doggly, a one-time farmer reduced to driving for Dr. Physicker, and Horace Guester, the first settler in this place, and still prospering. Who'd've thought they could fit together so smooth? But it was because each one knew who the other was, knew it pure and true, knew it as sure as an atom might know the name God gave him; each one in his place, doing his work.

All these thoughts rushed through Alvin's mind so fast he hardly noticed himself thinking them, yet in later years he'd remember right enough that this was when he first understood: These two men, together, made something between them that was just as real and solid as the dirt under his feet, as the tree he was leaning on. Most folks couldn't see it—they'd look at the two of them and see nothing but two men who happened to be sitting in a boat together. But then, maybe to other atoms it wouldn't seem like the atoms making up a bit of a iron was anything more than two atoms as happened to be next to each other. Maybe you have to be far off, like God, or anyhow bigger by far in order to see what it is that two atoms make when they fit together in a certain way. But just because another atom don't see the connection don't mean it isn't real, or that the iron isn't as solid as iron can be.

And if I can teach these atoms how to make a string out of nothing, or maybe how to make iron out of gold, or even—let it be so—change Arthur's secret invisible signature all through his body so the Finders wouldn't know him no more—then why couldn't

a Maker also do with people as he does with atoms, and teach them
a new order, and once he finds enough that he can trust, build them
together into something new, something strong, something as real
as iron.

"You coming, Al, or what?"

Like I said, Alvin hardly knew what thought it was he had. But
he didn't forget it, no, even sliding down the bank into the mud he
knew that he'd never forget what he thought of just then, even
though it'd take him years and miles and tears and blood before he
really understood it all the way.

"Good to see you, Po," said Alvin. "Only I kind of thought we
was doing something a mite secret."

Po rowed the boat closer in, slacking the rope and letting Alvin
spider his way on board without getting his feet wet. Alvin didn't
mind that. He had an aversion to water, which was natural enough
seeing how often the Unmaker tried to use water to kill him. But
the water seemed to be just water tonight; the Unmaker was invisible
or far away. Maybe it was the slender string that still hooked Alvin
to Arthur—maybe that was such a powerful Making that the Unmaker plain hadn't the strength to turn even this much water against
Alvin.

"Oh, it's still secret, Alvin," said Horace. "You just don't know.
Afore you ever got to Hatrack River—or anyway I mean afore you
came back—me and Po, we used to go out and fetch in runaway
slaves and help them on to Canada whenever we could."

"Didn't the Finders ever get you?" asked Alvin.

"Any slave got this far, that meant the Finders wasn't too close
behind," said Po. "A good number that reached us stole their own
cachet."

"Besides, that was afore the Fugitive Slave Treaty," said
Horace. "Long as the Finders didn't kill us outright, they couldn't
touch us."

"And in those days we had a torch," said Po.

Horace said nothing, just untied the rope from the boat and tossed
it back onto shore. Po started in rowing the first second the rope
was free—and Horace had already braced himself for the first lurch

of the boat. It was a miracle, seeing how smooth they knew each other's next move before the move was even begun. Alvin almost laughed out loud in the joy of seeing such a thing, knowing it was possible, dreaming of what it might mean—thousands of people knowing each other that well, moving to fit each other just right, working together. Who could stand in the way of such people?

"When Horace's girl left, why, we had no way of knowing there was a runaway coming through here." Po shook his head. "It was over. But I knowed that with Arthur Stuart put in chains and dragged on south, why, there wasn't no way in hell old Horace wasn't going to cross the river and fetch him back. So once I dropped off them Finders and headed back away from the Hio a ways, I stopped the carriage and hopped on down."

"I bet Dr. Physicker noticed," said Alvin.

"Course he did, you fool!" said Po. "Oh, I see you're funning me. Well, he noticed. He just says to me, 'You be careful, them boys are dangerous.' And I said I'd be careful all right and then he says to me, 'It's that blame sheriff Pauley Wiseman. He didn't have to let them take him so fast. Might be we could've fought exerdiction if we could've held onto Arthur Stuart till the circuit judge come around. But Pauley, he did everything legal, but he moved so fast I just knew in my heart he wanted that boy gone, wanted him clean out of Hatrack River and never come back.' I believe him, Horace. Pauley Wiseman never did like that mixup boy, once Old Peg got the wind in her sails about him going to school."

Horace grunted; he turned the tiller just a little, exactly at the moment when Pauley slacked the oar on one side so the boat would turn slightly upstream to make the right landing on the far shore. "You know what I been thinking?" said Horace. "I been thinking your job just ain't enough to keep you busy, Po."

"I like my job good enough," said Po Doggly.

"I been thinking that there's a county election this fall, and the office of sheriff goes up for grabs. I think Pauley Wiseman ought to get turned out."

"And me get made sheriff? You think that's likely, me being a known drunk?"

"You ain't touched a drop the whole time you been with the doctor. And if we live through this and get Arthur back safe, why, you're going to be a hero."

"A hero hell! You crazy, Horace? We can't tell a soul about this or there'll be a reward out for our brains on rye bread from the Hio to Camelot."

"We ain't going to print up the story and sell copies, if that's what you mean. But you know how word spreads. Good folks'll know what you and me done."

"Then *you* be sheriff, Horace."

"Me?" Horace grinned. "Can you imagine me putting a man in jail?"

Po laughed softly. "Reckon not."

When they reached the shore, again their movements were swift and fit together just right. It was hard to believe it had been so many years since they worked together. It was like their bodies already knew what to do, so they didn't even have to think about it. Po jumped into the water—ankle deep is all, and he leaned on the boat so as not to splash much. The boat rocked a bit at *that,* of course, but without a bit of wasted motion Horace leaned against the rocking and calmed it down, hardly even noticing he was doing it. In a minute they had the bow dragged up onto the shore—sandy here, not muddy like the other side—and tied to a tree. To Alvin the rope looked old and rotten, but when he sent his bug inside to feel it out, he was sure it was still strong enough to hold the boat against the rocking of the river against the stern.

Only when all their familiar jobs was done did Horace present himself like militia on the town square, shoulders squared and eyes right on Alvin. "Well, now, Al, I reckon it's up to you to lead the way."

"Ain't we got to track them?" asked Po.

"Alvin knows where they are," said Horace.

"Well ain't that nice," said Po. "And does he know whether they got their guns aimed at our heads?"

"Yes," said Alvin. He said it in such a way as to make it plain that he didn't want no more questions.

It wasn't plain enough for Po. "You telling me this boy's a torch, or what? Most I heard was he got him a knack for shoeing horses."

Here was the bad part about having somebody else along. Alvin didn't have no wish to tell Po Doggly what all he could do, but he couldn't very well tell the man that he didn't trust him.

It was Horace came to the rescue. "Po, I got to tell you, Alvin ain't part of the story of this night."

"Looks to me like he's the biggest part."

"I tell you, Po, when this story gets told, it was you and me came along and happened to find the Finders asleep, you understand?"

Po wrinkled his brow, then nodded. "Just tell me this, boy. Whatever knack you got, you a Christian? I don't even ask that you be a Methodist."

"Yes sir," said Alvin. "I'm a Christian, I reckon. I hold to the Bible."

"Good then," said Po. "I just don't want to get myself all mixed up in devil stuff."

"Not with me," said Alvin.

"All right then. Best if I don't know what you do, Al. Just take a care not to get me killed because I don't know it."

Alvin stuck out his hand. Po shook it and grinned. "You blacksmiths got to be strong as a bear."

"Me?" said Alvin. "A bear gets in my way, I beat on his head till he's a wolverine."

"I like your brag, boy."

A moment's pause, and then Alvin led them off, following the thread that connected him to Arthur Stuart.

It wasn't all that far, but it took them an hour cutting through the woods in the dark—with all the leaves out, there wasn't much moonlight got to the ground. Without Alvin's sense of the forest around them, it would've taken three times as long and ten times the noise.

They found the Finders asleep in a clearing with a campfire dying down between them. The white-haired Finder was curled up on his bedroll. The black-haired Finder must've been left on watch; he was snoring away leaning against a tree. Their horses were asleep not far off. Alvin stopped them before they got close enough to disturb the animals.

Arthur Stuart was wide awake, sitting there staring into the fire.

Alvin sat there a minute, trying to figure how to do this. He wasn't sure how smart the Finders might be. Could they find scraps of dried skin, fallen-off hairs, something like that, and use it for a new cachet? Just in case, it wouldn't do no good to change Arthur right where he was; nor would it be too smart to head on out into the clearing where they might leave bits of their own selves, as proof of who stole Arthur away.

So from a distance, Alvin got inside the iron of the manacles and made cracks in all four parts, so they fell away to the ground at once, with a clank. The noise bothered the horses, who nickered a bit, but the Finders were still sleeping like the dead. Arthur, though, it didn't take him a second to figure out what was happening. He jumped to his feet all at once and started looking around for Alvin at the clearing's edge.

Alvin whistled, trying to match the song of a redbird. It was a pretty bad imitation, as birdcalls go, but Arthur heard it and knew that it was Alvin calling him. Without a moment's waiting or worrying, Arthur plunged right into the woods and not five minutes later, with a few more bad birdcalls to guide him, he was face to face with Alvin.

Of course Arthur Stuart made as if to give Alvin a big old hug, but Alvin held up a hand. "Don't touch anybody or anything," he whispered. "I've got to make a change in you, Arthur Stuart, so the Finders can't catch you again."

"I don't mind," said Arthur.

"I don't dare have a single scrap of the old way you used to be. You got hairs and skin and such all over in your clothes. So strip them off."

Arthur Stuart didn't hesitate. In a few moments his clothes were in a pile at his feet.

"Excuse me for not knowing a bit about this," said Po, "but if you leave those clothes a-lying there, them Finders'll know he come this way, and that points north to them sure as if we painted a big white arrow on the ground.''

''Reckon you're right,'' said Alvin.

''So have Arthur Stuart bring them along and float them down the river,'' said Horace.

''Just make sure you don't touch Arthur or nothing,'' said Alvin. ''Arthur, you just pick up your clothes and follow along slow and careful. If you get lost, give me a redbird whistle and I'll whistle back till you find us.''

''I knew you was coming, Alvin,'' said Arthur Stuart. ''You too, Pa.''

''So did them Finders,'' said Horace, ''and much as I wish we could arrange it, they ain't going to sleep forever.''

''Wait a minute anyway,'' said Alvin. He sent his bug back into the manacles and drew them back together, fit them tight, joined the iron again as if it had been cast that way. Now they lay on the ground unbroken, fastened tight, giving no sign of how the boy got free.

''I don't suppose you're maybe breaking their legs or something, Alvin,'' said Horace.

''Can he *do* that from here?'' asked Po.

''I'm doing no such thing,'' said Alvin. ''What we want is for the Finders to give up searching for a boy who as far as they can tell doesn't exist no more.''

''Well that makes sense, but I still like thinking of them Finders with their legs broke,'' said Horace.

Alvin grinned and plunged off into the forest, deliberately making enough noise and moving slow enough that the others could follow him in the near-darkness; if he wanted to, he could've moved like a Red man through the woods, making not a sound, leaving no whiff of a trail that anyone could follow.

They got to the river and stopped. Alvin didn't want Arthur getting into the boat in his present skin, leaving traces of himself all over. So if he was going to change him, he had to do it here.

''Toss them clothes, boy,'' said Horace. ''Far as you can.''

Arthur took a step or two into the water. It made Alvin scared, for with his inward eye he saw it as if Arthur, made of light and earth and air, suddenly got part of himself disappeared into the blackness of the water. Still, the water hadn't harmed them none on the trip here, and Alvin saw as how it might even be useful.

Arthur Stuart pitched his wad of clothes out into the river. The current wasn't all that strong; they watched the clothes turn lazily and float downstream, gradually drifting apart. Arthur stood there, up to his butt in water, watching the clothes. No, not watching them—he didn't turn a speck when they drifted far to the left. He was just looking at the north shore, the free side of the river.

"I been here afore," he said. "I seen this boat."

"Might be," said Horace. "Though you was a mite young to remember it. Po and I, we helped your mama into this very boat. My daughter Peggy held you when we got to shore."

"My sister Peggy," said Arthur. He turned around and looked at Horace, like as if it was really a question.

"I reckon so," said Horace, and that was the answer.

"Just stand there, Arthur Stuart," said Alvin. "When I change you, I got to change you all over, inside and out. Better to do that in the water, where all the dead skin with your old self marked in it can wash away."

"You going to make me White?" asked Arthur Stuart.

"Can you *do* that?" asked Po Doggly.

"I don't know what all is going to change," said Alvin. "I hope I don't make you White, though. That'd be like stealing away from you the part of you your mama gave you."

"They don't make White boys be slaves," said Arthur Stuart.

"They ain't going to make this partickler mixup boy a slave anyhow," said Alvin. "Not if I can help it. Now just stand there, stand right still, and let me figure this out."

They all stood there, the men and the boy, while Alvin studied inside Arthur Stuart, finding that tiny signature that marked every living bit of him.

Alvin knew he couldn't just go changing it willy-nilly, since he didn't rightly understand what all that signature was *for*. He just knew that it was somehow part of what made Arthur himself, and you don't just change that. Maybe changing the wrong thing might strike him blind, or make his blood turn to rainwater or something. How could Alvin know?

It was seeing the string still connecting them, heart to heart, that gave Alvin the idea—that and remembering what the Redbird said, using Arthur Stuart's own lips to say it. "The Maker is the one who is part of what he Makes." Alvin stripped off his own shirt and then stepped out into the water and knelt down in it, so he was near eye-to-eye with Arthur Stuart, cool water swirling gently around his waist. Then he put out his hands and pulled Arthur Stuart to him and held him there, breast to breast, hands on shoulders.

"I thought we wasn't supposed to touch the boy," said Po.

"Hush up you blame fool," said Horace Guester. "Alvin knows what he's doing."

I wish that was true, thought Alvin. But at least he had an idea what to do, and that was better than nothing. Now that their living skin was pressed together, Alvin could look and compare Arthur's secret signature with his own. Most of it was the same, exactly the same, and the way Alvin figured, that's the part that makes us both human instead of cows or frogs or pigs or chickens. That's the part I don't dare change, not a bit of it.

The rest—I can change that. But not any old how. What good to save him if I turn him bright yellow or make him stupid or something?

So Alvin did the only thing as made sense to him. He changed bits of Arthur's signature to be just like Alvin's own. Not *all* that was different—not all that much, in fact. Just a little. But even a little meant that Arthur Stuart had stopped being completely himself and started being partly Alvin. It seemed to Alvin that what he was doing was terrible and wonderful at the same time.

How much? How much did he have to change till the Finders wouldn't know the boy? Surely not all. Surely just *this* much, just *these* changes. There was no way to know. All that Alvin could do was guess, and so he took his guess and that was it.

That was only the beginning, of course. Now he started in changing all the other signatures to match the new one, each living bit of Arthur, one by one, as fast as he could. Dozens of them, hundreds of them; he found each new signature and changed it to fit the new pattern.

Hundreds of them, and hundreds more, and still he had changed no more than a tiny patch of skin on Arthur's chest. How could he hope to change the boy's whole body, going so slow?

"It hurts," whispered Arthur.

Alvin drew away from him. "I ain't doing nothing to hurt you, Arthur Stuart."

Arthur looked down at his chest. "Right here," he said, touching the spot where Alvin had been working.

Alvin looked in the moonlight and saw that indeed that spot seemed to be swollen, changed, darkened. He looked again, only not with his eyes, and saw that the rest of Arthur's body was attacking the part that Alvin changed, killing it bit by bit, fast as it could.

Of course. What did he expect? The signature was the way the body recognized itself—that's why every living bit of a body had to have that signature in it. If it wasn't there, the body knew it had to be a disease or something and killed it. Wasn't it bad enough that changing Arthur was taking so long? Now Alvin knew that it wouldn't do no good to change him at all—the more he changed him, the sicker he'd get and the more Arthur Stuart's own body would try to kill itself until the boy either died or shed the new changed part.

It was just like Taleswapper's old story, about trying to build a wall so big that by the time you got halfway through building it, the oldest parts of it had already crumbled to dust. How could you build such a wall if it was getting broke down faster than you could build it up?

"I can't," said Alvin. "I'm trying to do what can't be done."

"Well if you can't do it," said Po Doggly, "I hope you can fly, cause that's the only way you can get that boy to Canada before the Finders catch up with you."

"I can't," said Alvin.

"You're just tired," said Horace. "We'll all just hush up so you can think."

"Won't do any good," said Alvin.

"My mama could fly," said Arthur Stuart.

Alvin sighed in impatience at this same old story coming back again.

"It's true, you know," said Horace. "Little Peggy told me. That little black slave girl, she diddled with some ash and blackbird feathers and such, and flew straight up here. That's what killed her. I couldn't believe it the first time I realized the boy remembers, and we always kept our mouths shut about it hoping he'd forget. But I got to tell you, Alvin, it'd be a pure shame if that girl died just so you could give up on us at this same spot in the river seven years later."

Alvin closed his eyes. "Just shut your mouth and let me think," he said.

"I *said* that's what we'd do," said Horace.

"So *do* it," said Po Doggly.

Alvin hardly even heard them. He was looking back inside Arthur's body, inside that patch that Alvin changed. The new signature wasn't bad in itself—only where it bordered on the skin with the old signature, that was the only place the new skin was getting sick and dying. Arthur'd be just fine if Alvin could somehow change him all at once, instead of bit by bit.

The way that the string came all at once, when Alvin thought of it, pictured where it started and where it ended and what it *was*. All the atoms of it moving into place at the same time. Like the way Po Doggly and Horace Guester fit together all at once, each doing his own task yet taking into account all that the other man did.

But the string was clean and simple. This was hard—like he told Miss Larner, turning water into wine instead of iron into gold.

No, can't think of it that way. What I did to make the string was teach all the atoms what and where to be, because each one of them was alive and each one could obey me. But inside Arthur's body

I ain't dealing with atoms, I'm dealing with these living bits, and each one of *them* is alive. Maybe it's even the signature itself that makes them alive, maybe I can teach them all what they ought to be—instead of moving each part of them, one at a time, I can just say—Be like this—and they'll do it.

He no sooner thought of it than he tried it. In his mind he thought of speaking to all the signatures in Arthur's skin, all over his chest, all at once; he showed them the pattern he held in his mind, a pattern so complex he couldn't even understand it himself, except that he knew it was the same pattern as the signatures in this patch of skin he had changed bit by bit. And as soon as he showed them, as soon as he commanded them—Be like this! This is the way!—they changed. It all changed, all the skin on Arthur Stuart's chest, all at once.

Arthur gasped, then howled with pain. What had been a soreness in a patch of skin was now spread across his whole chest.

"Trust me," Alvin said. "I'm going to change you sure now, and the pain will stop. But I'm doing it under the water, where all the old skin gets carried off at once. Plug your nose! Hold your breath!"

Arthur Stuart was panting from the pain, but he did what Alvin said. He pinched his nose with his right hand, then took a breath and closed his mouth. At once Alvin gripped Arthur's wrist in his left hand and put his right hand behind the boy and plunged him under the water. In that instant Alvin held Arthur's body whole in his mind, seeing all the signatures, not one by one, but all of them; he showed them the pattern, the new signature, and this time thought the words so strong his lips spoke them. "This is the way! Be like this!"

He couldn't feel it with his hands—Arthur's body didn't change a whit that he could sense with his natural senses. But Alvin could still see the change, all at once, all in an instant, every signature in the boy's body, in the organs, in the muscles, in the blood, in the brain; even his hair changed, every part of him that was connected to himself. And what wasn't connected, what didn't change, that was washed away and gone.

Alvin plunged himself under the water, to wash off any part of Arthur's skin or hair that might have clung to him. Then he rose up and lifted Arthur Stuart out of the water, all in one motion. The boy came up shedding waterdrops like a spray of cold pearls in the moonlight. He stood there gasping for breath and shaking from the cold.

"Tell me it don't hurt no more," said Alvin.

"Any more," said Arthur, correcting him just like Miss Larner always did. "I feel fine. Except cold."

Alvin scooped him up out of the water and carried him back to the bank. "Wrap him in my shirt and let's get out of here."

So they did. Not a one of them noticed that when Arthur imitated Miss Larner, he didn't use Miss Larner's voice.

Peggy didn't notice either, not right away. She was too busy looking inside Arthur Stuart's heartfire. How it changed when Alvin transformed him! So subtle a change it was that Peggy couldn't even tell what it was Alvin was changing—yet in the moment that Arthur Stuart emerged from the water, not a single path from his past remained—not a single path leading southward into slavery. And all the new paths, the new futures that the transformation had brought to him—they led to such amazing possibilities.

During all the time it took for Horace, Po, and Alvin to bring Arthur Stuart back across the Hio and through the woods to the smithy, Peggy did nothing more than explore in Arthur Stuart's heartfire, studying possibilities that had never before existed in the world. There was a new Maker abroad in the land; Arthur was the first soul touched by him, and everything was different. Moreover, most of Arthur's futures were inextricably tied with Alvin. Peggy saw possibilities of incredible journeys—on one path a trip to Europe where Arthur Stuart would be at Alvin's side as the new Holy Roman Emperor Napoleon bowed to him; on another path a voyage into a strange island nation far to the south where Red men lived their whole lives on mats of floating seaweed; on another path a triumphant crossing into westward lands where the Reds hailed Alvin as the great unifier of all the races, and opened up their last refuge to him, so perfect was their trust. And always by his side was Arthur Stuart, the mixup boy—but now trusted, now himself gifted with some of the Maker's own power.

Most of the paths began with them bringing Arthur Stuart to her springhouse, so she was not surprised when they knocked at her door.

"Miss Larner," called Alvin softly.

She was distracted; reality was not half so interesting as the futures revealed now in Arthur Stuart's heartfire. She opened the door. There they stood, Arthur still wrapped in Alvin's shirt.

"We brought him back," said Horace.

"I can see that," said Peggy. She *was* glad of it, but that gladness didn't show up in her voice. Instead she sounded busy, interrupted, annoyed. As she was. Get on with it, she wanted to say. I've seen this conversation as Arthur overheard it, so get on with it, get it over with, and let me get back to exploring what this boy will be. But of course she could say none of this—not if she hoped to remain disguised as Miss Larner.

"They won't find him," said Alvin, "not as long as they don't actually see him with their eyes. Something—their cachet don't work no more."

"Doesn't work anymore," said Peggy.

"Right," said Alvin. "What we come for—came for—can we leave him with you? Your house, here, Ma'am, I've got it hexed up so tight they won't even think to come inside, long as you keep the door locked."

"Don't you have more clothes for him than this? He's been wet—do you want him to take a chill?"

"It's a warm night," said Horace, "and we don't want to be fetching clothes from the house. Not till the Finders come back and give up and go away again."

"Very well," said Peggy.

"We'd best be about our business," said Po Doggly. "I got to get back to Dr. Physicker's."

"And since I told Old Peg that I'd be in town, I'd better be there," said Horace.

Alvin spoke straight to Peggy. "I'll be in the smithy, Miss Larner. If something goes wrong, you give a shout, and I'll be up the hill in ten seconds."

"Thank you. Now—please go on about your business."

She closed the door. She didn't mean to be so abrupt. But she had a whole new set of futures. No one but herself had ever been so important in Alvin's work as Arthur was going to be. But perhaps that would happen with everyone that Alvin actually touched and changed—perhaps as a Maker he would transform everyone he loved until they all stood with him in those glorious moments, until they all looked out upon the world through the lensed walls of the Crystal City and saw all things as God must surely see them.

A knock on the door. She opened it.

"In the first place," said Alvin, "don't open the door without knowing who it is."

"I knew it was you," she said. Truth was, though, she didn't. She didn't even think.

"In the second place, I was waiting to hear you lock the door, and you never did."

"Sorry," she said. "I forgot."

"We went to a lot of work to save this boy tonight, Miss Larner. Now it's all up to you. Just till the Finders go."

"Yes, I know." She really was sorry, and let her voice reveal her regret.

"Good night then."

He stood there waiting. For what?

Oh, yes. For her to close the door.

She closed it, locked it, then returned to Arthur Stuart and hugged him until he struggled to get away. "You're safe," she said.

"Of course I am," said Arthur Stuart. "We went to a lot of work to save this boy tonight, Miss Larner."

She listened to him, and knew there was something wrong. What was it? Oh, yes, of course. Alvin had just said exactly those words. But what was wrong? Arthur Stuart was always imitating people.

Always imitating. But this time Arthur Stuart had repeated Alvin's words in his own voice, not Alvin's. She had never heard

him do that. She thought it was his knack, that he was so natural
a mimic he didn't even realize he was doing it.

"Spell 'cicada,' " she said.

"C-I-C-A-D-A," he answered. In his own voice, not hers.

"Arthur Stuart," she whispered. "What's wrong?"

"Ain't nothing wrong, Miss Larner," he said. "I'm home."

He didn't know. He didn't realize it. Never having understood
how perfect a mimic he had been, now he didn't realize when the
knack was gone. He still had the near-perfect memory of what
others said—he still had all the words. But the voices were gone;
only his own seven-year-old voice remained.

She hugged him again, for a moment, more briefly. She understood now. As long as Arthur Stuart remained himself, the Finders
could have found him and taken him south into slavery. The only
way to save him was to make him no longer completely himself.
Alvin hadn't known, of course he hadn't, that in saving Arthur, he
had taken away his knack, or at least part of it. The price of Arthur's
freedom was making him cease to be fully Arthur. Did Alvin understand that?

"I'm tired, Miss Larner," said Arthur Stuart.

"Yes, of course," she said. "You can sleep here—in my bed.
Take off that dirty shirt and climb in under the covers and you'll
be warm and safe all night."

He hesitated. She looked into his heartfire and saw why; smiling,
she turned her back. She heard a rustle of fabric and then a squeak
of bedsprings and the swish of a small body sliding along her sheets
into bed. Then she turned around, bent over him where he lay upon
her pillow, and kissed him lightly on the cheek.

"Good night, Arthur," she said.

"Good night," he murmured.

In moments he was asleep. She sat at her writing table and pulled
up the wick on her lamp. She would do some reading while she
waited for the Finders to return. Something to keep her calm while
she waited.

No, she wouldn't. The words were there on the page, but she
made no sense of them. Was she reading Descartes or Deuteronomy?

It didn't matter. She couldn't stay away from Arthur's new heartfire. Of course all the paths of his life changed. He wasn't the same person anymore. No, that wasn't quite true. He was still Arthur. Mostly Arthur.

Almost Arthur. Almost what he was. But not quite.

Was it worth it? To lose part of who he had been in order to live free? Perhaps this new self was better than the old; but that old Arthur Stuart was gone now, gone forever, even more surely than if he had gone south and lived the rest of his life in bitter slavery, with his time in Hatrack as a memory, and then a dream, and then a mythic tale he told the pickaninnies in the years just before he died.

Fool! she cried to herself in her heart. No one is the same person today that he was yesterday. No one had a body as young as it was, or a heart so naive, or a head so ignorant as it was. He would have been far more terribly transformed—malformed—by life in bondage than by Alvin's gentle changes. Arthur Stuart was more surely himself now than he would have been in Appalachee. Besides, she had seen all the dark paths that once dwelt in his heartfire, the taste of the lash, the stupefying sun beating down on him as he labored in the field, or the hanging rope that awaited him on the many paths that led to his leading or taking part in a slave revolt and slaughtering dozens of Whites as they lay in their beds. Arthur Stuart was too young to understand what had happened to him; but if he were old enough, if he could choose which future he'd prefer, Peggy had no doubt that he would choose the sort of future Alvin had just made possible.

In a way, he lost some of himself, some of his knack, and therefore some of the choices he might have had in life. But in losing those, he gained so much more freedom, so much more power, that he was clear winner in the bargain.

Yet as she remembered his bright face when he spelled words to her in her own voice, she could not keep herself from shedding a few tears of regret.

☙ 19 ❧

The Plow

THE FINDERS WOKE up not long after Arthur Stuart's rescuers took him across the river.

"Look at this. Manacles still fastened tight. Good hard iron."

"Don't matter. They got them a good spell for sleeping and a good spell for slipping out of chains, but don't they know us Finders always find a runaway, once we got his scent?"

If you could've seen them, you'd think they was glad Arthur Stuart got loose. Truth was, these boys loved a good chase, loved showing folks that Finders just couldn't be shook loose. And if it so happened they put a fistful of lead shot through somebody's belly before the hunt was done, well, ain't that just the way of it? Like dogs on the trail of a bleeding deer.

They followed Arthur Stuart's path through the forest till they came to the water's edge. Only then did their cheerful looks give way to a kind of frown. They lifted up their eyes and looked across the water, searching for the heartfires of men abroad at this time of night, when all honest folk was bound to be asleep. The white-haired one, he just couldn't see far enough; but the black-haired one, he said, "I see a few, moving about. And a few not moving. We'll pick up the scent again in Hatrack River."

Alvin held the plow between his hands. He knew that he could turn it all to gold—he'd seen gold enough in his life to know the pattern, so he could show the bits of iron what they ought to be. But he also knew that it wasn't no ordinary gold that he wanted. That would be too soft, and as cold as any ordinary stone. No, he wanted something new, not just iron to gold like any alchemist could dream of, but a living gold, a gold that could hold its shape and strength better than iron, better than the finest steel. Gold that was awake, aware of the world around it—a plow that knew the earth that it would tear, to lay it open to the fires of the sun.

A golden plow that would know a man, that a man could trust, the way Po Doggly knew Horace Guester and each trusted the other. A plow that wouldn't need no ox to draw, nor added weight to force it downward into the soil. A plow that would know which soil was rich and which was poor. A sort of gold that never had been seen in all the world before, just like the world had never seen such a thin invisible string as Alvin spun between Arthur Stuart and himself today.

So there he knelt, holding the shape of the gold inside his mind. "Be like this," he whispered to the iron.

He could feel how atoms came from all around the plow and joined together with those already in the iron, forming bits much heavier than what the iron was, and lined up in different ways, until they fit the pattern that he showed them in his mind.

Between his hands he held a plow of gold. He rubbed his fingers over it. Gold, yes, bright yellow in the firelight from the forge, but still dead, still cold. How could he teach it to be alive? Not by showing it the pattern of his own flesh—that wasn't the kind of life it needed. It was the living atoms that he wanted to waken, to show them what they were compared to what they *could* be. To put the fire of life in them.

The fire of life. Alvin lifted the golden plow—much heavier

now—and despite the heat of the slacking fire, he set it right amid the glowing charcoal of the forge.

They were back on their horses now, them Finders, walking them calmly up the road to Hatrack River, looking into every house and hut and cabin, holding up the cachet to match it with the heartfires that they found within. But nary a match did they find, nary a body did they recognize. They passed the smithy and saw that a heartfire burned inside, but it wasn't the runaway mixup boy. It was bound to be the smith what made the manacles, they knew it.

"I'd like to kill him," whispered the black-haired Finder. "I know he put that spell in the manacles, to make them so that boy could slip right out."

"Time enough for that after we find the pickaninny," said the white-haired Finder.

They saw two heartfires burning in the old springhouse, but neither one was like what they had in the cachet, so they went on, searching for a child that they might recognize.

The fire was deep within the gold now, but all it was doing was melting it. That wouldn't do at all—it was life the plow needed, not the death of metal in the fire. He held the plowshape in his mind and showed it plain as can be to every bit of metal in the plow; cried out silently to every atom, It ain't enough to be lined up in the little shapes of gold—you need to hold this larger shape yourselves, no matter the fire, no matter what other force might press or tear or melt or try to maim you.

He could sense that he was heard—there was movement in the gold, movement against the downward slipping of the gold as it turned to fluid. But it wasn't strong enough, it wasn't *sure* enough. Without thinking, Alvin reached his hands into the fire and clung to the gold, showing it the plowshape, crying to it in his heart, Like this! Be like this! This is what you are! Oh, the pain of it burned something fierce, but he knew that it was right for his hands to be there, for the Maker is a part of what he makes. The atoms heard him, and formed themselves in ways that Alvin never even thought of, but the result of it all was that the gold now took the heat of the fire into itself without melting, without losing shape. It was done; the plow wasn't alive, exactly, not the way he wanted—but it could stand in the forgefire without melting. The gold was more than gold now. It was gold that knew it was a plow and meant to stay that way.

Alvin pulled his hands away from the plow and saw flames still dancing on his skin, which was charred in places, peeling back away from the bone. Silent as death, he plunged his hands into the water barrel and heard the sizzle of the fire on his flesh as it went out. Then, before the pain could come in full force, he set to healing himself, sloughing away the dead skin and making new skin grow.

He stood there, weakened from all his body had to do to heal his hands, looking into the fire at the gold plow. Just setting there, knowing its shape and holding to it—but that wasn't enough to make the plow alive. It had to know what a plow was for. It had to know why it lived, so it could act to fulfill that purpose. That was Making, Alvin knew it now; that was what Redbird come to say three years ago. Making wasn't like carpentry or smithy work or any such, cutting and bending and melting to force things into new shapes. Making was something subtler and stronger—making things *want* to be another way, a new shape, so they just naturally flowed that way. It was something Alvin had done for years without knowing what it was he was doing. When he thought he was doing no more than finding the natural cracks in stone, he was really making those cracks; by imagining where he wanted them to be, and showing it to the atoms within the bits within the pieces of the rock, he taught them to want to fulfill the shape he showed them.

Now, with this plow, he had done it, not by accident, but on purpose; and he'd taught the gold to be something stronger, to hold better to its shape than anything he'd ever Made before. But how could he teach it more, teach it to act, to move in ways that gold was never taught to move?

In the back of his mind, he knew that this golden plow wasn't the real problem. The real problem was the Crystal City, and the building blocks of *that* weren't going to be simple atoms in a metal plow. The atoms of a city are men and women, and they don't believe the shape they're shown with the simple faith that atoms have, they don't understand with such pure clarity, and when they act, their actions are never half so pure. But if I can teach this gold to be a plow and to be alive, then maybe I can make a Crystal City out of men and women; maybe I can find people as pure as the atoms of this gold, who come to understand the shape of the Crystal City and love it the way I did the moment I saw it when I climbed the inside of that twister with Tenskwa-Tawa. Then they'll not only hold that shape but also make it act, make the Crystal City a living thing much larger and greater than any one of us who are its atoms.

The Maker is the one who is part of what he makes.

Alvin ran to the bellows and pumped up the fire till the charcoal was glowing hot enough to drive any regular smith outside into the night air to wait till the fire slacked. But not Alvin. Instead he walked right up to the forge and climbed right into the heat and the flame. He felt the clothes burning right off his body, but he paid no mind. He curled himself around that plow and then commenced to healing himself, not piecemeal, not bit by bit, but healing himself by telling his whole body, all at once, Stay alive! Put the fire that burns you into this plow!

And at the same time, he told the plow, Do as my body does! Live! Learn from every living bit of me how each part has its purpose, and acts on it. I can't show you the shape you've got to be, or how it's done, cause I don't know. But I can show you what it's like to be alive, by the pain of my body, by the healing of it, by the struggle to stay alive. Be like this! Whatever it takes, however hard it is for you to learn, this is you, be like me!

It took forever, trembling in the fire as his body struggled with the heat, finding ways to channel it the way a river channels water, pouring it out into the plow like it was an ocean of golden fire. And within the plow, the atoms struggled to do what Alvin asked, wanting to obey him, not knowing how. But his call to them was strong, too strong not to hear; and it was more than a matter of hearing him, too. It was like they could tell that what he wanted for them was good. They trusted him, they wanted to be the living plow he dreamed of, and so in a million flecks of time so small that a second seemed like eternity to them, they tried this, they tried that, until somewhere within the golden plow a new pattern was made that knew itself to be alive exactly as Alvin wanted it to be; and in a single single moment the pattern passed throughout the plow and it was alive.

Alive. Alvin felt it moving within the curve of his body as the plow nestled down into the coals of the fire, cutting into it, plowing it as if it were soil. And because it was a barren soil, one that could bear no life, the plow rose quickly out of it and slipped outward, away from the fire toward the lip of the forge. It moved by deciding to be in a different place, and then being there; when it reached the brink of the forge it toppled off and tumbled to the smithy floor.

In agony Alvin rolled from the fire and also fell, also lay pressed against the cold dirt of the floor. Now that the fire no longer surrounded him, his body gained against the death of his skin, healing him as he had taught it to do, without him having to tell it what to do, without need of direction at all. Become yourself, that had been Alvin's command, and so the signature within each living bit of him obeyed the pattern it contained, until his body was whole and perfect, the skin new, uncallused, and unburned.

What he couldn't remove was the memory of pain, or the weakness from all the strength his body had given up. But he didn't care. Weak as he was, his heart was jubilant, because the plow that lay beside him on the ground was living gold, not because he made it, but because he taught it how to make itself.

The Finders found nothing, nowhere in town—yet the black-haired Finder couldn't see anyone running away, neither, not within the farthest distance that any natural man or horse could possibly have gone since the boy got taken back. Somehow the mixup boy was hiding from them, a thing they knew full well was pure impossible—but it must be so.

The place to look was where the boy had lived for all these years. The roadhouse, the springhouse, the smithy—places where folks were up unnatural late at night. They rode to near the roadhouse, then tied up their horses just off the road. They loaded their shotguns and pistols and set off on foot. Passing by the roadhouse they searched again, accounting for every heartfire; none of them was like the cachet.

"That cottage, with that teacher lady," said the white-haired Finder. "That's where the boy was when we found him before."

The black-haired Finder looked over that way. Couldn't see the springhouse through the trees, of course, but what he was looking for he could see, trees or not. "Two people in there," he said.

"Could be the mixup boy, then," said the white-haired Finder.

"Cachet says not." Then the black-haired Finder grinned nastily. "Single teacher lady, living alone, got a visitor this time of night? I know what kind of company she's keeping, and it ain't no mixup boy."

"Let's go see anyhow," said the white-haired Finder. "If'n you're right, she won't be putting out any complaint on how we broke in her door, or we'll just tell what we saw going on inside when we done it."

They had a good little laugh about that, and set off through the moonlight toward Miss Larner's house. They meant to kick in the door, of course, and have a good laugh when the teacher lady got all huffy about it and made her threats.

Funny thing was, when they actually got near the cottage, that plan just clean went out of their heads. They forgot all about it. Just looked again at the heartfires within and compared them to the cachet.

"What the hell are we doing up here?" asked the white-haired Finder. "Boy's bound to be at the roadhouse. We *know* he ain't here!"

"You know what I'm thinking?" said the black-haired one. "Maybe they killed him."

"That's plain crazy. Why save him, then?"

"How else do you figure they made it so we can't see him, then?"

"He's in the roadhouse. They got some hex that hides him up,

I'll bet. Once we open the right door there, we'll see him and that'll be that.''

For a fleeting moment the black-haired Finder thought—well, why not look in this teacher lady's cottage, too, if they got a hex like that? Why not open *this* door?

But he no sooner had that thought than it just slipped away so he couldn't remember it, couldn't even remember *having* a thought. He just trotted away after the white-haired Finder. Mixup boy's bound to be in the roadhouse, that's for sure.

She saw their heartfires, of course, as the Finders came toward her cottage, but Peggy wasn't afraid. She had explored Arthur Stuart's heartfire all this time, and there was no path there which led to capture by these Finders. Arthur had dangers enough in the future—Peggy could see that—but no harm would come to the boy tonight. So she paid them little heed. She knew when they decided to leave; knew when the black-haired Finder thought of coming in; knew when the hexes blocked him and drove him away. But it was Arthur Stuart she was watching, searching out the years to come.

Then, suddenly, she couldn't hold it to herself any longer. She had to tell Alvin, both the joy and sorrow of what he had done. Yet how could she? How could she tell him that Miss Larner was really a torch who could see the million newborn futures in Arthur Stuart's heartfire? It was unbearable to keep all this to herself. She might have told Mistress Modesty, years ago, when she lived there and kept no secrets.

It was madness to go down to the smithy, knowing that her desire was to tell him things she couldn't tell without revealing who she was. Yet it would surely drive her mad to stay within these walls, alone with all this knowledge that she couldn't share.

So she got up, unlocked the door, and stepped outside. No one around. She closed the door and locked it; then again looked into Arthur's heartfire and again found no danger for the boy. He would be safe. She would see Alvin.

Only then did she look into Alvin's heartfire; only then did she see the terrible pain that he had suffered only minutes ago. Why hadn't she noticed? Why hadn't she seen? Alvin had just passed through the greatest threshold of his life; he had truly done a great Making, brought something new into the world, and she hadn't seen. When he faced the Unmaker while she was in far-off Dekane, she had seen his struggle—now, when she wasn't three rods off, why hadn't she turned to him? Why hadn't she known his pain when he writhed inside the fire?

Maybe it was the springhouse. Once before, near nineteen years ago, the day that Alvin was born, the springhouse had damped her gift and lulled her to sleep till she was almost too late. But no, it couldn't be that—the water didn't run through the springhouse anymore, and the forgefire was stronger than that.

Maybe it was the Unmaker itself, come to block her. But as she cast about with her torchy sight, she couldn't see any unusual darkness amid the colors of the world around her, not close at hand, anyway. Nothing that could have blinded her.

No, it had to be the nature of what Alvin himself was doing that blinded her to it. Just as she hadn't seen how he would extricate himself from his confrontation with the Unmaker years ago, just as she hadn't seen how he would change young Arthur at the Hio shore tonight, it was just the same way she hadn't seen what he was doing in the forge. It was outside the futures that her knack could see, the particular Making he performed tonight.

Would it always be like that? Would she always be blinded when his most important work was being done? It made her angry, it frightened her—what good is my knack, if it deserts me just when I need it most!

No. I didn't need it most just now. Alvin had no need of me or my sight when he climbed into the fire. My knack has never deserted me when it was *needed*. It's only my desire that's thwarted.

Well, he needs me now, she thought. She picked her way carefully down the slope; the moon was low, the shadows deep, so the path was treacherous. When she rounded the corner of the smithy, the light from the forgefire, spilling out onto the grass, was almost blinding; it was so red that it made the grass look shiny black, not green.

Inside the smithy Alvin lay curled on the ground, facing toward the forge, away from her. He was breathing heavily, raggedly. Asleep? No. He was naked; it took a moment to realize that his clothing must have burned off him in the forge. He hadn't noticed it in all his pain, and so had no memory of it; therefore she hadn't seen it happen when she searched for memories in his heartfire.

His skin was shockingly pale and smooth. Earlier today she had seen his skin a deep brown from the sun and the forgefire's heat. Earlier today he had been callused, with here and there a scar from some spark or searing burn, the normal accidents of life beside a fire. Now, though, his skin was as unmarked as a baby's, and she could not help herself; she stepped into the smithy, knelt beside him, and gently brushed her hand along his back, from his shoulder down to the narrow place above the hip. His skin was so soft it made her own hands feel coarse to her, as if she marred him just by touching him.

He let out a long breath, a sigh. She withdrew her hand.

"Alvin," she said. "Are you all right?"

He moved his arm; he was stroking something that lay within the curl of his body. Only now did she see it, a faint yellow in the double shadow of his body and of the forge. A golden plow.

"It's alive," he murmured.

As if in answer, she saw it move smoothly under his hand.

Of course they didn't knock. At this time of night? They would know at once it couldn't be some chance traveler—it could only be the Finders. Knocking at the door would warn them, give them a chance to try to carry the boy farther off.

But the black-haired Finder didn't so much as try the latch. He just let fly with his foot and the door crashed inward, pulling away from the upper hinge as it did. Then, shotgun at the ready, he moved quickly inside and looked around the common room. The fire there was dying down, so the light was scant, but they could see that there was no one there.

"I'll keep watch on the stairs," said the white-haired Finder. "You go out the back to see if anybody's trying to get out that way."

The black-haired Finder immediately made his way past the kitchen and the stairs to the back door, which he flung open. The white-haired Finder was halfway up the stairs before the back door closed again.

In the kitchen, Old Peg crawled out from under the table. Neither one had so much as paused at the kitchen door. She didn't know who they were, of course, but she hoped—hoped it was the Finders, sneaking back here because somehow, by some miracle, Arthur Stuart got away and they didn't know where he was. She slipped off her shoes and walked as quietly as she could from the kitchen to the common room, where Horace kept a loaded shotgun over the fireplace. She reached up and took it down, but in the process she knocked over a tin teakettle that someone had left warming by the fire earlier in the evening. The kettle clattered; hot water spilled over her bare feet; she gasped in spite of herself.

Immediately she could hear footsteps on the stairs. She ignored the pain and ran to the foot of the stairs, just in time to see the white-haired Finder coming down. He had a shotgun pointed straight at her. Even though she'd never fired a gun at a human being in her life, she didn't hesitate a moment. She pulled the trigger; the gun kicked back against her belly, driving the breath out of her and slamming her against the wall beside the kitchen door. She hardly noticed. All she saw was how the white-haired Finder stood there, his face suddenly relaxing till it looked as stupid as a cow's face. Then red blossoms appeared all over his shirt, and he toppled over backward.

You'll never steal another child away from his mama, thought Old Peg. You'll never drag another Black into a life of bowing under the whip. I killed you, Finder, and I think the good Lord rejoices. But even if I go to hell for it, I'm glad.

She was so intent on watching him that she didn't even notice that the door out back stood open, held in place by the barrel of the black-haired Finder's gun, pointed right at her.

Alvin was so intent on telling Peggy what he had done that he hardly noticed he was naked. She handed him the leather apron hanging from a peg on the wall, and he put it on by habit, without a thought. She hardly heard his words; all that he was telling her, she already knew from looking in his heartfire. Instead she was looking at him, thinking, Now he's a Maker, in part because of what I taught him. Maybe I'm finished now, maybe my life will be my own—but maybe not, maybe now I've just begun, maybe now I can treat him as a man, not as a pupil or a ward. He seemed to glow with an inner fire; and every step he took, the golden plow echoed, not by following him or tangling itself in his feet, but by slipping along on a line that could have been an orbit around him, well out of the way but close enough to be of use; as if it were a part of him, though unattached.

"I know," Peggy told him. "I understand. You *are* a Maker now."

"It's more than that!" he cried. "It's the Crystal City. I know how to build it now, Miss Larner. See, the city ain't the crystal towers that I saw, the city's the people inside it, and if I'm going to build the place I got to find the kind of folks who ought to be there, folks as true and loyal as this plow, folks who share the dream enough to want to build it, and keep on building it even if I'm not there. You see, Miss Larner? The Crystal City isn't a thing that a single Maker can make. It's a city of Makers; I got to find all kinds of folks and somehow make Makers out of them."

She knew as he said it that this was indeed the task that he was born for—and the labor that would break his heart. "Yes," she said. "That's true, I know it is." And in spite of herself, she couldn't sound like Miss Larner, calm and cool and distant. She sounded like herself, like her true feelings. She was burning up inside with the fire that Alvin lit there.

"Come with me, Miss Larner," said Alvin. "You know so much, and you're such a good teacher—I need your help."

No, Alvin, not those words. I'll come with you for those words, yes, but say the other words, the ones I need so much to hear. "How can I teach what only you know how to do?" she asked him—trying to sound quiet, calm.

"But it ain't just for the teaching, either—I can't do this alone.

What I done tonight, it's so hard—I need to have you with me.''
He took a step toward her. The golden plow slipped across the floor
toward her, behind her; if it marked the outer border of Alvin's
largest self, then she was now well within that generous circle.

''What do you need me for?'' asked Peggy. She refused to look
within his heartfire, refused to see whether or not there was any
chance that he might actually—no, she refused even to name to
herself what it was she wanted now, for fear that somehow she'd
discover that it couldn't possibly be so, that it could never happen,
that somehow tonight all such paths had been irrevocably closed.
Indeed, she realized, that was part of why she had been so caught
up in exploring Arthur Stuart's new futures; he would be so close
to Alvin that she could see much of Alvin's great and terrible future
through Arthur's eyes, without ever having to know what she would
know if she looked into Alvin's own heartfire: Alvin's heartfire
would show her whether, in his many futures, there were any in
which he loved her, and married her, and put that dear and perfect
body into her arms to give her and get from her that gift that only
lovers share.

''Come with me,'' he said. ''I can't even think of going on out
there without you, Miss Larner. I—'' He laughed at himself. ''I
don't even know your first name, Miss Larner.''

''Margaret,'' she said.

''Can I call you that? Margaret—will you come with me? I know
you ain't what you seem to be, but I don't care what you look like
under all that hexery. I feel like you're the only living soul who
knows me like I really am, and I—''

He just stood there, looking for the word. And she stood there,
waiting to hear it.

''I love you,'' he said. ''Even though you think I'm just a boy.''

Maybe she would've answered him. Maybe she would've told
him that she knew he was a man, and that she was the only woman
who could love him without worshipping him, the only one who
could actually be a helpmeet for him. But into the silence after
his words and before she could speak, there came the sound of a
gunshot.

At once she thought of Arthur Stuart, but it only took a moment to see that his heartfire was undisturbed; he lay asleep up in her little house. No, the sound came from farther off. She cast her torchy sight to the roadhouse, and there found the heartfire of a man in the last moment before death, and he was looking at a woman standing down at the foot of the stairs. It was Mother, holding a shotgun.

His heartfire dimmed, died. At once Peggy looked into her mother's heartfire and saw, behind her thoughts and feelings and memories, a million paths of the future, all jumbling together, all changing before her eyes, all becoming one single path, which led to one single place. A flash of searing agony, and then nothing.

"Mother!" she cried. "Mother!"

And then the future became the present; Old Peg's heartfire was gone before the sound of the second gunshot reached the smithy.

Alvin could hardly believe what he was saying to Miss Larner. He hadn't known until this moment, when he said it, how he felt about her. He was so afraid she'd laugh at him, so afraid she'd tell him he was far too young, that in time he'd get over how he felt.

But instead of answering him, she paused for just a moment, and in that moment a gunshot rang out. Alvin knew at once that it came from the roadhouse; he followed the sound with his bug and found where it came from, found a dead man already beyond all healing. And then a moment later, another gunshot, and then he found someone else dying, a woman. He knew that body from the inside out; it wasn't no stranger. It had to be Old Peg.

"Mother!" cried Miss Larner. "Mother!"

"It's Old Peg Guester!" cried Alvin.

He saw Miss Larner tear open the collar of her dress, reach inside and pull out the amulets that hung there. She tore them off her neck, cutting herself bad on the breaking strings. Alvin could hardly take in what he saw—a young woman, scarce older than himself, and beautiful, even though her face was torn with grief and terror.

"It's my mother!" she cried. "Alvin, save her!"

He didn't wait a second. He just tore on out of the smithy, running barefoot on the grass, in the road, not caring how the rough dirt and rocks tore into his soft, unaccustomed feet. The leather apron caught and tangled between his knees; he tugged it, twisted it to the side, out of his way. He could see with his bug how Old Peg was already past saving, but still he ran, because he had to *try*, even though he knew there was no reason in it. And then she died, and still he ran, because he couldn't bear not to be running to where that good woman, his good friend was lying dead.

His good friend and Miss Larner's mother. The only way that could be is if she was the torch girl what run off seven years ago. But then if she was such a torch as folks around her said, why didn't she see this coming? Why didn't she look into her own mother's heartfire and forsee her death? It made no sense.

There was a man in front of him on the road. A man running down from the roadhouse toward some horses tied to trees just over yonder. It was the man who killed Old Peg, Alvin knew that, and cared to know no more. He sped up, faster than he'd ever run before without getting strength from the forest around him. The man heard him coming maybe thirty yards off, and turned around.

"You, smith!" cried the black-haired Finder. "Glad to kill you too!"

He had a pistol in his hand; he fired.

Alvin took the bullet in his belly, but he didn't care about that. His body started work at once fixing what the bullet tore, but it wouldn't've mattered a speck if he'd been bleeding to death. Alvin didn't even slow down; he flew into the man, knocking him down, landing on him and skidding with him ten feet across the dirt of the road. The man cried out in fear and pain. That single cry was the last sound he made; in his rage, Alvin caught the man's head in such a grip that it took only one sharp jab of his other hand against the man's jaw to snap his neckbone clean in half. The man was already dead, but Alvin hit his head again and again with his fists, until his arms and chest and his leather apron was all covered with the black-haired Finder's blood and the man's skull was broke up inside his head like shards of dropped pottery.

Then Alvin knelt there, his head stupid with exhaustion and spent anger. After a minute or so he remembered that Old Peg was still lying there on the roadhouse floor. He knowed she was dead, but where else did he have to go? Slowly he got to his feet.

He heard horses coming down the road from town. That time of night in Hatrack River, gunshots meant only trouble. Folks'd come. They'd find the body in the road—they'd come on up to the road-house. No need for Alvin to stay to greet them.

Inside the roadhouse, Peggy was already kneeling over her mother's body, sobbing and panting from her run up to the house. Alvin only knew for sure it was her from her dress—he'd only seen her face but once before, for a second there in the smithy. She turned when she saw Alvin come inside. "Where were you! Why didn't you save her! You could have saved her!"

"I never could," said Alvin. It was wrong of her to say such a thing. "There wasn't time."

"You should have looked! You should have seen what was coming."

Alvin didn't understand her. "I can't see what's coming," he said. "That's *your* knack."

Then she burst out crying, not the dry sobs like when he first came in, but deep, gut-wrenching howls of grief. Alvin didn't know what to do.

The door opened behind him.

"Peggy," whispered Horace Guester. "Little Peggy."

Peggy looked up at her father, her face so streaked with tears and twisted up and reddened with weeping that it was a marvel he could recognize her. "I killed her!" she cried. "I never should have left, Papa! I killed her!"

Only then did Horace understand that it was his wife's body lying there. Alvin watched as he started trembling, groaning, then keening loud and high like a hurt dog. Alvin never seen such grieving. Did my father cry like that when my brother Vigor died? Did he make such a sound as this when he thought that me and Measure was tortured to death by Red men?

Alvin reached out his arms to Horace, held him tight around the shoulders, then led him over to Peggy and helped him kneel there beside his daughter, both of them weeping, neither giving a sign that they saw each other. All they saw was Old Peg's body spread out on the floor; Alvin couldn't even guess how deeply, how agonizingly each one bore the whole blame for her dying.

After a while the sheriff came in. He'd already found the black-haired Finder's corpse outside, and it didn't take him long to understand exactly what happened. He took Alvin aside. "This is pure self-defense if I ever saw it," said Pauley Wiseman, "and I wouldn't make you spend three seconds in jail for it. But I can tell you that the law in Appalachee don't take the death of a Finder all that easy, and the treaty lets them come up here and get you to take back there for trial. What I'm saying, boy, is you better get the hell out of here in the next couple of days or I can't promise you'll be safe."

"I was going anyway," said Alvin.

"I don't know how you done it," said Pauley Wiseman, "but I reckon you got that half-Black pickaninny away from them Finders tonight and hid him somewhere around here. I'm telling you, Alvin, when you go, you best take that boy with you. Take him to Canada. But if I see his face again, I'll ship him south myself. It's that boy caused all this—makes me sick, a good White woman dying cause of some half-Black mixup boy."

"You best never say such a thing in front of me again, Pauley Wiseman."

The sheriff only shook his head and walked away. "Ain't natural," he said. "All you people set on a monkey like it was folks." He turned around to face Alvin. "I don't much care what you think of me, Alvin Smith, but I'm giving you and that mixup boy a chance to stay alive. I hope you have brains to take it. And in the meantime, you might go wash off that blood and fetch some clothes to wear."

Alvin walked on back to the road. Other folks was coming by then—he paid them no heed. Only Mock Berry seemed to understand what was happening. He led Alvin on down to his house, and there Anga washed him down and Mock gave him some of his own clothes to wear. It was nigh onto dawn when Alvin got him back to the smithy.

Makepeace was setting there on a stool in the smithy door, looking at the golden plow. It was resting on the ground, still as you please, right in front of the forge.

"That's one hell of a journeyman piece," said Makepeace.

"I reckon," said Alvin. He walked over to the plow and reached down. It fairly leapt into Alvin's hands—not heavy at all now— but if Makepeace noticed how the plow moved by itself just before Alvin touched it, he didn't say.

"I got a lot of scrap iron," said Makepeace. "I don't even ask for you to go halves with me. Just let me keep a few pieces when you turn them into gold."

"I ain't turning no more iron into gold," said Alvin.

It made Makepeace angry. "That's *gold,* you fool! That there plow you made means never going hungry, never having to work again, living fine instead of in that rundown house up there! It means new dresses for Gertie and maybe a suit of clothes for me! It means folks in town saying Good morning to me and tipping their hats like I was a gentleman. It means riding in a carriage like Dr. Physicker, and going to Dekane or Carthage or wherever I please and not even caring what it costs. And you're telling me you ain't making no more *gold*?"

Alvin knew it wouldn't do no good explaining, but still he tried. "This ain't no common gold, sir. This is a living plow—I ain't going to let nobody melt it down to make coins out of it. Best I can figure, nobody could melt it even if they wanted to. So back off and let me go."

"What you going to do, plow with it? You blame fool, we could be kings of the world together!" But when Alvin pushed on by, headed out of the smithy, Makepeace stopped his pleading and started getting ugly. "That's my iron you used to make that golden plow! That gold belongs to *me*! A journeyman piece always belongs to the master, less'n he gives it to the journeyman and I sure as hell don't! Thief! You're stealing from me!"

"You stole five years of my life from me, long after I was good enough to be a journeyman," Alvin said. "And this plow—making it was none of your teaching. It's alive, Makepeace Smith. It doesn't belong to you and it doesn't belong to me. It belongs to itself. So let me just set it down here and we'll see who gets it.''

Alvin set down the plow on the grass between them. Then he stepped back a few paces. Makepeace took one step toward the plow. It sank down into the soil under the grass, then cut its way through the dirt till it reached Alvin. When he picked it up, it was warm. He knew what that had to mean. "Good soil," said Alvin. The plow trembled in his hands.

Makepeace stood there, his eyes bugged out with fear. "Good Lord, boy, that plow *moved*."

"I know it," said Alvin.

"What are you, boy? The devil?"

"I don't think so," said Alvin. "Though I might've met him once or twice."

"Get on out of here! Take that thing and go away! I never want to see your face around here again!''

"You got my journeyman paper," said Alvin. "I want it."

Makepeace reached into his pocket, took out a folded paper, and threw it onto the grass in front of the smithy. Then he reached out and pulled the smithy doors shut, something he hardly ever did, even in winter. He shut them tight and barred them on the inside. Poor fool, as if Alvin couldn't break down them walls in a second if he really wanted to get inside. Alvin walked over and picked up the paper. He opened it and read it—signed all proper. It was legal. Alvin was a journeyman.

The sun was just about to show up when Alvin got to the springhouse door. Of course it was locked, but locks and hexes couldn't keep Alvin out, specially when he made them all himself. He opened the door and went inside. Arthur Stuart stirred in his sleep. Alvin touched his shoulder, brought the boy awake. Alvin knelt there by the bed and told the boy most all that happened in the night. He showed him the golden plow, showed him how it moved. Arthur laughed in delight. Then Alvin told him that the woman he called Mama all his life was dead, killed by the Finders, and Arthur cried.

But not for long. He was too young to cry for long. "You say she kilt one herself afore she died?''

"With your pa's own shotgun."

"Good for her!" said Arthur Stuart, his voice so fierce Alvin almost laughed, him being so small.

"I killed the other one myself. The one that shot her."

Arthur reached out and took Alvin's right hand and opened it. "Did you kill him with this hand?"

Alvin nodded.

Arthur kissed his open palm.

"I would've fixed her up if I could," said Alvin. "But she died too fast. Even if I'd been standing right there the second after the shot hit her, I couldn't've fixed her up."

Arthur Stuart reached out and hung onto Alvin around his neck and cried some more.

It took a day to put Old Peg into the ground, up on the hill with her own daughters and Alvin's brother Vigor and Arthur's mama who died so young. "A place for people of courage," said Dr. Physicker, and Alvin knew that he was right, even though Physicker didn't know about the runaway Black slave girl.

Alvin washed away the bloodstains from the floor and stairs of the roadhouse, using his knack to pull out what blood the lye and sand couldn't remove. It was the last gift he could give to Horace or to Peggy. Margaret. Miss Larner.

"I got to leave now," he told them. They were setting on chairs in the common room of the inn, where they'd been receiving mourners all day. "I'm taking Arthur to my folks' place in Vigor Church. He'll be safe there. And then I'm going on."

"Thank you for everything," said Horace. "You been a good friend to us. Old Peg loved you." Then he broke down crying again.

Alvin patted him on the shoulder a couple of times, and then moved over to stand in front of Peggy. "All that I am, Miss Larner, I owe to you."

She shook her head.

"I meant all I said to you. I still mean it."

Again she shook her head. He wasn't surprised. With her mama dead, never even knowing that her own daughter'd come home, why, Alvin didn't expect she could just up and go. Somebody had to help Horace Guester run the roadhouse. It all made sense. But still it stabbed him to the heart, because now more than ever he knew that it was true—he loved her. But she wasn't for him. That much was plain. She never had been. A woman like this, so educated and fine and beautiful—she could be his teacher, but she could never love him like he loved her.

"Well then, I guess I'm saying good-bye," said Alvin. He stuck out his hand, even though he knew it was kind of silly to shake hands with somebody grieving the way she was. But he wanted so bad to put his arms around her and hold her tight the way he'd held Arthur Stuart when he was grieving, and a handshake was as close as he could come to that.

She saw his hand, and reached up and took it. Not for a handshake, but just holding his hand, holding it tight. It took him by surprise. He'd think about that many times in the months and years to come, how tight she held to him. Maybe it meant she loved him. Or maybe it meant she only cared for him as a pupil, or thanked him for avenging her mama's death—how could he know what a thing like that could mean? But still he held onto that memory, in case it meant she loved him.

And he made her a promise then, with her holding his hand like that; made her a promise even though he didn't know if she even wanted him to keep it. "I'll be back," he said. "And what I said last night, it'll always be true." It took all his courage then to call her by the name she gave him permission last night to use. "God be with you, Margaret."

"God be with you, Alvin," she whispered.

Then he gathered up Arthur Stuart, who'd been saying his own good-byes, and led the boy outside. They walked out back of the roadhouse to the barn, where Alvin had hidden the golden plow deep in a barrel of beans. He took off the lid and held out his hand, and the plow rose upward until it glinted in the light. Then Alvin took it up, wrapped it double in burlap and put it inside a burlap bag, then swung the bag over his shoulder.

Alvin knelt down and held out his hand the way he always did when he wanted Arthur Stuart to climb up onto his back. Arthur did, thinking it was all for play—a boy that age, he can't be grieving for more than an hour or two at a time. He swung up onto Alvin's back, laughing and bouncing.

"This time it's going to be a long ride, Arthur Stuart," said Alvin. "We're going all the way to my family's house in Vigor Church."

"Walking the whole way?"

"*I'll* be walking. *You're* going to ride."

"Gee-yap!" cried Arthur Stuart.

Alvin set off at a trot, but before long he was running full out. He never set foot on that road, though. Instead he took off cross country, over fields, over fences, and on into the woods, which still stood in great swatches here and there across the states of Hio and Wobbish between him and home. The greensong was much weaker than it had been in the days when the Red men had it all to themselves. But the song was still strong enough for Alvin Smith to hear. He let himself himself fall into the rhythm of the greensong, running as the Red men did. And Arthur Stuart—maybe he could hear some of the greensong too, enough that it could lull him to sleep, there on Alvin's back. The world was gone. Just him, Arthur Stuart, the golden plow—and the whole world singing around him. I'm a journeyman now. And this is my first journey.

⊁ 20 ⋈

Cavil's Deed

CAVIL PLANTER HAD business in town. He mounted his horse early on that fine spring morning, leaving behind wife and slaves, house and land, knowing all were well under his control, fully his own.

Along about noon, after many a pleasant visit and much business well done, he stopped in at the postmaster's store. There were three letters there. Two were from old friends. One was from Reverend Philadelphia Thrower in Carthage, the capital of Wobbish.

Old friends could wait. This would be news about the Finders he hired, though why the letter should come from Thrower and not from the Finders themselves, Cavil couldn't guess. Maybe there was trouble. Maybe he'd have to go north to testify after all. Well, if that's what it takes, I'll do it, thought Cavil. Gladly I'll leave the ninety and nine sheep, as Jesus said, in order to reclaim the one that strayed.

It was bitter news. Both Finders dead, and so also the innkeeper's wife who claimed to have adopted Cavil's stolen firstborn son. Good riddance to her, thought Cavil, and he spared not a second's grief for the Finders—they were hirelings, and he valued them less than his slaves, since they weren't *his*. No, it was the last news, the worst news, that set Cavil's hands to trembling and his breath to stop. The man who killed one of the Finders, a prentice smith named Alvin, he ran off instead of standing trial—and took with him Cavil's son.

He took my son. And the worst words from Thrower were these: "I knew this fellow Alvin when he was a mere child, and already he was an agent of evil. He is our mutual Friend's worst enemy in all the world, and now he has your most valued property in his possession. I wish I had better news. I pray for you, lest your son be turned into a dangerous and implacable foe of all our Friend's holy work."

With such news, how could Cavil go about the rest of the day's business? Without a word to the postmaster or to anybody, Cavil stuffed the letters into his pocket, went outside, mounted his horse, and headed home. All the way his heart was tossed between rage and fear. How could those northerner Emancipationist scum have let his slave, his son, get stole right out from under them, by the worst enemy of the Overseer? I'll go north, I'll make them pay, I'll find the boy, I'll—and then his thoughts would turn all of a sudden to what the Overseer would say, if ever He came again. What if He despises me now, and never comes again? Or worse, what if He comes and damns me for a slothful servant? Or what if He declares me unworthy and forbids me to take any more Black women to myself? How could I live if not in His service—what else is my life *for*?

And then rage again, terrible blasphemous rage, in which he cried out deep within his soul, O my Overseer! Why did You let this happen? You could have stopped it with a word, if You are truly Lord!

And then terror: Such a thing, to doubt the power of the Overseer! No, forgive me, I am truly Thy slave, O Master! Forgive me, I've lost everything, forgive me!

Poor Cavil. He'd find out soon enough what losing everything could mean.

He got himself home and turned the horse up that long drive

leading to the house, only the sun being hot he stayed under the shade of the oaks along the south side of the road. Maybe if he'd rode out in the middle of the lane he would've been seen sooner. Maybe then he wouldn't have heard a woman cry out inside the house just as he was coming out from under the trees.

"Dolores!" he called. "Is something wrong?"

No answer.

Now, that scared him. It conjured up pictures in his mind of marauders or thieves or such, breaking into his house while he was gone. Maybe they already killed Lashman, and even now were killing his wife. He spurred his horse and raced around the house to the back.

Just in time to see a big old Black running from the back door of the house down toward the slave quarters. He couldn't see the Black man's face, on account of his trousers, which he didn't have on, nor any other clothing either—no, he was holding those trousers like a banner, flapping away in front of his face as he ran down toward the sheds.

A Black, no pants on, running out of my house, in which a woman was crying out. For a moment Cavil was torn between the desire to chase down the Black man and kill him with his bare hands and the need to go up and see to Dolores, make sure she was all right. Had he come in time? Was she undefiled?

Cavil bounded up the stairs and flung open the door to his wife's room. There lay Dolores in bed, her covers tight up under her chin, looking at him through wide-open, frightened eyes.

"What happened!" cried Cavil. "Are you all right?"

"Of course I am!" she answered sharply. "What are you doing home?"

That wasn't the answer you get from a woman who's just cried out in fear. "I heard you call out," said Cavil. "Didn't you hear me answer?"

"I hear everything up here," said Dolores. "I got nothing to do in my life but lie here and listen. I hear everything that's said in this house and everything that's done. Yes, I heard you call. But you weren't answering *me*."

Cavil was astonished. She sounded angry. He'd never heard her sound angry before. Lately he'd hardly heard a word from her at all—she was always asleep when he took breakfast, and their dinners together passed in silence. Now this anger—why? Why now?

"I saw a Black man running away from the house," said Cavil. "I thought maybe he—"

"Maybe he what?" She said the words like a taunt, a challenge.

"Maybe he hurt you."

"No, he didn't *hurt* me."

Now a thought began to creep into Cavil's mind, a thought so terrible he couldn't even admit he was thinking it. "What *did* he do, then?"

"Why, the same holy work that you've been doing, Cavil."

Cavil couldn't say a thing to that. She knew. She knew it all.

"Last summer, when your friend Reverend Thrower came, I lay here in my bed as you talked, the two of you."

"You were asleep. Your door was—"

"I heard everything. Every word, every whisper. I heard you go outside. I heard you talk at breakfast. Do you know I wanted to kill you? For years I thought you were the loving husband, a Christlike man, and all this time you were rutting with these Black women. And then sold all your own babies as slaves. You're a monster, I thought. So evil that for you to live another minute was an abomination. But my hands couldn't hold a knife or pull the trigger on a gun. So I lay here and thought. And you know what I thought?"

Cavil said nothing. The way she told it, it made him sound so bad. "It wasn't like that, it was holy."

"It was adultery!"

"I had a vision!"

"Yes, your vision. Well, fine and dandy, Mr. Cavil Planter, you had a vision that making half-White babies was a good thing. Here's some news for you. I can make half-White babies, too!"

It was all making sense now. "He raped you!"

"He didn't rape me, Cavil. I invited him up here. I told him what to do. I made him call me his vixen and say prayers with me before and after so it would be as *holy* as what you did. We prayed to your damned Overseer, but for some reason he never showed up.''

''It never happened.''

''Again and again, every time you left the plantation, all winter, all spring.''

''I don't believe it. You're lying to hurt me. You *can't* do that —the doctor said—it hurts you too bad.''

''Cavil, before I found out what you done with those Black women, I thought I knew what pain was, but all that suffering was nothing, do you hear me? I could live through that pain every day forever and call it a holiday. I'm pregnant, Cavil.''

''He raped you. That's what we'll tell everybody, and we'll hang him as an example, and—''

''Hang *him*? There's only one rapist on this plantation, Cavil, and don't think for a moment that I won't tell. If you lay a hand on my baby's father, I'll tell the whole county what you've been doing. I'll get up on Sunday and tell the church.''

''I did it in the service of the—''

''Do you think they'll believe that? No more than I do. The word for what you done isn't holiness. It's concupiscence. Adultery. Lust. And when word gets out, when my baby is born Black, they'll turn against you, all of them. They'll run you out.''

Cavil knew she was right. Nobody would believe him. He was ruined. Unless he did one simple thing.

He walked out of her room. She lay there laughing at him, taunting him. He went to his bedroom, took the shotgun down from the wall, poured in the powder, wadded it, then dumped in a double load of shot and rammed it tight with a second wad.

She wasn't laughing when he came back in. Instead she had her face toward the wall, and she was crying. Too late for tears, he thought. She didn't turn to face him as he strode to the bed and tore down the covers. She was naked as a plucked chicken.

''Cover me!'' she whimpered. ''He ran out so fast, he didn't dress me. It's cold! Cover me, Cavil—''

Then she saw the gun.

Her twisted hands flailed in the air. Her body writhed. She cried out in the pain of trying to move so quickly. Then he pulled the trigger and her body just flopped right down on the bed, a last sigh of air leaking out of the top of her neck.

Cavil went back to his room and reloaded the gun.

He found Fat Fox fully dressed, polishing the carriage. He was such a liar, he thought he could fool Cavil Planter. But Cavil didn't even bother listening to his lies. "Your vixen wants to see you upstairs," he said.

Fat Fox kept denying it all the way until he got into the room and saw Dolores on the bed. Then he changed his tune. "She made me! What could I do, Master! It was like you and the women, Master! What choice a Black slave got? I got to obey, don't I? Like the women and you!"

Cavil knew devil talk when he heard it, and he paid no mind. "Strip off your clothes and do it again," he said. Fat Fox howled and Fat Fox whined, but when Cavil jammed him in the ribs with the barrel, he did what he was told. He closed his eyes so he didn't have to see what Cavil's shotgun done to Dolores, and he did what he was told. Then Cavil fired the gun again.

In a little while Lashman came in from the far field, all a-lather with running and fearing when he heard the gunshots. Cavil met him downstairs. "Lock down the slaves, Lashman, and then go fetch me the sheriff."

When the sheriff came, Cavil led him upstairs and showed him. The sheriff went pale. "Good Lord," he whispered.

"Is it murder, Sheriff? I did it. Are you taking me to jail?"

"No sir," said the sheriff. "Ain't nobody going to call this murder." Then he looked at Cavil with this twisted kind of expression on his face. "What kind of man are you, Cavil?"

For a moment Cavil didn't understand the question.

"Letting me see your wife like that. I'd rather die before I let somebody see my wife like that."

The sheriff left. Lashman had the slaves clean up the room. There was no funeral for either one. They both got buried out where Salamandy lay. Cavil was pretty sure a few chickens died over the graves, but by then he didn't care. He was on his tenth bottle of bourbon and his ten-thousandth muttered prayer to the Overseer, who seemed powerful standoffish at a time like this.

Along about a week later, or maybe longer, here comes the sheriff again, with the priest and the Baptist preacher both. The three of them woke Cavil up from his drunken sleep and showed him a draught for twenty-five thousand dollars. "All your neighbors took up a collection," the priest explained.

"I don't need money," Cavil said.

"They're buying you out," said the preacher.

"Plantation ain't for sale."

The sheriff shook his head. "You got it wrong, Cavil. What happened here, that was bad. But you letting folks see your wife like that—"

"I only let *you* see."

"You ain't no gentleman, Cavil."

"Also, there's the matter of the slave children," said the Baptist preacher. "They seem remarkably light-skinned, considering you have no breeding stock but what's black as night."

"It's a miracle from God," said Cavil. "The Lord is lightening the Black race."

The sheriff slid a paper over to Cavil. "This is the transfer of title of all your property—slaves, buildings, and land—to a holding company consisting of your former neighbors."

Cavil read it. "This deed says all the slaves here on the land," he said. "I got rights in a runaway slave boy up north."

"We don't care about that. He's yours if you can find him. I hope you noticed this deed also includes a stipulation that you will never return to this county or any adjoining county for the rest of your natural life."

"I saw that part," said Cavil.

"I can assure you that if you break that agreement, it will be the end of your natural life. Even a conscientious, hardworking sheriff like me couldn't protect you from what would happen."

"You said no threats," murmured the priest.

"Cavil needs to know the consequences," said the sheriff.

"I won't be back," said Cavil.

"Pray to God for forgiveness," said the preacher.

"That I will." Cavil signed the paper.

That very night he rode out on his horse with a twenty-five-thousand-dollar draught in his pocket and a change of clothes and a week's provisions on a pack horse behind him. Nobody bid him farewell. The slaves were singing jubilation songs in the sheds behind him. His horse manured the end of the drive. And in Cavil's mind there was only one thought. The Overseer hates me, or this all wouldn't have happened. There's only one way to win back His love. That's to find that Alvin Smith, kill him, and get back my boy, my last slave who still belongs to me.

Then, O my Overseer, will You forgive me, and heal the terrible stripes Thy lash has torn upon my soul?

❧ 21 ❧

Alvin Journeyman

ALVIN STAYED HOME in Vigor Church all summer, getting to know his family again. Folks had changed, more than a little—Cally was mansize now, and Measure had him a wife and children, and the twins Wastenot and Wantnot had married them a pair of French sisters from Detroit, and Ma and Pa was both grey-haired mostly, and moving slower than Alvin liked to see. But some things didn't change—there was playfulness in them all, the whole family, and the darkness that had fallen over Vigor Church after the massacre at Tippy-Canoe, it was—well, not *gone*—more like it had changed into a kind of shadow that was behind everything, so the bright spots in life seemed all the brighter by contrast.

They all took to Arthur Stuart right off. He was so young he could hear all the men of the town tell him the tale of Tippy-Canoe, and all that he thought of it was to tell them his own story—which was really a mish-mash of his real mama's story, and Alvin's story, and the story of the Finders and how his White mama killed one afore she died.

Alvin pretty much let Arthur Stuart's account of things stand uncorrected. Partly it was because why should he make Arthur Stuart out to be wrong, when he loved telling the tale so? Partly it was out of sorrow, realizing bit by bit that Arthur Stuart never spoke in nobody else's voice but his own. Folks here would never know what it was like to hear Arthur Stuart speak their own voice right back at them. Even so, they loved to hear the boy talk, because he still remembered all the words people said, never forgetting a scrap it seemed like. Why should Alvin mar what was left of Arthur Stuart's knack?

Alvin also figured that what he never told, nobody could ever repeat. For instance, there was a certain burlap parcel that nobody ever saw unwrapped. It wouldn't do no good for word to get around that a certain golden object had been seen in the town of Vigor Church—the town, which hadn't had many visitors since the dark day of the massacre at Tippy-Canoe, would soon have more company than they wanted, and all the wrong sort, looking for gold and not caring who got harmed along the way. So he never told a soul about the golden plow, and the only person who even knew he was keeping a secret was his close-mouthed sister Eleanor.

Alvin went to call on her at the store she and Armor-of-God kept right there on the town square, ever since before there *was* a town square. Once it had been a place where visitors, Red and White, came from far away to get maps and news, back when the land was still mostly forest from the Mizzipy to Dekane. Now it was still busy, but it was all local folks, come to buy or hear gossip and news of the outside world. Since Armor-of-God was the only grown-up man in Vigor Church who wasn't cursed with Tenskwa-Tawa's curse, he was also the only one who could easily go outside to buy goods and hear news, bringing it all back in to the farmers and tradesmen of Vigor Church. It happened that today Armor-of-God was away, heading up to the town of Mishy-Waka to pick up some orders of glass goods and fine china. So Alvin found only Eleanor and her oldest boy, Hector, there, tending the store.

Things had changed a bit since the old days. Eleanor, who was near as good a hexmaker as Alvin, didn't have to conceal her hexes in the patterns of hanging flower baskets and arrangements of herbs in the kitchen. Now some of the hexes were right out in the open, which meant they could be much clearer and stronger. Armor-of-God must've let up a little on his hatred of knackery and hidden powers. That was a good thing—it was a painful thing, in the old days, to know how Eleanor had to pretend not to be what she was or know what she knew.

"I got something with me," said Alvin.

"So I see," said Eleanor. "All wrapped in a burlap bag, as still as stone, and yet it seems to me there's something living inside."

"Never you mind about that," said Alvin. "What's here is for no other soul but me to see."

Eleanor didn't ask any questions. She knew from those words exactly why he brought his mysterious parcel by. She told Hector to wait on any customers as came by, and then led Alvin out into the new ware-room, where they kept such things as a dozen kinds of beans in barrels, salt meat in kegs, sugar in paper cones, powder salt in waterproof pots, and spices all in different kinds of jars. She went straight to the fullest of the bean barrels, filled with a kind of green-speckle bean that Alvin hadn't seen before.

"Not much call for these beans," she said. "I reckon we'll never see the bottom of this barrel."

Alvin set the plow, all wrapped in burlap, on top of the beans. And then he made the beans slide out of the way, flowing around the plow smooth as molasses, until it sank right down to the bottom. He didn't so much as ask Eleanor to turn away, since she knew Alvin had power to do *that* much since he was just a little boy.

"Whatever's living in there," said Eleanor, "it ain't going to die, being dry down at the bottom of the barrel, is it?"

"It won't ever die," said Alvin, "at least not the way folks grow old and die."

Eleanor gave in to curiosity just enough to say, "I wish you could promise me that if anybody ever knows what's in there, so will I."

Alvin nodded to her. That was a promise he could keep. At the time, he didn't know how or when he'd ever show that plow to anybody, but if anybody could keep a secret, silent Eleanor could.

So anyway he lived in Vigor Church, sleeping in his old bedroom in his parents' house, lived there a good many weeks, well on toward July, and all the while he kept most of what happened in his seven-year prenticeship to himself. In fact he talked hardly more than he had to. He went here and there, a-calling on folks with his Pa or Ma, and without much fuss healing such toothaches and broken bones and festering wounds and sickness as he found. He helped at the mill; he hired out to work in other farmers' fields and barns; he built him a small forge and did simple repairs and solders, the kind a smith can do without a proper anvil. And all that time, he pretty much spoke when people spoke to him, and said little more than what was needed to do business or get the food he wanted at table.

He wasn't glum—he laughed at a joke, and even told a few. He wasn't solemn, neither, and spent more than a few afternoons down in the square, proving to the strongest farmers in Vigor Church that they weren't no match for a blacksmith's arms and shoulders in a rassling match. He just didn't have any gossip or small talk, and he never told a story on himself. And if you didn't keep a conversation going, Alvin was content to let it fall into silence, keeping at his work or staring off into the distance like as if he didn't even remember you were there.

Some folks noticed how little Alvin talked, but he'd been gone a long time, and you don't expect a nineteen-year-old to act the same as an eleven-year-old. They just figured he'd grown up to be a quiet man.

But a few knew better. Alvin's mother and father had some words between the two of them, more than once. "The boy's had some bad things happen to him," said his mother; but his father took a different view. "I reckon maybe he's had bad and good mixed in together, like most folks—he just doesn't know us well enough yet, after being gone seven years. Let him get used to being a man in this town, and not a boy anymore, and pretty soon he'll talk his leg off."

Eleanor, she also noticed Alvin wasn't talking, but since she also knew he had a marvelous secret living thing hidden in her bean barrel, she didn't fuss for a minute about something being *wrong* with Alvin. It was like she said to her husband, Armor-of-God, when he mentioned about how Alvin just didn't seem to have five words altogether for nobody. "He's thinking deep thoughts," said Eleanor. "He's working out problems none of us knows enough to help him with. You'll see—he'll talk plenty when he figures it all out."

And there was Measure, Alvin's brother who got captured by Reds when Alvin was; the brother who had come to know Ta-Kumsaw and Tenskwa-Tawa near as well as Alvin himself. Of course Measure noticed how little Alvin had told them about his prentice years, and in due time he'd surely be one Alvin could talk to—that was natural, seeing how long Alvin had trusted Measure and all they'd been through together. But at first Alvin felt shy even around Measure, seeing how he had his wife, Delphi, and any fool could see how they hardly could stand to be more than three feet apart from each other; he was so gentle and careful with her, always looking out for her, turning to talk to her if she was near, looking for her to come back if she was gone. How could Alvin know whether there was room for him anymore in Measure's heart? No, not even to Measure could Alvin tell his tale, not at first.

One day in high summer, Alvin was out in a field building fences with his younger brother Cally, who was man-size now, as tall as Alvin though not as massive in the back and shoulders. The two of them had hired on for a week with Martin Hill. Alvin was doing the rail splitting—hardly using his knack at all, either, though truth to tell he could've split all the rails just by asking them to split themselves. No, he set the wedge and hammered it down, and his knack only got used to keep the logs from splitting at bad angles that wouldn't give full-length rails.

They must have fenced about a quarter mile before Alvin realized that it was peculiar how Cally never fell behind. Alvin split, and Cally got the posts and rails laid in place, never needing a speck of help to set a post into soil too hard or soft or rocky or muddy.

So Alvin kept his eye on the boy—or, more exactly, used his knack to keep watch on Cally's work—and sure enough, Alvin could see that Cally had something of Alvin's knack, the way it was long ago when he didn't half understand what he was doing with it. Cally would find just the right spot to set a post, then make the ground soft till he needed it to be firm. Alvin figured Cally wasn't exactly planning it. He probably thought he was finding spots that were naturally good for setting a post.

Here it is, thought Alvin. Here's what I know I've got to do: teach somebody else to be a Maker. If ever there was someone I should teach, it's Cally, seeing how he's got something of the same knack. After all, he's seventh son of a seventh son same as me, since Vigor was still alive when I was born, but long dead when Cally came along.

So Alvin just up and started talking as they worked, telling Cally all about atoms and how you could teach them how to be, and they'd be like that. It was the first time Alvin tried to explain it to anybody since the last time he talked to Miss Larner—Margaret— and the words tasted delicious in his mouth. This is the work I was born for, thought Alvin. Telling my brother how the world works, so he can understand it and get some control over it.

You can bet Alvin was surprised, then, when Cally all of a sudden lifted a post high above his head and threw it on the ground at his brother's feet. It had so much force—or Cally had so ravaged it with his knack—that it shivered into kindling right there where it hit. Alvin couldn't hardly even guess why, but Cally was plain filled with rage.

"What did I say?" asked Alvin.

"My name's Cal," said Cally. "I ain't been Cally since I was ten years old."

"I didn't know," said Alvin. "I'm sorry, and from now on you're Cal to me."

"I'm *nothing* to you," said Cal. "I just wish you'd go away!"

It was only right at this minute that Alvin realized that Cal hadn't exactly invited him to go along on this job—it was Martin Hill what asked for Alvin to come, and before that, the job had been Cal's alone.

"I didn't mean to butt into your work here," said Alvin. "It just never entered my head you wouldn't want my help. I know I wanted your company.''

Seemed like everything Alvin said only made Cal seethe inside till now his face was red and his fists were clenched tight enough to strangle a snake. ''I had a place here,'' said Cal. ''Then you come back. All fancy school taught like you are, using all them big words. And *healing* people without so much as touching them, just walking into their house and talking a spell, and when you leave everybody's all healed up from whatever ailed them—''

Alvin didn't even know folks had noticed he was doing it. Since nobody said a thing about it, he figured they all thought it was natural healing. ''I can't think how that makes you mad, Cal. It's a good thing to make folks better.''

All of a sudden there were tears running down Cal's cheeks. ''Even laying hands on them, I can't always fix things up,'' said Cal. ''Nobody even asks me no more.''

It never occurred to Alvin that maybe Cal was doing his own healings. But it made good sense. Ever since Alvin left, Cal had pretty much been what Alvin used to be in Vigor Church, doing all his works. Seeing how their knacks were so much alike, he'd come close to taking Alvin's place. And then he'd done things Alvin never did when he was small, like going about healing people as best he could. Now Alvin was back, not only taking back his old place, but also besting Cal at things that only Cal had ever done. Now who was there for Cal to be?

''I'm sorry,'' said Al. ''But I can teach you. That's what I was starting to do.''

''I never seen them bits and what-not you're talking about,'' said Cal. ''I didn't understand a thing you talked about. Maybe I just ain't got a knack as good as yours, or maybe I'm too dumb, don't you see? All I can be is the best I figure out for myself. And I don't need you proving to me that I can't never measure up. Martin Hill asking for you on this job, cause he knows you can make a better fence. And there you are, not even using your knack to split the rails, though I know you can, just to show me that *without* your knack you're a match for me.''

"That's not what I meant," said Alvin. "I just don't use my knack around—"

"Around people as dumb as *me*," said Cal.

"I was doing a bad job explaining," said Alvin, "but if you'll let me, Cal, I can teach you how to change iron into—"

"Gold," said Cal, his voice thick with scorn. "What do you think I am? Trying to fool me with an alchemist's tales! If you knew how to do *that*, you wouldn't've come home poor. You know I once used to think you were the beginning and end of the world. I thought, when Al comes home, it'll be like old times, the two of us playing and working together, talking all the time, me tagging on, doing everything together. Only it turns out you still think I'm just a little boy, you don't say nothing to me except 'here's another rail' and 'pass the beans, please.' You took over all the jobs folks used to look to me to do, even one as simple as making a stout rail fence."

"Job's yours," said Alvin, shouldering his hammer. There was no point in trying to teach Cal anything—even if he *could* learn it, he could never learn it from Alvin. "I got other work to do, and I won't detain you any longer."

"*Detain* me," said Cal. "Is that a word you learned in a book, or from that ugly old teacher lady in Hatrack River that your ugly little mix-up boy talks about?"

Hearing Miss Larner and Arthur Stuart so scornfully spoken of, that made Alvin burn inside, especially since he had in fact learned to use phrases like "detain you any longer" from Miss Larner. But Alvin didn't say anything to show his anger. He just turned his back and walked off, back down the line of the finished fence. Cal could use his own knack and finish the fence himself; Alvin didn't even care about collecting the wages he'd earned in most of a day's work. He had other things on his mind—memories of Miss Larner, partly, but mostly he was upset about how Cal hadn't wanted Alvin to teach him. Here he was the person in the whole world who had the best chance to learn it all as easy as a baby learning to suck, since it was his natural knack—only he didn't want to learn it, not from Alvin. It was something Alvin never would have thought possible, to turn down the chance to learn something, just because the teacher was somebody you didn't like.

Come to think of it, though, hadn't Alvin hated going to school with Reverend Thrower, cause of how Thrower always made him feel like he was somehow bad or evil or stupid or something? Could it be that Cal hated Alvin the way Alvin had hated Reverend Thrower? He just couldn't understand why Cal was so angry. Of all people in the world, Cal had no reason to be jealous of Alvin, because he could come closest to doing all that Alvin did; yet for that very reason, Cal was so jealous he'd never learn it, not without going through every step of figuring it out for himself.

At this rate, I'll never build the Crystal City, cause I'll never be able to teach Making to another soul.

It was a few weeks after that when Alvin finally tried again to talk to somebody, to see if he really could teach Making. It was on a Sunday, in Measure's house, where Alvin and Arthur Stuart had gone to take their dinner. It was a hot day, so Delphi laid a cold table—bread and cheese and salt ham and smoked turkey— and they all went outside to take the afternoon in the shade of Measure's north-facing kitchen porch.

"Alvin, I invited you and Arthur Stuart here today for a reason," said Measure. "Delphi and me, we already talked it over, and said a few things to Pa and Ma, too."

"Sounds like it must be pretty terrible, if it took that much talking."

"Reckon not," said Measure. "It's just—well, Arthur Stuart, here, he's a fine boy, and a good hard worker, and good company to boot."

Arthur Stuart grinned. "I sleep solid, too," he said.

"Fine sleeper," said Measure. "But Ma and Pa ain't exactly young no more. I think Ma's used to doing things in the kitchen all her own way."

"That she is," sighed Delphi, as if she had more than a little reason for knowing exactly how set in her ways Goody Miller was.

"And Pa, well, he's tiring out. When he gets home from the mill, he needs to lie down, have plenty of quiet around him."

Alvin thought he knew where the conversation was heading. Maybe his folks just weren't the quality of Old Peg Guester or Gertie Smith. Maybe they couldn't take a mix-up boy into their home or their heart. It made him sad to think of such a thing about his own folks, but he knew right off that he wouldn't even complain about it. He and Arthur Stuart would just pack up and set out on a road leading—nowhere in particular. Canada, maybe. Somewhere that a mix-up boy'd be full welcome.

"Mind you, they didn't say a thing like that to *me*," said Measure. "In fact, I sort of said it all to them. You see, me and Delphi, we got a house somewhat bigger than we need, and with three small ones Delphi'd be glad of a boy Arthur Stuart's age to help with kitchen chores like he does."

"I can make bread all myself," said Arthur Stuart. "I know Mama's recipe by heart. She's dead."

"You see?" said Delphi. "If he can make bread himself sometimes, or even just help me with the kneading, I wouldn't end up so worn out at the end of the week."

"And it won't be long before Arthur Stuart could help out in my work in the fields," said Measure.

"But we don't want you to think we're looking to hire him on like a servant," said Delphi.

"No, no!" said Measure. "No, we're thinking of him like another son, only growed up more than my oldest Jeremiah, who's only three and a half, which makes him still pretty much useless as a human being, though at least he isn't always trying to throw himself into the creek to drown like his sister Shiphrah—or like you when you were little, I might add."

Arthur Stuart laughed at that. "Alvin like to drowned *me* one time," said Arthur Stuart. "Stuck me right in the Hio."

Alvin felt pure ashamed. Ashamed of lots of things: The fact that he never told Measure the whole story of how he rescued Arthur Stuart from the Finders; the fact that he even thought for a minute that Measure and Ma and Pa might be trying to get rid of a mix-up boy, when the truth was they were squabbling over who got to have him in their home.

"It's Arthur Stuart's choice where to live, once he's invited," said Alvin. "He came home along with me, but I don't make such choices for him."

"Can I live here?" asked Arthur Stuart. "Cal doesn't much like me."

"Cal's got troubles of his own," said Measure, "but he likes you fine."

"Why didn't Alvin bring home something useful, like a horse?" said Arthur Stuart. "You eat like one, but I bet you can't even pull a two-wheel shay."

Measure and Delphi laughed. They knew Arthur Stuart was repeating something Cal had said, word for word. Arthur Stuart did it so often, folks came to expect it, and took delight in his perfect memory. But it made Alvin sad to hear it, because he knew that only a few months ago, Arthur Stuart would have said it in Cal's own voice, so even Ma couldn't've known without looking that it wasn't Cal himself.

"Is Alvin going to live down here too?" asked Arthur Stuart.

"Well, see, that's what we're thinking," said Measure. "Why don't you come on down here, too, Alvin? We can put you up in the main room here, for a while. And when the summer work's done, we can set to fixing up our old cabin—it's still pretty solid, since we ain't moved out of it but two years now. You can be pretty much on your own then. I reckon you're too old now to be living in your pa's house and eating at your ma's table."

Why, Alvin never would've reckoned it, but all of a sudden he found his eyes full of tears. Maybe it was the pure joy of having somebody notice he wasn't the same old Alvin Miller Junior anymore. Or maybe it was the fact that it was Measure, looking out for him like in the old days. Anyway, it was at that moment that Alvin first felt like he'd really come home.

"Sure I'll come down here, if you want me," Alvin said.

"Well there's no reason to cry about it," said Delphi. "I already got three babies crying every time they think of it. I don't want to have to come along and dab your eyes and wipe your nose like I do with Keturah."

"Well at least he don't wear diapers," said Measure, and he and Delphi both laughed like that was the funniest thing they ever heard. But actually they were laughing with pleasure at how Alvin had gotten so sentimental over the idea of living with them.

So Alvin and Arthur Stuart moved on down to Measure's house, and Alvin got to know his best-loved brother all over again. All the old things that Alvin once loved were still in Measure as a man, but there were new things, too. The tender way Measure had with his children, even after a spanking or a stiff talking to. The way Measure looked after his land and buildings, seeing all that needed doing, and then doing it, so there was never a door that squeaked for a second day, never an animal that was off its feed for a whole day without Measure trying to account for what was wrong.

Above all, though, Alvin saw how Measure was with Delphi. She wasn't a noticeably pretty girl, though not particular ugly either; she was strong and stout and laughed loud as a donkey. But Alvin saw how Measure had a way of looking at her like the most beautiful sight he ever could see. She'd look up and there he'd be, watching her with a kind of dreamy smile on his face, and she'd laugh or blush or look away, but for a minute or two she'd move more graceful, walking partly on her toes maybe, like she was dancing, or getting set to fly. Alvin wondered then if he could ever give such a look to Miss Larner as would make *her* so full of joy that she couldn't hardly stay connected to the earth.

Then Alvin would lie there in the night, feeling all the subtle movements of the house, knowing without even using his doodlebug what the slow and gentle creaking came from; and at such times he remembered the face of the woman named Margaret who had been hiding inside Miss Larner all those months, and imagined her face close to his, her lips parted, and from her throat those soft cries of pleasure Delphi made in the silence of the night. Then he would see her face again, only this time twisted with grief and weeping. At such times his heart ached inside him, and he yearned to go back to her, to take her in his arms and find some place inside her where he could heal her, take her grief away, make her whole.

And because Alvin was in Measure's house, his wariness slipped away from him, so that his face again began to show his feelings. It happened, then, that once when Measure and Delphi exchanged such a look as they had between them, Measure happened to look at Alvin's face. Delphi was gone out of the room by then, and the children were long since in bed, so Measure was free to reach out a hand and touch Alvin's knee.

"Who is she?" Measure asked.

"Who?" asked Alvin, confused.

"The one you love till it takes your breath away just remembering."

For a moment Alvin hesitated, by long habit. But then the gateway opened, and all his story spilled out. He started with Miss Larner, and how she was really Margaret, who was the same girl who once was the torch in Taleswapper's stories, the one that looked out for Alvin from afar. But telling the story of his love for her led to the story of all she taught him, and by the time the tale was done, it was near dawn. Delphi was asleep on Measure's shoulder—she'd come back in sometime during the tale, but didn't last long awake, which was just as well, with her three children and Arthur Stuart sure to want breakfast on time no matter how late she stayed up in the night. But Measure was still awake, his eyes sparkling with the knowledge of what the Redbird said, of the living golden plow, of Alvin in the forgefire, of Arthur Stuart in the Hio. And also a deep sadness behind that light in Measure's eyes, for the murder Alvin had done with his own hands, however much it might have been deserved; and for the death of Old Peg Guester, and even for the death of a certain runaway Black slave girl Arthur Stuart's whole lifetime ago.

"Somehow I got to go out and find people I can teach to be Makers," said Alvin. "But I don't even know if somebody without a knack like mine can learn it, or how much they ought to know, or if they'd even want to know it."

"I think," said Measure, "that they ought to love the dream of your Crystal City before they ever know that they might learn to help in the making of it. If word gets out that there's a Maker who can teach Making, you'll get the sort of folks as wants to rule people with such power. But the Crystal City—ah, Alvin, think of it! Like living inside that twister that caught you and the Prophet all those years ago."

"Will you learn it, Measure?" asked Alvin.

"I'll do all I can to learn it," said Measure. "But first I make you a solemn promise, that I'll only use what you teach me to build up the Crystal City. And if it turns out I just can't learn enough to be a Maker, I'll help you any other way I can. Whatever you ask me to do, Alvin, that I'll do—I'll take my family to the ends of the Earth, I'll give up everything I own, I'll die if need be—anything to make the vision Tenskwa-Tawa showed you come true."

Alvin held him by both hands, held him for the longest time. Then Measure leaned forward and kissed him, brother to brother, friend to friend. The movement woke Delphi. She hadn't heard most of it, but she knew that something solemn was happening, and she smiled sleepily before she got up and let Measure take her off to bed for the last few hours till dawn.

That was the beginning of Alvin's true work. All the rest of that summer, Measure was his pupil and his teacher. While Alvin taught Making to Measure, Measure taught fatherhood, husbanding, manliness to Alvin. The difference was that Alvin didn't half realize what he was learning, while Measure won each new understanding, each tiny shred of the power of Makery, only after terrible struggle. Yet he *did* understand, bit by bit, and he did learn more than a little bit of Making; and Alvin began to understand, after many failed efforts, how to go about teaching someone else to "see" without eyes, to "touch" without hands.

And now, when he lay awake at night, he did not yearn so often for the past, but rather tried to imagine the future. Somewhere out there was the place where he should build the Crystal City; and out there, too, were the folks he had to find and teach them to love that dream and show them how to make it real. Somewhere there was the perfect soil that his living plow was meant to delve. Somewhere there was a woman he could love and live with till he died.

* * *

Back in Hatrack River, that fall there was an election, and it happened that because of certain stories floating around about who was a hero and who was a snake, Pauley Wiseman lost his job and Po Doggly got him a new one. Along about that time, too, Makepeace Smith come in to file a complaint about how back last spring his prentice run off with a certain item that belonged to his master.

"That's a long time waiting to file such a charge," said Sheriff Doggly.

"He threatened me," said Makepeace Smith. "I feared for my family."

"Well, now, you just tell me what it was he stole."

"It was a plow," said Makepeace Smith.

"A common plow? I'm supposed to find a common plow? And why in tarnation would he steal such a thing?"

Makepeace lowered his voice and said it all secret-like. "The plow was made of gold."

Oh, Po Doggly just laughed his head off, hearing that.

"Well, it's true, I tell you," said Makepeace.

"Is it, now? Why, I think that I believe you, my friend. But if there was a gold plow in your smithy, I'll lay ten to one that it was Al's, not yours."

"What a prentice makes belongs to the master!"

Well, that's about when Po started getting a little stern. "You start telling tales like that around Hatrack River, Makepeace Smith, and I reckon other folks'll tell how you kept that boy when he long since was a better smith than you. I reckon word'll get around about how you wasn't a fair master, and if you start to charging Alvin Smith with stealing what only he in all this world could possibly make, I think you'd find yourself laughed to scorn."

Maybe he would and maybe he wouldn't. It was sure that Makepeace didn't try no legal tricks to try to get that plow back from Alvin—wherever he was. But he told his tale, making it bigger every time he told it—how Alvin was always stealing from him, and how that golden plow was Makepeace Smith's inheritance, made plowshape and painted black, and how Alvin uncovered it by devil powers and carried it off. As long as Gertie Smith was alive she scoffed at all such tales, but she died not too long after Alvin left, from a blood vein popping when she was a-screaming at her husband for being such a fool. From then on, Makepeace had the story his own way, even allowing as how Alvin killed Gertie herself with a curse that *made* her veins pop open and bleed to death inside her head. It was a terrible lie, but there's always folks as like to hear such tales, and the story spread from one end of the state of Hio to the other, and then beyond. Pauley Wiseman heard it. Reverend Thrower heard it. Cavil Planter heard it. So did a lot of other folks.

Which is why when Alvin finally ventured forth from Vigor Church, there was plenty of folks with an eye for strangers carrying bundles about the size of a plowshare, looking for a glint of gold under burlap, measuring strangers to see if they might be a certain run-off prentice smith who stole his master's inheritance. Some of those folks even meant to take it back to Makepeace Smith in Hatrack River, if it happened they ever laid their hands upon the golden plow. On the other hand, with some of those folks such a thought never crossed their minds.

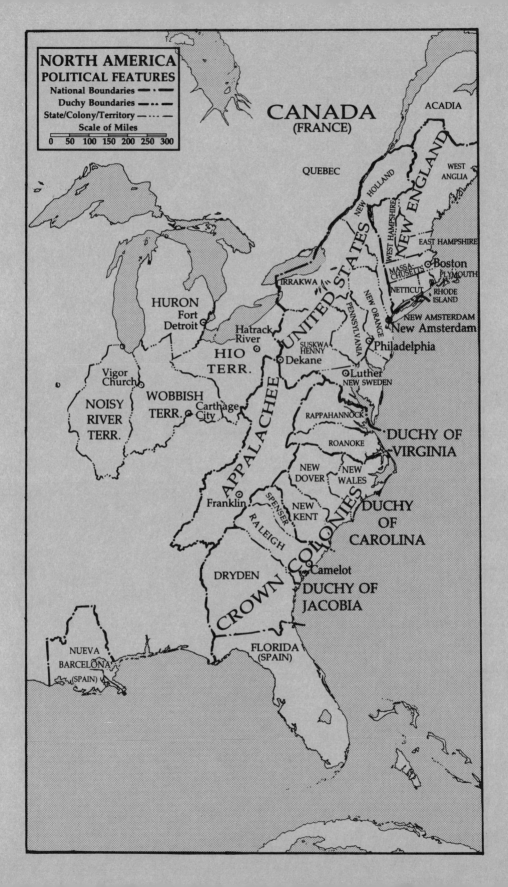

NORTH AMERICA
POLITICAL FEATURES
National Boundaries ▬ ▪ ▬
Duchy Boundaries ▬ ▪ ▪ ▬
State/Colony/Territory ▬ ▪ ▬
Scale of Miles
0 50 100 150 200 250 300

CANADA
(FRANCE)

ACADIA

QUEBEC

WEST ANGLIA

NEW HOLLAND

NEW ENGLAND

WEST HAMPSHIRE

EAST HAMPSHIRE

IRRAKWA

UNITED STATES

MASSA-CHUSETTS

Boston

PLYMOUTH

NETTICUT

RHODE ISLAND

NEW ORANGE

PENNSYLVANIA

NEW AMSTERDAM
New Amsterdam

HURON

Fort Detroit

Hatrack River

HIO TERR.

SUSKWA-HENNY

Dekane

Philadelphia

Luther
NEW SWEDEN

Vigor Church

NOISY RIVER TERR.

WOBBISH TERR.

Carthage City

APPALACHEE

RAPPAHANNOCK

ROANOKE

DUCHY OF VIRGINIA

NEW DOVER

NEW WALES

Franklin

SPENSER

NEW KENT

DUCHY OF CAROLINA

RALEIGH

DRYDEN

CROWN COLONIES

Camelot

DUCHY OF JACOBIA

NUEVA BARCELONA
(SPAIN)

FLORIDA
(SPAIN)